"In KL Smith's latest, *Tropical Ice*, you can taste the rum, feel the heat, and smell the blood."

Alan Dean Foster
Award-winning novelist, *Star Wars*, *The Chronicles of Riddick*, *Star Trek*

"One of the best adventure thrillers I've ever read and I've read a million! Listen, do you like Clive Cussler's novels? Ken Smith is a better writer than old Clive, and he's actually lived the life he writes about. Go! Buy! Trust me! You won't be sorry."

Homer Hickam
Author, *Rocket Boys/October Sky* and *Carrying Albert Home*

"Not enough mainstream fiction confronts the wanton killing of wildlife, but Smith attacks it head on: jaguar trophy hunting, shark finning, reef raping for phony Asian aphrodisiacs, lavish dinners featuring endangered species, you name it. Even for environmentalists, this book is an eye opener."

Rodger Schlickeisen
Past President, Defenders of Wildlife

"KL Smith's *Tropical Ice* chills like a good thriller should. Smith's unflinching look at the cruel practice of shark finning, his skillful storytelling, and one very hot plot—chock full of intrigue—engage readers from start to finish. What a ride!"

J. Jill Robinson
Award-winning novelist, *More in Anger* and *Lovely in her Bones*

"*Tropical Ice* is full of intrigue, corruption, murder, revenge, romance, and the quest of morally-minded individuals for justice in many forms. I was hooked from the beginning. While it is fiction, it might be a new breed—its story embraces today's realities of environmental degradation through greed and need and the people who fight against such forces."

Steven Ross Smith
Award-winning poet, former Director of Literary Arts, Banff Centre.

Tropical Ice

~

KL Smith

Angela~
Hope you
enjoy the diving,
and lets
save the reefs
Ben
"K. J. Smith"

WATER STREET
CRIME

Designer Credits
Cover art by Mark Bartman
Interior design by Typeflow

Produced in the USA

ISBN 978-1-62134-340-0

For Lucia

Mexico

Ambergris Caye

Rum Caye/Cap'n Jack's

Bucky's Caye

Tikal

The Shark Dive

Belize City

Turneffe Islands

Spanish Lookout

Lord's Caye

Jaguar Lodge

Belmopan

Snapper Caye

Blue Hole

Guatemala

Belize

Dangriga

Shark
Finning

N

Placencia

Livingstone/Puerto Barrios

Honduras

I

~

CAPTAIN JACK AFRICA pinched his nostrils to shut out the stench, but the acrid smell of rotting flesh hung so heavy in the humid air he still gagged. Squinting his watery eyes, he took one last look at the purple strands of bloated snapper guts . . . the severed moray eel head, one opaque eye gazing skyward . . . the bony skeleton of a parrotfish, its decaying head and tail still intact . . . all floating in the bloody, icy slush slowly hardening in his rusty Kelvinator freezer.

Jack turned away. Tomorrow, frozen solid and dangling sixty feet below the surface of the sea, that block of ice would be ripped apart in minutes by a score of sharks with razor-sharp teeth and no manners. And at least one of the divers who had paid good money to kneel twenty feet away and watch the gory shark jamboree would probably lose his breakfast. Some folks just didn't have the stomach for the show.

"Buck," Jack yelled at the reed-thin man standing nearby with a bucket of fetid fish scraps. "For chrissake, dump that shit in the freezer. It's time to call it a day."

Buckmaster Jones raised his bucket and then took a step back. "How'd that freezer get so full of guts? Fishing hasn't been that good."

Little Man, who had been throwing around forty-pound scuba tanks like Presto logs, grabbed Buck's pail and dumped the offal into the five-foot-long freezer. "Just because you're too old to catch much anymore doesn't mean the other guys don't." He slammed the lid shut.

Jack, wearing only a faded maroon T-shirt and black bikini swim trunks, pulled a Belizean five-dollar bill from his waistband and shoved it at Buck, who stared at the money. "Look, Buck, who else would pay you for fish guts? Nobody. But then nobody else in these islands had the smarts to pull off these shark parties, did they?"

Saying nothing, Buck took the five and sauntered across the sand to the water's edge. A quiet ripple from the bay washed over his feet, dissolving the blood caked on his toes, and spinning crimson swirls into the clear Caribbean Sea.

Jack walked the other direction, past the scuba shack, a tin-roofed, garage-sized building stinking of unwashed neoprene wetsuits and compressor exhaust. A large driftwood slab leaned against the building with Cap'n Jack's Rum Point Inn painted on it, the letters bleached from the sun. He hadn't got around to hanging it back up since tropical storm Malvina ripped it off the siding last year.

Ahead, a few steps from the beach, his open-air tiki bar, built from scraps nearly forty years ago, rose from the sand. Blinking Christmas tree lights dangled from the frayed thatched roof. Stepping behind the circular bar, he reached into a Styrofoam chest and pulled out a Belikin beer, his third of the early evening. At last, the searing sun slipped into the sea, and a cool breeze freshened the air.

Inside his lodge, fourteen guests, mostly from Texas, Colorado, and California, chattered noisily, some nervously, as they dug into Monday night dinner: shrimp Creole, fried plantains, rice, and beans. Twelve were scuba divers. They had flown in for Captain Jack's Shark Week, to swim with sharks and to watch them dance. Tomorrow, God willing, they would do just that.

At nine o'clock the next morning, Jack picked up a spear gun shaft and clanged the rusty steel scuba tank hanging from a low branch of a sea grape tree. The divers milled about, picking out weights, tugging their thin dive skins over their swimsuits, some smiling and chatting incessantly, others stone silent, their grim faces hiding their anxiety, but all were staying busy.

Jack, who had stayed up drinking long after everyone else had gone to bed, kept a distance to hide his foul breath. Now, clad only in faux leopard skin Speedo trunks, his leathery, sunbaked skin stretched taut over his thick bones, he climbed atop a splintered and soiled picnic table. He had fashioned his thinning blond hair, streaked with silver and bleached by the sun, into a short ponytail, wrapped tight by a red rubber band. His straggly Van Dyke beard had turned gray. In his left ear, he wore a dime-sized rubber O-ring, a gasket from the neck valve of a scuba tank. Years ago, he had sported an 18K gold ring in his ear lobe, but when New York City doctors and L.A. lawyers started showing up wearing gold earrings in their pierced ears, he switched to rubber.

"All right, divers, listen up. Sharks. Doing what they do best—feeding with a frenzy." He surveyed the divers, who were mainly in their fifties, plus or minus, most carrying extra pounds around their waists and their arms, faces, and legs slathered with sunscreen. One couple, twenty-something honeymooners, held hands, focusing on Jack's every word. A tall, slender woman in a tie-dyed bikini, long, straight brown hair, in her early twenties, listened carefully, her eyes intense. She reminded him of the woman he had fallen for years ago, the one who had never returned.

"You're going out on the *Shark Hunter* with me and Little Man and Smokey, the guy in the dreadlocks over there. Charlie, my dive instructor, who took you out yesterday, never comes on these dives, so you won't be seeing him." Jack wasn't about to tell his divers that Charlie wanted nothing to do with turning wild animals into circus performers. Frankly, neither did Jack, but it was his only shot at keeping his doors open. Too many divers had stopped coming to Rum Point when all he could show them was fished-out, algae-covered reefs, so Jack had done what he needed to do and began orchestrating shark feeds.

"Little Man, here, is our videographer." All of five feet, four inches tall, Little Man, his head down, eyes averted, flexed his considerable biceps. "He will be on the bottom shooting video as you descend. It's sixty feet down.

Then it slopes another fifteen feet to where the vertical wall starts. If you go over that wall, you can swim a mile straight down . . . but if you do, you're on your own. I won't be coming after you."

The divers laughed, a nervous laugh, Jack thought. Good. It's the nervous ones who buy the shark videos.

"Little Man will show you where to kneel 'round the circus ring. You must get your buoyancy under control. I don't want anyone bouncing up and down like a blob in a lava lamp.

When you're settled, we'll push over the ice block and let it dangle ten feet off the bottom. The ice is like a time-release vitamin capsule. The goodies drip out for thirty, maybe thirty-five minutes, and it's party time for the sharks."

A woman in an XL *Divers Do It Deeper* T-shirt that almost covered her knees waved her hand. "Has anyone ever been bitten?"

"Of course not." Jack wasn't about to tell her about the Chicago guy in the Bahamas who had bled to death a few years back after being bitten in a shark feed. Nor would he mention the Hawaiian divemaster who lost her forearm when she tried to feed a shark by hand. Not good stories to tell the tourists.

"They don't want a piece of you. Fish heads are what they want because your flesh is too bland. Now, if one of those boys gets too close for comfort, bump it with your camera or punch its snout. He'll run off. But remember your training. Don't freak out and hold your breath. That's a no-no. If you rise a few feet, that air in your lungs will expand like a balloon and bubbles will lodge in an artery." Jack paused. The divers stared at him, each breathing harder. "That's an embolism, folks, and it's no way to end your life."

Heads nodded.

"Now, you will be having the time of your life, but don't stir up the sand because Little Man needs clear water so he can get a good video of you in the middle of the shark rally. When you check out Saturday morning, you can buy your own shark dive DVD for only sixty bucks a pop. Your friends will never forget it." Jack was pleased. None of the divers was a serious photographer; one had an old video camera, two more had point-and-shoots with some video capacity in cheap housings, and another, who had just learned to dive, had an expensive housed Nikon he said he had never operated underwater. Little Man's dive DVD should bring in enough to meet payroll.

"One last thing. Do not, I say, do *not* swim up to the boat if the screws are turning. Stay clear. Don't become a one-armed diver. OK?" Heads bobbed. "Now grab your gear and let's get wet."

AN HOUR LATER, the 42-foot *Shark Hunter*, its twin engines leaving a trail of black diesel smoke, arrived at Shark Alley. From the flying bridge, Jack could see sixty feet down where two reef sharks, their dorsal fins tipped in white, circled slowly. The boat was half a mile off the nearest island, Goofy Bird Caye, and to keep shark fishermen away, Jack had never marked the site with mooring balls. Once satisfied he had positioned the *Shark*

Hunter over the exact spot, he waved and Little Man lowered the anchor.

Jack watched the divers gear up, keeping an eye on the novices, their jaws tight, their moves unsure. One wetsuit-clad diver with his tank on his back sat on the railing, a leg over the side, fiddling with his dive computer. Sweat dripped from the tip of his nose. "How much weight are you wearing?" Jack asked.

"Ten pounds."

"What's that then?" Jack pointed to five two-pound lead weights strung on a black belt lying on the deck. "Looks like you forgot to put it on.

"All right, the first six of you sit on the railing," Jack said. "On the count of three, back roll over the side and then kick out about twenty feet away from the boat to make room for the next wave of divers. Stay on the surface until I say, dive."

Below, the sharks were congregating, accustomed to being fed. Eight gunmetal-gray reef sharks zipped about, disappearing as the divers hit the surface, then reappearing just as quickly. The last of the divers hit the water and bobbed to the surface. After they had adjusted their equipment, all twelve signaled OK to Jack. "Dive," he shouted.

A crimson stream trickled through the scuppers at the boat's stern. Smokey leaned against the ice block and shoved, losing his footing and slipping to his knees when the block failed to budge. "Smokey," Jack shouted, "I told you to lay off the ganja in the morning. Divers are down. Get this thing moving."

Smokey pushed again, and this time the block

slid off the transom, hitting the water with a bloody smack, scattering the sharks in all directions. But it was a clarion call. Four more sharks streamed up over the wall, their bodies shuddering like cats when they hear an electric can opener turn. Dangling from the hawser, the sharksicle slowly sank, a gory lure.

SIXTY FEET BELOW, twelve divers were kneeling on the bottom. Those with cameras had positioned themselves elbow-to-elbow twenty feet from the block, ready for action. The other divers had spread out behind them, the more timid sitting in back near the reef's top, as far away as they could get. Little Man kneeled at one end, filming the suspended ice block, and then turned the video camera on the divers.

Eight reef sharks circled the block warily, like cinema Indians circling a wagon train, looking for an opening. A dozen more, both whitetip and blacktip reef sharks, lingered in the background while a nine-foot hammerhead, a long ragged scar down its side, crossed above.

A whitetip reef shark bumped the ice with its round gray nose, testing it, making sure it wouldn't fight back. Its second nose-bump broke off a chunk of scarlet ice. A ten-foot bull shark shot up over the wall, scattering the other sharks, then shut its eyes as it ripped off a dangling snapper head. Now the block was under attack as reef sharks, the hammerhead, and the bull shark tore at it with the rows of saw blades in their mouths.

A black-tip ripped off a hunk of offal, leaving a two-foot eel tail hanging free. Quickly, the bull shark returned, rushing the block, hitting it with such force that it swung into the head of a small blacktip, momentarily stunning it. The blacktip sank toward the sand, then gave a quick tail flip and disappeared into the blue.

The vicious hammerhead returned, speeding in from behind the divers and slapping a diver's snorkel with its powerful tail fin. Another diver ducked, but the hammerhead had passed so close he could have run his hand along the scar on its side.

Not only sharks came to feast. Dozens of mottled Nassau groupers hung below the ice block, catching droppings. Yellowtail snappers swirled around the sharks, scurrying above the divers, between them, past their faces, everywhere. Rainbow wrasses, striped grunts, and French angelfish darted around the ice block and nosed into the sand for scraps. One excited diver opened his mouth so far that his mouthpiece fell out. Before he could panic, Little Man grabbed it and stuck it back in.

Over the roar of exhaust bubbles growing louder as the divers breathed faster, the sharks smacked the ice, ripping out globs of entrails. The frenzied sharks, so lost in their own senses, jerked and shivered and shook, oblivious to the divers, electrified by the smell of rotting fish corpses. Sand clouds began to obscure the action as a six-foot nurse shark, its tail propelling its outsized club head, dug into the sand for remains.

At the bottom of the block, what appeared to be a long, slender moray dangled from the ice. One black-tip locked it in its jaw, twisting his head violently to rip it from the ice. The hammerhead's tail hit the black-tip across his head, knocking the eel loose. A bull shark, snatching it in mid-water, surged toward the divers. It was not a moray eel. The shark's jaws were clamped on an arm — a human forearm.

As the bull shark passed over the kneeling divers, the hand on the arm waved in the turbulent water. In shock, some divers dropped to their hands and knees, while others bolted upright. One diver started toward the surface, but his partner grabbed his fin and held him back. Another diver, with vomit oozing from her mouth, yanked out her regulator, engulfing herself in an opaque cloud, but shoved the mouthpiece back between her teeth as she kicked toward the surface.

Exhaled air bubbled, gurgled and streamed upward, bouncing around like silvery flying saucers as flailing divers kicked to escape. One diver grabbed another's hand — she had been sitting motionless, paralyzed by the horror — yanking her so hard that her mask nearly slipped off, but she hung on as he pulled her upward toward the boat. A dozen sharks continued to rip at the icy coffin.

As a human foot became visible, a frenzied bull shark tore out the remains of a leg. When a black-tip uncovered a human torso, it jammed its snout into the belly, clamped its jaws, and shook its head viciously. Human bowels popped free like so much sausage, unfurling in the currents created by the rushing animals.

When the last bull shark swam over the rim of the wall with a human head in its mouth, no one was watching. On the surface, divers clamored into the boat, screaming, crying, stunned. One woman scampered up the ladder still wearing her fins, only to slip on the top rung and fall backward, landing on her husband floating on the surface. Blood spurted from where her tank valve had creased his skull.

A diver crawled on his hands and knees across the deck, sliding through pools of his own puke. Off the stern, one diver bobbed like a cork, his eyes shut, his head held above the surface by his inflated vest. The first to reach the surface, he had shot up too fast, but the others had ignored him in the chaos. Little Man, the last diver up, swam to the floating man and pushed him to the boat. Jack dragged him over the transom and then helped the last diver clamber up the ladder.

"Smokey, get the oxygen," Jack shouted, but Smokey, his jaw slack, could only stare at the limp diver on the deck. Jack whacked him, and he jumped into the cabin, returning with the oxygen bottle and mask. Little Man climbed the ladder to the bridge and fired up the *Shark Hunter* while Jack strapped the mask on the injured diver's face and turned on the oxygen. Little Man started the full-throttle run back to Cap'n Jack's.

Only then was someone finally able to tell Jack what had happened below.

2

~

Every second, every day, somebody among Mother Earth's seven billion squatters is carving his name in a living coral reef, cutting down old-growth redwood trees, letting her house cat pounce on disappearing songbirds, even slicing gall bladders out of bears for phony rheumatism cures. Matthew Oliver looked out the window of Continental Flight 1627 to Belize City, knowing that someone in the vast rain forest below was doing more of the same. Whoever they were, he despised them.

He shrugged. So what? Confrontation wasn't his thing, at least not any longer. He wasn't looking to do anything more than to write a travel story—*Eight Days in Beautiful Belize, from Reef to Rainforest*—send it to his agent and be paid by the dozen Sunday newspapers that had bought it. He would make a few easy dives, watch howler monkeys swing from branches, take notes, drink a few beers, and go back home to Sausalito. He would write about pristine Belize, the lush reefs, the steaming rainforests, and maybe his words would encourage a reader somewhere to preserve a lingering slice of nature. It was time for others to act. It was no longer his calling.

As his flight crossed from Mexico into Belize, the verdant rainforest rambled off to the distant mountains. A patch of smoke meant someone was cutting timber, clearing land, baring the fragile soil to the searing sun. A giant new dam was flooding the pristine Macal River Valley. Endless miles of virgin forest were disappearing, displacing monkeys, small cats like the margay, and magnificent toucans and scarlet macaws. And jaguars. A female jaguar needs her own range of as much as two hundred square miles, maybe twice as much. Force a big cat into another's homeland and one either moves on, or it's a rumble in the jungle, winner takes all.

And magnificent trees fall. A timber company slips a new Land Rover into a politician's garage, then chainsaws more mahogany for toilet seats, fancy English walking sticks, and engraved caskets. Four-bedroom beachfront condominiums will get cheap electrical rates. The Belize Biltmore can leave its neon highway sign on all night long for no increase in electrical rates.

Matt, take a deep breath, he told himself. No need to tie yourself in a knot even before you walk off the plane. He had tried to leave all that anger behind when he quit the Wilderness Foundation and cashed in his thirty-five-thousand-dollar retirement fund. He had resigned from a sixty-hour-a-week job because his bosses, even board members, too often insisted he sanitize his articles and the speeches and congressional testimony he wrote. They complained his words were too strong, too unforgiving, too strident. Be more political, more mainstream, they told him. But the administration deserved no quarter, and he wasn't about to give it. He left downtrodden, stifled, disappointed that the big environmental organizations cared more about getting along with politicians than calling them to account. With George W. Bush having two years left in his presidency, Matt had refused to waste his time politely trying to get the administration's attention on matters such as stopping logging companies from willy-nilly clear-cutting old growth forests or letting mining companies burrow at the boundaries of national parks and fill their skies with toxic dust. To the administration, they were mundane matters; to Matt, they were the future of the wilderness.

Maybe he should have never left Greenpeace, where before the Wilderness Foundation he had put in three long years making waves internationally, but they, too, had lost their way, abandoning their risky protests trying to save the whales while making snide remarks about Sea Shepard's reckless confrontations with Japanese harpooners at sea. It seemed like these days organized environmental action meant little more than issuing pronouncements to urge consumers to carry home their groceries in reusable cotton bags.

The 737 began its descent to the Belize City airport. He pressed his nose against the window to view the river directly below and smelled peppermint. The mousy young woman sitting on the aisle, who had been eating Altoids, one after another, was trying to look around him. She couldn't be older than eighteen, but she dressed like his grandmother, with a dark blue and white floral print dress that fell to her ankles. Since takeoff, she had kept her face buried in a leather-bound Bible, but now she was stretching to peer out the window. He turned quickly, almost bumping her nose. She fell back into her seat.

"Oh, I'm sorry." Her face reddened, brightening a complexion that looked like it had never seen the sun.

"Think nothing of it. First time in Belize?"

She shook her head, blushing even more. "I live here. But when we flew to America it was night time," she said, without looking at him. She wore no makeup, no earrings, no jewelry. Eyeglasses with translucent rims the color of her pale skin perched on her nose. She had braided her sandy hair and wrapped it around her head like a skullcap, then partially covered it with a long black scarf. A Mennonite. Matt had seen others board the plane, including two men in dull plaid shirts and black pants held up with suspenders, wearing identical straw hats. One sat directly behind Matt, and the grim-faced other was across the aisle, keeping a watchful eye on the girl. Matt figured they probably had small farms, raised cows, and made cheese. No one in Belize paid much attention to the Mennonites, which was why hundreds had emigrated from Canada through Mexico and into Belize more than half a century ago.

"Here, let's change seats so you can look out the window." Matt unbuckled his seat belt. The girl kept her head buried in Ecclesiastes. He pushed himself up from the seat. "You ought to see it from the air. The jungle. Those mountains. You can see all the way to Guatemala." She glanced at him from the corner of her eye, as if

Lucifer was coaxing her, but girls in Summer-of-Love granny dresses were never Matt's thing.

"That's very kind of you, sir," she said, closing her Bible. "But they did tell us to buckle our seat belts." Her English was slow, guttural, maybe a trace of German from her grandparents, among the first Mennonite immigrants.

"I think they'll overlook your little indiscretion. It's not a cardinal sin, you know."

She smiled, her face not so mousy after all. Moving into the aisle, she kept her distance when Matt stepped behind her, then she slid into the window seat and gazed out.

In a few minutes, the plane banked as it began a wide U-turn, preparing for its final approach. She pushed herself from Matt's seat. "Thank you very much, sir. I'd better switch back to my seat now."

Matt again slipped into the aisle, and she followed, eyes averted. He sidestepped back toward his window seat; she dropped into her seat, ignoring the elder across the aisle who was shaking his head.

Suddenly, with a roar, the 737 lunged upward, throwing Matt off balance. He caught himself on the center seat armrests, but his left hand slipped off and plunged directly into the girl's lap. As the plane accelerated, he tumbled onto her, his face flush against hers. Her hysterical scream paralyzed him.

Across the aisle, the elder gasped; the elder behind Matt pulled himself up and stared back over the seat. Matt's hand had become buried between the girl's legs, held firm by the force of the plane's rapid climb. The girl, her mouth wide open, hooked her fingernails into his arm.

As the 737 finally leveled off, Matt was able to pull himself up and off her. Two meaty hands from behind grabbed Matt's ears and yanked them hard. As his head flew back, an arm wrapped around Matt's throat. He gagged and gasped for air, jabbed his elbow back, and felt warm blood on his forearm. The arm around his neck released and Matt heard the man moan as he fell back into his seat. Matt shuddered; he had never hurt someone like that before.

A flight attendant rushed to the sobbing girl while the elder across the aisle pointed at Matt, shouting "heathen, heathen."

"I'm so sorry," Matt mumbled. "I hope I didn't hurt you. The plane, it jerked, you know." Mortified, she didn't look up.

Blood gushed from the nose of the elder behind. Matt handed him a paper napkin.

3
~

It took ten more minutes for the Continental flight to land. The Mennonite girl kept her eyes studiously averted from Matt the entire time. As the plane taxied toward the terminal, over the intercom the pilot ordered everyone to remain seated until the passenger in seat 18E had been escorted off the plane.

Once the plane stopped on the tarmac, fifteen restless minutes passed while passengers grumbled, cabin temperature climbed, and babies cried. A flight attended pulled Matt's backpack from the overhead bin and took it to the front of the plane. When the door finally opened, a police officer, Inspector Barnstable, according to his badge, tramped down the aisle. A muscular man with a trimmed mustache and black eyes, dressed in a crisply pressed gray uniform shirt and black pants, he grabbed Matt's wrist, pulled him down the aisle, out the cabin door, and into Belize's summer steam bath. As soon as Matt began descending the portable stairway to the tarmac, sweat pearled on his forehead. At the bottom of the stairway stood a round-faced constable, his fat belly nearly pulling the buttons on his shirt back through the buttonholes, holding Matt's backpack. He stepped in behind Matt and the three men marched across the tarmac to a terminal door sporting a red and white store-bought sign. *No Admittance.*

Painted the color of dried peas, the room had one sturdy government-issued table, a straight-backed chair on one side, a metal folding chair on the other. There were no windows but, at the far end, a second door held a red and white sign stating *Terminal*, as if this was it — it was all over.

Above the door, an air conditioner groaned without mercy. Inspector Barnstable pointed at the folding chair, and Matt sat down. Barnstable flipped a wall switch and the air conditioner fan slowed and finally halted with a series of pings. By the time Barnstable took his seat, the temperature had bounced up five degrees.

The inspector reached across the table with his right hand, palm up, and stared straight at Matt. "Your papers, please."

Matt unbuttoned his left shirt pocket and fished out his passport. Between the pages were the Belize customs and immigration forms he had filled out on the flight. Barnstable thumbed through the passport, looking at each stamp: Belize… Grenada… Fiji… Mexico… Honduras… Guatemala.

"Mr. Parson Matthew Oliver. Sausalito, California. Thirty-two years old. Six feet, one inch tall. Hundred eighty-five pounds. Brown hair. Blue eyes. Born in Seattle. Is this you?"

Matt cringed. "Yes, that's me. But call me Matt, not

Parson." He hated being called Parson, the name his father had put on his birth certificate.

"This picture. The long hair. You look like a hippie." Barnstable glanced at him, and then looked back at the passport. "Married?"

"No."

"Never?"

"Nope."

Barnstable shook his head and smacked his lips. He slipped the forms back in the passport, and Matt reached for it, but the inspector smiled, or maybe just curled his upper lip, and put it into his shirt pocket, tamping it down several times as if to ensure it would not pop out.

"So, Mr. Oliver. We understand you broke a passenger's nose after groping the young Mennonite girl. How do you explain yourself?"

"Grope her? The plane lurched. I fell on top of her."

The inspector's eyes narrowed. "Mr. Oliver, three passengers, including the flight attendant, said otherwise. One man tried to stop you, and you punched him."

"That's bullshit." As soon as the last syllable rolled off his tongue, Matt knew he had just made a huge mistake. This little windowless room in a country not his own was no place to talk as Californians do.

Inspector Barnstable pushed back his chair and stood straight up. Then he leaned forward, supporting himself on the table with his strong black hands, displaying carefully manicured fingernails painted with clear nail polish.

"Mr. Parson Oliver, you are a visitor here, and you will

not talk that way to Belize police officers. More important, sir, you will not talk that way to me." He smelled of sweat and Aqua Velva. Matt's eyes watered.

"Very sorry, sir. But please, don't call me Parson. I prefer Matt."

"And why is that?"

"Well, my father was a minister, sir. Presbyterian. So he named me Parson. But I go by Matt, my middle name." For a moment, he missed his parents, both gone, his mother dead from an aneurysm at his high school graduation party. He had last seen his father alive, his back turned, as he entered the security lines at the Seattle/Tacoma airport.

Barnstable pulled his chair back under him and sat down. "Let's talk about what you did to that poor girl."

"Inspector, we were switching seats. The plane lurched, and I fell on her. That's all. I'm not one for accosting girls half my age. I'm a liberal. Affirmative action and all that stuff." Matt stopped himself. What was he talking about?

Barnstable leaned back in his chair, keeping his eyes fixed firmly on Matt, the left side of his jaw rippling. "And you start a fight on the plane while it is landing and smash the face of one of our citizens? We call that terrorism here in my country. We lock up terrorists until they're too old to walk anymore."

Matt imagined a Belize jail cell, 120°F, surrounded by massive Creole-mumbling felons, a fate not for him. "Inspector, please. I'm not a troublemaker. I'm here to write a newspaper story about why Americans should visit your beautiful country."

"Not tourists like you, I would hope. Do you have any proof you're a writer?"

Matt reached into his backpack, retrieved an envelope, and handed it to Barnstable, who removed a letter, unfolded it, slowly and silently mouthed the words, and handed it back to Matt. "I'd prefer to put you back on that plane and send you home." He stroked his chin, scratched his head. "But those are good newspapers. What are you writing about?"

"Your great country. How a tourist can spend eight glorious days here, snorkeling, river rafting, seeing the monkeys."

Barnstable nodded. "Well, we do need the publicity." He slid open the drawer underneath the table, pulled out a small metal box and flipped back the lid. Inside were a purple ink pad and a rubber stamp. As he reached for them, he glared and then pointed at his own eyes with the first two fingers of his right hand. "I'll be watching you."

He pulled Matt's passport from his shirt pocket, flipped through it until he found an empty page, thumped the stamp three times on the ink pad, slammed it square in the middle of the passport page, then scribbled in a date and initialed it. "I'll give you six days to write your story. I'm sure you will tell tourists just how welcome they are in Belize." Barnstable leaned forward. "But only six days."

Matt shook his head. "The story's about eight days in Belize, sir. I need more time."

"Six days is all you get. If you have not passed through Immigration by day seven, Mr. Parson, my men will track you down and lock you up. Is that clear?"

"Couldn't be clearer."

Barnstable held up the immigration form Matt had filled out on the flight. "Says here that you are staying at Cap'n Jack's. On Rum Caye."

"Yes, for the first few days." Matt had vacationed at Jack's, four years running. Jack had even stayed at his home when he once visited California. He fashioned Jack as a friend, even family, maybe like a crazy old uncle. But Jack had been there for Matt when he needed him.

Barnstable scratched off Cap'n Jack's on the immigration form. "There was an incident out there this morning. Jack's is closed. You are to stay away. Write about some other place. Not Rum Caye."

"Incident?" Matt stiffened, putting his hands on the table. "Is Jack all right?"

"Nothing happened to him. It's just that he won't be having guests for a while, that's all. You go out to Ambergris Caye. Americans prefer it there."

Ambergris Caye? Forget it. Barnstable was not going to chase him away from Jack's, no matter what he said.

Someone opened the door. It was the fat constable. Barnstable walked toward him; they whispered, and Barnstable turned back to Matt. "Wait here." The two men exited.

Wiping sweat dripping from his face with the back of his hand, Matt flipped on the air-conditioner switch, but no sooner had the fan started to rumble then the door opened and Barnstable peered in. "Turn off the air conditioning. We conserve electricity in this country."

Matt flipped the switch; the air conditioner slowed and then shut down. Ping. Ping. Ping. Innocent of all charges, and still feeling guilty. He pictured his father's stern face.

His microfiber shirt had stopped wicking away sweat long ago. He sat on the floor, stretched, worked through a few yoga positions, then stood and paced, wondering what had happened at Jack's. Outside, he could hear the 737's roaring engines as it taxied before takeoff. In his mind's eye, he could picture his father walking down the jetway at Sea/Tac airport, headed off on the tour Matt had paid for, a tour of six Mayan ruins, private plane flights in Honduras, Guatemala and Belize, unique rain-forest lodges, everything. His father had been reluctant to go, but Matt had insisted. His father needed to live a little.

After watching his father's plane pull back from the gate, a smiling blonde working at an insurance kiosk had caught his eye. He stopped to chat, hoping to walk away with her phone number, but instead he walked away with a million-dollar flight insurance policy she had talked him into buying. Ten days later, Matt flew alone to Guatemala and the seedy town of Puerto Barrios to claim his father's body. His father's plane, a chartered single-engine Cessna heading to Belize City, had crashed after takeoff, killing the pilot, his father, and two other tourists aboard. When Matt arrived, no one would take him four miles into the roadless jungle to the crash site. The Guatemalan charter company had cut off its phones and locked its doors. A day later, the police finally carried out the bodies, refusing to discuss the accident.

Jack showed up the next day to help him deal with the insufferable Guatemalan bureaucracy. It was no easy matter to claim his father's body—without Jack, he would have been lost—and hold a proper burial. With no brothers or sisters to help, not even aunts and uncles, he was now a family of one, last in the gene pool, living off his father's blood money. The thought of his father's death made Matt ill.

Matt lay back on the dusty floor, stretched himself full length, and counted the holes in the acoustical ceiling tiles, waiting for Barnstable. He checked his watch: 6:00 PM. More than an hour had passed. No word from Barnstable. No water even. That was enough.

He knocked on the door marked *Terminal*. No answer. He tried the knob, and the door opened into the departure waiting lounge, empty except for a grizzled police officer reading a newspaper.

"Excuse me, sir. Is Inspector Barnstable here?"

The old man looked up, peering over his reading glasses. He turned a page of his newspaper and folded it neatly before he answered. "The inspector has gone for the day."

"I can leave?"

"Could have left long ago." The guard nodded toward the door. "The inspector said the girl's father might press charges. Didn't know yet. Said you should stay in town tonight at the Radisson before you go to Ambergris. Here's your passport."

Matt put the passport back in his shirt pocket. "Thanks for your help."

"It's that airplane liquor. Too many tourists get liquored up and cause problems. They think they can do anything here because they're not at home anymore."

"I suppose."

"You can find a cab outside," the guard said, gesturing toward the door. "And by the way, the inspector said he doesn't want to see you again." He returned to his newspaper. "Take my advice. Don't test him."

4

~

Matt flipped open his cell phone to call Jack.
Getting no signal, he headed to the outside payphone,
tapped in Jack's number, then his VISA number. Still
no answer, not even voice mail. Across the way, a small
sign advertised Randolph's Fancy Inn. *Air-Conditioned
Rooms for Travelers, Quiet, Clean, $80, Victoria Street,
286-5987.* He called and booked a room.

Matt climbed into a battered 1992 Toyota Camry
cab, with a coughing driver smelling of weed. Twenty
minutes later, in the center of town on Mapp Street,
dust-covered SUVs and rusting Chevrolets jammed
the streets. Traffic was stopped cold. Matt handed the
driver thirty dollars Belize. "We're a couple blocks away.
I'll just walk."

Swinging his pack over his shoulder, he stepped over
a broken rum bottle and started down the street. At
the first intersection, a policeman leaned against a post,
occasionally dipping his head to look into passing cars.
One of Barnstable's boys, no doubt. Deciding to avoid
him, Matt took the first right turn. Empty lots and

half-finished houses scarred the neighborhood. Doors and ground floor windows of the two-story tin-roof buildings were either shuttered or protected by iron bars. Beside the curb, in a ditch covered with cracked concrete slabs, sewage gurgled as it flowed to Haulover Creek in the town's center. Bitter sweat, leaded exhaust, and musty decay filled the low hanging humid air, sweetened only by discarded mango peels rotting in puddles left from the last downpour. Empty lots and half-finished houses reminded him of New Orleans after Katrina, although Belize City hadn't seen a serious hurricane since Hattie in 1961.

Money didn't stay in Belize City. Neither did tourists. The restaurants had no stars, the dark, smoky bars were no haven for visitors, and the beaches had no sand, only mud. In the distant harbor, a sparkling white Carnival cruise ship glowed blood-orange from the rays of the setting sun passing through the smoky haze. Cautioned not to venture out at night in the perilous city, the last tourists were already safe onboard after trips to the zoo or raft rides down distant rivers.

Ahead, half a dozen men, none older than thirty, stared hard at Matt as he approached. Three were shirtless, their chests black and shiny, their hair in dreadlocks, their lips tight. One passed a rum bottle to another, both keeping their eyes fixed on Matt. They stood next to a faded Ford flatbed truck in a barren lot surrounded on three sides by a foot-high crumbling cinderblock foundation. Two horn-shaped loudspeakers on the truck's roof broadcast unintelligible Creole and Belize English, delivered by another dreadlocked man inside the cab shouting into a hand-held microphone. Something about politicians taking bribes, the U.S. and China, disappearing fish, tourists, crooked police, money, rich foreigners, bribes, and more bribes.

When the speaker saw Matt, he changed his dialect. "And de Americans? Dey turned dere backs on us, mon. De developers takes our money and pays off de politicians, and you and me, we got nothing. Would you believe dat? And Chinee, de buy Belize passports for big money and move here and de politicians put dat money in dere own pockets. What about dat? Did you vote for dat?" He pointed at Matt, who started to walk. "No, mon, you just a tourist, but don't turn your back on us, mon. We be a beautiful country, mon. Don't go slouching off."

Matt waved, embarrassed. The man holding the rum bottle took a step toward him and Matt quickened his stride. *Eight Days in Beautiful Belize.*

An EIGHT-FOOT CINDER-BLOCK wall topped off with jagged shards of green and brown glass to deter intruders surrounded Randolph's Fancy Inn. An envelope posted on the office's padlocked door had *Oliver, Room J* written in pencil on the outside. Inside was a key with a paperclip through the hole. At the bar, two old men in blue baseball caps stared at a twenty-six-inch television screen, watching the Cubs and Dodgers on WGN. In the corner, four younger men played a spirited game of dominoes, arguing whether a murdered politician was a robbery victim or just getting payback.

Behind the bar, the blinking sign—Belikin, the Beer of Belize—quickly persuaded him to order a beer from a tiny Hispanic woman bartender who was wearing an embroidered blouse and who wouldn't look him in the eye. He left a five-dollar tip, the same he had paid for the Belikin, and took it to his room. As he turned on the overhead light, thumb-sized cockroaches slipped into cracks in the wall. Kicking off his shoes, he dropped down on the single bed, its chenille cover threadbare, its only pillow smelling of mildew. He was back in the tropics. He took his cell phone from his pack to call Jack, but he expected no signal and got none. He tried the room phone, but it was dead. He lay awake for nearly two hours, wondering what had happened at Jack's, hoping he was not in trouble, guessing he would find out first thing in the morning when he took a water taxi out to the island. Finally, he pulled his legs into the fetal position without bothering to take off his clothes or turn out the light. Quickly he was asleep, oblivious to the hard summer's rain that burst from the night sky.

5

$\sim$

David Mallard pulled his rain jacket hood over his head, tightening the nylon drawstring to cover his shaggy beard. His mustache, softened by the warm rain, hung over his lower lip like dripping moss. His hazel eyes peered into the darkness.

He hadn't expected rain tonight, especially since the afternoon winds seemed to blow the last drops from the gray sky. His assistants could predict rain hours before it fell, but he had sent them home. No one could know what he was doing.

Mallard brushed raindrops from the face of his watch. The luminous dial read 10:30 PM. He should have worn his full poncho and rain pants, but sloshing back down the trail to his Land Rover to get them would only eat up time. Besides, in the hot jungle night, his own sweat would soak him thoroughly. He pulled his bare knees up under his chin, and then stretched his parka over them, hoping to keep his socks dry, though it didn't matter much. In the jungle, socks sucked up water like a blotter.

Water streamed down his jacket, seeking tiny crevices and soaking into his bush shorts. He shifted slowly, hoping the pounding rain muffled his movements. From fifty yards away, a jaguar could hear a twig break under his boot and a jaguar, he expected, would be a lot closer tonight.

Occasionally, when the clouds thinned, filtered moonlight revealed the enormous mahogany tree twenty feet away alongside the muddy trail, but Mallard could see little else. His patience shortened. He had sat through too many nights like this. Each one he liked less.

It was all for the cats, he reminded himself. As a field biologist for the Global Fund for Wildlife, he had been tracking Belize jaguars nearly three years. Only twice had he left the country and returned to D.C., once to present his initial research about the jaguar's range in the Cockscomb Basin, focusing outside the Belize Jaguar Preserve, the second time to plead for more funding. Requests by email were not good enough, they had told him. They needed to ask him personally why he couldn't stop the locals from stealing his cameras from the bush, as if he, himself, should hide out waiting for thieves to show up.

The Washington people were idiots who had never spent a night in the rainforest but insisted on asking him meaningless questions and then making bad decisions. It cost nineteen-hundred dollars for the flight to D.C. and three nights in the downtown Marriott Court Hotel, the price of ten Bushnell tracking cameras, the number he needed. "Dr. Mallard, we'll fly you here so you can make your case, but we'll send you home empty-handed." That was not even a biologist talking to him. It was a goddamn accountant.

But ten more cameras weren't enough. He also needed about thirty thousand dollars to hire more help to finish the census and range verification, and he was running out of time, fast. The cats had expanded their range beyond what he had expected. He once thought the Monkey River was the outer reaches of MK2's range, but he was no longer certain. The young female, FK11, had certainly crossed the Sittee River, and may have gone as much as ten miles farther. He had not seen her tracks for eighteen days. Now that the cats had broadened their travels, the Belize Forestry Department was unwilling to preserve this land any longer. Money talks. Rumor was that someone had slipped a satchel loaded with American greenbacks into a politician's BMW as it went through a car wash. The price for a hundred thousand more acres of logging? If the loggers or developers grabbed any more land, the jaguars were finished.

Rain dripped from Mallard's hood, beating on his nose. He pulled the hood down further, nearly to his eyelids. And he listened through the rain. Not that he expected to hear anything other than the drops beating on his hood. Even on a dry night, a jaguar could slip through the dark like a black ghost. He could only hope that FK7, the old lady, would trigger the strobe. Tonight, he just needed to know that she was still here, to see her majestic coat with his own eyes. Then he would return, track her down again, and drop her with an anesthetizing dart. It was his last resort but with that accomplished, his project would get the money he needed.

For now, he had nothing to do but wait for a flash in the dark.

"Fucking rain," he grumbled. And then suddenly it stopped.

The staghorn fern next to the mahogany tree rustled slightly. Then again. He could smell her wildness, feel her presence. And there she was. Just for a moment. Staring at him. Illuminated by a lightning flash.

The black crescent on the orange fur between her eyes gave her away as FK7. Reflected lightning rippled over her, creating an ethereal god-like presence, a presence the Mayans had once revered. Instantly the night was black, blacker than ever as Mallard had been momentarily blinded by the lightning. In milliseconds, a sharp crack of thunder shook the jungle, and his strobe flashed, illuminating FK7's flanks as she dashed into the forest.

Mallard sat still for a moment, breathless after seeing such a beautiful creature, so important, so valuable. Then, it was time to pack up and go. His plane would depart from Belize City in six hours.

6

~

Seven o'clock and already the sun was piercing the foliage, heating up Randolph's courtyard and drying the puddles. Empty beer bottles, cigarette-clogged ash-trays, and dirty glasses cluttered the bar, their sour smell diluted by sweet bougainvillea. The office door was open. From behind the dull wood desk, a man nearly bald save for long tufts of white hair poking from his ears, stood and extended his hand.

"Morning, sir," he said. "You must be Matt Oliver. I'm Randolph. How did you sleep?"

"Other than a few cockroaches tiptoeing across the wall calendar, I didn't hear a thing."

Randolph snorted. "They sleep in your shoes, so if you don't shake them out, they crunch when you walk, like Rice Crispies." He motioned toward the tattered love seat wrapped in plastic that filled the postage-stamp-sized office, but Matt remained standing.

"You a Canadian, Mr. Matt?"

"No, American. From California."

"Oh. Too bad. We usually get Canadians. Americans

worry too much about crime. There was a time you never had nothing to fear in Belize City, but these days tourists get into trouble walking where they shouldn't." Randolph looked down at the sturdy Teva sandals on Matt's feet, then his tattered shorts. "You don't have to worry, though. They're looking for money."

Matt straightened up, making himself look taller. Curly hair he should have had cut two months ago, khaki cargo shorts, a rumpled navy blue polo shirt, a sweat-stained San Francisco Giants' cap. When it came to stealing money, he wasn't worth a second glance.

"Where are you headed, may I ask?"

"Rum Caye. Jack Africa's."

Randolph lowered his head. "Hmm. Unless you have business there, you might be safer here in Belize City. They found a body out there yesterday. The sharks were eating it."

"What?" Matt jerked up on his tiptoes, landing back hard on his heels. His voice raised a pitch. "A body? At Jack's?"

"That's what they say. Don't know much more, but the body was in that ice ball he uses to attract sharks."

Matt dropped down into the loveseat. No wonder Barnstable had tried to shoo him away.

"Heard about it from my brother last night," Randolph said. "Hasn't been on the news or anything."

"That's all? Nothing else?"

"No, but that Jack is a troublemaker. He's American, you know. Got no respect."

Matt laughed—Jack was a cantankerous bastard. Last time Matt was here, Jack had yet to start his shark dives, but he had described how he would freeze fish guts to woo the sharks and the customers. Matt pulled out his cell phone to call Jack, but the battery was dead. "Mind if I use your phone, Randolph?"

"To call Jack Africa's? Two dollars a minute."

Matt unzipped the side pocket on this pack, retrieved his address book.

Randolph crossed his arms and squinted. "How come you still carry a ripped up old phone book?"

"It's backup. The electricity and cell service around here are about as dependable as the weather. This way I don't need to charge my phone to get a number," he said. Randolph shrugged as Matt punched Jack's number into the desk phone, got a dozen rings, but no answer. He thumbed through his address book again, this time looking for Charlie Turner. Years ago, Jack let Charlie build a house and cottage on Jack's property across the lagoon from the lodge. Charlie ran Jack's dive operation, managed his books, and probably cooked them as well. His number was under Tuna, "Charlie Tuna," as everyone called him. He answered on the first ring.

"We were expecting you yesterday," Charlie said, his voice gruff. "Probably a good thing you didn't come. You can't stay at Jack's, you know."

"I heard. Tell me what happened."

"No time for that now."

"Then how about I stay in your cottage? I'll pay you." Matt figured if Barnstable came looking for him, he probably wouldn't look there.

"Things are cluttered. The place is a mess. Jack is a mess. Go up to Ambergris. Come back in a few days."

"Three days from now I have to be at Jaguar Lodge. So I have to come out now."

"Well, I don't know, I suppose I can work it out. So happens I'm in town right now, which is why you caught me on my cell. You know the pier at Cooley's Hardware on the river, where we always pick up? Be there at a quarter to nine."

It was a ten-minute walk at best. "I'll be there." Matt hung up the phone. "How much do I owe you, Randolph?"

"Eight dollars for the calls, eighty for the room."

Matt handed him eighty-eight dollars in Belizean bills. Randolph fingered them. "American dollars, not Belize."

"Your airport sign said eighty dollars. That's not Belize dollars?"

"Always American. Never Belize. Total is eighty-eight. American."

Matt shook his head. Two Belize dollars equaled one American dollar. He did not like being conned. "You're doubling up on me, Randolph." Matthew Oliver's first travel rule: Get the quote in local currency. He hadn't, and he would have to eat it.

Randolph grunted when Matt handed him a credit card. "Got to charge you five percent to use the credit card." Matt groaned, and Randolph smiled, revealing a tiny mark carved into the enamel covering his gold front tooth.

IT WAS A six-block walk to Front Street, where passengers from the anchored-out cruise ship were already mingling with locals. Women vendors in small booths covered with blue tarps sold all things plastic: children's backpacks with an Asian-looking Mickey Mouse on the pocket, battery-powered clocks with soccer star David Beckham's face; a twelve-inch plate — marked down from twenty dollars to six dollars — picturing Olympian Marion Jones, her mother a Belizean, wearing three gold medals and carrying the nation's flag.

Matt dipped his hand into a woven reed basket with a sign: *Crikey! Here's What Killed the Crocodile Man. Two for $10.* He pulled out a polished object about the size of his pinky, feeling the prick of its pointed end against his finger. A stingray barb, the type that had pierced that Aussie guy's chest, the one on Discovery Channel, and killed him. Who even comes up with the idea to sell these things? Stingrays weren't fished commercially here. Matt dropped the barb back into the basket. Behind it for thirty dollars was a baseball-size *Amazon Shrunken Human Head,* with its eyelids sewn shut, tiny teeth, flattened ears, lips skewered with a bamboo peg, a dried spider monkey head, with some hair plucked to make it more human-like.

He crossed the swing bridge over Haulover Creek and walked to Albert Street. At the end of the block, he saw a welcome sign: *Inside. Air Conditioned. Chin's Chinese Grocery.* As he opened the door, a sharp buzzer signaled his entry. The cold air took his breath away. Behind the counter sat an ancient woman, nearly toothless, wearing a tattered silk jacket, its collar frayed, its sleeves stained, its buttons missing. Her face was colored and cracked like a dry mudflat. She greeted him in Chinese.

Matt bowed and headed to the musty back of the store, where above the cooler a glowing plastic polar bear was drinking a Coke. He pulled a sixteen-ounce bottle of orange Fanta out of the cooler, popped the cap, and took a swig. The barren shelves held a few cans of food, all labeled in Chinese with faded photos of greens and fish and vegetables he didn't recognize. Matt stuck his head into a dusty back room lined with shelves stacked with jelly and mayonnaise jars filled with powders, grasses, twigs, and buds. Labeled in Chinese, they were no doubt cures for everything from gallstones to flatulence. He glanced toward a shrouded doorway even farther in the back, where the curtains were pulled tight. Whatever Chin's Grocery was selling in that last room, they weren't about to show Matt. Fifty years ago, Matt figured, it would have been opium poppies.

He finished his Fanta and headed to the front door to pay the woman. Her hand trembled like a beggar's as she held it out to take his money. He felt sorry for her. "Uh, I'll take that, too," he said, pointing at a can of water chestnuts. "Make it two." Outside, he handed both cans to a small, dark-skinned boy who looked at the label and shrugged his shoulders. Matt shrugged back. He should have just given the woman a tip.

Matt hurried over the swing bridge, and then scampered four blocks to Cooley's Hardware, worrying he would hold up Charlie. Half a dozen rotted wooden steps led down the riverbank to a small dock. Haulover Creek crept along, its flat, oily surface carrying decaying bananas, ragged plastic sacks, even a soiled diaper. Down river, Charlie Turner, his watermelon belly hanging over his faded board shorts, was standing in the stern of his *Tuna Too*, steering his Belizean skiff with his foot on the outboard throttle arm. He wore no shirt or shoes, but a woven cotton bracelet encircled his thick left wrist, matching another he wore on his right ankle. He dropped the Evinrude 75 into idle, easing his skiff to the dock, then jumped out with a line in hand, lashed it to the deck cleat, and watched the current pull the rope taut.

"Howdy, Matt. Not the best time to be here, but welcome back, anyhow." Charlie's mouth was barely visible under the tangle of his salt-and-pepper beard. According to Jack, Charlie had come to Belize from Florida in the late eighties, captained a dive boat in Placencia to the south, and worked odd jobs, even hauling marijuana to Key West in a rented schooner. The last ten years he had been leading dives for Jack.

Matt tossed his backpack into the boat. "Thanks for picking me up."

"Sorry to see you're alone," Charlie said. "I was hoping you brought along that girlfriend of yours. The one you had with you last year."

"Maxie? No. We called it quits, but she is coming to Belize City day after tomorrow for a conference. I hope to see her, but she's only a friend these days."

"Too bad she's not coming out to the Caye. We don't see many string bikinis down here." Charlie waggled his eyebrows. "Little Man said he'd clean up my place for you. So, your stay is gratis on me. The cops will probably be all over Jack's today, so no staying there."

"So, what exactly happened? There was a body in the ice block he drops to attract the sharks?"

"So I'm told. I didn't work yesterday. I won't do that shark dive—it just ain't natural. But when Jack lowered that fish popsicle, the sharks ripped out a body and the divers scattered from hell to breakfast. Now, that's making a long story short, but I've been in town the last two days, so I don't know what the long story is. But I'll bet it's a doozy." Charlie laughed, his beard jerking up and down against his broad bare chest.

"That's all you know?" Matt didn't see the humor.

"As I said, I wasn't there. You'll have to get it from Jack himself. If he's talking." Charlie picked up Matt's backpack and put it on a bench seat. "But you're here to write a story, right?"

"A tourist piece on Belize. Figured Jack's would be a good place to start. But Jesus, Charlie, that seems irrelevant. I'm worried about Jack. And the body, for godsake."

"I wouldn't get into that if I were you. Stick to what you're here to do. Jack needs some good publicity. We haven't been doing well. Last year's big blow ripped sixty feet off the little runway on the island, and those island hoppers still can't land out there, so the tourists now have to come by water taxi. Adds a couple hours to their trip, so they say 'screw it' and go to Ambergris instead— though the reefs up there are beat to holy hell and there ain't any fish. 'Course, there ain't any bodies, either." He pointed at the hardware store. "I have to pick up a few things. You stay here and watch your stuff."

Charlie returned with a roll of fine netting, four squirt bottles, a monofilament roll, and two five-gallon gas cans. "Thought I'd better get this stuff while there's still money around. Government's been on Jack's ass about his sewage and garbage and even his liquor license, and now this stuff. Don't see how the man can stay in business."

Matt helped Charlie stack the supplies in the bow. "So, Charlie, anyone say whose body it is?"

"Nah, and I'm sure the sharks made short order of it."

"What about making a dive there? Never tell what's been left behind."

Charlie turned on the boat's ignition and then hopped back out to unfurl the lines from the dock cleats. "That ain't for me to do. Or you. That's police work. You got to mind your own business in Belize. Besides, I'm busy all week."

"Can't imagine you're working at night, too?"

Charlie glanced at Matt. "If you're suggesting a night dive where the body was, forget it." The *Tuna Too* floated down Haulover Creek with the engine a notch above idle, Charlie standing at the wheel, Matt sitting alongside. Cars rattled across the medieval hand-powered swing bridge, its center span forming a five-foot ceiling over the waterway. Matt pulled his compact Casio digital from his backpack and began snapping pictures. Maybe he would even sell a shot or two.

"Watch your head," Charlie yelled and dropped to his knees on the deck. "You don't want to get knocked into the river, here. Ain't enough antibiotics in Belize to cure your ass." Matt put his head between his knees, his back passing less than two feet below the rusting iron span.

Once past the bridge, Charlie jumped up. "This is the tricky part." The creek widened and two hundred yards ahead, it emptied into the broad sea. Scores of turquoise- and mustard-colored single-masted fishing boats lashed together at the bows and sterns jammed the waterway, their shabby captains smoking hand-rolled cigarettes or curled up sleeping. Deckhands in tattered clothes mending ragged green nets gazed menacingly at the gringos slipping through. Charlie brought *Tuna Too* to a halt. Two faded boats, their hulls scratched and scraped, sat stern-to-stern, blocking Charlie's passage. With one foot on the gunwale a Mestizo, a tall muscular man with bronze skin in a greasy yellow T-shirt, lifted cartons marked *Lobster, Republic of Honduras* and handed them to the next boat, where another shirtless worker—a Mayan Indian, a foot shorter than his partner, his copper skin glistening as if it had been oiled, a red bandanna tied around his head like a skull cap—stacked them on the deck.

Neither man said a word. The first man picked up a dirty rag and wiped his face. A scar ran from under his ear to his Adam's apple. His eyes fixed on Charlie, squinting as if to sharpen focus. Charlie glared back, waiting for an opening to head seaward. A dozen more boxes passed before the Mestizo pushed the boats apart, just enough for the *Tuna* to squeeze through. Matt took two quick photos, trying not to be seen. As Charlie guided his boat through the gap, he gave a quick salute. "Thank you, gentlemen." He gunned the engine, and the skiff's stern swung into the other's bow, just hard enough to knock the Mestizo off balance. He fell backward, landing on the gunwale with a thud and sliding over the side into the dark water. Grabbing the gunwale with his powerful arms, he lifted himself back into the boat and was instantly on his feet, lurching for a machete. "Motherfucker!"

Charlie gunned the boat. "Sorry, man," he yelled. "Unintentional." The noise from the whining engine drowned out the Mestizo's shouts. Charlie waved and then turned to Matt. "Play by these guys' rules and there's never trouble. Break the rules, and your boat will end up in Honduras, traded for drugs."

"Didn't look to me that you were playing by the rules."

"An accident. They didn't give me enough room." Matt nodded but said nothing.

As they moved out the creek's mouth, Charlie shoved the throttle full forward, lifting the boat's bow. The muddy sea gradually turned azure as Belize City's low profile slowly disappeared behind them. As they ripped past a clump of mangrove trees, a dozen snowy egrets scrambled into the air and headed for the next mangrove patch.

An hour after leaving Belize City, Matt could see Rum Caye's low scrub brush, trees no higher than telephone poles, an occasional cluster of palm trees, and a low-rise building. Charlie pulled back on the throttle and the roar of the motors dropped to a murmur. "I'll let you off at the water taxi dock. Little Man is picking up the day's groceries, and he'll ride you to the lodge in the golf cart. I've got to head over to Turneffe Island." They pulled up to the dock and Matt climbed out, his pack slung over one shoulder. Charlie gave a quick wave, then spun the wheel, and the runabout roared away.

7

"WELCOME BACK, MON." Little Man was in his mid-twenties, with skin the color of eggplant, close-cropped hair that was starting to recede, and a broad smile. He was built like an iron pumper thanks to bone hard work and the exceptional genes of his African forebears, who had escaped from Caribbean slavery three centuries ago.

"Good to see you again." Matt shook his hand, trying to gauge Little Man's emotions, but Little Man stayed in character, the tourist greeter. "How's Jack?"

"He be fine." Little Man pointed to the torn vinyl seat next to him. "Hop in." Matt did, dropping his backpack into the back, on cardboard boxes of papayas, peppers, potatoes, onions, and canned food Little Man had picked up from the water taxi. The cart lurched forward, humming as it meandered down the sandy road along the calm, shallow lagoon. A lone brown pelican skimmed the surface, scattering a cloud of bonefish.

Little Man wiped the sweat and dust off his brow. "Charlie said to take you to his place, at least until the policeman leaves Jack's."

"Right. He told me about the shark dive. What happened?"

Little Man clenched his jaw, saying nothing. Matt glanced at him, but Little Man gazed straight ahead.

"Say, last time I was here, Jack was trying to turn you into a diver. You ever take him up on it?"

"I did, mon. Yes, I did, even got a certificate for it." Gleefully, he slapped Matt on the thigh. "But to tell you the truth, I'd rather just drive the boat. Keep the hull between me and them sharks." He turned to Matt. "I go out nearly every day. Charlie goes some days when he's not off working on his photo book."

Matt remembered Charlie's underwater photos, but he didn't remember him having much of an eye. "So now Charlie's a professional photographer?"

"Nah, that Charlie ain't no professional. He's got thousands of pictures on his computer, none you can pass around or hang on the wall." Little Man stuck out his chest, poked it with his index finger, and chuckled. "But, I'm the pro. I do the shark videos. Jack sells them to the divers for sixty dollars, and he gives me five bucks for each one."

"Not a bad deal."

"For Jack, that's for sure."

"Did you video the shark dive with the body?"

Little Man pointed at a feral cat scampering into the dusty underbrush. "Look at dat. Those cats are takin' over this place." He kept on driving.

HALF-MILE WIDE AND two miles long, Rum Caye was separated by a narrow channel on the north side. Jack owned ninety percent of it, which he had bought decades ago when investors had no interest in a mosquito-covered caye in a country no one had heard of. A hundred fishing families had lived on the north end in houses built on stilts to survive occasional storm-driven waters. But over the years, the fishermen had stripped the conch from the sandy bottom and pulled the last lobsters from beneath coral bunkers. The money fish— grouper, hogfish, snappers—had all but disappeared, and most families had left as well. The few remaining fishermen refused to move to Belize City to get work cleaning hotel toilets, so they spent their days playing dominoes and drinking cheap rum. Some still fished, selling what they could to Jack or taking their slim pickings into Belize City, if they thought their proceeds would cover gas for their tired boats, with enough left over for a few bottles of white rum.

After driving a half-mile, Little Man stopped on a large sandy beach, at the foot a rickety boat dock. Ahead, near the dive shop, eight cottages fashioned from rough local wood lined the lagoon, their decks cantilevered over the water. They were simple, functional cottages with queen-sized beds built on platforms, dark wood interiors, and thatched roofs, stylish when Jack built them decades ago. Today they were Spartan, even primitive.

It was the coffin-sized freezer behind the dive shop that caught Matt's attention. Lying on its side, unplugged, its lid ajar, it was marked off limits by a line cobbled together from rope strands and strung across the pathway. A dozen strips of red cloth had been tied randomly on the rope, a sloppy effort to make an official police barrier. Matt leaned forward, staring at the freezer. "So, what do the police think?"

Little Man sighed. "There's only one cop so far, and he don't tell me. Just said to keep my mouth shut or else." He turned off the cart's motor, pulled out Matt's pack and headed to Jack's Zodiac inflatable boat at the end of the dock. "I'll take you over to Charlie's."

Fifty yards across the lagoon, Charlie Tuna's ramshackle house stood on thick poles four feet above a stretch of million-dollar real estate. The grounds were cluttered with plastic gasoline cans, a rusty outboard motor clamped to a bench, torn plastic seat cushions spewing stuffing, a burned out engine cowling, an overturned dinghy patched with fiberglass—a poor man's boatyard. A small cottage, its bare wood siding flecked with old turquoise paint, sat away from the house, near two storage sheds, their doors double-padlocked.

"Charlie said to take the cottage and help yourself to whatever's in his refrigerator. Probably not much except Seven-Up and a beer or two." Matt gave Little Man five bucks and watched as he jumped into the Zodiac and headed back to Jack's.

In the sultry oppressive air, Matt felt like he was wearing a hot soggy blanket. He dropped his shorts and pulled a swimsuit from his pack. At the lagoon's edge, a fifteen-foot runabout, crudely painted yellow and red, sat at the water's edge, its motor lifted to keep the prop above the sand. A ragged fishing net lay in the beat-up boat, and fishing lures filled a white plastic bucket with *The Tuna* painted on the side. Snorkeling gear lay alongside. The mask and black rubber Rocket fins would do just fine.

The Caribbean Sea was as warm as a baby's bath, but to Matt it was a welcome relief from the burning sun and humid air. He dived forward and then remained motionless, the only sound his breath whooshing through the snorkel. A few juvenile turquoise wrasses flitted among small patches of bleached finger coral. As he kicked out farther from the beach, the bottom fell away, and the sea turned bright blue. For six months the water temperature had been three degrees above normal, he had read, killing colorful corals, leaving only their ghastly white bones. He surfaced, took a deep breath, and then kicked down again looking for life. Behind one snowy cerebrum-like brain coral, a familiar Nassau grouper as long as his arm floated nearly motionless. It was Nick, a resident for years, and so named by Charlie because some voracious creature had ripped a chunk from its tail. Matt reached down to stroke its chin. The grouper didn't move. As Matt edged backward, it moved toward him, keeping less than an arm's length away. His arms crossed, Matt watched Nick watching Matt. When his chest began to ache from oxygen deprivation, he kicked upward, blowing water from his snorkel as he broke the surface, then pulling air deep into his lungs.

Last year Jack had taken him to "Critter Corral," a plateau fifty yards out covered with finger and tube and long-stemmed soft corals. Jack had pointed out three yellow longsnout seahorses the length of his ring finger, all with tails wrapped around the same coral branch. Nearby had been another, yellow with black marks, and another with a distended belly filled with eggs, and scores more clinging to other corals.

When Matt reached the plateau, he kicked down to the candelabra coral where those three perfect little seahorses had lived. He hovered, studying the bleached branches, which were gradually being enshrouded with brown filaments of algae. Not a single seahorse remained. Where had they gone? He dived again and again. No seahorses anywhere. Where last year huge pufferfish had been under ledges, there were only empty caverns. He remembered sea cucumbers, soft and pliable like unbaked baguettes. None. He had seen brilliant schools of silvery snapper and yellow grunts in a Disney-like panorama, but now it was more like a moss-covered dying coral forest, with no surviving inhabitants.

He headed upward toward the sun, breaking the surface with his arms above him. In the distance, a black wetsuit-clad diver swam near a white runabout, and then disappeared under the surface. Another diver appeared sixty feet to Matt's left but quickly submerged. Matt headed downward, catching only a glimpse of the diver's black fins as he moved away. He stopped kicking. There, in fifteen feet of water, its tail wrapped around a small coral branch, was a beautiful little brown-splotched pike seahorse. Its eye, not much bigger than a poppy seed, followed Matt's every move. Its gossamer pectoral fins fluttered as rapidly as hummingbird wings. Like the last critter in a dying sea. In the distance, a jumble of reef fish, grouper, hogfish, snappers, thirty or more, trapped in a chicken-wire cage—a solitary fish trap long ago declared illegal—struggled to swim free. Matt could feel his heart pound, his blood pump, and his anger rise. He tore open the funnel-shaped entrance, tipped the cage on its side, and hammered at it with his hands, sending the fish scurrying. As Matt surfaced, a diver in a black wetsuit watched him, then turned and kicked away.

Swimming toward shore, wondering if he had freed the bounty of a dirt-poor fisherman, he spotted something below. A hawksbill turtle, its carapace as big as a wheel rim, ripped at a purple vase sponge, pulling out fist-sized chunks like a dog tearing meat from a bone. Near its tail, a small barnacle had attached itself next to a thumb-sized hole in its mottled shell, the hole perhaps the remnant of a spear point from a failed hunter. Seeing Matt, the turtle lifted its head, flicked its flippers, and headed upward to replenish its air.

As Matt watched the turtle rise, he heard the throaty groan of an inboard motor, the pitch rising. The boat was coming fast. The noise grew louder, stronger, closer, and Matt hungered for air. He had been underwater nearly a minute. He needed air now.

Kicking hard, he popped through the surface next to the resting hawksbill. The boat was screaming, bearing down, the bow dead on. Without taking a breath, he flipped his body head-down, grabbing the startled hawksbill's shell. The turtle paddled downward; Matt kicked downward, nearly devoid of oxygen, his carbon dioxide load so painful he wanted to vomit.

The panicked turtle swam with great strength and speed, pulling Matt farther down. The boat flew overhead, the prop wash jostling them. Matt felt the boat clip his foot, tumbling him sideways. And then his world turned dead black and disappeared altogether.

8

~

JACK AFRICA SAT at his circular beach bar, chewing on a matchstick, his hands shaky. The bar's *Welcome to Miller Time* thermometer registered 88 degrees at eleven in the morning. Jack gripped a hot coffee cup with both hands, inhaling the aroma of Appleton rum drifting up with the steam, and then took a gulp. When the rum finally took hold, his body quieted.

Yesterday, it had taken ninety minutes at full throttle to get the injured diver to the recompression chamber on Ambergris Caye. The diver had breathed pure oxygen during the entire trip and was alert; his wife sat alongside him, pale and trembling. By 3:00 PM, Jack had the boatload of remaining divers back at his dock. Nine immediately checked out and demanded cart rides to the water taxi dock. The rest of the afternoon and into the evening Jack listened to the guests try to make sense of what they thought they had seen.

This morning a constable had arrived from Ambergris, but all he had accomplished was to cordon off the freezer with a found rope. The officer now leaned against the porch railing, his arms crossed, chatting up Cleo, Jack's cook, who had put on a dress for the occasion. A remaining guest, Junie Pavlo, sat at the bar, looking over her bill. "There are rum drinks on here we didn't order," she said, not looking up.

"Then scratch them off," Jack said.

"And when do we get our refund for you ruining our vacation?"

How was he going to manage that? These folks had sent their money six months ago, and he had spent it the following day to cover bills. "I'll mail it next week, but you can stay, you know, and I'll still take you diving."

She scoffed, and then slid backward off the barstool. "If I don't see that money in a week, you're dead meat." She marched off to the main building.

"I already am," Jack yelled after her. In the distance, a runabout skimmed across the water, a red light flashing. Police. From Belize City. Jack watched the driver guide the boat up to his pier, with one hand on the wheel. Another officer, dressed in a khaki police shirt, his face grim, stood erect. The aviator glasses and stiff back meant it was Inspector Barnstable, who for years had made it his job to sniff around Jack's like a sorry-eyed old bloodhound. He had written up Jack for selling liquor without a license (Jack had missed the renewal date by three days), for failing to charge his guests the hotel tax (though Jack had paid the proper tax from his proceeds, he just hadn't passed it through on the customers' bills), and for other petty charges he could no longer remember. Sure, Jack fudged a little, but he didn't cheat. When he had tried to do like other expats do—answer a minor police complaint with a few crisp greenbacks folded inside an old paperback book— Barnstable just grew tougher. He was the only cop Jack knew who would not accept a gratuity for a little leniency.

Barnstable walked across the sand to the Ambergris cop, who was now all business, pad in hand, interviewing Cleo. Barnstable pulled him aside. The Ambergris cop pointed toward the dive shack and the two men walked around the main house.

Fifteen minutes later, they reappeared, and Barnstable walked briskly toward Jack as if he thought Belize was still in the British Empire and he worked for the Queen. He carried a beaten-up government-issue vinyl attaché case, which he carefully set on the bar. "Mr. Jack, this is not my day to work. You continue to cause Belize more trouble than you are worth. And now you have a murder on your hands."

"Murder? What are you talking about?" Jack motioned toward the barstool.

Barnstable didn't move. Jack slicked back his thinning hair and sat down anyway. "Inspector, my divers think they saw a body. At least that's what they told me. Nobody said they saw a murder."

"A body in an ice block is a murder."

"Is that so? Then go find the remains and gather some evidence. Right now, all you have is the active imagination of those crazy divers. And no body, that's for sure."

Barnstable peered at Jack over the rim of his sunglasses. He snapped open his attaché case and extracted a yellow legal pad on which he wrote something and then underlined it, finishing with an orchestra conductor's flair. Sweat blotches appeared where his shirt bunched under his armpit. "There are no human traces in your freezer, none on the boat, not a button, not a hair, not a piece of flesh. No tracks in the sand, which there might be if a body had been dragged. Nothing." He leaned closer to Jack. "But people know what they see. It was not their imagination. So, tell me what happened, from the time you woke up yesterday morning until the time you stepped off the boat."

"It's a long story, Inspector. Let me wet my whistle first." Jack could feel the disapproval through Barnstable's dark glasses, but he added a half-shot of Appleton to his coffee and managed a sip. It took him ten minutes to review his day for Barnstable and when he finished he took another sip, coughed, and pounded his chest with his fist. "But, Inspector, what I did yesterday makes no difference. Yesterday that ice was frozen rock-hard. Day before that it was slush, but the freezer was filled to the brim. So, if someone climbed in there and died, they did it days before that. Besides, the day before yesterday we had a squall that would have washed away any tracks in the sand."

Barnstable flipped pages of his pad. "You never looked into the freezer before you put that block on your boat?"

"Would you stick your nose in that rot? That's what I pay my boys to do."

"And who are your boys?"

"Little Man and Smokey, mainly. But there are fishermen, like Buckmaster and a few old guys from the village who I pay to drop their trimmings in the freezer.

Hard to get enough guts every week. No one's catching any fish."

"But you had enough to cover up the body, so who put it in there?"

"None of my guys, that's for sure. They're good kids. And the fishermen are all too damn old even to wrestle a twenty-pound grouper into the boat, let alone lift a stiff into the Kelvinator."

"My constable says none of your diving employees are here today."

"There's no work for them. Not much reason to be here."

Barnstable reached into his briefcase and waved a paper at Jack. "Your advertising flyer says you provide guests with a video of their dives. Did you film that dive?"

"Well, Little Man did have a camera down there." Jack walked behind the bar where his Sony video camera was wrapped in a towel. He slid out the camera and sat down on a barstool. "Here, Inspector, have a seat." He turned on the camera and held it so they could both watch it stream. He ran through Jack's shark briefing so Barnstable could see the divers, then fast-forwarded to the divers jumping into the water. The camera ran as Little Man submerged, then it pointed back at the surface, capturing the divers in a mass of bubbles as they headed down and settled in the sand then focused on a woman diver. The camera had been switched off, apparently, and the next scene showed the ice block, burgundy and dirt brown from the blood and guts, an occasional snapper head visible, but nothing more. Barnstable shuddered as the first shark smacked into the ice.

The camera turned to the divers, panning them slowly, showing them waving their arms, squirming, as exhaust bubbles rushed upward when the divers exhaled. Little Man went in for a close-up of the slender woman who had water in her mask and was holding it, blowing through her nose to push out the water and clear her mask. She was on screen for nearly thirty seconds, then she waved, and Little Man slowly panned to another diver. Then upward, to a shark zipping overhead, then jerky shots of everyone panicking, scattering, kicking toward the surface, and then the screen went blank.

"That's it?" Barnstable asked. Jack nodded.

"Why did he stop filming?"

"I suppose he decided to take care of the divers. That's his job."

Barnstable pointed at the Sony. "I saw other divers on that video with cameras. What about them?"

"One diver had an expensive Nikon, but he flooded it. First time he had used it. One woman had a point-and-shoot and just captured flailing arms and legs. The diver with the video got scared when a shark buzzed him. He dropped his camera and shot to the surface when all hell broke loose. He's the one in the recompression chamber on Ambergris right now. The last guy was on his third dive ever and was so mesmerized he just flat out forgot to take pictures. Happens all the time."

"What about the dropped camera?"

"He had it clipped on a lanyard, so it came up with him. It's in the lodge."

"No pictures of the body?"

"Not a one. If there were, I'd have already called Rupert Murdoch and the cash would be in my account."

Barnstable flipped his tablet closed and put the pen into his shirt pocket. "You know more than you're telling me, Jack."

"Now why should I hold something back, Inspector?"

Barnstable crossed his arms. "Well, let's talk about those three cocaine bundles that washed up here a few years back."

"It was four bundles, as I recall. Until your cronies hauled them away for evidence, and one bundle disappeared."

Barnstable frowned. "A body fed to sharks is what you would expect from someone in the drug business."

"Bullshit, Inspector. Point your finger at someone else. Colombian scum lost those bundles of nose candy on the way north. I run a clean business. You ought to know, all the times you been out here sniffing around, making up infractions. You're over your head, Inspector, and you don't have a clue where to begin."

Barnstable walked around the bar and grabbed Jack's arms, yanking him inches from his face. "I'm beginning right here, Jack, with you." He pushed Jack back and glared at him.

Jack held up his hands, palms out. "Inspector, sorry, I've had a little rum. Had to settle my nerves, so no offense."

Barnstable grunted. "Any disturbances the night before last or the night before that? Any strangers around?"

"Nothing I heard. Cleo lives in the cottage behind the lodge. Three or four days ago, she told me people were outside jabbering after midnight. Just drunken guests. Happens all the time."

Barnstable put the tablet in his briefcase and snapped the lid shut. "And what about the fellow who lives in the house over there." Barnstable pointed across the lagoon at Charlie's house.

"Charlie? I haven't seen him for two days."

"I want to talk to him. Tell him to call me. Immediately. In the meantime, you think about who put that body in the ice."

Barnstable lifted his head and glanced at a framed photo hanging behind the bar. It was Jack, posed on an old *Skin Diver* magazine cover. *Cap'n Jack Africa, Founding Father of Belize Diving.* Barnstable scoffed. "You're good at getting press attention, Jack, but we don't want publicity for this incident. Tourism isn't good these days. If you have anything to say, say it to me."

"I thought you didn't like tourists, Inspector."

"I don't." He started toward the lodge but then turned around. "You know, we never pursue matters like this when an American sells out and leaves the country. It's no longer worth the trouble. Think about it." Barnstable headed back to the lodge.

Sell out? Leave the country? Forget it. Sailing from San Francisco years before, Jack had weathered a dozen bar fights, losing half a thumb to a machete, and spent a week in a Honduras slammer before he finally reached Belize. The first thing he did was jump overboard with a mask and fins. When he saw all those rainbow-colored fish swirling around immaculate coral reefs, he swore he would never leave. He cleaned out his California bank account to buy his island and settled in, intent on preserving it forever.

But what brought him here thirty years ago was disappearing fast. Where there had been a dozen manatees, maybe two now remained. Only one old crocodile, the last of a family, still lived in the channel. The developers, the goddamn politicians, all the moneygrubbers who saw only cash in crocodile-hide handbags and hotels on turtle-nesting beaches could kiss his ass. When his day came, he would give his land to the Global Fund for Wildlife, buy a case of Appleton, chain his leg to the bar, and let the next hurricane take him away.

Maybe that storm was beginning to blow. He poured himself another Appleton.

9

M‌ATT REGAINED CONSCIOUSNESS in the bright surface sunlight, coughing furiously and expelling a geyser of seawater from his lungs. He threw back his head and yanked the snorkel from his mouth, gasping for air, and coughing repeatedly while bouncing on the surface with each violent jerk of his body.

He had blacked out underwater as the boat roared overhead and the propeller's turbulence pulled him upward. Buoyant enough to float, Matt had popped to the surface, still unconscious. His first breath pulled the water from his snorkel into his lungs, but that was followed by a rush of air that revived him. Coughing, he pulled the snorkel from his mouth, rolled over on his back and kicked, but pain shot through his right foot. The boat's propeller had severed his right fin blade and nicked his toes. Blood trickled from a gash in his big toe. He started kicking with his good foot and fin, paddled with his hands, and headed to shore.

Exhausted, he pulled himself up on the beach, climbed into a string hammock stretched between two coconut palms, and lay motionless, his head pounding, his coughing slowing. Blood still dripped from his toe, but there were no other marks. Had he saved the hawksbill turtle? Had it saved him?

Matt fell into a deep sleep for more than an hour, waking with a start from the loud splash as a pelican hurled itself into the water. He took a deep breath and then crawled out of the hammock. "Looks like I just dodged a bullet," he mumbled to himself. Nearby, in a Styrofoam cooler, two cans of diet Seven-Up lay in an inch of water. Matt downed one, coughing between swallows, then drank the other more slowly. Across the way, alongside Jack's pier, was a runabout with a red light mounted atop a pole on the stern. Shit, he thought to himself, I've been run down, lacerated, and damn near decapitated by that police boat. Matt was in no mood for sitting still.

He pulled his shorts over his swimsuit and limped toward the end of the lagoon where a shallow mangrove swamp separated the lagoon from the sea on the other side. To traverse the muck, villagers had cobbled together a walkway with rotted planks, an overturned hull of a worm-eaten skiff, and palm and mangrove trunks. Matt negotiated the path carefully, remembering Jack's story about the rum-soaked villager who became stuck waist-deep in the muck, only to be found dead, covered with mangrove crabs, his flesh pitted like a golf ball. By the time Matt broke into the opening on the sand road leading to Jack's, welts from mosquitoes were rising on his bare back.

He walked past the rope that marked the freezer as

off-limits and passed a half-dozen rusty mountain bikes crammed into racks. As he rounded the corner of the lodge, a whiff of Aqua Velva hit him an instant before he crashed into Inspector Barnstable.

"Oliver! You came here when I distinctly ordered you to stay away?"

"Well, sir, I thought —"

"This hotel is closed. It's a crime scene."

Matt motioned toward Charlie's house. "I'm staying over there. He's a friend."

"This is a police investigation. There is no story here. Keep your nose out of this."

Matt scratched his head. "Inspector, I didn't know my six-day stay came with writing restrictions. Freedom of the press and all that."

Barnstable pulled his glasses down over his nose. Matt, half a foot taller, looked down at him, annoyed that Barnstable was more interested in what he was doing at Jack's than in the Iceman. "So, Inspector, any idea about the body? Who it was?"

"Oliver, you're one question away from a flight home. You're only a visitor in my country, and an unwanted one at that."

"Maybe so, but you're not treating me much like a guest. You nearly killed me. And a turtle, too."

"You're talking nonsense."

"I was in the water out there," Matt said, pointing south across the lagoon, "when your driver damn near decapitated me."

"Mr. Oliver, we came around the other end of the island." Barnstable pointed north.

Matt looked back at the water. The boat he had seen when he was snorkeling had disappeared. "Sorry, sir," he said. "My mistake."

"Mistake? Hardly. I won't tolerate such rude disrespect. Your stay is over." He put two fingers in his mouth and whistled, snapping the boat driver, the fat constable Matt had seen at the airport, to attention. "Constable," Barnstable shouted, "bring me handcuffs. Mr. Oliver is going to town with us."

Matt froze. Oh, shit. He imagined a Belize prison, filled with all those nothing-to-lose Creole felons. Without thinking, he turned and began sprinting across the sand and down the path. By the time he hit his stride he knew he was in deep trouble. Of his own making.

"Oliver, stop!" Barnstable started after him, the constable right behind. Matt looked over his shoulder to see the two officers struggling to run in the soft sand, with the constable trying to pry his pistol from his holster. A hundred yards later, the path cut abruptly to the right. Out of sight from his pursuers, Matt stopped to catch his breath. My God. This was the most stupid thing he had ever done. But it was too late. He leaped from the path and pushed deep into the underbrush so that he was no longer visible from the trail, but he could still see it through the foliage. The inspector and the constable arrived, both panting, the constable wheezing. The constable whipped out his gun and fired a shot down the road, snapping off a tree limb.

"You idiot," Barnstable shouted. "Stop it. Let him go. He's not worth the chase."

"But we should lock him up, sir. All the trouble he's caused."

"Put that pistol away. Shooting him will just cause us more trouble. If he hasn't left Belize in five days, we'll hunt him down and put him on the first flight out." Barnstable headed back down the path, the constable behind him. "I want to be back to Belize City before my shift is over."

Matt watched the two men disappear down the path. For now, he could forget those Creole felons. He relaxed, and then he remembered that white boat with blue railings bearing down. It wasn't a simple navigation error, a drunken boat driver out for a romp. Whoever was driving that boat had tried to hit him.

Matt waited until he heard the police runabout fire up and knew that Barnstable and the constable were pulling out of the lagoon and into the sea. Soon, the sound of its engine slowly dissipated in the trade winds. Above, heavy clouds forming in the sky expanded rapidly as he walked back toward Jack's. A breeze off the water had picked up, rustling the trees and lifting the waves, so they now slapped on the shore. The cloud cover shimmered from distant lightning bolts, followed by the low growl of thunder. Raindrops exploded in the sand, leaving BB-sized craters, as Matt dashed for the beach bar.

"Jack?" Matt held his arms out. "How are you?"

Jack just stood there, his jaw tight, and squinted at Matt but showed no recognition. He looked older than just a year ago, his beard untrimmed, his skin dark and wrinkled. Matt tugged nervously at his shorts and glanced away. When he looked back, Jack was staring at the sea. "Hey, Jack. It's me, Matt. You look shell-shocked."

"Matt Oliver? You should have stayed home."

"Don't be crazy. Besides, I have a dozen newspapers waiting for a story about you— well, at least I did."

Jack shrugged his shoulders, poured two fingers of Appleton into a tumbler, dropped in two ice cubes and handed it to Matt. "Here. If I remember right, you're a rum drinker. Join me."

Matt lifted the glass, sniffed it, and gagged. Staring at him from inside an ice cube was a cockroach. "Jesus, Jack, you still pulling that same dumb stunt?"

"Just for you, Matty. The diver who goes to a hundred and eighty feet chasing a dropped camera when he's already out of air. I still haven't forgiven you. Weren't for me grabbing you and then Tuna bringing you another tank, you'd be playing wheelchair basketball."

"At best. Yeah, I owe you. And thanks again for helping me with my father."

"For you, anything. Good to see you. First laugh I've had in a day." He threw his arms around Matt and hugged him. "Now, Matty, how you been doing these past months? OK?"

"Yeah, I'm hanging in there," Matt mumbled, then raised his glass. "But you, Jack. A cockroach in an ice cube, a body in an ice block. What's with this ice fixation? What's the story?"

"I was topside, so I only know what the divers who were down there told me." Jack stared into his cup, his eyes drooping.

"But, the body. Was it intact?"

Jack jerked up his head, squinted. "Hell, I don't know if it was whole or fricasseed, come to think of it. All I know is they saw an arm, a leg, a string of guts. As far as I'm concerned, it was a burial at sea, nothing more, nothing less."

"A burial at sea? What are you talking about?"

"Frozen in his casket and buried at sea. That's how you preserve a sailor's body when you can't embalm him. Put him on ice. Like a tuna." Jack's eyes were glazed, his hands shaky. "Makes sense, doesn't it?"

Matt shook his head. This was serious stuff, and Jack was drunk and in denial. "Why go to so much trouble? Makes no sense to me, Jack."

"Not to me, neither." Jack took a sip and leaned back.

"Well, it seems likely someone's either trying to pin a murder on you or send you a message. Pick one."

"I don't like either choice. But they did get my attention, whoever 'they' are. No postmark, no return address on that message."

"They must figure you'd know. Who's on your enemy list?"

"Can't say that I have many friends, frankly. Barnstable's certainly not the chairman of my fan club."

"Barnstable nailed me at the airport." Matt told him the story. "He told me to steer clear of you and then I ran into him here."

"There you go. Now we're both on his shit list." Jack went behind the bar, filled a glass with ice, added a splash of Appleton, and topped if off with water. "But I got to get my doors open. I have bills and staff to pay."

"Jack, you have bigger problems than that. Are the Colombians still bringing coke through the islands?"

"Of course. Down south. The little cayes. They drop the shit off at night. Belizeans haul it out before dawn. But don't go thinking I'm in that business."

"Doesn't look like it to me, Jack." The tiki bar's thatched roof had holes in it, paint peeled from the siding on the lodge, and half-a-dozen burned-out light bulbs needed replacing. "But what about Barnstable? Is he in cahoots?"

"Some of his cronies are but not him. He's just a bureaucratic play-by-the-rules prick." He looked out the corner of his eye at Matt. "But I don't want to talk about it anymore. Barnstable told me to keep my mouth shut, and maybe I should, especially since you're a writer. So, no more questions."

Matt shrugged. He thought about Barnstable. The boat nearly gunning him down. The dead reefs. The constable shooting into the bush. He was already swimming with sharks. Like the Iceman. And he wasn't ready to let it go.

As DARKNESS FELL, Matt carried two bowls of what Cleo called "Shrimp Surprise" to the bar. Christmas tree lights hung from the beams of the bar, out of season and out of place.

"Jack, I thought you might want something to eat."

Jack picked up a fork and started picking at the rice. "'Shrimp Surprise,' she calls it. Used to make this dish with lobster, but I won't buy it anymore. They're too depleted. They farm the shrimp down the coast, and then they pump the wastewater into the ocean so all the reefs there are dead. Just to keep Bubba Gump's happy. But you have to feed tourists some kind of seafood. So just eat the rice. I don't want to be surprised."

Matt poked at his rice. "The reef off Charlie's looked dead today. Algae all over it, not many fish."

Jack set his fork down and looked at Matt. "Every January there used to be thousands of groupers out there at full moon, one big mating game. This January, maybe a hundred. Guys were dropping nets after dark. I ran them off, but they were right out there the next night."

"You didn't turn them in?"

"See that boat out there in the middle of the lagoon?" Jack pointed to a partially sunk thirty-two-footer, water over the gunwales, the cabin scarred by fire. "About a year ago, I called Belize Fisheries and told them that two guys with spears were tracking a manatee in the north end channel. Even gave them the bastards' names. Guess what? Two days later, my boat became a midnight bonfire."

"The Fisheries guy?"

"The poachers. Fisheries called them in for a chat. They know the game. No doubt, they handed over a few bills to a lousy bureaucrat and left with my name. And there goes my boat. If I turn them in again, they'll burn down my lodge. With me in it."

To Matt, it sounded like the frontier without a sheriff. "What about the reef off Charlie's? It looked like it had been harvested. And there was a trap jammed with fish."

Jack dropped his fork. "They're trapping again? The poor bastards in the village are struggling to make a buck, but they're wiping out the fish. Next year they won't make a nickel."

"But the little stuff's gone too, Jack. Are you sure it's guys from the village? People aren't eating seahorses or sea cucumbers or two-inch fish."

"Well, the Asians eat the sea cucumbers, but not the others." Jack speared a shrimp, studied it, and put it back on his plate.

"You must know what's going on, Jack. It's not just poor old fishermen cleaning out the reef."

"I don't know. Not many fishermen are left, but fish are disappearing, even up into Mexico and down into Honduras. That's something you ought to write about. Find out what's really happening. Expose the bastards." Suddenly, Jack threw his glass across the bar, shattering it. "Remind me to sweep that up in the morning. If I'm still alive."

"Calm down, for godsake. I'm not a crime reporter."

"How much do you make, a few hundred bucks an article? I thought you'd be living off insurance money."

Matt stiffened.

"Sorry, Matt, I didn't mean that. Your father's not coming back, but you can still do something to make him proud."

Matt's jaw was tight. Jack had him pegged, but it wasn't Jack who had made him angry. He imagined the barren reef, not much different from his life in a way. He took a deep breath. "That's not what I do, Jack. I wouldn't know where to begin."

"How about starting at the freezer, for openers?" Jack pushed away his plate and looked at Matt. "Never mind,

Matty, forget it. You have Barnstable on your ass, who's now seen you in the company of a suspected murderer." Jack yawned, folded his arms, and lay his head on them. In a minute, his snoring drowned out the soft lapping waves.

Starlight cast shadows on the sand. Matt felt sheepish, as if he were letting Jack down, maybe letting himself down. He was too tired to walk back to Charlie's, so he let Jack sleep and headed inside the lodge to say hello to Cleo, who was putting away the last dishes, and told him he could stay in Cottage 8. On his way to the cottage, he strolled behind the dive shack. A spear gun was propped against the wall, the ancient Kelvinator lay on its side, still rank. Dried fish guts were stuck in crevices. A parrotfish gill shimmered like a silver dollar in the rays of a flickering floodlight.

Matt studied the freezer, estimated the dimensions—nearly two meters long, a meter high and a little less wide. He pictured the body, imagined it being dropped in, arranged, rearranged; he could see it all, except who had done it. A story had begun here, but where would it end? It wasn't the story Matt had come to write.

AN HOUR LATER, still sitting on his bar stool, Jack woke with a start. Across the lagoon, Charlie was pulling his skiff onto his beach in the moonlight. Jack headed to his dock, struggling to walk a straight line in the heavy sand. He stumbled into his runabout, landing square on the seat next to the outboard. He picked up his plastic Clorox bottle with the bottom sliced off, dipped it into the ocean, poured water over himself, and then motored over to Charlie's. When he pulled his skiff up on the beach, Charlie slammed shut the door on one shed, fastened the latch with a padlock, and walked toward Jack, waving his beefy hand to greet him.

Jack shook his head, one last effort to clear away the fog. "So, where were you today? Barnstable thinks you were in hiding."

"I had work to do. The sun was perfect. Plenty of good light."

"Work? Taking more pictures? How many do you need for that book of yours?"

"Enough to finish," Charlie said.

"You don't even know how to write. How you going to finish it?"

Charlie lunged at Jack, who stepped aside too slowly. Charlie's shoulder, with his medicine-ball chest behind it, buried into Jack's stomach, knocking him down on the sand. As Charlie hovered over him, fists clenched, Jack held up both hands.

"Sorry, Tuna, no disrespect for your talents, but your disappearing act didn't go down well with Barnstable. Or me." Jack stood up and brushed at the sand sticking to his body.

"What did you tell him?"

"I didn't tell him you were out taking snapshots. Otherwise, he'd think you were avoiding him. Now, you got to help me out here."

"And you got to pay me. I'm about four weeks out of pocket," he said, poking a finger into his own fleshy chest, "and Charlie, here, has a little cash flow problem."

"We're all going to have cash flow problems if Barnstable stops sending my guests away."

"Maybe so, but you being out of money is nothing new, Jack, and your new job as a shark circus ringmaster hasn't saved your ass. Just sell your place, put a million bucks in your pocket, and buy a bar on Ambergris. Upgrade to twenty-one-year-old Appleton Estate rum. You deserve it."

"My liver's big enough as it is. Be looking like your belly in no time."

Charlie took a step forward and crossed his arms, as if to hold himself back from another wrestling match. "Well, my uncle's still serious. He'd be happy to write you a big check for this little island of yours and give me a serious salary. He likes it down here."

"And so do I. Someday you can bury me over there, Charlie. Then let the mangroves reclaim it."

"That could happen sooner than you think, Jack. You already had your first body. Who's next?"

"Now just what the hell does that mean? Some sort of threat?"

"No, Jack, I'm just saying if this were my property there would be a fire sale."

"Well, Jack Africa's isn't on the market. And if you want to keep working for me, you'll get your ass in to see Barnstable, so he gets off my ass."

"I'll call him, but I'm telling you, I can't wait forever to get paid."

"Tell that to Barnstable. Now, let me see what photos you took today."

"They aren't edited. A hundred shots, maybe half a dozen I'd care to show."

"I can make that call myself. Fish shots never bore me."

Charlie took his Canon from the skiff and handed it to Jack, who started clicking through the images. "Took these today, did you? Some of your surface shots have rain clouds in them. Didn't rain here until dinner time."

"I was twenty miles south," Charlie said.

Jack grunted, then flipped through another twenty images before he handed the camera back to Charlie. "Here. Let me know what Barnstable says."

As Jack climbed into his skiff to motor back across the lagoon, Charlie unlocked his shed and disappeared inside.

10

$\sim$

FROM THE HEAD table, Robert Turnbull III, the guest of honor, surveyed the crowd of four hundred, most older than fifty, except for the Internet millionaires easily recognizable by their blue jeans and black shirts worn under their black blazers. Seats at the Global Fund for Wildlife dinner were five hundred dollars apiece, a price people happily paid to rub elbows with those who mattered. And to stay on Trey Turnbull's good side.

The evening had begun with an obligatory welcome by the Executive Director, an ethnobiologist who droned on about an orangutan project in Malaysia, while guests drank wine and busied themselves with their Caeser salads. Then it was vegetarian lasagna, followed by Ben and Jerry's Chunky Monkey ice cream, and finally time for Trey's pet project—preserving a pristine corridor through Central America and Mexico for jaguars and smaller cats, such as margays and jaguarondi, wanting to make the journey.

Sitting next to Turnbull was Nancy Pareto, President

of the Fund. She squeezed Turnbull's hand. "It's time to get started," she said. "Ready?"

"My pleasure," Turnbull replied, rubbing his forefinger across the back of her hand.

She slipped her hand away and walked to the lectern, smiling at the attendees, who had been fueled by all the donated wine. Turnbull scribbled a few last-minute notes as Pareto tapped the microphone with the two carats on her ring finger. The crowd quieted. "Wasn't that a lovely dinner?" A respectful applause. She thanked the staff, the volunteers — the "little people," as Turnbull called them. As he wondered what the hell these two hundred staff members in Washington did, he recognized a shock of red hair and the bushy beard on a mountain man standing in the back of the room. Trey squinted, trying to focus. Yes, it was David Mallard, a desperate man, a trait that interested Trey.

Pareto turned toward Turnbull and smiled. "We're here tonight to honor a great benefactor of the Global Fund for Wildlife, Mr. Robert Turnbull. I first met Trey three years ago in Kenya's Masai Mara. I was leading a group on a ten-day safari, and we had just watched a magnificent pack of wild dogs on a twilight hunt. We returned to camp as the sky turned black and, in the glow of our campfire, I saw a stranger sitting there. He looked as if he had just stepped off the *L.L. Bean* catalog cover.

"He said he'd been in the Mara for two weeks with only his guide and two helpers, so he could see the animals without disturbing them. When he saw our campfire, he dropped by to say hello. As you know, Trey is a charmer, and we talked until midnight. By the time he left, we had a new board member."

The crowd clapped politely. "As we have come to learn, Trey is a conservation pioneer. A rancher in Texas, he has bequeathed a substantial parcel from his considerable holdings to the Fund, so we may preserve his ecologically sensitive land for generations to come."

The crowd applauded with more vigor. Turnbull smiled and nodded.

"But Trey is more than just a rancher. He is a lover and patron of the wild. His private West Texas animal sanctuary educates thousands of children annually. On his own ranch, he protects hundreds of endangered African animals. His successful breeding program demonstrates just how a businessman can give back to his community."

Trey glanced at his watch and drummed his finger on his leg. It was nearly nine-thirty; this damned dinner had dragged on long enough.

"Trey has served many organizations, including the Natural Land Conservancy, but for the last three years, he's been ours. Not only has he given his time freely, but each year Trey has been generous financially. His leadership in our land acquisition program to create a wildlife corridor from Mexico to Panama and even restore Belize's coral reefs and mangrove islands is unparalleled."

The crowd stood and clapped.

"I need go no further. We all know what he means to the Fund, and we are all here to honor him. So, ladies and gentlemen, let us acknowledge our distinguished board member and benefactor, Mr. Trey Turnbull."

Trey pushed his chair back from the table and rose to

the applause. Broad shouldered and six feet three inches tall, he was imposing in the bright spotlight. Everyone in the room was standing. Trey basked in the adulation. He waved to his Mara development partner, Barnes Wellington, who had helped him cut a personal tourist development deal with the Masai the morning of the day he had met Nancy Pareto at the campfire.

Turnbull gave Nancy a brief kiss on the cheek then pulled a dozen notecards from his coat pocket.

IN THE REAR, David Mallard craned forward. The sleeves on his rental tuxedo hung to his knuckles, the pants legs drooped over his black Earth shoes. His Fund grant manager had told Mallard to fly to Washington to discuss his project. Because there were empty seats at the donor tables, he had been "allowed" to join the event.

Mallard had spent the afternoon explaining one last time that he needed at least $32,000 more to finish collecting data to determine the actual jaguar range before the pending dam project was finalized. The Fund told him that he had run out of time. And that they had run out of money. The Fund now had other priorities.

Mallard knew better. He had become too political for Belize, too demanding of government officials who had far more to gain from developers than from saving wildlife. He had either to raise his own money or to give up. Neither option was easy. Big cat donors loved tigers, lions and leopards, and Africa and Asia. Jaguars put less money in the bank. Besides, their habitat was Central America, where all those illegal immigrants come from.

And Belize? Where was that? But he would do whatever was necessary.

When the evening ended, Mallard lingered, watching Trey get his final handshakes and pats on the back. Trey glanced at him, his eyebrows flickering recognition. Mallard waited near the door, and when Trey finally approached, Mallard extended his hand. "Excellent speech. Well done. Congratulations."

Trey grabbed Mallard by the elbow and led him away from the crowd. "Did you get a cat? A margay maybe?"

"I released an ocelot out there. Everything is fine."

"All right. I'll be back in Belize tomorrow. I know where to find you. The money is yours if you do what I say."

Mallard started to speak. Trey squeezed his elbow harder until Mallard grimaced. "This is just between you and me, of course."

Mallard nodded. Trey let go and walked away to shake more hands. Mallard headed out the door, his hands deep in his pockets, knowing how it felt to make a deal with the devil.

II

~

T HE DAY BEGAN at Jack's as usual, with a soft rap on every cottage door and a melodious "good morning." Cleo had placed a pot of Guatemalan coffee and a carafe of fresh orange juice on Matt's porch. He sat naked on the side of his bed. Crumpled on the floor lay his single dull white sheet, pushed off in the night's hanging heat. He slipped on his shorts, opened his cabana door, poured a cup of black coffee, and sat down in the bamboo chair. The bay was still, the only sign of life a single pelican sitting atop a piling ruffling its wing feathers with its massive beak.

Today his shoulders felt heavy, his body like lead. Too much baggage. Writing came easy to him, but how could he produce a tranquil picture of Belize while Jack was being hung out to dry? He thought about an investigative piece, but starting at the beginning—the Kelvinator, as Jack said—gave him no inspiration. What else was there?

Matt finished his coffee, showered, and brushed his teeth. A little sign next to the mirror read, "The tap water is pure rainwater, collected in a cistern, but use it sparingly. Don't drink the toilet water, it's from the sea." He threw on yesterday's polo shirt, because his pack was still at Charlie's, and headed into the morning heat.

Across the way, Charlie climbed into his Zodiac, destroying the solitude with the sudden ripsaw sound of the outboard. In seconds, he was at Jack's dock. He wore only faded blue swim trunks, which hung below the plumber's line. "Morning, Matt. I see you made it through the night. I brought over your pack," he said, setting it on the dock.

"Thanks. Yeah, made it through the night but barely made it through yesterday."

"I told you there'd be police around."

"It wasn't that. I went snorkeling off your beach, Charlie. Saw guys diving, maybe spearfishing. And there was a fish trap."

"Fish trap? The guys in the village know better than to drop traps."

"The diver was wearing a wetsuit."

"He had to be local. The Guatemalans and Hondurans are all poaching down south. They're not coming up this far." He shook his head. "Anyhow, I have to go boot up the computer and try to explain to Jack's future guests, who are probably already packing their bags, why they have to rebook. There won't be no refunds coming." He shook his head. "It ain't no happy task." Charlie started toward the lodge, his spidery legs too thin for his tank-like torso.

Three dull, scuffed plastic yellow kayaks, solid shell and hollow, just like one he docked at home, sat near the water's edge. He needed a morning cruise. Matt pulled one off the beach, waded knee-deep alongside, and climbed in. With two quick paddle flicks he was in the center of the lagoon, headed toward the sea. He paddled hard for ten minutes, following the shore's northward curve, not even breaking into a sweat.

Rounding the north point, he guided the kayak into the cut between the two cayes and rested the paddle on his lap. From down the channel, he could hear the faint rumble of an outboard, but the sound soon stopped, leaving only the wind whispering through the mangroves. The channel, more than a half a mile long, eventually ended near the water taxi dock.

Just beneath the surface, he could see a shiny, slender needlefish concealing itself between mangrove roots. Nearby floated a finely woven net, shaped like a dome, its base invisible due to the dark, rich water. As he lifted it, thousands of tiny fish furiously flapped inside. He flipped the net over, freeing the captives. These were not baitfish, Matt knew, but juvenile reef fish, no doubt destined for home aquariums, probably in the U.S. This mangrove fish nursery was being cleaned out before the fry were old enough to migrate to their permanent coral homes, so that the reefs would soon become little more than vacant apartments. Half the captured fish would never live through the commercial flight north; most others would die soon after they were placed in private tanks. And another shipment would go out next week.

He dipped his paddle into the water and glided to a submerged rope that was tied to trees on both sides of the channel. Below the water line, a gill net lay hidden in the dark, nutrient-rich water. Somebody was hell-bent on cleaning out every last living fish. Matt untied one end of the rope and then pulled himself along to the other side to release the net. It was still empty, so it had just been set. He stashed it in the mangroves, thinking he would pick it up on his way back. If there was even one last manatee in the channel, he had hopefully saved it from becoming entangled and drowning.

Matt paddled quietly around the bend in the channel. There. Ahead. The white boat. Blue rails. The runabout that yesterday had nearly decapitated him. With a powerful backward stroke, he stopped the kayak, and then slipped behind an overhanging mangrove clump. The white boat looked empty though heat waves rose from the outboard cowling. In the distance, a muddy streak appeared near the channel's bank, moving toward him, a foraging manatee, Matt figured. Matt watched the murky cloud slowly rise. There. The surface turned to a rapid boil. Bubbles. From the manatee. The water boiled again, closer, then again. That manatee must weigh half a ton, Matt guessed, spellbound. More bubbles.

Fear jolted him. Those weren't manatee bubbles. They came from a scuba diver. He thrust the paddle into the water and pushed hard to back away, but the kayak's bow bolted upright, tossing Matt backward. Between his legs, a thin, metal shaft zoomed through the kayak's yellow hull, its point quivering inches from his chin. The only sounds Matt could hear were his thumping heart and the bubbles gurgling from the invisible diver.

Then the spear slid back through the hole until its

hinged barbs caught on the kayak's hull. Pulled from below, the kayak began moving through the water toward the white boat. Matt leaned over the side, but could see nothing in the muddy water. He jabbed his paddle through the surface, but the diver was too far down for him to reach. His kayak slid forward, dragged by the mysterious diver. With a few quick turns, Matt unscrewed the spear tip and jammed the bare shaft back through the hole in the hull, freeing his kayak. Water spurted into the seat pocket as he paddled furiously backward, sending his kayak spinning. Left, right, left, right. Finally, straightening out his kayak, he could sprint away. But with each strong stroke, he moved more slowly, as water poured through the spear hole, flooding the plastic hull.

Matt dug his paddle deeper, pulling harder, finally emerging from the channel into the open ocean. There was no engine sound behind him, only the trade winds rustling the palms and his paddle whacking at the surface. But much of the hull was now filled with seawater. It took him fifteen minutes to cover the last half-mile to Jack's.

When Jack saw him coming, he rushed to the water's edge to help drag the flooded kayak onshore. He tipped it over, letting the water spill out. "What the hell's this about?"

Matt pointed at the hole in the yellow hull. "Somebody tried to spear me, Jack. The guys from yesterday." He told Jack what had happened.

"If those were local poachers, Matty, they'd sink your boat, but they'd never try to kill you."

"Do you know a white boat with blue rails? Twenty-four feet, maybe."

"There's a hundred like that around here. No telling who owns that one."

"Well, I'm pissed. I didn't come here to get skewered." Matt was shaking. Fight and flight played tug-of-war inside him. He took several deep breaths and tried to calm himself.

Jack put his arm around Matt's shoulders. "Look, there's nothing we can do about it right now. Do me a favor, don't go telling stories around the breakfast table. There are still two guests left, and they've had enough to worry about. Now let's eat and get ready for a dive."

"You're going diving?" Matt was incredulous. But Jack sported a big smile, showing no effects from the Iceman or the Appleton.

"Rum Caye therapy. Relaxes your mind. Besides, I still have paying customers. We'll go an hour away where there won't be any trouble. Can't think of a better way to spend the day."

INSIDE THE DINING room, Dr. Herb Freeman, a Dallas plastic surgeon, and his wife Betty, the only guests left, had gathered for breakfast and were chatting with Charlie. Matt introduced himself. "Glad to meet someone else staying here," Freeman said. "I don't believe in letting a little gore ruin a good vacation." Matt tried to smile.

It was only eight-thirty, but Freeman's wife appeared dressed for a cocktail party, with diamond studs in both earlobes and a sparkling pendant resting against her black silk tank top. It was not the usual attire at Cap'n Jack's.

Cleo sauntered from the kitchen and placed a platter of mango pancakes and rashers of bacon on the table. She returned to the kitchen, re-emerging with a mush of refried beans, a bowl of salsa, and plates of toast and bananas. Jack lifted the white porcelain bowl filled with chocolate-colored refries and dropped a spoonful on his plate. "Have your beans, people. You need your fiber when you travel. About the only complaint I get here is from those who don't eat their beans."

"Well, I have plenty of complaints," Betty said, sitting up straight. "We finally got a flight, and we're leaving tomorrow morning. I wish we had never come."

Herb put his hand on her arm. "Dear—"

"Don't dear me. We're not safe here. I would have gone back to Belize City yesterday, but the hotels are dreadful, and the shopping is worse. My only bright moment in this entire disaster is this little pendant I bought while we waited for that horrible water taxi." She held it up.

Matt raised his head and saw Charlie lean over to look, his eyes widening. "Nice. How much you pay for it?"

"Hundred dollars American, mounted in twenty-four karat gold. At Robert's Import Jewelers on Front Street."

"Incredible," Charlie said, "I didn't know they charged so much for those things."

She sniffed. "It would be four times as much in Houston." She placed three pieces of bacon on her napkin and pressed out the grease.

"Herb," Jack said, between mouthfuls of beans,

"because you paid to dive, I'm taking you to Devil's Caye. Matt, here, will be joining us." He looked at Betty. "You can come along for the ride if you'd like."

She glared. "I'm going nowhere." Jack shrugged and glanced at Charlie, who had just pulled four more bacon slices from the serving plate. "And, Charlie? You're talking to Barnstable today, right?"

"Don't have much choice, now, do I?"

"Not if you want to get paid."

THE TRIP ON Jack's twenty-four-foot Boston Whaler, *Jumpin' Jack Flash*, was fast. Herb kept belching like a water buffalo, trying to keep his breakfast down. Matt stood alongside Jack near the wheel. As the boat hit the wind-blown water between islands, Matt softened at the knees, imagining spear after spear shooting through the hull.

"Hell of a ride," Jack shouted over the engine roar. "I could slow it down, but I need a little extra time to check on the flock of red-footed boobies that nest there. Been a pet project over the years."

Seventy minutes after they had left, they reached Devil's Caye, and he cut the Whaler to half speed. "It's one big island, about the size of Central Park, but it's crisscrossed by a bunch of narrow channels through the mangroves. You can't pass through them all. In the olden days, it was a good hiding place for pirates. Drug runners, these days."

"You ever see them?" Herb asked.

"Nope, I stay home at night." Jack glided his boat

through the turquoise waters of a small cove surrounded by a powdery sand beach, low scrub brush, and scores of coconut palms. He turned off the engine, clambered onto the foredeck, and tossed the anchor overboard, tugging on the line until the hook dug into the sand bottom.

"OK, Herb, on the lee side here it's all easy diving. You'll probably see nurse sharks and southern stingrays in the sand. Eighty feet is our maximum depth, and then we'll spend the last ten minutes in the shallows to burn off some nitrogen. Now let's get wet."

AFTER THE DIVE, Jack motored near the shore. He cut the engines, leaped from the *Jumpin' Jack Flash* with the anchor, and carried it ashore, pulling the line behind him. He dropped it thirty yards from the beach and waded back to the boat. "Lunch time," he said, standing knee-deep in water. "Hand me the cooler and c'mon ashore."

Jack pulled a large tablecloth from the chest, spread it on the sand, and put out plastic containers of salad, sandwiches wrapped in waxed paper, bananas and papaya, and coconut squares. "There's lemonade and Belize Crystal Water. Keep yourself hydrated." He walked back to secure his boat.

Herb turned to Matt. "So, what do you think about this Iceman business?"

"I don't know. I wasn't there to see it. What about you?"

"I think Jack ought to get the hell out of Belize. That's what I think. Sell out. Take the money and run." Herb stared at Matt as if he wanted him to agree.

"I didn't know that was an option."

"It's always an option, my Belize friends tell me. Buyers chasing land. All the time, everywhere."

Matt reached for a bottle of water and unscrewed the cap. "Maybe, but my bet is Jack will ride it out. He's a survivor."

"Sure, but why survive if you don't have a pot to piss in. Doesn't sound like he has many friends down here. Without friends, this country will eat you alive." Herb slapped at a mosquito. "See that, it's eating me alive, and I got friends down here. Good friends."

As Jack returned, Matt stood, brushing the sand from his legs. Herb fell back into the sand, folded his hands on his belly, and shut his eyes. Grabbing his machete, Jack started down the beach, beckoning Matt to join him. A hundred yards away, where a mangrove clump marked the end of the beach, a small sign proclaimed, *No Trespassing, Global Fund for Wildlife.*

Jack tapped the sign with the blunt end of his machete. "New sign. I didn't know the Fund owned anything out here."

"You'd think they would, at least, call it a preserve."

"Don't know that it is. I would have heard about it. C'mon, let's keep walking."

Disintegrating coconut husks, their sprouting stalks staking a new claim, marked the opening of the leaf-covered trail that disappeared into the bush. Jack whacked at the underbrush until they reached a small clearing with a twenty-foot-high wobbly wooden tower, a rickety ladder leading to a small platform on top. "You first," Jack said, "but be quiet, don't scare the birds."

Vines had wrapped themselves around the tower legs. The bottom ladder rung was missing. Matt climbed several rungs, snapping one as it took his full weight. Both his legs dropped into space and his butt landed on the rung below.

"Careful," Jack said, from ten feet below.

"Thanks for the advice." Matt pulled himself up. With each step, the tower swayed, but he made it to the top, an eight-foot square platform with broken planks, and a railing on one side only. Jack followed.

Perched in the bushes, no more than thirty feet away, were a dozen snow-white red-footed boobies, larger than seagulls, preening, cooing, and cackling, with one eye focused on the intruders. "Odd," Jack said. "Those treetops are usually covered. At least a hundred birds, sometimes more." As he spoke, several birds flew off but quickly returned.

"When were you last here?"

"Four or five months ago."

The two men watched silently until Jack headed back down the ladder, jumping the last three feet. When Matt reached the ground, he walked into the thick growth under the nesting birds. "Look at this," Matt said. A pile of torn feathers, half a red booby foot, and a dismembered beak. Six feet away, another pile with similar remains.

Jack pushed through the brush. "Something got them."

"What's out here?" Matt asked.

"Damned if I know." He shook his head. "There aren't any predators."

"What about cats? I saw a feral on your island."

"Could be, but boobies would be too big for them. On the mainland, there are ocelots and little margays, but they don't live out here."

"Jack, look at this." Matt pulled a long stick from the underbrush. Bamboo, close to ten feet long. On one end was lashed a small woven basket, a foot in diameter. "Looks like some sort of dipping basket. Maybe someone stands on the platform and uses this to pick up the chicks or steal their eggs."

"I'll be damned —" Jack grabbed it from Matt and broke the handle over his knee. He threw the remains into the brush. "I don't like it, Matt, not at all. You have to help me out here."

"And how would I do that?"

"Stop being a cub reporter. If investigating the Iceman is too much for you, maybe you can look into a few dead birds."

"Screw you, Jack."

Jack shrugged. "C'mon, let's head back. I'm hotter than a ten-cent tin roof."

"No. Wait a minute." Matt put his hand on Jack's shoulder and spun him around. "What do you want from me?" Jack looked tired. Matt could see the anguish in his eyes.

"Just step up to the plate, for Christ sakes. Write about something that does some good, has an impact. Maybe earn yourself a Pulitzer, Matty." He slapped at a mosquito. "Or, maybe just save an old man's life." Jack tapped himself on his chest. "And quit hoping I might fill in for your father."

Matt took a deep breath but said nothing.

"Think about it," Jack said.

They walked in silence until they reached the beach. Matt put his arm around Jack's shoulder. "Look, I leave for the rainforest lodge tomorrow, but there's one more dive I want to do. Tonight. Where the Iceman disappeared."

12

$\sim$

Matt put the cooler back on the *Jumpin' Jack Flash* as they prepared to depart for their second dive. Jack, chewing on a wooden matchstick, motored the craft five minutes out, carefully dropped anchor, then helped Herb don his tank. "Go over when you're ready, Herb. Bottom's only twenty feet here, then it drops away to ninety."

Matt climbed into his gear, flipped backward over the side and headed to the bottom, mesmerized by darting reds and yellows and blues of finger-sized fish flitting between dusky brown soft corals. Herb dropped like a rock, sending up a thick sand cloud as he crashed into the bottom. Jack floated down behind him.

Herb flashed the OK sign and started kicking. The three divers zigzagged between narrow coral canyons. Traveling as a squadron, scores of small Creole wrasses, royal blue with an orange splash, disappeared into the blue. A stoplight parrotfish, its mottled body sparkling from the sunlight piercing the surface, chewed at live coral, and then swam away, excreting a milky trail. Matt stopped breathing to listen to the faint snaps and clicks, the critter voices in surround sound, like an undersea Morse code.

Suddenly Jack stopped kicking. With a flip of his fins, he jerked upright and started at the surface. Matt's eyes followed, searching for an eagle ray, maybe a shark passing overhead. Then he heard the distant drone growing louder. A boat. Matt saw its hull cut through the surface leaving a frothy trail. Then the engine cut to idle.

Jack pointed at Matt and Herb, hit his fists together, and then drew circles with his fingertip. You two stay together and swim around, he was signaling. With a quick kick, he headed to the surface. Ignoring Jack's instructions, Matt kicked slowly upward, signaling Herb to follow. Surfacing, twenty feet from the *Jumpin' Jack Flash*, Matt saw Jack, with a hardy kick, pull himself up on his boat's transom, jump to his feet, peel off his mask, nearly ripping the O-ring from his ear, and pull off his fins. Sitting in the small boat alongside, bare-chested with a bandana around his neck and a machete lying across his lap, was the muscular Mestizo Matt had seen on Haulover Creek when he and Charlie were leaving Belize City.

"Ah, Jack, thanks for comin' up, mon. I wanted to talk to you. I thought this might be a good way to get your attention." A scar ran down the Mestizo's left cheek; on his left arm, "King" was engraved under a tattoo of Jesus's face. His partner was a Mayan, smaller, with a flatter nose, mocha skin, small gold studs in both ears and a greasy ponytail poking out of the dirty red bandana tied around his head. Strapped to his calf, a black rubber sheath held a bone-handled diver's knife.

"I've got divers down there, assholes," Jack said.

"They came up, they're behind you," the Mestizo said, pointing to them. He pulled a rusty file from a plastic bucket and ran it down his machete blade. Without looking up, he said, "These are private cayes, you know."

"Bullshit. There's a sign that says the Fund owns them, but maybe you never learned to read."

The Mestizo, his right eyebrow cocked, looked at Jack. "Fuck you. I said you won't be going on that caye no more. Or diving in this lagoon. You go dive some other place." He resumed sharpening his machete.

"What kind of crap is that?"

"This is a preserve. I'm paid to protect it." He looked like a cat about to pounce, his mouth tight, his eyes fixed on Jack.

"News to me. And it's always been open for diving."

"No more. You be going now."

"Who do you guys work for? What are your names?"

"What the fuck is his name," yelled the Mayan, shaking his finger at Matt bobbing in the water, his mask pulled and resting on his chest. "That's the prick who took our picture."

Matt looked at Jack, whose teeth were clenched, his right hand balled into a fist. The Mestizo pointed his machete at Matt. "Your ass is next," he said, "if you don't stay the fuck out of here." The Mayan slipped the outboard into gear, lifting the bow from the water, lurching toward Matt, then quickly turning, its wake pushing the two divers backward as the boat headed away.

Matt and Herb kicked to the *Flash* and Jack extended

his hand to Herb to help him up the ladder. "Assholes, trying to tell me I can't dive here," Jack mumbled.

"So, who are those thugs? Can they do that?" Matt asked.

"Who cares," Herb said. "I'd just find some other place to dive."

"Over my dead body," Jack said. "Maybe someone can keep me from walking on that piece of real estate, but they can't keep me out of the water. What the hell is a boatload of divers once a week going to do to it?"

"I saw those two guys when I came out from Belize City with Charlie," Matt said. "I think they'd kill you just for looking at them." Matt started pulling off his gear. "I can't believe the Fund would hire them. It's supposed to be a classy group."

"Nobody's classy in Belize, sonny." Jack pointed to the anchor line. "Give me a hand with that, will you?"

Matt tugged the anchor line, but it wouldn't budge. Jack started the engine and swung the Whaler around, looking for an angle to pull the hook off the reef, but it was wedged tight.

"Matty, how about going down and freeing the anchor?"

Matt grabbed his mask and fins. Jack lifted the tank to his back and Matt stepped into the water with a splash. Kicking down toward the anchor, he saw a nurse shark sequestered under a coral ledge. Matt touched its tail, expecting it to shoot from beneath the ledge and head for the next sand patch, but it only edged forward. Only when Matt swam to the shark's head did he realized it was not a bottom-feeding nurse shark, but a reef shark, its mouth moving up and down as if it were trying to speak.

Matt pulled back, and the shark's eye followed him, but it was dull, confused, like the sad eye of a dying dog.

Matt exhaled, letting his body sink slowly to the sand. Then he stopped breathing, choking back the raw taste in his throat. Where the shark's dorsal fin had once been, a crab picked at open flesh. Damselfish poked at another fleshy wound, where its pectoral fin had been cut off. The shark repeatedly opened and closed its mouth, desperately trying to draw oxygen from the water it pulled through its gills. Otherwise, it lay motionless. Unable to swim, it would be picked to death by surgeonfish, snappers and sharks and all the bottom dwellers.

Matt rushed to the surface. "Jack, you need to see this." Without waiting, Matt headed back down, kicking hard. Jack was alongside him moments later. Matt pointed; they both stared at the gaping shark, and then looked at each other. Signaling for Matt to stay, Jack headed to the surface and returned gripping a knife. The shark's gills barely rippled. Jack carefully placed the knife directly behind the shark's head, over its spine, and then, like a bullfighter, plunged the sharp tip through the tough skin, deep between the vertebrae. The shark offered no resistance.

AT THE LODGE before dinner, Matt and Jack sat at the bar in silence while Charlie and Little Man engaged in a spirited game of dominoes. All Matt could think about was that shark, its fins no doubt headed for somebody's soup bowl. His chest burned as his anger and sadness fused.

The crack of dominoes hitting the table sounded like

cap guns firing, snapping Matt out of his fog. "Gotcha," Little Man yelled. "Six for me, nothing for you, Charlie. You don't even know how to play the game."

Little Man went behind the bar, returning with two orange Fantas. Charlie grabbed his and downed half, a trickle of orange staining his beard. "I never beat this guy," he mumbled. Laughing, Little Man headed to the lodge. Jack passed a half-empty bottle of Appleton to Matt, who waved it off, so he poured two fingers for himself.

Charlie finished off his Fanta. "While you guys were out diving, I checked out the local Internet bulletin boards. The police don't want the Iceman publicized, but the electronic tom tom has the story bouncing around the islands. Seems like the police interviewed the divers when they arrived in Belize City and not one could give any positive ID. Some saw a black arm; others thought it was white."

Jack shook his head. "And Little Man, that dumb shit, who should have captured it all on his Sony, was getting his jollies filming that good looking babe clearing her mask. Chaos at the ice block and Little Man missed it all. He could have made a fortune off that video."

"Fortune, my ass," Charlie scoffed. "The five bucks you'd have paid him would have been it."

"I'd given him a piece of it. But he's got no excuse for missing that scene. He had the camera on that woman for maybe a minute. Ten seconds a diver is what I've told him all along."

"He liked the way she looked," Charlie said. "She was a fox."

"Give me a break. By the way, what did you tell Barnstable today?"

"I told him what I knew, which is nothing."

"What about the night or two before? When the body got dumped. You were in your house. Did you hear anything?"

"With these ears," Charlie said, tugging at a fleshy lobe, "if you were cutting down a coconut palm with a chainsaw, I'd never hear it. In fact, Barnstable says the Iceman might be a hoax. No body, just a mannequin."

"Well, I'll be a son-of-a-bitch," Jack said.

"Barnstable said no one's turned up missing."

"Barnstable's covering his ass. He's dying to pin it on me, but he can't. And he's not about to chase down other leads. No telling what he'll turn up. Probably some politician. By the way, Tuna, you know what we found out there today? A reef shark with its fins cut off. You know what that means, Tuna? Soup. Shark fin soup."

Charlie ran his fingers through his beard, gritting his teeth. "No shit. If I ever caught a guy doing that, I would cut off his arm and beat him over his head with it. But there you go, Jack, what did I tell you? You train those sharks to show up for a dinner bell, and they're easy pickins for any fisherman. Now you got their blood on your hands, as well."

"It wasn't where we do the rodeo, Tuna. The shark was at Devil's Caye."

"Makes no difference where it was, Jack, it's just a matter of time. That's all it is."

Matt, who was listening to Charlie and Jack bicker like cranky brothers, jumped to his feet. "Guys, neither of you have dived the shark feed site since Tuesday, right?"

"Nope," Charlie said, "but police divers were supposed to, or so I heard."

"Hey, Jack!" It was Little Man, coming out of the lodge. "Cleo needs you in the kitchen."

Jack slid off his stool. "You guys figure it out. We still have some guests to feed before they leave in the morning."

As Little Man took Jack's barstool, Matt put his hand on Charlie's arm. "Charlie, I want to see the shark dive site. Take me out there tonight."

"Not me. I got work to do."

"Look, I'll pay you."

Charlie looked at his watch, adjusting the bezel. "Aren't you flying to that jungle lodge in the morning? Thought I was taking you and the Freemans to Belize City bright and early. You can't dive twenty-four hours before you fly. You'll get bent."

"My flight's not until four o'clock in the afternoon, and the plane flies so low the rules don't apply, anyhow. Don't make excuses for me."

"Come back after your trip to that lodge and we'll go then. You can help us close down here, nail the doors shut."

"Jack says he's going to reopen."

Charlie shook his head. "They'll never let him reopen. Trust me."

Little Man's eyes opened wide. "What? That would be no good, mon, not for either of us. You never thought about that, Charlie."

"What do you mean, never thought about it? I'm tellin' you right now we'll all need another job."

Little Man jumped up. "Then you should be taking this man diving, because he's paying you. You wanted me to go. Take him instead."

"You were going to take Little Man out there?" Matt asked.

Charlie slid off his barstool and headed for another Fanta. "The police won't take kindly to us rooting around that reef, considering it's a crime scene."

"Bullshit. Barnstable called it a hoax."

"It's just not something you ought to bother yourself with—or write about."

"You know something I don't, Charlie?"

"Nah. But you don't live here. I'm not trying to warn you off or anything; I'm just saying there's nothing in it for you."

"I'm not doing it for me, Charlie. I'm doing it for Jack."

13

Two ViewSonic computer monitors glimmered in the dark room, one displaying unopened emails in Mandarin, the second a financial spreadsheet in English. Martin Chin sat at his wooden desk, eating a gelatinous chicken and noodle soup with chopsticks from a ceramic bowl, last week's *South China Morning Post* spread before him. Though the current edition was online, the words on newsprint seemed more truthful to Chin. And they fueled his nostalgia.

From inside a tiny canary cage atop a filing cabinet, a magnificent scarlet macaw stared at him. Whenever the bird straightened up, its head hit the top of the cage. A dime-sized bald spot had appeared where the feathers had been rubbed off. Chin had a larger cage, but when he put the macaw into it, the bird would cackle, drawing the unwanted interest of passersby on the street outside. In the canary cage, the macaw just sat and stared, unable to move more than a few inches.

Chin checked his Blackberry, but no messages. Perhaps

the ambassador had left town. He went back to the *Post*. He would be patient.

Chin had been in Belize fifteen years. To the day. But he had no intention of celebrating his anniversary. He had work to do, as he had every day. By Belize standards, he was a very rich man, but still not rich enough for him, though he was far better off than when he lived in Hong Kong.

In the early nineties, he had begun to fear the coming English withdrawal and what dire economic fate the communist government would surely bring in the 1997 Hong Kong takeover. Tearoom rumors were rampant that little import businesses such as his would be expropriated. Or at best, the government would force him to pay such high taxes he would have to shut down. Gossip was also rife that the Hong Kong stock market would drop through the floor. So, when he read that the Belize government was selling passports to citizens of the British Empire, no strings attached, Chin scraped up the last of his money, knowing only that Belize had also once been part of the British Empire, British Honduras as he recalled from his school days. It was tropical, democratic, close to the United States, undeveloped, with only 200,000 citizens. From the few people he could find who knew anything about Belize, he learned the government eagerly sought foreign investors, relaxing rules to attract their money. Best of all, the size of the expected bribes had not caught up with what you had to slide under the table in other countries; a case of Johnny Walker would do just fine to encourage an official to turn a blind eye, at least on small deals. So, paying the Belize government $23,800 for full citizenship seemed like a splendid investment, though he had no idea what he would do once he arrived.

Across from him in a small room, a stack of folded cartons, each stenciled with Chinese and English lettering, almost touched the ceiling. Upstairs, four women were canning soup, producing twenty cases a day, sometimes thirty. Annoyed by their constant chatter about the old country, Chin stayed away from them. In another room, Chin's son sorted herbs bought from farms in Belize and Mexico.

When Chin had arrived in Belize, tourists had nothing to spend their money on, so he opened a small store near the swing bridge over Haulover Creek. He sold plastic black Jesuses nailed on crosses, with "Belize" printed on the stands; bracelets with painted dinosaurs; woven Chinese baskets with dancing natives. Belizeans had no craft-making skills, so Chin imported carvings and pottery and tapestries from Mexico and Guatemala.

One morning, while standing outside his store smoking a Marlboro, he watched two women, one fingering a ceramic ashtray shaped like a Mayan temple, the other studying a hairbrush with a crude drawing of Michael Jackson on the back.

"Nothing but tchotchkes, Barbara, nothing but tchotchkes."

Chin responded, "You like them? What did you call them?"

"Tchotchkes," she said. "Tchotchkes."

"American word. I don't know it. Say it again, please?"

"Tchotchke. Like 'choch key.'" Laughing, the women bought six fist-sized plaster Mount Rushmore replicas, with Ronald Reagan replacing Teddy Roosevelt, then sauntered off, telling Chin it was "Mai Tai Time."

The next day a sign went up. *Chin's Chotchkes*.

His tchotchke business kept him alive and, thanks to the Chinese economic attaché in Hong Kong who accepted Chin's generous gift of a Honda motorcycle, he became the sole Belizean importer of Chinese goods. Soon, his wife, their two children, her sister, and his mother joined him. He added goods that the "natives," as he called them, would buy—hair clips, coin purses, CDs—and set up women in his street stands to sell them. He bought a building, then another, opened a Chinese restaurant, bought a water taxi business with six fast boats, started a small taxidermy business, imported herbs and made traditional medicines to sell to other Chinese who had moved to Belize—they now numbered about six thousand—and to Asian immigrants in Mexico and Honduras. His export business to Central America and China was growing, so he'd bought a small plane, which he leased when he was not using it to move his goods throughout the area.

Chin was about to pick up the *Post* again when his Blackberry started vibrating noisily. A text message: *Greetings Chin. Deliver the usual to the main gate before five tonight, thank you, sir.* No abbreviations like *ty* or *u*. No doubt, the sender was too old to learn.

Chin opened his right-hand drawer, fished out a small ring of keys, ignoring the pistol. Behind his desk, a padlock secured a wooden door decorated with a

1993 calendar, a memorial to Hong Kong as it had been. Unlocking the padlock, he pulled open the door. An odd, earthy aroma crept deep into his lungs. In what was once a large bathroom, shelves ran from floor to ceiling, framing the toilet tank. Jars by the score were filled with powders or crushed leaves or stems. On the shelf above the toilet, brown Kraft bags overflowed with dry flora.

As Chin reached for an empty jar, he cried out; a searing pain shot through his lower back as if he had been stabbed with a thin stiletto. He stopped, stood still, rubbed his back, let the pain subside, and then reached again slowly for the jars. The tiny jars, which once held Knott's Berry Farm strawberry jam, had been stolen by a Radisson Inn waiter, sold to Chin, and boiled clean by his wife. Some customers preferred tiny brown sacks, but for the embassy, the jars seemed more appropriate.

Chin spooned a thimble's portion of powder into one jar; in the other, he placed twice the amount. He stuck a small white label on one, a yellow label on the other, and wrote on them with Chinese characters. After placing both jars into a small, maroon-colored cotton sack, he pulled the drawstrings tight, dropped it into a leather diplomatic pouch, shut the door to the storage room, and fastened the padlock. The macaw slept.

It was a ten-minute walk to the embassy, but he had nothing pressing to do, so he would drop off his package early. The ambassador would appreciate it. He always did.

14

Without even a sliver of moon in the sky, darkness came quickly. The trade winds stopped; the water lay still with only an occasional wave lapping at the shore. The distant islands were only a black silhouette, rimmed by faint light from faraway stars.

Matt arrived at the dock at half past seven, pleased that Charlie was already onboard. Illuminated by a floodlight atop a pole at the end of the dock, Little Man unwrapped the stern line, tossed it on the deck, and pushed the boat away with his foot. Charlie slid the throttle forward, and they slipped into the lagoon, then into open water at half throttle. Matt pulled on his wetsuit top as protection against the evening breeze.

"So, Matt? How are you and sharks?"

"I have a mantra: I don't eat sharks, and they don't eat me."

"Looks like it's worked so far. Anyhow, I doubt we'll see many. Then again, in the dark one could be sniffing at your fanny and you would never know it. But these are mainly whitetip sharks. Puppy dogs."

"Mainly?"

"Mainly. You get an occasional bull. They're the ones to keep an eye out for."

"So advised." Inside his wetsuit, sweat rolled down Matt's chest. He unzipped it to let the breeze blow in.

"Tell me, Matt, why are you so eager to make this dive? Still playing journalist?"

"Just curious. Never know what you might find, that's all."

Like sparklers, bioluminescent plankton glowed in the prop wash until Charlie finally cut the engine nearly to idle, an hour after departing. "The site's ahead about half a mile. I'm going to sneak up on it, just so those puppies don't think we're bringing them a midnight snack. I'd just as soon they don't spoil our party."

Matt fiddled with his equipment, trying not to think about sharks. Mainly whitetips. Mainly. With only starlight, the surface looked like a shimmering black hole.

"I've got to get positioned right. I haven't dived here since Jack started his shark wrangling. I tried to talk him out of it, but I lost that fight long ago. I told him it would come back and haunt him. And now it has." As Charlie's skiff drifted, he turned on his halogen dive light and let the beam skim along the water. Two hundred yards away, a white float the size of a basketball bobbed on the surface. "Looks like the police marked the site. I'm going to snip the line to keep the fishermen away from the sharks."

He took a quick compass reading and turned off the light. The compass glow illuminated his face. He uncoiled the anchor line and lowered it to the reef, giving it a tug to set the hook.

"Behind us is Goofy Bird Caye." It was pitch-black, only its vague profile visible against the starry sky. "It's about a quarter mile away, so if you lose me or can't see the boat, set your compass for it. One hundred sixty-five degrees. The bottom is forty feet down, if I recall right, and it pretty much stays that way until we get to the site, which is about sixty feet from the edge of the big wall and the drop-off."

"Where the sharks carried the Iceman."

"That's the claim. It drops off a thousand feet or more there. On the swim over, we'll stay about ten feet deep. Probably take us about fifteen minutes."

They geared up silently, but as Matt lifted his tank from the rack, it banged against another, sending a sharp report into the clear night air. "Quiet," Charlie whispered. "Enter the water off the transom. And check your light."

Matt pointed his light downward and flipped the switch. The beam reflected off the fiberglass deck, casting light skyward.

"Keep your light off. It has plenty of battery. I'll use mine. Just follow me. When we get there, switch on yours. If you find anything interesting, wiggle the beam at me." Charlie slipped into the water and slowly sank until all Matt could see was the eerie glow of his light. Matt jumped in and followed.

After a fifteen-minute swim, Matt turned on his light. A lead weight lay in the sand attached to the police mooring ball floating on the surface. Charlie pulled his knife from the sheath on his leg and cut the line, freeing the float.

As Matt moved his beam around, pinpricks of light reflected back from the eyes of critters hidden in crevices. Like a ten-legged ballerina, a lobster tiptoed on point across the sand. Against a lump of dead coral, a midnight-blue parrotfish slept in a protective cocoon it had spun from its own mucus.

Charlie finned slowly, weaving his light back and forth across the bottom. Matt moved to Charlie's left, fanning the sand, hoping to uncover anything unusual. He turned his light toward the surface, imagining a wide, gaping mouth lunging at him, but saw nothing. Sweeping his light in wide arcs across the sand, he looked for straight lines or perfect circles, shapes that did not come naturally to the reef.

His beam hit a bright white object, two feet long, nearly straight, with a knob on one end. A femur. Matt stopped breathing; his heart pounded inside his chest. He kicked toward it. No, not a femur, only a staghorn coral branch, bleached and broken.

His mind wandered to the brilliant reds and oranges and yellows illuminated by his light. He passed above a green moray, its mouth slowly opening and closing, and then he picked up a slender coral finger and began probing the sand, for what he didn't know.

Wham! Something slammed into his chest, knocking the wind out of him. Matt's head jerked back violently, hitting the valve on his tank, sending a searing pain through his skull. Swirling sand engulfed him, like a desert storm. He thrust out the light like a shield. With the other hand, he grabbed at the burning pain at the back of his head. The blow had flipped him up and spun him around. He could see nothing in the blizzard.

Smack. Another blow. This one against his right leg, knocking him sideways. As he tumbled, he waved his arms, hoping to frighten whatever had struck him, but he fanned only water. He landed on a jagged coral head and rolled off onto the sand. He saw Charlie's light moving toward him, and then he saw his attacker. Burying himself in the sand twenty feet away, a southern stingray scooted away to hide from the idiot who had just jammed a piece of coral into its back. Shaking, Matt took a deep breath and relaxed, trying to settle down. The ray's dagger-like barb had been inches from his stomach.

Charlie pulled his regulator from his mouth, shined his light on his face, and grinned. Still trembling, Matt gave him the finger.

After pointing at his watch, Charlie flashed five fingers twice and drew circles with his index finger: hang out here for ten minutes. Matt shone his light where the stingray had initially buried himself. Something dull yellow, the size of a fingernail was disappearing as sand particles settled. Matt grabbed it. He held his light on it. A gold tooth. A front tooth. He waved his beam at Charlie, who was sixty feet away, absorbed in his own search, so he put the tooth in his vest pocket and dug for more. Ten minutes later, Charlie banged his knife against his tank, waved his light, and pointed it in the direction of the boat. Time to go.

Matt signaled OK, but fanned the sand a few more times, keeping an eye on Charlie's light, which grew fainter as Charlie headed back. Matt turned his compass bevel to 135 degrees and as he did the beam from his own light flashed in his eyes, blinding him. He sat for a moment until he could see again and then kicked off, following his compass arrow. Ahead, he could see only black. Charlie and his light had dissolved into the darkness.

Matt stayed on course, weaving his light back and forth across the bottom. He bolted upright. A squirrelfish shot through his light beam just inches away. Charlie's light had kept his fears at bay, but now he was alone, surrounded by black water where the Iceman had disappeared.

He kicked harder and breathed faster. The features of the sand floor dimmed, the fish in the distance became tougher to see. His light was fading, dimming, slowly disappearing. Charlie had said he had plenty of battery. Why had Matt trusted him? He kicked harder, nine minutes to go, eight, seven, and then it was dark, as dark as death. Matt stiffened. His heart banged against his chest wall, reverberating in the steel tank on his back. He looked up. Or was it up? A sharp pain sliced across his forehead. He slapped at it. A black tomb, no directions, no light. No up, no down. Only black.

Tears flushed his eyes as the pain soared. He gritted his teeth, took a deep breath, and felt himself beginning to float upward. Exhaling, he kicked a few times. As he broke the surface, sharp electrical pulses shot through his head. Letting out a scream, he swiped at his head, and a jellyfish, the size of an omelet, plopped into the water and floated away. He swiveled full circle, but he could not see the boat.

Which way to go? The boat couldn't be gone. He would have heard the engine. His eyes were nearly closed as the lids swelled from the jellyfish venom. He couldn't read his compass. Goofy Bird Caye, he remembered, was a quarter mile away. Though he thought he had been swimming a straight line between the shark dive site and the boat, he had no idea where the boat should be. He could only swim toward the island, if he could see it.

Then, roaring across the surface came Charlie's voice. "Some fucker stole my boat." Matt saw Charlie's light dance across the surface. He rolled over on his back and started kicking toward Charlie.

"My boat. It's gone. The line's been cut."

Matt kicked hard, the splashing water sparkling from the rising moon. "Who? Who did it?" He could hear Charlie smacking the water with both hands, his roars ringing across the surface.

"How should I know?" Charlie yelled. They both bobbed in the black sea, ten feet from each other, Charlie screaming, "Son of a bitch. Son of a bitch."

Matt splashed seawater at his head, but his flesh felt seared. They were floating a quarter-mile from an island, in the middle of a dark Belizean night, with Charlie's skiff nowhere in sight.

"Start swimming," Charlie said. He wiggled his light toward the island, but the beam just disappeared without reaching shore. All Matt could see was the vague black outline of treetops. "Keep your tank on. No reason to ditch our gear. No need to make Jack hoppin' mad."

Matt rolled over on his back and started kicking,

wondering if the sound of his fins stirring the surface would attract sharks. He kicked steadily, and with each kick inched ahead of Charlie, whose rumbling exhalations sounded like a humpback whale blowing.

Forty minutes later, Matt stood in three feet of water, the stinging subsiding. He could hear Charlie's overworked lungs bellowing before he could see him. After he had crawled onto the shore, it took minutes before Charlie had absorbed enough oxygen to talk. "Those motherfuckers stole my boat." He pushed himself up and sloshed through the water, his fins in one hand, and his mask in the other.

Sweat poured down Matt's face from the long swim in the humid 80-degree night, yet he still shivered, from fear, not from cold. He peered into the undergrowth on the island, not knowing what to expect. It was dead quiet. He pulled off his tank, letting it drop to the sand, and unzipped his wetsuit. "So now what?" Matt asked, swatting a mosquito from his face.

Charlie dropped his tank and climbed out of his wetsuit. "Somebody will find us in the morning—Little Man, most likely. You better leave your wetsuit on, otherwise you'll be eaten to death by mosquitoes."

Matt nodded. "Charlie, what makes you think that was just a boat thief and not somebody trying to tell us something."

"Like what?"

"Like stay the hell out of here."

"You don't know that."

Matt wasn't sure what he knew. He had heard no motor, so whoever took the boat must have paddled out to it. He scoured the horizon. Nothing moved, no sounds, it was far too quiet. Reaching into his buoyancy vest pocket, he fished around for the gold lump he had stashed. He dug it out from a corner with one finger. "Shine your light here."

It was a dull gold, with what seemed like a chip on one side. Charlie took the tooth from Matt and rolled it around between his thumb and third finger, inspecting all facets. "Where'd you get this?"

"The stingray dug it up."

"It's a tooth." Charlie kept rolling it around.

"It has to be the Iceman's."

"Could be," Charlie said. Matt reached for it, but Charlie pulled back his hand, poked the tooth into the key pocket in his shorts, and patted it. "I'll let Barnstable worry about this."

"Let me know what he says." Swarms of mosquitoes and no-see-ums circled, sensing Matt's bare legs, chest, and neck. He walked back into the water and sat down, scooting forward, so the water touched his chin.

"Little Man gets to work about six in the morning. When he sees the boat gone, he'll be over here in a flash. In the meantime, you just sit in the water and keep swinging at the mozzies."

Charlie was right. Little Man had them back to the lodge by half past eight and then headed off to Belize City with the last of Jack's guests.

Matt covered the mosquito bites ringing his neck with cortisone cream. On his swollen cheeks, fading squiggles marked where the jellyfish tentacles had stung him below his mask.

He had two hours before taking the eleven o'clock water taxi to meet Maxie in Belize City. After that, he would fly to Jaguar Lodge. He stuffed his clothes and laptop into his backpack and carried it to the lodge.

"Your face looks like a pink pumpkin," Charlie said when Matt walked in.

"It feels like one, as well. Looks like that bush on your face saved you a lot of pain."

Charlie scratched the one bite on his fleshy cheek. "That and the resistance you develop after being eaten alive a few times." Charlie slapped the cover on his laptop closed. "Told you Little Man would come find us."

"But you didn't think he'd be towing your boat."

"Nope, I figured it would be halfway to Honduras. Surprised he found it before he found us."

Matt walked out into the fresh breeze blowing across the deck. So it wasn't a boat theft. It was one more warning, maybe for Charlie, maybe for Jack.

Maybe for him.

15

Maxie McCaw was one tough chick. Matt wished now he had never shared a bed with her; he had felt like shark prey. She could lift all one hundred and eighty-five pounds of him over her head and had done just that at a Wilderness Foundation picnic. She drank her Bushmills neat, drove a souped-up mini-Cooper, and carried a 9mm Glock, which Matt had once told her she didn't need because she had drop-dead looks. That was the only time he had seen her blush.

The business card in her purse read: *Maxie McCaw, Special Agent, Environmental Protection Agency*. Matt had met her four years before at a seminar that she had led on cleaning up oil spills in San Francisco Bay wetlands. He had asked her a couple of questions, the last being "What are you doing for lunch?" They'd ordered pork tacos from a street truck, then became an item for a very long year, before splitting up and becoming friends, fellows from the same environmental cloth. Safe friends.

When she told Matt that she would be participating

in a Central American conference on illegal river and ocean dumping in Belize City, it was easy enough for him to set up his trip to coincide with hers. He would like some companionship and figured they might find time to take a river-rafting trip, but now he no longer had time to play. When he called her to meet, he wanted advice and Maxie was always ready to give it.

Miss Frankie's café was a block from Randolph's, on the second story of a white clapboard building. Pointing up crumbling staircase, a hand-lettered sign read:

Miss Frankie's breakfast & lunch restrant,
Freid fish, plantains, Beers, iced cream
dinner sometimes, come after Church

Matt climbed the stairs and entered the long, narrow restaurant. The aroma of frying fish and goat stew drifting from the kitchen trumped the dead smells of Belize City. He took a window table with a red-flowered plastic tablecloth and a crusted bottle of Marie's Hot Sauce. As he ordered a Belikin beer from the waitress, in strode Maxie, her auburn hair clipped nearly to a crew-cut, wearing black jeans, a black leather front fanny pack, a black blazer, and black cowboy boots — the wrong outfit for the tropics, Matt thought, but that was Maxie. He had once seen her rip open the invisible Velcro seal on her fanny pack and whip out her Glock. Just for fun.

When she saw him, she started laughing. "What's with your puffy face? You look like you've been up all night binging."

"How about starting with something like, 'Hello, Matt, good to see you?'"

"Hello, Matt. Didn't I just see you in Sausalito last month? Now, what about the puffy face?"

"Just a midnight swim."

"With some hotty, I presume."

"With a jellyfish. How's your conference going?"

"These people are thirty years behind the environmental curve. If you drank a gallon of that river water out there," she said, motioning vaguely toward Haulover Creek, "your gut would rot away before you could piss out all the microbes."

The waitress arrived with a Belikin for Matt and Maxie ordered one for herself along with a plate of conch fritters. "What about you? Having fun?"

"I wouldn't call it that." He told her everything that had happened.

"You? Groping a Mennonite?" She laughed so loud that the waitress walked from the kitchen to check on the commotion. "Your father, the preacher, God bless him, would roll over in his grave." Matt cringed.

"Oh, just a figure of speech. But sorry for my insensitivity. I forgot about your father. But I can't see you groping anyone. So tell me, who was the guy in the ice block?"

"Who knows? No body. No ID. No evidence. No nothing."

"Only the tooth?"

"Right, but somebody stuffed the body in the slush in the dark of the night. At least, that's the assumption."

"So here's your chance to boost your career, to join the big leagues of investigative reporting. It's a piece *Outside* magazine would kill for."

"Yeah, and I'd get killed doing it. I'm not one for being hunted. That spear between my legs was enough."

"Oh, come on. That was just a warning shot under your bow. If they wanted to kill you, they would have. Don't be scared of being scared. You're sitting on a hot story. Dump your depression and get a life. I'd love going after the bastard who did that."

"Be my guest. I don't do murder investigations, especially in Belize."

"You haven't done much of anything since you left the Wilderness Foundation to become a 'writer,'" Maxie said, sketching air quotation marks with her fingers.

He wanted to say, "Fuck off." Instead, he took a deep breath. "I'm selling travel stories, Maxie."

"Five days in beautiful Belize? Come on. You're beyond that stuff. I thought you had a social conscience."

"I do. And I'm committed to a paid assignment. And, by the way, Maxie, it's eight days."

"Make it a month. Who cares? A hundred people have written that story a hundred times for a hundred publications. Now it's soon to be a hundred and one. Congratulations."

Matt looked out the window.

"No offense, Matthew, it's just that you've stumbled onto something pretty unusual. If you don't like the body angle, what about that finned shark? Jesus, Matthew, the reefs are being raped right under your nose, somebody's gunning for you, and you're writing about fun in the sun. You'd be doing yourself a favor chasing this one down. And your father would be proud."

"Look. Somebody's dead, the cops want me out of here,

I was nearly run over—these are mean bastards. And my bet is they're just getting started."

"Then get yourself a weapon. Maybe a machete, because as I recall, you are morally opposed to guns." She put half a conch fritter in her mouth, then looked Matt square in the eye while she slowly chewed the fritter.

"C'mon, Maxie. I came for advice and all I get is shit." He waved to the waitress and signaled for another Belikin to oil his body armor.

"All right, my apologies, I went a little overboard." Her brow furrowed, and she leaned forward on her arms. "Do you think this is about drugs?"

"I don't know. Maybe. But why they picked on Jack is beyond me."

"Then go find out. If you can understand why someone might frame Jack, then you might come up with a suspect or two." She reached for another fritter. "Oh, I forgot. You're not much of a people person. I suppose if someone were beating dogs or shooting deer in the park, you'd jump in." She took a swig of beer, staring hard at Matt. "Well, sharks without fins and dead reefs seem to be in the same ballpark."

He leaned back in his chair. "OK, Maxie, you're the trained investigator. What's my next step?"

"Simple. Forget about that trip to the jungle. Root around here. Go turn over a few rocks. See who crawls out. Then grind them into the ground with those Teva sandals of yours. But hold on for a second—I need to hit the loo." She slid from her chair and disappeared behind a yellow plastic curtain.

In the street below, a boy passed by on a bicycle with a wooden box mounted over the rear tire; inside were two small jungle cats, ocelots maybe, just kittens, their paws wrapped together with duct tape. As Matt watched the boy disappear around a corner, he wondered who the buyer might be. Or whether the kid would try to raise them as pets, as some do until it gets too expensive to feed them. He pulled his cell phone from his pocket, got the number for Jaguar Lodge, and called.

"Hello, this is Maria, may I help you?"

"This is Matt Oliver. I'm supposed to arrive there tonight, but it looks like I can't make it."

"Oh, yes, Mr. Oliver. You're the writer. You should talk with Miss Mandell, but she's off in the bush. She'll be back in half an hour. Can she reach you?"

"Sure." He left his number and put the phone back in his pocket just as Maxie returned.

"Making a date?"

"Canceling one. I think I'll stick around."

She slapped him on the back. "Good for you, Matt, good for you. Count on me to help." She looked at her watch. "Now, I have to run. I'm lecturing on the practical use of night scopes, but no telling what those guys are going to use them for."

"Thanks for coming, Maxie." He stood and they hugged. Her arms tightened around him, and she drew her head back, looking him in the eye. "I'm staying at the Princess Hotel at the Marina. Call me if they come after you."

After she left Matt settled the bill and headed out the door, his pack over one shoulder. His head was spinning.

He sat on a low cinder-block wall, shut his eyes, took several deep breaths, then stood up and started walking. "OK, Matt," he said to himself, "let's go look under a few rocks."

The streets were alive with hundreds of passengers from the sparkling white *Carnival Princess* anchored off shore. At one booth, a buffed, aging, shirtless man with cropped bleached-blond hair fingered a hammock. Behind him, a jockey-sized fellow half his age watched. The grandmotherly shopkeeper kept her eyes on the hammock, averting her eyes from the half-naked torso.

"That's the matrimonial hammock," she said. "Big enough for two."

"Well, I do think we need one, don't you, sweetheart?" he said to his partner.

The shopkeeper rolled her eyes and turned to another patron who held aloft a delicate seashell with curled arms. "Nice, don't you think?" the woman said to her companion. "It would look nice on top of our toilet."

"Yes, indeed," her friend said. "We could put dried daisies in it."

The shopper waved it at the shopkeeper. "How much is it?"

"Twenty dollars. My son, he dives for them."

Matt recognized it, a scorpion spider shell, dredged up in the Philippines by power shovels that rip up the reef to get the buried shells. On the shelves were China clamshells, feather coral, helmet shells, and polished black coral—all endangered species. Matt poked through the items, one ear tilted to the conversation, as a slow burn grew in his chest.

"How old is your boy?"

"He's twelve, ma'am," the shopkeeper said.

"Wonderful." The woman handed her an American twenty-dollar bill, and the shopkeeper wound the spider shell in bubble wrap. After the woman had carried it away, the shopkeeper pulled a Belizean twenty from her pocket and put it into the cash register, stuffing the U.S. bill into her pocket.

Matt held up a hollow puffer fish, blown up to the size of a softball, its prickly spines extruding like those of a frightened porcupine. Then he noticed a plastic fob hanging from a key chain that contained a tiny curled seahorse, its head bent almost in prayer, its tail curled behind it. He picked it off the wall, rubbing the plastic between his fingers. Son of a bitch. Seahorses dangling from fifty-cent key chains.

"Ten dollars," the shopkeeper said.

"Where are these from?" he asked.

She looked as if he had accused her of something. "China, they come from China."

"Not Belize?"

"Oh, no."

Matt looked at the bottom of the pufferfish stand, on the back of the seahorse fobs, but none was labeled with the country of origin. He pulled two more seahorse fobs down, inspecting each, staring into their tiny dead eyes. "How do you know these are from China?"

"That what Mr. Chin says. He's the owner."

"Chin? The same guy who owns the grocery store?"

"Yes, very wealthy man. He's from Hong Kong."

"Oh, that makes sense. Where can I find him?"

"He comes after the cruise ships leave to pick up the money, but he has an office on Broad Street. By the shave ice cart," she said.

He thanked her then walked ten minutes to Chin's building, three stories high and painted a bright yellow. The windowless third story looked like an afterthought. The downstairs windows, covered with black bars, were shuttered tight; the yellow door, with a chest-high center peephole, was shut tight. Matt knocked, and then knocked harder until a black pupil filled the lens. "Do you have business here? asked the voice behind the eye.

"I'd like to talk with Mr. Chin."

"And what is your business?"

"I'm writing a story on Belize tourism. For an American newspaper. It would be helpful to speak with Mr. Chin."

From under the door, a white business card appeared. "You call this number tomorrow. Set up an appointment." And the eye disappeared.

Matt knocked again. "Hey, how about now?" No one responded. As he turned away and started down the street, his cell phone vibrated in his pocket.

"Hello?"

"Matt Oliver? This is Cat Mandell at Jaguar Lodge. Sorry I missed your call, but I've been trying to track down a missing troop of howler monkeys."

"Missing monkeys?"

"Yes. A family has been working the treetops on the north edge of the property for years, but they seem to have disappeared. It's strange."

"Disappeared or just moved on?"

"I'm not sure, but I'm concerned. I can't imagine they've been hunted, because the villagers protect them, but not hearing them hoot and holler worries me. Anyhow, you're the fellow doing the travel story, aren't you? Maria says you won't be coming up."

Matt looked back at Chin's place, the bars on the window, the drawn curtain. He thought about the stingray barbs in the basket, the missing boobies, the shrunken head, which was, in fact, a monkey head. Was there more to this? "There's been a change. I still have a reservation on the four PM flight. Maybe I can help you find the monkeys."

16

Every time he walked from his office to the American embassy, Trey Turnbull felt as if he were in a 1950s political film set in some mysterious tropical country. The colonial era building, originally erected in New England, had been shipped as ballast in freighters in the nineteenth century. Once the residence of the wealthiest American in Belize, it now sported security cameras under the eaves to spot unwanted visitors, but Trey knew it wouldn't take much for an angry crowd to scale the eight-foot wrought iron fence and make a sixty-foot dash across the lawn to the doorway. However, the likelihood of that happening in Belize was less than zero.

The female guard at the gate couldn't be much more than twenty years old, probably fifteen years younger than his own daughter, who would have never considered the Marine Corps. "I'm here to see Ambassador Barber," he said, handing her his passport. She checked his name against a list on her computer screen and typed something.

Handing him back his passport, she nodded. "You may enter, sir."

"Thank you, Corporal," Trey said, tipping his Panama hat.

Trey had met Laddie B. Barber more than two decades ago when he bought the ranch owned by Laddie's deceased father, land adjacent to his own eighty thousand acres in West Texas. Trey, slick as a rattlesnake's belly, walked away with sixty thousand acres for half their value, sealing the deal by granting Barber annual hunting rights to Trey's exotic animals.

Barber, a good old boy, threw money to politicians as if he were throwing hay to his horses. For the last election, he raised more than three million for the primary and another three million for the general election, assuring himself a big payback. Barber insisted on becoming Ambassador Barber, preferably somewhere in the Far East, perhaps Bangkok. "Trey, I have to tell you, those little ladies from Thailand are the best." But the president's political staff, who could distinguish between money and intelligence, assigned him to Belize, where he couldn't do much harm.

A young man in a light blue seersucker suit led Trey to the ambassador's office. Barber's door was wide open, and he sat with his hand-tooled cowboy boots propped up on his king-sized desk, cigar smoke curling from behind a day-old *Dallas Herald*. When he saw Trey, he jumped up to shake his hand. "My old buddy. Such a pleasure to see you."

"Mr. Ambassador," Trey said, aware of how ridiculous that sounded when applied to Laddie B. Barber, "nice to be here."

"You can stop that ambassador crap right now, Trey."

"Good enough. But it did take me two weeks to get an appointment with you, so I flew in from Washington this morning just to keep it. You're never in town."

"Would you spend time in Belize if you didn't have to? Hell no, and I don't either. The only thing America cares about is keeping the Colombians from using Belize as a drug stopover on the way to the U.S. But I let my staff worry about that."

"So you can do more important things."

"Like helping Americans make a fortune here, which I can do just as easily on my cell while I'm back home bass fishing." Barber motioned to one of four dark leather overstuffed chairs surrounding a circular coffee table. Trey let Barber pick a seat and then sat across from him. Barber pointed to the adjacent wall and the stuffed head of a Thompson gazelle, its marble eyes appearing to blink as the overhead fan blades spun slowly. "I don't spend much time here, but I wanted a few reminders of home, so I brought my Tommy down. Remember that? She was one quick animal, but I nailed her, didn't I?"

"That you did, Laddie."

"Some of my best times have been shooting Tommies, bongos, all them fellows on your ranch."

"Just don't tell the folks in this building where they come from. And while we're on the subject, put the twentieth and twenty-first on your calendar. I'm going to get you another trophy."

"You didn't bring more Tommies into Texas, did you?"

"Tommies? No, better than that." Trey looked around. "Say, this room isn't wired, is it?"

Barber laughed. "I sure as hell hope not. I'd have some

explaining to do. I don't think much of these Belize girls, but being that I'm the ambassador I find a good one now and then." Laddie stood and walked to the armoire, pulling out a bottle of Maker's Mark and two glasses. He poured them each a couple of fingers in glasses embossed with the seal of the United States of America. They clinked glasses. Trey sipped, Barber swigged.

"And how is the dinner coming, Laddie?"

"It's all set. Exotic as ever. Thirty people have confirmed, all the movers and shakers. They want to hear what you have to say."

"It's all about the land, Laddie. We need to get our hands on those forty thousand acres before the Belize government makes them off-limits forever. That might be awhile, but I don't want to risk it."

"You'll have the right people in the room, that's for sure."

"And the menu?"

"Martin has it set. If the invitees don't want to listen to you, they'll at least show up to eat."

"I appreciate that."

"And you are welcome, sir. You know, if Ambassador Laddie B. Barber picks up the phone, every politician down here listens. It's America calling. The embassy career guys don't like it when I make calls, but the President appointed me, not them, so you know what I say?"

"And the horse they rode in on." They both laughed.

Trey sipped his Maker's Mark and put down the glass. "Say, speaking about women, is my good friend Martin taking care of you?"

"In spades and I'll repay the favor. I don't know what he has in those little jelly jars he brings over, but I perform like Balboa when he discovered the fountain of youth."

Trey frowned but decided not to embarrass Barber by correcting him. A buzzer sounded on Barber's desk. He pushed a button and a voice over the intercom announced, "Ambassador, it's Washington. The Under Secretary is on the line."

Barber glanced at his watch. "I have to talk to this lady. Might be a while. Stay in touch. I'm flying to Houston in the morning to check on my ranch, but I'll be back in a couple of days, in time for our dinner." They shook hands and, as Trey headed for the door, Barber picked up the phone. "Ambassador Laddie B. Barber here, Madam Secretary. How can I be of service?"

17

As the single-engine Tropic Air Cessna 172 taxied down the grass runway, the Aussie pilot popped open his door, letting the breeze fill the stifling cabin. He pulled the plane to a halt near a small thatched-roof palapa, the only structure in sight. With the prop winding down, he jumped from the cockpit, walked around the tail of the plane, and pulled open the passenger door. Matt crawled out. The pilot reached behind his seat, grabbed Matt's backpack, and carried it to the thatched-roof lean-to.

"The Lodge is ten minutes away, mate, but they never leave to pick up a guest until they hear us overhead." He glanced at his watch. "Should be here in about three or four minutes. It's a beautiful place. You won't want to leave." He shook Matt's hand.

After the pilot had returned to his Cessna, Matt walked to the edge of the underbrush forty feet away. As he unzipped his fly to pee, a mud-splattered Land Rover rounded the corner and pulled up next to the palapa. As he hurriedly zipped up, out hopped a woman dressed in bush shorts, a white T-shirt, and sun visor. She was tall, maybe five-ten, with a sprinter's long legs, dark blonde hair pulled back in a ponytail, and a tanned, welcoming face.

"I see you found the men's room. There used to be a door on it, but a villager took it to make a cooking fire."

"Ha. You must be Cat."

"Right you are. Cat Mandell, welcome to the lodge." After a quick handshake, she grabbed his pack and pushed it through the back window, letting it drop onto the back seat. Matt climbed into the front alongside her. Pulling hard on the steering wheel, she spun the vehicle around and headed back up the rutted dirt road, expertly dodging holes and mounds.

"I know you're doing a story but don't remember for what publication," Cat said.

"It's for several newspapers, a travel piece on Belize."

"You'll like our place, but then I'm biased. Maybe it's not on par with Coppola's Blancaneaux Lodge, but what is?" She swerved hard left, dodging a crater. Matt fell against her, but a hard right turn threw him back against the door.

"With all that movie money, I guess old Francis has to put it someplace," Matt said.

The road flattened, and she gunned the engine. "So, if this is the rainforest, what's the reef?"

"Well, it was going to be Cap'n Jack's."

She took her foot off the gas. "Oh. Now that's a story. I've been following it on the local bulletin boards. It's as if the New Jersey mob has moved in. I don't even want to think about it."

"I don't blame you. Doesn't look like he'll be having customers for a while."

She shook her head. "Yeah, that's a business killer."

"And what about these howler monkeys of yours? Isn't that what tourists come for?"

"They do. And for our birds, as well, but the monkeys mean more to me than just a tourist attraction. They're almost family. I'm going to look again for them in the morning. Come along if you want."

"Count me in. But tell me, what do you mean they went 'missing'?"

"There were eight in the northern troop, ten in the southern troop, and often at war with each other. It's a civil war with lots of screaming, so I call them the Blues and the Grays. They each protect their own turf, but the Grays have a fig tree and the Blues try to get to it. The Grays scream bloody murder, then stomp and snarl until the Blues back off. Starting a couple of days ago, I heard only the Grays. The locals say they don't know why since the two troops have been here forever."

"Maybe the Blues just found another fig tree."

Cat downshifted as she took the Land Rover over a two-foot deep pothole. "I hope so, but my gut tells me otherwise."

"The locals still eat monkey meat?"

"A few people still hunt them, but no one in the village. We hire them and contribute to their school, so in turn they protect the baboons. That's what they call them—'baboons'. It's monkey in Creole." After one last bend in the road, they arrived at an open wooden gate with a sign alongside, *Jaguar Lodge, Guests Only*. A long driveway wound through a manicured lawn and gardens, ending at the open-air reception area, under a cantilevered roof. Matt pointed at a plump bird poking in the grass, with "eyes" embossed on its tail feathers, similar to a peacock's. "Ocellated turkey? Nice to see them hanging around here."

"As I said, the locals leave the animals alone. Nobody shoots the wildlife."

Hopping out of the Land Rover, she motioned toward the reception desk. "You can check in there. Cocktail hour is six, dinner seven to eight-thirty. In the morning, I'll show you around." She pulled Matt's bag from the back seat and carried it inside. "After dinner, a wildlife biologist is giving his weekly talk. He's tracking jaguars around here so you might want to catch it."

He completed the reception form and handed over his credit card, but Cat grabbed it. "No problem. The stay is on us. Just write something nice."

Matt hesitated. "Thanks, much appreciated, but I'll pick up my own tab. Can't get in bed with our subject, so to speak."

Cat smiled. "Just an offer, not a bribe." The receptionist recorded the credit card numbers, and Cat grabbed his bag. "When you own a resort in the bush, you get used to doing everything yourself. I even made the beds today. Only one girl showed up, so tonight I chop onions and slice tomatoes. Otherwise, you won't eat."

Cat led the way to the long bar in the lobby. The only patron, a tall man with wavy silver hair reading the newspaper, nodded at Matt but returned to his paper without waiting for a response.

Cat stopped. "Want a welcome drink? Rum punch?"

"No thanks. I'll pass." Matt followed her down a path lined with bougainvillea, past three identical thatched-roof cabanas, each sixty feet apart, bordered by the forest. She seemed to dance as she walked. Stopping at the last cabana, Cat unlocked the door and entered, setting his bag next to the king-sized bed. She brushed her hair away from her green eyes and then twisted the gold band on her left thumb.

"Here's your home for two days. I hope you like it."

"What's not to like?" Three walls were half-screened, with bamboo curtains to roll down for privacy. Mosquito netting shrouded the bed. A small bowl holding candies sat on the nightstand, beneath a cane lamp. A writing desk and a chair were against another wall, with a stuffed chair nearby.

"The walls are tight, so you really don't need the netting." She winked. "It's mainly for effect. The water is drinkable. It's well water. But if you don't trust it, there's bottled water in the little fridge there." She walked into the bathroom and flipped on the light. "You have both a Jacuzzi soaking tub and a shower. The water gets hot fast. Don't burn yourself."

"Very nice." Matt opened the opaque glass door to the shower. Room for two, he noticed.

"We have individual tables for dinner, so you can eat alone if you wish. Or, I can introduce you to other guests if you want company. Or you can eat at the bar."

"I'll take the bar."

"I figured so." She looked him over. "Luciano's a good bartender. Makes a killer cinnamon rum punch.

Anyway, enjoy the evening and I'll see you in the morning."

Matt pulled back the mosquito netting and plopped down on the bed. He hadn't expected such a woman in the middle of the Belize jungle. She wore a silver thumb ring and no others. Did she have a husband, partner, significant other? So what? He shut his eyes, his thoughts falling back to Jack, the barren reef, Chin's kiosks at the cruise ship terminal. And now the baboons. Mulling over the events of the past few days, he pictured each as a domino, each placed end to end, then end to side, then side to side. Finally, he got up and splashed water on his face, pulled a maroon polo shirt from his backpack, tried to shake out the wrinkles before putting it on, then headed into a night filled with cries and calls from the rainforest.

After dinner—Belizean chicken, with lots of tomatoes and onions, rice, zucchini and okra, and a glass of Chilean merlot—he settled into a big corduroy chair in the open-air lounge. A dozen lodge guests sat on couches and cushioned rattan chairs, some sipping coffee, others having drinks.

The evening's speaker, dressed in dirty forest-green long pants and a khaki shirt with the sleeves rolled above his elbows, looked like he belonged in the rainforest. His unkempt red beard crept up his cheeks. His bushy eyebrows looked like little caterpillars.

"Welcome, everyone, my name's David Mallard. I've been studying jaguars in these mountains for nearly three years." He pointed at his pants leg. "If you look at the mud on my knees," he said, "you might think I've been praying. I have. An hour ago I moved two trip-cameras just in case a couple of my favorite jaguars came this way. I've been praying that no one will steal the cameras and that they will work if a jaguar passes."

Mallard turned off the overhead light, turned on his laptop, flashed the first frame of his powerpoint presentation on the screen he had set up, then flipped through his program: here's the jaguar range ... Belize should have twice as many jaguars as it does ... depending upon prey, females roam up to two hundred square miles, males often twice as much ... as many as thirty pass through the Catscomb basin ... deforestation is constantly reducing their range ... I've been tracking seven ... I'm supported by the Global Fund for Wildlife, hoping to set aside more range ... Jaguars don't stay put; they roam and we need to create unfettered corridors throughout the Americas ...Of course, you may never see one because they are mainly nocturnal and avoid humans ... Poachers are active ...The pelt is worth about five-thousand dollars American on the open market, maybe more, but cubs are just as valuable. He turned off the powerpoint and turned on the overhead light.

Mallard fielded a few questions from the guests, and then Matt waved his hand. "Dr. Mallard, where's the market for jaguar pelts? In Belize? Or elsewhere?"

"I'm sure most if not all get smuggled out of the country," Mallard said.

"Besides pelts, I know in some Asian cultures tiger penises are thought to be an aphrodisiac. What about jaguar penises?"

"I've never heard of a black market for jaguar penises,

but I suppose someone might claim they're a logical substitute. Of course, those phony aphrodisiac claims have no basis in science. However, I'm not an expert in the underground animal trade. I study the living animal and its habitat."

Mallard answered a few more questions from other guests, thanked them, and started collecting his equipment. Matt walked over to him. "Dr. Mallard, I'm Matt Oliver. Very informative presentation."

"Thanks, glad you enjoyed it," he responded, without looking up. "Always something new to learn about the cats. Always more to study."

"I'm writing a travel piece on the lodge, and I'd like to mention your work. You present here weekly, right?"

Tugging at his beard, he looked directly at Matt. "Every Wednesday. Just what are you writing about?"

"The lodge, wildlife, items of interest to tourists. Any chance of talking with you in more detail?"

"Wish I could, but I just flew in from Washington this afternoon and rushed up here to move a couple of cameras before dark. I'm heading back to camp tonight." He dropped his laptop into a leather case, slipped it over his shoulder, and headed for the door. "Sorry."

Matt watched him hurry to his Range Rover. Odd that he didn't want to talk. Matt had never met a field scientist who would not go out of his way to publicize his project if it gave him the chance to raise more money. The Fund must treat him well.

A half-dozen people were perched on bar stools, four more stood behind them, drinks in their hands, arguing about macaws. Matt took a stool and ordered an inexpensive port. He thumbed through his notes from Mallard's presentation, adding a few words here and there. He could work with what he had though he wondered if his heart was still in his original assignment. Anyhow, he would give the jaguar program only a paragraph or two. Maybe not even that. The monkeys were more important.

Someone pulled up the adjacent stool, brushing his arm. It was the silver-haired man who had been at the bar earlier. Without looking at Matt, he opened the *Belizean Times*. The bartender poured him a plain soda water with a squeeze of lime. Anyone reading a paper at a bar was asking to be left alone, but a guy in a beige linen suit at a jungle lodge might have a story in him. "So, what's the local scoop? Anything big in Belize worth noting?" Matt asked.

The man glanced at Matt and then started to fold the paper. "Culinary news is about the most important thing in this god-forsaken land today. Says here it wasn't chicken in the chop suey in a Chinese restaurant in Belmopan. It was a house cat. Somebody found its hide in the garbage can." He drank half the sparkling water and pushed the stool back. "I'm leaving at the crack of dawn. Enjoy your stay." He put an American ten-spot on the bar and walked away.

18

~

In the morning, the fresh jungle air, washed clean by a midnight thunderstorm, was filled with the distant hoots, howls, and screams from a howler monkey troop making its way through the treetops. Matt sat in a wicker chair on his porch watching the rising sun peek through the forest leaves. He sipped slowly from a cup of coffee, wondering how it might be to wake up here every morning. Cap'n Jack's seemed like another world.

"Ready for a morning stroll?" Cat's voice, an anomaly among the sounds of the forest, surprised Matt, and he tipped his coffee cup, spilling drops on his shirt. She threw up her hands. "Oh, sorry, I didn't mean to startle you."

Matt laughed. "I shouldn't have been startled, with all that monkey chatter, but your voice didn't seem to be part of the pack."

"I should hope not. That's the Gray troop making the ruckus." She pointed to a small post marking the trail. "Let's have a look."

They took off across the lawn, Cat leading the way.

"Ask any questions you want. We haven't had many people write about us. Those who do always write about the
same things — the black howler monkeys, the turkeys
on the lawn, how the silent but deadly jaguar lurks in
the bush." She snarled like a jaguar and laughed.

"And tourists never see them."

"Never. Mallard's trip-cameras get photos now and
then, but the animals are nocturnal and reclusive.
They're only dangerous if you get one cornered, but
that's not too likely." She made an abrupt left onto a
narrow trail. "Of course, whenever you see an ad for
Belize tourism, a jaguar's featured. It's always the same
cat. Check the markings. It's the Belize Zoo jaguar, lapping water from a pool or sitting in a tree. They just
don't show the cage."

Sunlight streaming through the trees illuminated
eyespots on the wings of an owl butterfly settling on
a branch. A coatimundi, the size of a house cat, its rac-
coon-like bushy tail pointing skyward, scampered across
the trail. A stream of tiny leaf pieces flowed between
Matt's legs, hiding the leaf-cutting ants carrying them
to their hideout.

"So, Cat, what brought you to Belize?"

She looked back over her shoulder and smiled. "Is this
an interview question or do you just want to know the
truth?"

Matt offered a weak smile. "Well, if there are two
answers, tell me the more interesting one."

"I'll give you the short answer, but it's not for publication, OK?"

"Sure." .

"I jumped bail."

"You're on the run?" *Not only beautiful but also danger-ous*, he thought.

"I'm not looking over my shoulder, if that's what you mean." She laughed. "I don't know why I'm telling you this. I never trust that 'off the record' stuff. Let's just say I came here to start a new life."

"Fair enough, but it would add a little color to my story."

"I doubt your editor would approve if the innkeeper is a wanted woman. Anyhow, there's a nice place to sit around the bend and sometimes the baboons are there." She flipped her head as if trying to toss hair out of her eyes.

Tree branches swayed, dipped, undulating in a wave that moved slowly through the forest canopy. The mon-key chatter increased. Black forms slipped through the thick foliage. A howler seemed to be sporting a back-pack until it reached an opening and revealed a baby monkey clutching its back. A larger howler followed, staring down at Matt.

"Oops, watch it," Cat shouted as she jumped off the trail. Matt looked up but froze. Drops fell through leaves like a morning rain shower. The monkey was try-ing to piss on him.

"He's not taking kindly to you." She laughed. Sixty feet above on a wild lime tree branch stood a two-foot-high creature, scowling and screaming. Matt didn't need to understand a word of monkey talk to recognize one ornery animal. The howler grabbed a branch and swung back to his tribe.

"I should have warned you."

"Not to worry. Might have made a better story had the little rascal hit me. Maybe I'll just write that he did."

The howlers peered down at them, some eating leaves, others hooting and hissing, but the troop eventually moved on, and their chatter faded.

"Quite a display," Matt said. "They're not happy campers."

"Not with us around, but they're safe here — or, well, they have been safe."

The large trunk of a fallen mahogany tree bordered the trail. Cat hoisted herself up and sat down. "Have a seat. I often come here to get away from the guests."

They sat quietly for a moment, and Cat put her hand to her ear. "Listen." She cocked her head. "Hear that? 'Erk, Erk.' Like a rasp. It's a toucan. Keel-billed toucan."

Matt nodded. "Amazing call. Now, as you were saying about bail?"

"I won't say any more, OK? I sometimes say things I regret. Interview me instead."

"Good enough. So, why did you open the lodge?"

"Well, I love the Caribbean. My junior year in college I went to St. Lucia for a semester in marine biology research, stayed a second semester on my own to study iguana habitat, and never went back to school. I spent nine years in St. Lucia, five as a tourist guide and four as a divemaster, and then came to Belize five years ago. My fantasy was to find a little beach lodge with diving, but I ended up here."

"The lodge is beautiful — quite an investment, I imagine. Do you have partners?"

"I have investors, but it's my lodge. I run it. It's very

special to me." She looked at her watch. "Oh, oh. I'd better get back. Breakfast is about over, and I have guests departing. I need to say goodbye."

They walked along the trail without words, until the shriek of howler monkeys broke the silence. However, these screams were more vivid, urgent, and angrier than earlier. Cat started running toward the noise. Matt took off after her. She stopped abruptly. A rumpled hairy body lay in the trail. Cat threw her hand over her mouth and stepped back. "Oh, my God."

"Jesus," was all Matt could muster. The body of a monkey lay still, its tiny fists clenched, its tail wrapped around it like a ribbon, its head missing, sliced off at the neck. The howlers continued to scream, even louder.

"Over there," she yelled, pointing into the bush. Matt took off running, unsure why, in the direction she had pointed, where the howlers were thrashing through the treetops, screaming. To the side of the trail, he saw a flash of yellow cloth, and then another flash. Branches snapped as someone crashed through the underbrush.

Matt charged toward him, struggling to push through the dense scrub, catching streaks of yellow. A man, short, black hair, running away from him. Vaulting over a fallen tree, Matt got within sixty feet of him. Turning to head him off, Matt crashed headlong into a tangle of thorny vines, as sharp as barbed wire. Blood spurted from his hand. He struggled through the growth. Razor sharp leaves tore at his skin, but he pushed ahead until he could go no farther. He retraced his steps, back over the fallen tree, when he heard an ignition turn over and a car start. When

Matt reached the road, no vehicle was in sight. Nor was the man in the yellow shirt.

By the time he returned to Cat she was sobbing. "I can't believe this. My God." She was sitting on the trail, cross-legged, cradling the monkey's headless body. "It can't be the people from around here. They'd never do anything like this."

"I heard a car. When I reached the road, he was gone."

"Could you tell who it was?"

"No, I couldn't make out his features, but he had a yellow shirt and black hair. That's all I know, other than he was no biologist collecting skulls for his classroom."

Cat placed the monkey's body in the bushes, then ripped off a hanging branch and flung it down the path. Matt put his arms around her. He sighed, wiped the tears from her face, then peeled long fronds from a fern and covered the body. She gave the sign of the cross. Matt did, too, but he did not know why. She took his hand, and they walked back to the lodge in silence.

MATT SPENT THE afternoon walking the trails with a map in hand, deep in thought. As he walked, his anger grew until he suddenly stopped and screamed, a deep, guttural scream. Birds scattered from the bush. And then the rainforest was quiet again. It was forty-eight hours until Barnstable's deportation deadline. He needed more time.

Returning to his room, he took a quick shower and headed to the lodge. Behind the front desk, Cat was ruffling through papers. She waved, and then wiggled her finger toward the two chairs where they had sat when he first arrived. He kept his eyes on her as she walked over, but she ignored his stare and sat down. "I can't get that image out of my mind," she said. "It was horrible."

"Worse than horrible."

"I went back to get the poor monkey's body. I thought I'd better show it to someone. But it was gone."

"You're sure people in the village weren't involved?" Matt wanted to hold her hand, comfort her.

"It's not the villagers. They protect the animals. People farther west still hunt bush meat, but they cook the whole animal over a fire. They don't take a head and leave the body behind."

"Remember Indiana Jones? They served monkey brains still in the skull."

"Please, Matt, don't make light. This is Belize, not Asia. We have enough trouble." Shaking her head, she rose from her chair. "Let's forget about it. What more do you need for your story? And, what can I bring you to drink?"

"A beer. Belikin."

She walked behind the bar and returned with two bottles. "Most cocktail hours I sit with guests and look at pictures of their grandkids. You're too young to have grandkids."

"Or kids. Or even a wife. But I have dog pictures. At home."

She undid the rubber band that held her ponytail, shaking her head several times to let her hair fall to her shoulders. "Those I'd be happy to see. More my style."

"By the way, is Cat your real name?"

"Catherine. My dad called me Cat. He's an animal

149

lover. I moved to Florida with my mom when I was three, but the name stuck with me."

"You ever get back to the states?"

"Once a year. To visit my mom and friends. Florida, mainly. Sometimes I stop over in Texas."

"Like I suppose all your guests say: if you're ever in San Francisco…" He thought he saw a smile, but maybe not. "Well, besides this story I'm supposed to write, I'm trying to figure out what's going on in this adopted country of yours. What do you know about Jack?"

"Jack's a colorful guy, you might say. Last time I saw him, he said the government was accusing him of polluting the Rum Caye water table by burying his garbage. He seems paranoid, but they're probably after him."

"Jack says they're after him and his land, but why? Thousands of Americans own property here. Why go after Jack?"

"His property blocks development of the island. A developer would need it to do anything on either end that makes financial sense. Jack won't sell, he won't build, and he won't move."

"Why should he? He lives in paradise. What's he going to do with millions of dollars?"

"People can get ruthless in this country. Just keep in mind: it's not your crime to solve. Stick your nose in it and somebody will slice it off. This can be a nasty place."

"Thanks for the advice." Matt smiled. "Now, back to my article." He asked more questions to fill in the details, but his mind kept wandering. After ten minutes, he closed his notebook. "One more question."

"Only one. I have to get back to work."

"If I nose around Belize a few extra days, can you help me out? Not sure doing what, but maybe you can fill me in about people, things I come across, whatever —"

"Well, so much for my advice to stay out of it." She sighed. "Sure, you can always call me. Where will you stay?"

"Probably the Radisson. I stayed at Randolph's once but not again."

"Never heard of it." She stood up abruptly. "Now I do have to run. I won't see you tonight, but I'll be around in the morning and maybe even take you to your plane. Ten o'clock?"

"Right."

"It's often late, so we leave only when we hear it circling. But you can call and confirm if you're anxious. Use my office. Tropic Air. Cell phones aren't working today." Cat pointed at a hallway behind the front desk. "Down there, the door at the end — it's open. See you in the morning."

Her office was cluttered. Her telephone had a list of numbers next to buttons marked Continental Airlines, Global Fund for Wildlife, American Embassy, Tropic Air. He picked up the phone and made a reservation at the Radisson, left a message for Maxie, and then dialed Martin Chin.

19

Rain had pummeled the land all night, turning the dirt roads into muck deep enough to suck a boot off a hiker. It had taken Trey two hours to travel thirty miles south from Jaguar Lodge. He wondered if he were wise to attempt the last six miles to Mallard's camp. But Mallard needed money, and he needed Mallard. He pushed on.

Keeping the Land Rover out of the deep muddy ruts in the road, he angled one set of wheels in the bush, the other on the center hump, then downshifted as the road dropped into a gully. A barefoot Indian wearing a ragged blue T-shirt and muddy khaki shorts squatted ahead, eyeing the Rover, a machete stuck in the ground before him. When Trey got within ten yards of the man, a second Indian stepped from the bush.

The Rover crept forward, but the pair didn't move. He stopped ten feet from the stone-faced Indians, leaned over, popped open the glove compartment and pulled out the pearl-handled Colt 45 he always kept there, resting it in the cup holder. He stuck his head out the window. "Say, boys, would you mind moving over? I'd like to drive on that ground there, so I don't get stuck in the mud."

The squatting Indian shouted back. "No problem. We'll help."

"Not a chance, boys. Move it. I'm only asking once."

They said nothing. If the Rover became stuck in that mud, they would be all over him like jackals. Pushing open the door, he stepped out with his left foot, leaving his right foot still in the cab, the pistol hidden. "You're not being helpful."

The squatting Indian stood, pulling the machete from the ground. "Go ahead, señor, we'll give you a hand if you need it."

Trey lifted the pistol between the open door and the car, pointed it above their heads and squeezed the trigger. A crow dropped from the branch of a sapodilla tree, its black feathers floating silently after it. The two men disappeared into the bush. Trey climbed back into the Rover and continued driving. An hour later, he heard the hum of Mallard's generator just before he saw his camp.

Three crumbling cinder-block buildings were clustered together. Alongside the door of the largest building, a wooden *Global Fund for Wildlife* sign was bolted to the wall. A well-fed iguana waddled out the door, followed by David Mallard, his khaki shirt sleeves rolled above his elbows, revealing thick, browned forearms. He stuck out a large hand to greet Trey.

"Welcome to my little piece of Belize," he said.

"Thank you, Dr. Mallard. Anytime I can see the Fund's work, it's a pleasure."

Sweat had pasted Mallard's hair to his forehead and made his beard glisten. Mud covered his boots. "Rainy season's started early," he said. "Same thing last year. Climate change will hit Belize hard."

"A couple degrees won't matter much. It's like a year-round sauna here, anyhow."

"Well, I suppose we'll find out."

They walked to the back building, its open windows covered with steel bars. Mallard lifted the combination padlock, did a quick left, right, left, and opened the lock. He turned to Trey. "People take anything they can carry that's not locked up."

"No respect for scientists?"

"No respect for property. Some guys living back here used to be hunters, but with the land around here preserved, they poach what they can and make it up other ways."

Mallard opened the door. The musty smell of concrete floated up from the floor, where water puddled. Tables built against two walls were cluttered with two computers, papers, and open books. On three walls hung several jaguar photos, each with a Post-it identifying the cat and the location. Mallard pointed out cat FK7.

"Jaguars are solitary, and the females protect a range up to 15 miles square, depending upon the habitat quality. Males want more space than females—twice as much. The center of this cat's range is about eight miles from here, at the base of the Cockscombs. The government wanted to sell off that property, but when I showed them this cat, it slowed them down. They want more proof she's living there, and I need more photos."

"And just where is this habitat?"

A topographical map covered half of another wall. Mallard pointed to a strip of land between two mountain ranges. "It's about eight miles long. Cats travel it though they don't reside there. If I can prove the number of cats, we may be able to convince them to preserve parcels at each end, maybe eighty miles square, total. It's roadless now, but both an American and an Asian lumber company want that land. So far, the Belize government is dragging its feet. They want to avoid the bad publicity they'd face by destroying the habitat of its own national symbol."

"The government's been offered about forty million, I heard."

"So far, but that's chump change."

"And you think the government will say no if you provide more proof that the cats are there."

"To tell you the truth, I don't know. Too many politicians have their hands out, so I don't have a lot of time."

Sweat poured down Trey's head, his shirt sticking to him like Saran Wrap.

"Sorry I don't have air conditioning," Mallard said. "Let's sit outside, maybe there's a breeze." Mallard spread a blue plastic tarp under a cashew tree.

"As I've told you, Mr. Turnbull, I'm out here to save the jaguar. That's my life. Just because the government puts a jaguar on every single advertisement to attract tourists doesn't mean it will protect the animals.

Tourists never see jaguars in the wild because they're night travelers. So whether there is one or a thousand doesn't make much difference to most Belize politicians."

"The American ambassador tells me that if the government doesn't sell, it will build more roads. That's something the Fund would like to stop."

"It has to. The jaguar can't survive if its territory is split with asphalt and lined with gas stations and tourist traps."

"You're pretty fond of those animals, aren't you?"

"We biologists don't say we're 'fond' of the animals that we're studying. Adds a bias. Let's just say I'm committed. Whatever I must do, I will do." Mallard stood. "How about something to drink? Iced tea OK?"

"Perfect."

Mallard returned with two Mason jars of ice tea, each with half a lime. "You'll excuse my stemware, I trust, but everything has to do double here." Trey didn't want to think about what other uses the jars might have had.

"So, did you bring good news from the Fund? Like another fifty-two thousand dollars?"

"I'm not exactly here on Fund business."

"I didn't think so. But you know the Fund has let me down. I'll be flat broke in two months, and I need a year to get my work finished."

"Nancy Pareto knows your work's crucial, but money is the problem. Donations are down, needs are up."

"Sure, and the Fund sits on an endowment of a hundred and forty-nine million, so if they get into financial trouble thirty years from now, they can still pay into executive retirement funds. Meanwhile, the jaguars are goners."

"Well, that's beyond what a single board member can do. The Fund's bylaws dictate the endowment. But tell me, did you find out whether you could trap old cat FK-7, as you call her?"

"I can dart her. She's an aging cat. Beyond breeding age, not much of a life left."

"And you're sure?"

"I'm sure I can find her, but I'm not sure what you want from her. And I'm not sure I even want to know. So, what's the deal?"

"You sound upset, maybe a little desperate."

Mallard didn't respond.

"Well, the money can be yours. But this isn't Fund business, this is personal business."

"I understand."

"And from now on out, I've never visited your camp, no matter who asks."

"That's not a problem."

"By the way, last night I saw that writer, Oliver, try to get your ear."

"I blew him off, as you requested."

"And you damn well better again if he shows up here. Word is, that guy is making trouble." Trey put his hand on Mallard's shoulder. "OK, Mallard. I asked you to test Devil's Caye as a cat habitat. What do you think?"

"I took an ocelot out there a couple weeks ago. He's found plenty to eat."

"Good, and then I'll tell you what you need to do for the money you want. Not from the Fund. Money from me. I want that big cat delivered to Devil's Caye. Can you manage it?"

"It shouldn't be a problem, given a couple days' notice."

"Consider this your notice. Get the cat out there in two days. But don't let anyone see you. If someone does, you and your jaguar friends will be in more trouble than you can imagine."

20

THAT MORNING, UNDER a darkening sky, Cat threw Matt's bag into the back of her truck. "Thanks for visiting. It was a pleasure. It's been a tough year, so any publicity will help."

"Thanks for having me."

"Not at all. Anyhow, take care of yourself. But stick to travel writing. Leave the true-crime reporting to Truman Capote."

"Capote's dead."

"And so will you be if you're not careful." They both laughed.

"By the way, Matt, my staff thinks that one of the stoners probably massacred that monkey. The people in the village will put a stop to it."

"Do you think the stoners have something to do with the missing Blues?"

"I don't know, but we'll find out." She glanced skyward. "Your plane is coming." Matt heard the Cessna overhead, the pilot circling to make sure an alligator had not wandered onto the airstrip. He reached out to hug

Cat, but she extended her hand. He clasped it, and they locked eyes.

"If you stick around Belize and need my help, let me know," she said. She patted the back of his hand. "I have to get lunch started. My driver will take you to the plane. Have a safe flight."

Matt jumped into the Land Rover with Luciano behind the wheel, and they arrived at the grass airstrip just as the Cessna touched down. The pilot swung the plane to the palapa, brought it to a jerky stop, and climbed out of the cockpit. "Howdy, mate, sorry, but we're going to sit awhile. There's a squall headed here from Belize City, but it should pass in a few minutes. They usually do. Got a flight to catch?"

"Not today, anyhow."

The pilot looked at this watch. "You alone? I'm expecting another bloke, that Mr. Turnbull. Brought him up a couple of days ago and thought he was heading back today."

"No one said anything to me."

"Tall man, Texan, nice looking fellow, white hair."

"I saw him at the bar the other night. Said he was leaving yesterday."

"He has a Rover up here, so maybe he's on the road." The pilot pointed at a dark cloud on the horizon. "That nimbostratus was tailing me on the way up, but looks like it's swinging away. If you don't mind a bumpy ride, we can slip around it and get to town in a flash."

The clouds were dark, billowy, moving fast. "I'm not keen on flying alongside that storm. My father went down in a little Cessna like this. A year ago in Guatemala."

"The crash at Puerto Barrios?"

"Yes, that one. You knew about it?"

"Yes, of course." He looked at Matt. "Your father was on that flight? My friend was the pilot, an English guy. So sorry for your father."

"Thanks. Sorry about your friend, too."

The pilot shook his head. "He should have refused to fly. Rumor is that besides the three passengers, every last inch was jammed with cargo; too much weight for that Cessna."

"Cargo? It was supposed to be a tourist plane."

"It was leased by the Mayan Touring Company. But it was carrying some freight, probably an undisclosed leasing deal by whoever owned the plane. I heard it barely lifted off the ground. Got buffeted by a crosswind and took a nose dive."

"The cops never said anything about that to me."

"Course not. People were paid to keep quiet. My mate's wife wanted to sue, but the investigators said people from a nearby village had cleaned out the wreck, so there was no evidence of any cargo. I heard they had talked to workers at the airport who watched the plane being loaded, but they wouldn't go on record. Probably had their jobs threatened. Her lawyer told her there was too much corruption to squeeze a penny out of anyone, and the fight would just prolong her grief. Eventually, she received a small insurance check. Five thousand bucks, I think."

"That's what I got. From a Belize insurance company," Matt said, failing to mention the airport insurance payout.

"You were both lucky to get anything, mate."

The pilot reached across Matt and pulled the door handle down, latching it. Matt watched the dark clouds slowly move away, revealing a blue sky. The Cessna bounced down the bumpy grass strip and, as its nose lifted, Matt didn't even notice they were airborne.

OUTSIDE THE AIRPORT, two drivers tried to usher Matt toward their taxis. A young Rasta grabbed Matt's backpack, ignoring the other driver who called him a good-for-nothing prick. At the Radisson, the desk clerk handed Matt a note from Maxie—*meet you in the bar at 5 pm.* He glanced at the wall clock: 1:45. He gave the bellhop five bucks to take his backpack to his room and headed out the lobby door to meet Martin Chin.

Matt knocked on the faded yellow door, and an eye quickly appeared at the peephole. The door latches clicked, and there stood a grinning man, a head shorter than Matt, wearing a starched white shirt over gray slacks, with cuffs drooping over his leather sandals.

"I'm Martin Chin. You want to write about me?" Martin Chin had no chin. His neck began at the bottom of his lower lip and ran uninterrupted to his clavicle. He parted his coal-black hair precisely, and the smooth, hairless face surrounding his uncharacteristic pointy nose made him look like a newborn rat.

"Yes, Mr. Chin, I would like to include you in my article. I see cruise tourists flocking to your tents. My readers would be interested in the genius behind it all."

"Yes, of course, my pleasure." He opened the door.

Matt extended his hand, and Chin shook it. How

easy to get behind closed doors if you tell a narcissist that you want to write about him. Chin hadn't even asked for credentials.

Matt followed him down a dark hallway that smelled foreign and earthy, a familiar blend of aromas, but he could not place it. Footsteps shuffled on the floor above. Chin ushered Matt into a dull room where light streamed through security bars fastened over the tall windows. The top shades were rolled up, the bottom shades drawn. From inside a canary cage atop a filing cabinet, a sad-eyed scarlet macaw stared at Matt, unnerving him.

Notebooks labeled with Chinese characters filled three wall-to-ceiling bookcases. The bottom half of each bookcase had rows of narrow drawers, some labeled. On one shelf was a single-engine model plane, with Chinese characters on the side.

A gurgling aquarium the size of a bathtub sat on a sturdy metal table. It was filled with reef fish, snappers, coneys, soapfish, puffer fish, even sea cucumbers, all species he would have seen off Charlie's beach just last year. Matt couldn't take his eyes off it.

Chin motioned Matt to a straight back chair as he dropped into his red leather office chair. "You like my aquarium?"

Matt felt sickened by it. It housed at least a hundred tightly packed fish, maybe more, with a dozen foot-long Nassau groupers stacked like cordwood. In each corner, aerators mixed air into the water, but the fish were all struggling to move water through their gills to extract enough oxygen.

"Looks more like a holding tank than an aquarium," Matt said.

"We're cleaning out their normal tanks. I'll move them back tonight. Very beautiful fish."

"From around here?"

"No, not around here. I bring them up from Panama and Honduras." Chin walked to the tank and draped it with a towel. "Now, what can I tell you about me?" His English was graced with a slight British accent. "Who do you write for?"

Matt hesitated. "I'm on assignment for several Gannet newspapers, a dozen, in fact.

"*USA Today* maybe? Great newspaper."

"Well, others, but with all the cruise passengers shopping at your kiosks, I thought you'd be just the one to tell me how tourism is helping Belize."

"I do a good business. I came from Hong Kong in nineteen-ninety-eight, when the cruise ships first arrived. I started by importing cheap things Belizeans didn't have. Calculators, Swatch watches. Then Game Boys, Nintendo, cell phones. Of course, I opened a Chinese restaurant, with chop suey, what else?" Chin let out a laugh, too big for a man his size. Matt laughed with him.

"Must be hard to get exotic ingredients here."

"I can get anything I want. I go to Houston every month, Mexico City, Honduras, Colombia, wherever I need to."

"Do any items you sell to tourists come from Belize?"

"Only baskets, paintings, a few carvings from the religious groups. Belize has no crafts. I even get my hammocks from India."

"What about those seashells? Or the little seahorses on key chains?"

Chin blinked. "No, I don't take anything from Belize. Either illegal or too many people complain. I got those from the Philippines, some from Indonesia. When tourists come to a country by the sea, they want to take the sea back home with them."

A beep indicated a message had popped up on one of Chin's computer screens. He typed in a brief answer then, saying nothing, he pushed his chair back and stepped to the door behind him. Removing an unlocked padlock, he cracked the door slightly, careful not to expose anything behind it, and shouted in Chinese. The reply came back in Chinese. Chin turned to Matt. "Excuse me, please," he said, "it's my son."

He stepped through the door and shut it behind him. A strong musty, herbaceous smell filled the room. Matt, pinching his nose so as not to sneeze, stood up and peered at the two computer screens, but both were blank. Chin's desk was bare of papers, so he tried to open the top desk drawer, but it was locked. He slid open the drawer below and saw a single check made out to Chin and drawn on a Hong Kong bank—$88,000, a sizeable sum for a little guy in an invisible country. A third drawer held two small paper bags, taped shut, and marked in Chinese characters. He tried another drawer. Same thing. In the next one, he found a box of bullets. Another drawer was filled with seahorses, dry and dead, each about the size of his thumb. He picked out two, hesitating when he heard the thump of footsteps coming down the stairs. He dropped them in his polo shirt pocket just as Chin opened the door.

"I'd like to talk more," Chin said, "but I must go to your American embassy."

"Very well. Thanks for your time. Mind if I email you other questions?"

"Please do." Chin reached into his pocket and pulled out a card. As he handed it to Matt, it slipped from his fingers. "So sorry."

Matt stooped to pick it up, and one seahorse slid from his pocket, landing next to the card. On pure impulse, he fell forward, as if off balance, dropping to his knees, covering the seahorse with his left hand, his right hand landing hard on Chin's foot. Chin shrieked and started hopping on the other foot, grabbing at his lower back. Matt scooped up the seahorse and put it back in his shirt pocket.

"Please, let me help you," Matt said.

Chin waved him off. He pulled another card from his pocket and handed it to Matt. "Please. Send me the article when it comes out," he said, rubbing his spine and directing Matt to the door. "When do you go home, Mr. Oliver?"

"Tomorrow morning."

Chin nodded. "Have a good trip."

IN THE RADISSON'S dark, windowless Bayman's Tavern, five men wearing white short-sleeved shirts with thin neckties sat around a small table arguing loudly in Creole. Matt took a chair as far away as he could, ordered a gin and tonic, and carefully pulled one of the two seahorses from his shirt pocket. It was twice as large as those that had been embedded in plastic. It was curled into a perfect S shape as if it were praying. Brown, stiff and dry, it was no longer a candidate to be encased in plastic and hung from a key chain. Matt put it back in his shirt pocket.

"What are you hiding, there, Matthew?" It was Maxie, carrying a drink. She sat down across from him. Matt pulled out the seahorse and handed it to her. "There were hundreds of seahorses like this in Chin's drawer. I think he rips them off the reef, dries them, and sells them to tourists."

"Who's Chin?"

"The guy who owns the kiosks down by the harbor. Where you can buy stingray barbs and puffer fish turned into powder room lamps."

"I saw his stuff. You didn't steal this from him, did you?"

"I took it out from his drawer after he left the room. I visited him on the pretense that I wanted to feature him in the travel article I'm writing."

"Matthew, you've turned a corner, here."

"He's a looter, Maxie. I don't know how much comes from Belize, but I'd bet he's one reason those reefs are barren."

"The Chinese claim that seahorses can do what Viagra doesn't." She leaned over and tapped him on the forehead. "Desire. Works on the mind, not just the mechanics. There's a worldwide trade in them. They run a hundred bucks a pound. Wholesale. Cheap for an aphrodisiac, even a bogus one."

"With six thousand Chinese in Belize he could make a few dollars," Matt said.

"A lot more considering the number of Asians migrating into Central and South America. No doubt some of these guys would do anything to track down the ultimate aphrodisiac, tiger penis, and if they can't find it, Chin would be happy to provide them with a phony substitute."

"Chin's grocery store looked like a little apothecary. No telling what he's selling there. The jars and sacks were marked in Chinese."

"Probably the same stuff you can buy in San Francisco's Chinatown," Maxie said. "Legal and not-so-legal stuff. Seahorses, live or ground up into powder, aren't regulated, and too many environmental organizations avoid attacking traditional Asian remedies, no matter how bogus. They get tagged as racists for attacking cultural beliefs."

"So, what's the cultural belief in stuffing so many fish into a hundred-gallon aquarium that there's barely ten gallons of water left in it? Or keeping a scarlet macaw in a cage that's better suited as a coffin?

"There is none. And no one is going to expose Chin unless it's you."

"Expose him for what? A crowded aquarium?"

"For starters."

"I bet Chin's fish are destined to be sushi, Maxie, but not the kind you and I eat. Little hunks will be sliced out and savored while the fish is still alive and flopping. You can bet your ass on it."

"So, as I said, nail Chin. There is something else going

on with that guy, and you know it." Maxie stood and brushed specks off her jacket. "Now I've got to make an appearance at my seminar's social hour." She put two fingers in her drink, pulled out the lime, and chewed out the flesh. "Watch your back." She blew a kiss.

Finishing his gin, he left a tip for the waitress and headed out the door and into the street. He had just turned over a rock and Chin crawled out. How many more to go? And what, if anything, did this have to do with Jack?

Burning rubbish softened the late afternoon light, bringing dusk prematurely. Matt wandered aimlessly, thinking about Chin, Jack, Cat, careful to stay where street lamps illuminated the sidewalk as the evening darkened. He came to an intersection from where he could see the back of Chin's building, a block away. A row of spotlights mounted along the roof's edge overwhelmed the light from a lone street lamp. No one could breach that building without being bathed by security lights.

As Matt approached, a motion light flashed on. Behind a barred window, someone pulled back a blind. Matt could see fingers, but the bright light washed out the facial features. He kept walking, his head down, and turned a corner back to the Radisson.

CHIN WENT TO the side window and watched Matt disappear into the night. He pushed a button on his desk phone, setting off a buzzer in another room. His son walked into his office.

"The writer walked by again. You think he was the one who emptied the fish trap?"

His son nodded.

Chin walked to the aquarium and peered in at the fish. "Look at those hogfish, those grouper. Scratches on the sides. Those are no good. No good at all. Send the grouper to our restaurants. Those two large ones in the back have parasites. Scrape them off. And send the hogfish to our restaurants. Throw the rest out. Then get me a dozen beautiful fish, not a mark. That's what the rich people want on their plates."

His son nodded.

Chin went to his computer and scrolled through his messages. He opened the last one, from rumrunner109@belize.net: *I'm bringing another load to you. But if you're the one cutting off shark fins, you can keep your money. I'm off the job."*

Chin hit reply: *Of course not. But no threats from you. You have no leg to stand on.*

21

~

I<small>N HIS SIXTH-FLOOR</small> room in the Radisson, Matt plugged his laptop into the telephone to connect via modem to the Internet, reminded that he was in a third-world country. He waited five minutes for his email to pop-up. *You have an absolute deadline for your Belize story, and it's seventy-two hours away. And how about your next piece, Scuba's Seven Hot Spots, a week from Friday*, his agent had written.

"In your dreams," Matt said aloud. He searched the Internet for Martin Chin but could find only mentions of his restaurants and nothing else. He surfed to the Fund's website. Their projects ranged from Albania to Uganda — save the tiger, save the elephant, save the snow leopard. He clicked on Belize, then the *Donate Now* button, and read their pitch, stopping at the sentence: *From Devil's Caye, we have been conducting important research not only to save Belize's reefs but also to preserve coral reefs worldwide.* He read it again. He saw no evidence of research on Devil's Caye, only dead booby birds and two nasty thugs who ran them off.

But, it's a big island. Maybe he had missed it. He went to the minibar, grabbed a miniature Dewar's Scotch, unscrewed the cap, and drank it.

He resumed surfing the web, the archives of *Channel 5 Belize* and the *Belize Times*. No reader had posted comments, and the Iceman story had disappeared, supplanted by blurbs on a cross-dressing Mennonite teenager in the Cayos District and a child taken to a health clinic after being bathed in a toilet. He went to BelizeBlogSpot, but the site was "undergoing maintenance." Or had someone shut it down? He tried the *BelizeIslandLiving* bulletin board, but posts were the usual "fun in the sun" drivel, along with advertisements for beachfront house rentals. Nothing there likely to upset any tourist browsing for information.

Matt took another Dewar's from the minibar, this time pouring it into a glass. The phone rang.

"Matt, it's Maxie. I pulled up some interagency memos on wildlife trafficking and just emailed them to you. Nothing classified. They describe an underground trade in the Caribbean in anything that swims, flies, crawls, and walks. Reef fish census is way down everywhere. I can't talk now. I have to pack for an early flight to Miami. Just read it." She hung up before Matt could say a word.

He fell back on his bed, his heart racing, imagining a map of Belize, thinking about Chin, Charlie, Jack. And a flight to Houston.

At 4:30 AM, he jerked upright, his room still dark. Day six. His last lawful day in Belize. Tomorrow he would be an illegal alien with Barnstable in serious pursuit. A Houston flight left in less than three hours, arriving at George Bush International about 10:30 AM, with a 2:15 return flight that would get him back about 4:00 PM, thanks to the time zone switch. He might have just enough time in Houston to do what he needed. He had to chance it.

He booted up his laptop, brushed his teeth while it connected to the Internet, and then went to the Continental website. Only first class was available, but why worry about a few bucks when he was about to throw himself to the wolves? He had doubted that Barnstable would have informed immigration officials about the deadline he had imposed on him, so Matt would just have to gamble that no one at the airport recognized him, coming or going. He bought the ticket.

WHILE PASSING THROUGH airport security, an officer wearing latex gloves grabbed Matt's backpack, which carried his Dopp kit, the few clothes he had brought, and his laptop. He undid every zipper, stuck his hand into every pocket to feel around, then probed with a short baton. He unzipped Matt's Dopp kit, unscrewed the lid of his Advil bottle, peered in and with two fingers he extracted the seahorse. Dropping it into a small plastic bowl on the table, he motioned to a constable nearby. The officer walked over, looked into the bowl, and then looked at Matt. "Where did you get this?"

"I found it on a beach in Ambergris Caye. Dead."

"You can't take reef animals out of Belize, sir. Did you know that?"

"No, I didn't. In fact, I saw some being sold in town. Mounted inside plastic."

"Let me see your passport."

Matt pulled it out from his back pocket. The constable opened it, studied the page with his picture and vital statistics, and then searched for the entry stamp. He returned the passport to Matt, picked up the seahorse and motioned Matt to move on.

WITH NO LUGGAGE to pick up, getting through Immigration and Customs at George Bush International took Matt fifteen minutes. He slung his pack over his shoulder and hailed a cab. Houston's new Chinatown portrayed the city at its worst: colorless strip malls built on the cheap, with faux Chinese arches and characters painted on walls. With less than an hour to do what he needed to do, he scurried past the Red Dragon restaurant and opened the door of the Hong Kong Herb Company. A bell clanged as if he were entering a small town Rexall drug store.

A Chinese elder wearing wire-rimmed glasses on the tip of his nose bent over the counter, marking a red leather stock book. The bell got his attention. "May I help you?"

"I hope so. I was sent here by Martin Chin, from Belize." Matt held out Chin's card. "He said you would take care of me."

The man looked at the card and shook his head. "I don't know this Martin Chin. What do you need?"

"Hmm. Martin said you were business associates."

"No, never heard of him."

Matt took the card back. "Sorry. I must be in the wrong store." He visited a second apothecary a block away, again claiming Chin had sent him, but he saw no glimmer of recognition. It wasn't until the third and last apothecary that Martin Chin's business card raised an eyebrow.

"Are you a friend of Martin?" The man was probably mid-thirties, with a round face and a drooping mustache composed of so few hairs his skin shone through. Dressed in a sagging brown business suit, he wore his white shirt open at the collar with no tie, and smelled of must and ginger.

"I met with him in Belize last week. He suggested I look you up."

"Your name?"

"Matt Oliver," he said, extending his hand.

"I'm Luke Wong. Always a pleasure to meet a friend of Martin's. Did you drop by just to say hello?"

"No, actually, I'm shopping." Matt pulled from his pocket the second seahorse he had taken from Martin Chin. "Can you help me with this?"

Wong took the seahorse, turned it over in his hand, and disappeared into the back room, returning with a tray and two jars of dead, dried seahorses. "We have better." He pulled out a gunmetal gray seahorse, almost as long as a pencil. "This is from Peru. Twenty dollars. Much yang, the best, solves every male problem. The white ones are from Indonesia, three dollars." He lowered his head as if peering over imaginary glasses. "How do you know Martin?"

"I've been to Belize many times, and I'm a good customer."

Wong's left eye narrowed as if he were bringing Matt into focus. "You seem a little young to be a customer. Did you get this in his office on Albert Street?"

"On Broad Street. His grocery store is on Albert."

"Ah, yes, of course. Lovely building on Broad Street, isn't it?" He was clearly testing Matt.

Wong stroked his jaw, his eyes intense. "When I saw Martin last he had just started growing his beard back. How does it look?"

Did Martin Chin have a beard? Matt couldn't remember, and then he pictured his chinless face. "Must have shaved it. Not a hair on his face."

"So, you have seen him recently." Wong nodded and reached again for Matt's seahorse. "Belize seahorses aren't the same quality as Pacific seahorses. Martin sells these in Honduras and Mexico, not in China. I will only buy them if my supply dries up."

"What's the difference?"

"Desire. Cold Pacific water creates hot blood. My seahorses create desire." He stuck out his tongue and panted, then tapped two fingers on his forehead. "Not just for a man to get ready. Use Viagra for that. Mine are for passion, to put fire in you." He stepped into a back room and returned in a minute with a plastic sandwich bag holding fine brown powder. "Two ounces. Fifty dollars. The best."

"Martin doesn't have these?"

"Not in Belize. Maybe someday."

Matt pulled his wallet from his back pocket then

leaned forward and whispered. "Martin said you may have something traditional for me. He mentioned 'Belize tiger.'"

Wong lowered his voice. "That's not my business. Talk with Martin." He started pulling small boxes out of a larger box, putting them on his shelves. "I must get back to work. Next time you see Martin, say hello for me."

"I'll do that." Matt left the store, clutching a small paper sack of powdered seahorses that looked like ground allspice. He ran his fingers through it. Legal stuff. Listed by the Convention on the Trade of Endangered Species, but still legal, though useless. And Chin was in the middle. Wary of carrying the crushed seahorses back into Belize, he dropped the bag into a trashcan and hailed a cab for the airport.

In the Continental passenger area, Matt opened his laptop, and while he waited for a wi-fi connection, he pulled out his Casio and browsed the few photos he had taken — the Mestizo, his scowling face nearly burning an image in the lens; Jack, his head on the bar; Charlie's place; Cat, talking to a guest at her bar. And there was his father, a photo he had never deleted, waving before he boarded the flight for the trip of a lifetime, his last trip. As Matt waited for the boarding call to head back to Belize, he thought his father might be proud of him again.

He opened his email.

Mat - Charly went in his boat last nite but never come back. Someone called and said his boat was drifting, but I never found it. Charly isn't back. I'm worry he's in trouble. Maybe dead. If your in town, help - Little Man

22

As the 737 leveled off over Galveston Bay, its nose pointing toward Belize City, Matt reclined in his wide first-class leather seat. Charlie was in trouble. Matt remembered the day he had dived too deep chasing after the underwater SLR camera he had dropped, realizing too late the gravity of his error. It was Charlie who had taken down two full air tanks, risking his own life by staying with him so that Matt wouldn't be disabled by the bends. Matt now would return the favor. And after he did, he would get inside that three-story building where Chin kept his secrets. Assuming, of course, he could get back into Belize.

The odd little man sitting next to Matt grabbed the flight attendant by the arm. "I'll have an eye opener, little lady. In fact, I'll have one for each eye. A double Bloody Mary." He cackled, she squirmed, and he turned to Matt. "Only way to get going after a hard morning at work, son." He stuck out his hand. Matt groaned under his breath but obliged with his own hand. "Laddie B. Barber's my name, Ambassador Laddie B. Barber."

"I'm Matt Oliver. May I ask, ambassador to what?"

"Ambassador to Belize, sir. Wouldn't be going there if I didn't have to. What's your business?"

"I'm a writer. Doing a piece on Belize."

The Bloody Mary arrived and the ambassador, after dipping in his finger and licking it, drank it halfway down. "Well, that's good. Who do you write for?"

"Newspapers. Mostly Gannett."

"My, my. Impressive. You should come by my office and talk to me. I'll tell you all about Belize."

"That would be helpful. I look forward to it."

"Let me give you my card." He reached into the inside pocket of his steel-gray gabardine suit coat. "Here. You call me. It's my job, you know, telling people about America's interests down there." He tossed back the remainder of his drink, smacking his lips.

Matt looked at the card, the embossed gold seal. Impressive. Knowing the ambassador couldn't hurt.

"I'm also available for news profiles, you know. If you want to do a story on me, my friends at the *Houston Post* will publish it. Do you have a card, Oliver?"

Matt pulled his cracked leather wallet from his pocket, lifted out a card, and stuck it in the ambassador's soft hand.

He read it aloud. "Matthew Oliver, journalist, global assignments, Sausalito, *Cal-ee-for-nigh-A*. You must be doing well to ride up here in first class," he said, his eyelids drooping. When the flight attendant offered lunch a few minutes later, he said, "No thank you, darling," then lowered his seatback and folded his hands on his belly. His snores began to vibrate his nostrils as soon as his eyes shut. Matt's occasional elbow in the ribs curtailed the snoring but only briefly.

The ambassador awoke just as the plane pulled up on the tarmac near the terminal and the pilot cut the engines. He stood up and pulled his case from the rack above. "What did you say your name was again?"

"Matt Oliver."

"Well, Oliver, call me and I'll give you a good story." He squeezed toward the open door and then turned back. "In fact, Oliver, I want you to come to a dinner I'm having. The night after next, Black Coral restaurant, drinks at five-thirty. You can meet a few people who will tell you what America is doing for Belize. Lots to write about."

The 737 had parked a hundred yards from the terminal and a jitney navigated a mobile staircase to the plane's exit door. When Matt had arrived the first time, Barnstable had taken his immigration and customs cards and had looked at his passport, but he never scanned it in, so he suspected his entry was not in the system. Certainly, no one had paid attention to his departure earlier. Regardless, as the ambassador headed into the hanging heat of the day, Matt walked in his shadow, listening to his chatter, letting the ambassador run cover for him. After Matt had collected a perfunctory stamp in his passport, the customs inspector waved the first-class passengers through, more interested in observing returning Belizeans with too much luggage.

"Don't forget to call me," Laddie B. said, as Little Man appeared and grabbed Matt's pack.

"We haven't found Charlie yet," he said, panic in his voice.

"How come you're here? Why aren't you out looking for him?"

"The fishermen are out there, but I needed to talk to you," Little Man said, rushing them to a ragtag Ford pickup, its blue paint dulled by the Belize sun. They headed to the city boat ramp, Little Man talking all the way.

"Charlie said he would be doing a photo shoot off Goofy Bird Caye. He left about ten yesterday morning, saying he be back for lunch. He seemed in a hurry to leave, but I stopped him when I saw a little shark in his boat. Somebody had cut off the fins. Charlie said he found it on a dive. It was dead, but still fresh. I think he was taking it to someone."

With traffic nearly at a standstill, Little Man leaned on the horn, to no avail. "Late afternoon I tried to radio him, but no answer. Then I got a call from my uncle on Salt Caye that Charlie's skiff had drifted past. The wind was blowin' thirty knots, and it was dark as night. Jack was drunk, couldn't walk a straight line, so he couldn't help. That's when I emailed you. At first light, I went out and stayed until I come get you."

"Why didn't your uncle grab the boat?"

"He's old. Rickety knees." His voice quavered. "But this morning, about five miles before the Blue Hole, I passed Bucky's Caye. Not much of a caye, mon, maybe two acres and covered with bushes, but Bucky's been living out there since Jesus died. Comes in occasionally to bring Jack some fish guts. And there in his little lagoon was Charlie's boat. Not even tied up. Just sitting there bobbing.

"Did it drift there?"

"That's a long drift. I pulled up to the beach and didn't see Charlie, but Bucky comes out waving a machete. I asked him about the boat, but he told me to get off his land or he would chop off my arm. He was drunk, like all these old fishermen who ain't catching nothing no more, so I did what he say."

At the marina, they climbed into the whaler, worked their way under the bridge, and headed out to the islands. The roar of the Johnson was so loud there was no use talking. Nearly an hour later, with maybe two daylight hours left, Little Man cut the engine and pointed to a small island, half-a-mile ahead. "That's Bucky's."

The island was flat, covered with thick mangroves. Matt shuddered. "So, how are we going to avoid Bucky?"

"I think we should pull up on the backside and walk in," Little Man said. "Buck won't even know we're there 'til we're standing in front of him."

"I'm not much for being swung at with a machete."

"Well, boss, we're here now. So, I think we be doin' it."

Little Man shut down the engine, and the hull scraped on the sandy bottom. Taking the bowline, he jumped out, tied it to a sea grape tree, and motioned Matt to follow him. They squirmed and squeezed through the scrub without talking, the only sounds being rustling palm leaves. Little Man stopped. Ahead stood a ramshackle wood structure built on four-foot stilts. Between two coconut palms, Buckmaster Jones lay in a ragged cotton hammock, slowly swinging back and forth, his hands folded on his chest, one leg, its skin cracked like raku pottery, hanging over the side, his foot scraping the sand. The smell of rotting conch and decaying mangrove leaves filled the air. A scrawny tabby lay curled beneath Jones, licking its paws. Little Man shrugged. "Might as well tell him we're here," he said, starting down the narrow path.

Crack! It sounded like a gunshot. Little Man dropped to one knee; Matt dropped face down on the sand. He looked up. It was only the wind slamming a loose shutter against the window frame.

"Oh, my God," Little Man whispered. Matt saw it next. A crease ran along Buckmaster's forehead, an inch deep, the mark of a blunt machete blow that had landed so hard his irises bulged like black olives. Buckmaster Jones was dead. Little Man stared; Matt turned away.

"God help him," Matt whispered. He had never actually seen a dead man, not even his father. He had been too shocked to open the coffin and say goodbye.

When they reached Charlie's boat, the outboard engine was missing, and someone had slashed the seat cushions, scattering the foam. Matt opened the hatch in the bow where Charlie stored extra gas and gear. An empty green plastic Diet Seven-Up quart bottle floated alone in six inches of water. "Picked the boat clean," Matt said.

Little Man pointed at the split cushions. "They think he keeps his money in there?"

"Or drugs. Little Man, what's happening here? You knew Buckmaster."

"He's just an old washed up fisherman. No reason for this, mon."

"Is Charlie into something you don't know about?"

Little Man shrugged. "I don't know all his business, no reason to."

Little Man sat down on the gunwale; Matt took a bench seat. "Maybe someone stole Charlie's boat and left him somewhere to die, or at least to think things over. That seems to be the practice around here."

The faint whine of a boat engine brought them both to their feet. They ran down the path, hopscotching along the shore and in and out of the water. As Matt rounded the tip of the island, he spotted a white boat with blue rails, a quarter-mile off, coming fast, with two men standing tall.

"That looks like trouble, mon." Little Man jumped on the Whaler and started the motor. "Get the line," he shouted. Matt ran to the trees, popped the knot, dropped the line, and scampered to the boat.

The other craft was headed for them. Little Man jammed the motor into reverse, backed off the beach, pushed the throttle forward, and gave it a hard left.

Thwack! Matt hit the floor hard. Little Man landed on top of him. The free line had jammed between two rocks, jerking the Whaler to a halt. As the motor roared, the boat strained on the line like a wild beast. Little Man grabbed his machete and swung at the taut line, but the dull blade bounced off. A hundred yards astern, the white boat was coming on hard. Holding the machete with both hands, he swung again, this time severing the line and freeing the boat. Little Man gunned the Whaler and in under a minute he and Matt were on the lee side of Bonefish Caye. Little Man hung a hard right then a left, putting the island between them and their pursuers. "Yes," he yelled, turning into an invisible channel, cutting the speed to a crawl.

"What are you doing? They can follow our wake in here."

"I know, mon, but nowhere to hide." Little Man slowed the Whaler through the mangrove cut, with barely a foot of clearance on each side. Behind them, the pitch of an outboard grew louder and then dropped to a growl. Whoever was after them had just entered the channel.

A hundred yards into the cut, a small rotting wooden dock jutted into the channel. Edging past the wayward dock, Little Man cut the engine, pulled a line from below the console, and threw it to Matt. "Loop this over that piling. Quick."

"Are you nuts?"

"Do what the captain say," he yelled.

"Yes, sir." Matt threw the loop around the piling. Little Man wrapped the other end around one stern cleat, then around a second. He revved the engine.

"Hang on." The line stretched tight as a bridge cable, the outboard screamed. Little Man pushed the throttle farther, driving the prop harder and raising mud from the bottom. Behind them, the snarl of the pursuer boat grew more ominous as it rounded the bend. Little Man jammed the accelerator forward; the boat leaped, the engine roared, and the dock snapped from its rotting piers and tumbled into the tiny channel. He cut the line, slammed down the throttle and headed straight out the channel to the ocean.

In seconds, a piercing boom from the fiberglass hull striking the floating dock filled the air.

Little Man swung the Whaler far out to sea. "I don't think there's anyone else behind us, mon."

"Let's hope not. But who were those guys?"

"No telling and I don't want to find out."

In the distance, a light speck caught Matt's attention. A tiny flash and then nothing. He grabbed Little Man's arm. "Slow down. Look." He pointed at the horizon. "Something flashed out there."

"I don't see nothing, mon," he said, his hand over his brow to cut the glare.

"There. Again." But now all he saw were sparkles of sunlight reflecting off waves breaking at the distant Blue Hole. They sped ahead, finally slowing to a crawl to dodge submerged coral, and then pulled up to a barrel-chested sunburned man sitting on a coral head, wiggling his hand as he reflected sunbeams off a shiny CD.

"So what the hell are you doing here, Oliver," Charlie shouted. "I thought you went home."

"I never made it. Are you OK?"

"Cut, scraped, screwed and tattooed. And I need water bad," he said as they pulled him into the boat. Little Man went for the cooler, but Charlie pushed him aside, grabbed a bottle of Crystal Water, drank it, and then downed two more. He belched and sat down.

"So what happened?"

"I don't want to talk about it right now. Just get me

home. But go south around Turneffe Island in case those guys are still hanging around."

Matt looked at Little Man and shrugged. "Let's go."

Minutes later, speeding back toward Jack's, they passed Devil's Caye. In the twilight, scores of boobies circled, as if waiting to land, then scattering as a loud crack suddenly split the air. Little Man cut the engine and looked at Charlie. "Gunshot," he said.

"Probably drug runners," Charlie mumbled. He motioned to Little Man to pick up speed.

"That's the Fund's island," Matt said.

"Some of it is," Charlie said, "but I heard an American's got a piece of it. Can't say, for sure." Overhead, more boobies circled, in no hurry to land.

In an hour, they arrived at Charlie's. Without saying a word, he jumped over the gunwale and headed toward his house, not looking back. Little Man and Matt exchanged glances, and then Little Man spun the Whaler's wheel and headed across the lagoon to Jack's. "Few days ago," he said, "I went by Devil's Caye at night and saw a boat without running lights enter one of those channels. Probably poachers, but months before that I saw a boat with chain fencing, poles, construction stuff like that."

"The Fund claims to be doing research there, so maybe they put up a fence, but that wouldn't explain the gunshot. Anyhow, why's Charlie so mum?"

"May never know. Sometimes he talks a lot, sometimes he don't talk much."

"But, he ought to tell us what happened and who's fucking with him."

As the Whaler floated up to the dock, Little Man jumped out. "Might be better not to know. I'm going to tell Jack about Bucky. He needs a proper burial, and he's got no family, so far as I know."

Jack sat at the bar, a coffee cup in his hand, a Belikin bottle on the bar behind him. Matt walked up behind him. "Got a room?"

"So, you found the Tuna," Jack said, without turning around. "Sorry I couldn't join you. Little Man left too early this morning."

"He told you about Bucky?"

"He did."

"I'm sorry about that."

"Yeah. He was just a poor old fisherman, the first guy around here to realize that after fifty years of watching the fish get smaller ever year, he couldn't make a living anymore. Tried to convince others not to keep the biggest fish, to let them reproduce because they have the best genes. They just laughed at him." Jack bowed his head. "I'll miss him."

Matt lifted a Belikin from the cooler and sat down on a barstool. Gray stubble had sprouted on Jack's face. His eyes were puffy from days of drinking but, from a distance, his coffee didn't smell adulterated. Matt told him about the chase, the journey to the Blue Hole, how Charlie would not talk about what had happened.

"Something's up with that guy. I've been seeing less and less of him lately. Even been thinking about replacing him and probably would if I had any money coming in."

"Oh, and we heard a gunshot when we passed Devil's Caye. Charlie claimed they were drug runners."

"A gunshot? Drug runners? Not out there."

"I heard the shot. You say the Fund owns Devil's Caye?"

"You saw the sign. The Bodden family owned it for decades, but I think they sold to the Fund. Or it was bought by an American guy named Turnbull who gave it to the Fund, just not sure which. Point is, it looks like the Fund owns the island now."

"Turnbull?" Matt's sat up straight.

"Flashy rich guy. He seems to fashion himself as a philanthropist, but I think he's a crooked bastard. Began buying land down here thirty years ago and paid the locals next to nothing for it. He's probably in cahoots with the government. You have to be to make big money here."

"He was at Jaguar Lodge, at the bar. So, what's really happening out there on that Caye?"

Jack shook his head. "Don't know. I've only been where the boobies live, where I took you. Haven't set foot on the rest of it for twenty years. I used to dig for pirate's gold out there until I figured out that for decades every other Belizean and their mothers' uncles have been rooting around that island for treasure. Pipe dream, you know."

"Maybe so, but I want to know what's on it now. Can someone take me out there?"

Jack looked at Matt, and then took a sip of coffee. "Well, it ain't going to be Charlie. When you find Bucky dead, and Charlie's in the neighborhood, kind of makes you want to steer clear. And Little Man has work to do, so that leaves only me. Anyway, I owe you for coming back and finding Charlie, though I'm not sure that's a blessing. I'll take you out tomorrow, though we might get chased away again."

"Not soon enough. Let's go tonight."

"Tonight? OK, Matty, your call," Jack said, reaching for the Belikin. "Tonight it is."

23

It would take the hundred-and-twenty-pound jaguar half a day to recover from the Telazol drug dart. David Mallard had carefully monitored her heart rate and breathing, looking for any sign of cardiac failure. She seemed fine. As he carried FK-7 over his thick shoulder to his truck, Mallard stumbled, catching himself with one hand against a mahogany tree. He didn't worry about waking her, having added enough ketamine to the Telazol on the dart to keep her drugged throughout her journey.

When he reached his Land Rover, he laid her gently on a blue plastic tarp he had left unrolled on the ground. He opened the back door and then lifted her again, struggling with her weight. Once she was inside, he covered her with a tattered blanket and shut the door. It would be a two-hour drive to the dock and then another hour in the rundown fishing scow he had leased to reach Devil's Caye, putting him there well after midnight.

He parked at the back of the dusty lot, with his rear door facing the bush. Not a soul was in sight, the only sounds squeaks and groans from fishing skiffs pulling at their lines. He carried FK-7 down the dock, as he might carry his bride over the threshold. Careful not to fall as he stepped over the boat's rail, he set her down in the small cabin and pulled back the blanket. The jaguar's open eyes startled him, but she remained comatose. He listened to her steady, shallow breathing with a stethoscope, checked her heart rate. All was well. After returning to the Rover to get his pack and lock the doors, he fired up the boat and was underway in less than a minute.

Occasionally, an outboard engine droned in the distance, reminding him to be cautious, but he figured it would be only poachers setting gill nets. He skirted past a dozen islands, arriving at Devil's Caye in a little more than an hour. Turning on his spotlight, he could see mangrove branches hanging haphazardly over the entrance to the narrow channel. After motoring for several minutes up the cut, he saw the fresh planks of a new dock. When Mallard cut the engine, all he could hear were his bow waves slapping against the mangrove roots.

Mallard strained to lift the jaguar from the rocking boat, but once she was settled in Mallard's strong arms, he was able to carry her down the overgrown path, stumbling once before he reached the clearing, a small lean-to and padlocked shed. Under the lean-to were four canvas deck chairs, a case of bottled water, and an unrolled tarp. He placed the cat on the ground then turned on his light. He checked her mouth, her respiration, and heart rate again, and felt relieved to find nothing wrong.

He lay alongside her for nearly an hour, curled up with her, stroking the animal, inhaling the wild smells from her coat. At last, he felt a low growl rumble through her body, a sign the tranquilizer was wearing off. Mallard stroked her back one more time, rubbed his hand over her head, and then stood. He wondered if he would ever forgive himself.

He would wait until she found her legs and didn't need his attention, and then he would go. The only consolation, he supposed, was that she was an old female, no longer fecund, who probably wouldn't even live to the next breeding season. She couldn't have much left in her.

He doubted he would ever again see this magnificent jaguar. When Turnbull told him Martin Chin would be getting in touch, it meant that someone was expecting a trophy. He could only pray that her sacrifice would mean hundreds of other jaguars would survive. But Mallard knew that Turnbull would not settle for just one.

24

A HALF HOUR INTO the trip, Jack trimmed the Whaler's outboard to run as quietly as possible. Forty-five minutes later, two hundred yards off Devil's Caye, he cut it entirely. If people were on the island, he didn't want to pique their interest.

Jack picked up a splintered canoe paddle, handed Matt another, and sat on the left gunwale, opposite Matt. They started paddling in unison. "Just like Hawaiians, right, Matty?"

After several strokes, Matt stopped paddling so the *Flash* wouldn't go around in circles. "I think they're a little better at it, bro." The breeze pushed the boat away from the island, making silent paddling difficult, but after fifteen minutes, the bow crunched into the sand. Matt carried the anchor ashore, twenty feet into the underbrush, and stuck its prongs into the soil. Jack wrapped the slack around the bow cleat and waded ashore. He handed Matt a bottle of DEET. "Lather up or you'll be hamburger." Matt obliged.

As Matt started down a thin trail through the

underbrush, Jack grabbed his shoulder. "This is my country, I lead," he said, turning on a thumb-sized flashlight. Forty feet into the thick brush, well hidden from the shoreline, a chain link gate, secured by two half-inch chains, each with fist-sized padlocks, blocked the trail. Across the eight-foot top, coiled razor wire meant serious business.

Jack shined his light on the fence. "I'll be a son of a bitch. No way to get past that."

"Might try some wire cutters."

"You might. Not me. A fence like that means trouble. At best, there's a pack of dogs in there."

"Dogs would be here by now."

"Maybe so, but this is as far as I go." Jack started back, but Matt pointed at a palm tree.

"Look at that." While several trees gently curved a hundred feet upward from the water's edge, one tilted inward at a thirty-five-degree angle, its top fronds extending far over the fence. Matt walked down the narrow shoreline, studying the tree's arc.

"Watch this." He grabbed the trunk with both hands, hunched over, and started climbing upward, his toe touching his leading heel with each step. Twice, his weight shifted, and he almost fell off, but, steadying himself, he was soon fifty feet up the slanted trunk, fifteen feet off the ground. After a few more steps, he passed over the barbed-wire crown. He sat down, carefully lowered himself off the trunk, hung from it for a moment, and then dropped ten feet to the soft ground below. Matt clapped his hands together silently.

"Excuse me, Matty, but how in the hell are you going to get out?"

Matt's grin disappeared. "Didn't think that one through, did I?"

"No, you didn't. Let me grab a line from the boat. I'll toss it over to you." Jack disappeared into the brush, returning with thirty feet of coiled rope. He flung it over to Matt, but it caught on the barbed wire. "Shit." Jack yanked it back and started coiling it back up.

"Why are you throwing me the rope?"

"Tie knots in it, then toss it over the tree and climb back up."

"Impossible."

"Well, don't expect me to go over that fence. I'm no fucking monkey."

"Three beers didn't help you either, Jack. Here, slip the rope through the fence." Jack threaded the end through the fence, and Matt gathered and coiled it. "Stay there. Let me see what's happening."

"Take this," Jack said, waving the flashlight. "But turn it on only if you need it. No telling who's in there with you," he said, his gravelly voice just above a whisper. Jack switched on the light and threw it over the fence.

Matt leaped to catch it and quickly turned it off. "If anyone saw that, I hope they thought it was a shooting star." Slipping it into the back pocket of his shorts, he turned into the bush. The farther he walked, the thicker the undergrowth. And then it struck him. He backtracked to his entry point where Jack was kneeling by the fence waiting for him.

"This is a prison, Jack. I bet this fence surrounds the island."

"Like I said, get out. Tie knots in the rope and flip it over the palm."

"Not yet. I'm going in a different way." Someone had cut the foliage away from the inside perimeter, so he kept his left hand on the fence, soon coming to a rough, overgrown pathway heading toward the center of the island. Pushing branches from his face, he stumbled ahead through the underbrush. Stickers jammed between his toes, his sandals providing no protection. He squelched a scream when a pointed branch separated his big toenail from the quick. Blood gushed from his foot. Fifty yards in, the path widened, the flies thickened, and then, filling his nostrils, an acrid, cloying smell that could only mean death. Covering his nose and mouth with his hand was no defense against the bitter odor. He wanted to turn around, but he held his breath and staggered forward, into the thickening stench. Whatever was scattered on the ground, it was covered with what seemed like a billion botlass flies sizzling like a massive electrical short.

He tried to shake a cluster of flies from his bloody foot but lost his balance and fell to one knee, his hand landing on a sandpapery surface that nearly rubbed the skin off his palm. He pulled out the flashlight and flipped the switch. It was a shark fin, alive with flies and coated with dry blood where it had been sliced from the shark's body. Shark fins were scattered everywhere, all carved from hundreds of sharks, which had surely been thrown alive back into the sea, defenseless and immobile, fodder for smaller sea creatures that nipped and picked endlessly, as the helpless shark died a slow, painful, agonizing death.

All for a bowl of soup.

Matt circled the fins, careful not to step on any, his blood boiling. Why in God's name was the holier-than-thou Global Fund for Wildlife drying shark fins on Devil's Caye? Just who were these bastards? He had to get out of there.

A wooden wagon with large bicycle tires sat near the opening to another trail, rutted by the wheels. Maybe this was his exit. Keeping his head down, watching each step, the dim flashlight showed him the way. A dull thud, then a voice, broke his concentration. Dropping to one knee, he held his breath.

"Toss me the line."

"Over here."

"Take this."

Two voices from the canal, perhaps a hundred feet away, drifted through the undergrowth. A flashlight beam flickered through the leaves. The chatter continued, but Matt could catch only a word here and there. One melodic voice sounded familiar, but it was too distant for Matt to place. Who were they? What were they doing here well after midnight? What about Jack at the other end of the island? Had they seen his boat?

Matt heard thuds, maybe boxes being dropped on the dock. He crept forward, but the voices became softer. The men were walking down another path, toward the center of the island, where Matt had just been. Sweat ran down his forehead, stinging his eyes. He wiped it off with the hem of his shirt. He had nowhere to go but forward.

In a ten-foot-wide clearing alongside the mangrove channel, an open gate in the chain link fence revealed a water taxi tied to the dock, its two engines lifted above the water, the hull filled with stacks of flattened cardboard boxes. He took a deep breath. Tied to a mangrove root was his way out—a dinghy.

Matt crept behind cinder blocks, PVC pipe, wire, scattered detritus left behind from the earlier construction. He felt the knot on the frayed rope lashed to the dinghy. It was pulled tight. A dim light shone through the bushes, and he heard footsteps coming back down the trail. Matt froze. No place to hide. Grabbing a two-foot long PVC pipe, he slipped into the water next to the dock.

Whispering voices grew closer. "Look at that. Little ripples. Something went into the water."

"Maybe a crocodile," were the last words Matt heard before he submerged. Pushing the PVC pipe against those in one corner supporting the dock, he began breathing through the pipe as quietly as he could, frightened of meeting a crocodile himself. He heard footsteps on the dock, felt it vibrate. The water brightened as a light beam swept the surface, then darkened, and those footsteps returned down the dock. And then it was black, pitch black. Fully submerged under the dock, ankle deep in a soft muddy channel bottom, breathing through the pipe, he waited. And waited. Finally, he lifted his head from the water. Faint moon rays flickered on the surface, reflecting off the dinghy on shore.

He moved along the bottom, with every step sinking deeper into the morass, then finally pulled himself onto the shore and crawled to the dinghy. His fingers, chilled stiff, fumbled over the tight knot until he finally untied it. Carefully, he dragged the aluminum rowboat into the water. Grabbing a wooden paddle lying alongside, he put one foot into the boat and pushed off into the darkness. Paddling quietly, he soon left the channel and headed toward his landing point. Before he saw Jack, he heard him snoring like an exotic animal.

25

A LIGHT BREEZE RATTLED the louvered windows, waking Matt from a deep sleep. He pulled the pillow over his head, but the roar of an outboard killed any chance of falling back to sleep. His right eyelid felt pasted down, a mosquito having drawn blood, leaving a swollen lump behind. He found dry shorts and a T-shirt, pulled them on, and made his way out to the porch.

Inside the reef, the blue-tinted water was as clear and calm as a backyard swimming pool. He held his hand over his eyes and squinted. Somewhere out there, thirty miles away, he had attacked the beach like a Marine, dropped like a paratrooper from a palm tree behind enemy lines, sneaked through the underbrush like a Ranger, stumbled across the severed fins of a thousand sharks, and hid in the black water like a Navy Seal. Matt, the ex-Wilderness Foundation bureaucrat, struggling freelance writer, now turned soldier of fortune, was pissed.

In the lodge, Charlie was following his shirtless morning ritual of checking his email, typing answers to reservation queries with the index finger of his right hand while stroking his white beard with his other hand between sips of coffee.

"Any more news on the web?" Matt asked. Remembering Jack's suspicion about Charlie, he wasn't about to tell him about last night.

Charlie didn't look up. "Been surfing the local chat rooms." He looked at his watch. "Nine days, now. Still no one in Belize has turned up missing. Told you it was a mirage."

"Still bullshitting yourself, Charlie? What did Barnstable say about the engraved tooth?"

Charlie grunted. "Said he can't do much about it. Could be from anyone. Might have been there for months, maybe years."

"Then it would have been under a foot of sand," Matt said.

Charlie kept typing. "Barnstable will figure it out. In the meantime, we got no guests here and a shit-load of bills to pay. Not to mention payroll coming up Monday." Charlie threw up his hands.

"And what's that mean?"

"Jack has a problem. I have a roof to patch and a boat to repair. And it all costs money." Charlie closed the computer lid. "For now, I'm going to have breakfast, and I'll worry about it tomorrow. That's how we do things here in Margaritaville."

"Charlie, I still don't get what you were doing at the Blue Hole. Why the secrecy?"

"Personal stuff. I don't talk personal."

"Little Man said you had a shark in your boat with fins missing?"

"I found it the day before. Thought I might know who killed it, but I guess I didn't."

"And that got you stranded at the Blue Hole?"

"Nah, a couple of Guatemalan poachers saw me climb out of my boat and went for it. So, I went for them, but they pulled a gun and took me for a ride."

"They weren't finning sharks?"

"Nope, they're just fucking thieves. Probably the same ones that took our boat on the night dive. Now if you don't mind, I'm gonna eat and scram."

"There's more to the story, Charlie."

Charlie turned his back to Matt and hobbled into the kitchen. "OK, girls, let's get breakfast for the Tuna."

Matt headed to the computer, logged on to his account, and scrolled through a bunch of messages, stopping only for the last one — Sender: Cat. Subject: Nice Meeting You.

Matt, I guess you're home in Sausalito after sweating it out here. Everyone was shocked about the monkey, but I have suspects. Email me if you have more questions for your article.

Wish your short visit could have been longer. It's not that I get lonely here, with all the tourists tromping through, but rarely do I meet a kindred spirit. Off to Belize City. I can hear the plane. Stay in touch. Cat

Matt stared at the message. Was the jungle goddess showing interest? Sent yesterday, but she didn't say whether she would be staying over in Belize City. Matt jumped when a hand touched his shoulder. It was Jack, his breath stale.

"Recovered, have you?"

"Not from the stench. Or what I saw." Matt closed the laptop cover.

"I could smell it from the shore. And you still can't figure out who the guys were who sent you snorkeling in the dark?"

"No, but that one voice I heard. It seemed familiar. I just couldn't get a look. But we have more important matters. Who do we report all those fins to?"

"Report? Shit, Matt, I'm not even sure shark finning is illegal here. You can sure as hell fish for sharks, so you can probably sell their fins."

"Jack, those fins are sliced off, and the shark is dropped back into the water alive. That's not shark fishing, that's slaughter."

"And nobody will do a goddamn thing about it. My burned-out boat out in the lagoon is proof."

Matt walked to the window, where he could see the corpse of the partially submerged boat the poachers had burned. "This isn't small-time stuff. Guys running a shark-finning ring are guys who would ice anyone, you included. But why do they go to the trouble of dropping a body in your freezer when they could dump it on any deserted caye and let it rot. What's your connection, Jack?"

"Matty, this isn't just about me. Think about the poor guy who got toasted."

"Frozen, is more like it."

"And fed to the sharks."

"Judging by that pile of fins I saw last night, I'm surprised there were any sharks left to feed. Which is why I'm going to the Fisheries Department."

"You'll be dead and gone before they do anything. Call the Fund. It's their property. They have an office in town." Jack pulled out a phone book, its pages curled from the salt air. He picked up his reading glasses, pushed them up on his nose, and thumbed the pages. "By the way, Barnstable called today. Wanted to know if I'd seen you."

"And?"

"I told him you were back in California, writing your story. He said it better be good. Ah, here's the number. They're on Front Street." Jack handed him the phone book and house cell phone, a red Nokia with a stubby antenna.

Matt punched in the numbers. A staccato ring repeated itself six times, and then a woman with a southern accent, Texas style, said, "Global Fund for Wildlife."

"Hello, may I talk with the director?"

"Mr. Turnbull isn't here. May I take a message?"

"Hmm, just a moment, please." Matt turned to Jack and covered the phone with his hand. "Guess what? The philanthropist Turnbull also runs the Fund. Maybe we should talk to him."

"I hope that's the royal 'we' you're using, sonny. I'm going nowhere."

Matt lifted the receiver again. "Would it be possible to schedule a meeting with Mr. Turnbull?"

"I can only pass on the message. He's leaving town this afternoon."

"No message then. Thanks." Matt hung up the phone. "Can't get past the gatekeeper, so maybe I'll just drop in. Somebody has to be interested in this story."

Matt called an old friend at Greenpeace in Washington, only to be told they had no office in Belize, and no boat anywhere near the Caribbean. Two calls to the Belize Fisheries Department asking about shark finning ended with someone saying, "Can't hear you, mon, must be something wrong with the line." He tried the *New York Times* in Mexico City, but they had cut staff back so far they couldn't cover isolated events in Belize.

Channel Five News Belize told him, "We reported on the body and talked to the police, but no one's been reported missing, so we're not following the story. And there are no reliable reports of shark finning in the Caribbean, but we'll keep it on our docket." Whatever that meant.

Matt put down the phone in frustration. He knew he could not post anonymously online and expect results. In Belize, there were few citizen crusaders, no tough-nosed environmentalists, no independent journalists to take up the cause, and even if someone did try to investigate, the government—and whoever else—would silence him in no time. Belize lived on tourism. If Matt were to identify himself online, he would be tracked down and frog-marched out of Belize—or locked up, even shot up—before sunrise.

He walked outside and saw Jack sitting at the bar. "When's the next water taxi?"

Jack took a swig of Belikin. "The Whaler's out there. The tank's full. Be my guest. But put on something clean. You're going to see a wealthy man."

"What do you have that will fit me?"

"How about a nice powder blue guayabera shirt. That's the national dress-up shirt down here. Four big pockets to hold all your cash. I bought one when Queen Elizabeth came to town, back in ninety-four. You're welcome to it."

"I'll take it." Matt picked up the phone and dialed Cat's lodge, hoping she was in town. If so, he would start with a lunch date.

As soon as Matt reached the mouth of Haulover Creek, he turned down the throttle on the 75-horsepower Johnson, coasting through the scores of fishing boats choking off the channel. A half-mile later, he pulled up to the hardware store landing.

Inside the store, he found Charlie's rusty old bike, with a slipping chain and fat marshmallow tires. Matt wheeled it out the door and rode off to Frankie's, where Cat had suggested they meet. When he arrived a little past noon, she was sitting at the same table where he had sat with Maxie, engrossed in the *Belize Reporter*.

"Hi, what's the latest in Belize?"

She pushed the paper away and grinned. "Not much, other than old Matt, he's back in town. Anybody ever call you that, Matt the Knife? Never mind," she smiled, "why would they? It's Mack, anyway." She stood and gave him a quick hug. She smelled of the rainforest—misty, even mystical. Her light green tank top matched the color of her eyes, her blonde hair rested on her tanned shoulders.

He sat down opposite her, folding his arms on the flowery table covering. "And what are you doing in town?"

"Lettuce, tomatoes, bacon, flour, mangoes. Everything the kitchen needs for a week and then some."

"Big task. I wouldn't know where to start. I usually stock my kitchen for two days. A hunk of cheese, half a dozen apples, a loaf of bread."

"And a jug of wine for your company, I suppose." She smiled that little lip curl. Matt returned the smile, saying nothing.

"So, Matt, why are you back just two days after I thought you left forever? Truman Capote syndrome?"

Before he could answer, a gray-haired Belizean woman appeared at the table with a pad and pen in hand. "Well, Miss Cat, looks like you have company this afternoon."

"Hi, Frankie. This is a friend from California, Matt."

"Welcome. If you like Belizean food, there's none finer than mine. Grouper came in this morning already. I serve it with rice and plantains."

"I'll take it." Matt could see she recognized him from when he had been there with Maxie. He appreciated her discretion.

"Make it two." Cat gave a thumbs-up.

Frankie returned to the kitchen, and Matt told Cat his story, finishing just as Frankie arrived with their meals. Cat looked worried. "Why are you doing all this? Just for a story?"

"Chin's a sleazebag."

She leaned forward. "Let me add to the sleaze. As I drove to the lodge the night before last, a car flying down the road with its lights off almost hit me. I couldn't tell what it was or who was driving it. When I reached the lodge, one of our guides said he had heard the howlers going nuts, so he ran into the woods and chased away two guys who were stringing up a huge net." Cat shook her head. "Those guys were idiots. Monkeys don't fly into nets like birds."

Matt put his fork down on the plate. "This is out of control. Have you talked to your biologist friend, Mallard?"

"What's he going to do? Besides, he's in the bush for a couple of weeks."

"Well, I'd like to talk to him, at least about the Fund. How do I reach him?"

"Email him. He has a satellite computer at his camp, unless someone stole it when he was away." She wrote his email address on the napkin and handed it to Matt.

"What exactly does the Fund do in Belize?"

"I know only what Mallard tells me. Why all the interest in the Fund?"

"Fund signs were on Devil's Caye near where the boobies roost, where those goons stopped us from diving." Matt watched Cat poke at her food. "After lunch, I'm going to the Fund's office." Her eyebrows popped up. "Is there something wrong with that?" he asked.

"No, no, not at all. It's just that you were headed home to write a story, and now you're back with a vengeance. Aren't you worried about getting in over your head?"

"A little." He cut off a piece of fish and chewed it slowly, savoring the nutmeg in the batter. The thugs protected the island with a Fund sign. Mallard was a Fund scientist. Cat knew him. So what? It was a small country. He continued: "I didn't finish my story before Frankie brought the food. Night before last, Jack and I went out to Devil's Caye. You know what we found?" He didn't wait for an answer. "Shark fins drying. Thousands. All surrounded by a ten-foot chain-link fence."

She straightened up. "Shark fins? Who would do that? Belizeans don't eat shark fin soup."

"Chinese do. How big is the Chinese community here — five, six thousand?"

"Probably. Lots of Taiwanese and some from Hong Kong."

"I think Devil's Caye is a staging ground, probably one of many, where they drop off fins to dry, and then gather them up and send them somewhere for shipping. The fins have to come from the Caribbean. Nobody is going to sail through the Panama Canal with a load of shark fins."

Cat held her head in her hands, her face down, saying nothing. "You OK?" Matt asked.

"I thought about the monkeys." She looked up. A tear glistened in the corner of her eye.

Frankie appeared and refilled their coffee cups, turning to Matt. "This is a good lady, the best. I hope you're being nice to her."

Cat answered for him. "He is, Frankie."

"Then I hope you're being nice to him."

"She's being very nice," he said. Cat smiled.

Matt put his hand on Frankie's arm. "I hear you're one

of the best cooks in Belize. When you were a child, did your folks ever cook monkey meat?"

"Heavens, no, mon. I lived out on the cayes. We had manatee now and then, but never monkey. But that old-time food is long gone." She set the coffee pot down and started gathering the dishes. "But that man, Mr. Chin? He wants to do a cookbook with traditional recipes. I gave him a few from my family."

Matt nodded. "Well, good for you."

Frankie put the check on the table and Cat grabbed it. She put down twenty dollars Belize, took a last sip of coffee, and slipped from the booth. Matt followed her out the door and down the stairs.

"You're doing the smart thing by going to the Fund," she said. "You can't trust the government."

"I'm not sure who I can trust."

She shrugged. "Do you want a lift to the Fund's office?"

"Thanks, but I have the fastest bike in town." He pointed at Charlie's rusty two-wheeler.

She put out her arms and Matt hugged her, a little more tightly than last time. Leaning back, she grabbed his hands. "Stay in touch. Come out for a few days, if you can."

"Love to. And thanks for lunch." They looked at each other for a second, and then Cat released his hands and turned. When she reached her car door, she looked back. "The dead monkey. You think it was Chin's people?"

Matt nodded.

"Take care of yourself." She climbed into her Ranger, started the ignition, and disappeared into the traffic. When he turned for the bike, it was halfway down the street, a small boy pedaling it as fast as he could.

26

A TEN-DOLLAR CAB RIDE later, Matt arrived at Twenty-one Slaughterhouse Road, a two-story house with a small deck on the side. Below barred windows, a plaque on a glistening white door announced *Global Fund for Wildlife*. Before Matt could knock, a woman about forty, hair pulled back, reading glasses hanging from a chain around her neck, unlatched the door, opening it a foot. "May I help you?" she asked in a syrupy southern accent.

"I'm Matt Oliver. I was hoping to talk with Trey Turnbull."

"You called earlier. I believe I told you that he is not here. I hope you haven't made the trip from the cayes just to see him."

"No, I happened to be in town." Matt hadn't mentioned the cayes. How did she know where he called from? "It's important that I talk to him."

She raised her head to get a better look at him. "About what?"

"About Fund business. Urgent business."

She straightened up. "Very well. Wait outside for a moment," she said, shutting the door.

Across the street, a German Shepherd peered at Matt between rebar jutting upward through the second story floor of an unfinished house. The neighborhood felt dead, as if all the people had evacuated, leaving only animals behind.

The door behind him opened. "Mr. Turnbull will be sending a car to take you to his personal office. It should be here in ten minutes." With a forced smile, the receptionist closed the door.

He sat on the steps, deep in thought, looking up only when a voice asked, "You Mr. Oliver?" A limousine had quietly rolled up, and the driver leaned across the front seat to the open passenger-side window. "My name is Winston. I'm here to take you to see Mr. Turnbull."

Matt climbed in the back seat, separated from the driver by a closed glass barrier. In five minutes, they pulled into the driveway of a two-story colonial house on Lovely Lane, a name probably contrived a century ago by some tea-sipping English cartographer who had never visited British Honduras. Scarlet bougainvillea climbed the walls, clinging to the eaves of the red tile roof. Sprinklers cast a haze over the perfectly tailored Kentucky bluegrass.

Winston slid open the glass window. "Go around the left side and knock on the door there."

"What is this building? Looks like an embassy."

"It was a consulate, once upon a time. Now it's Mr. Turnbull's private residence when he's in Belize."

Matt walked around the side and down a slate walkway.

Before he could knock on the small white door, a short man with a shaved head opened it and ushered him in. "Mr. Oliver, Mr. Turnbull is waiting for you." Matt followed him up a narrow stairwell to the second floor and saw an open door at the end of the hallway. "You'll find him in there."

The walls had been elaborately paneled with Belizean hardwood. The wall behind Turnbull was plastered with framed and signed photographs of Turnbull shaking hands with Governor Ann Richards, Senator John Tower, Lady Bird Johnson, and sitting at tables with scores of other politicians, celebrities, and some Belizeans. Turnbull, with his back to the door and a phone pressed to his ear, stared out the window.

"Well, Herb, we'll take care of you just fine. I'm delighted you can come back on such short notice. I do appreciate your help." Turnbull listened and then laughed. "Us old Texas boys always have to stick together. It will be you, me, the ambassador, the superintendent, hopefully a couple of investors— My Comanche's at the airport now… Look forward to seeing you."

Trey spun around in his chair and dropped the receiver in the cradle. "Well, now. You're the fellow I saw at the lodge last week," Turnbull said.

"At the bar. You were appalled with the cat chop suey."

"That's right. Small country, this is." Turnbull reached across his desk to shake hands. "You know, last season three times more people went to Texas Stadium to see the Longhorns play than live in Belize."

"And I bet most couldn't point to Belize on a map."

Turnbull grunted, directing Matt toward a red leather

chair. In a photo on the wall alongside, Turnbull, dressed in a camouflage outfit, had his arm draped over the shoulder of another fellow in similar attire. It was Turnbull and Martin Chin, rifles at their sides, standing over an enormous African kudu, its spiral horns nearly as tall as Chin.

"I understand you're a travel writer," Turnbull said. He walked out from behind his desk and took a chair facing Matt. His perfectly pressed white linen trousers didn't even show a wrinkle.

"I am. Doing a newspaper piece on Belize. Reefs, rain-forests, all the usual stuff. That's why I was at the lodge. But that's not why I wanted to see you. I happened to be on Devil's Caye the other day. I think the Fund owns it, or so I've heard." Matt hesitated, catching Trey's eyes as they narrowed. "I was shocked at what I saw."

"That island is off limits. We allow only researchers on the grounds. What were you doing there?" Trey played with a Newton's Cradle on the coffee table between them, lifting a steel ball, letting it go, watching it strike the next with a click like a pistol hammer.

"Curiosity, I suppose, but that's not important. What I saw is what's important."

"The fence is there for a reason."

"Barbed wire atop a ten-foot chain link fence is not the kind of fence I'd expect on an island."

"There's critical research going on there. It involves bird nesting, native plants, and mangrove habitat. It's pristine habitat and can't be disturbed. That's why it's secure."

"Then why all the shark fins scattered around? There's

enough to make soup for all those fans at one of your Texas football games."

The balls kept clicking. Trey's silver eyebrows dropped, his eyelids tightened; only his irises were visible. "Shark fins, you say? What time of day were you there?"

"Dead of night, frankly, but with a little moonlight and a keen nose, it was pretty apparent they were fresh shark fins."

Trey watched the balls swinging back and forth, slowing, slowing, and finally stopping. "You're sure of what you saw?"

"As sure as the million swarming flies were."

Trey smirked, then pushed himself up from his chair, brushed the front of his slacks, and opened the door to the closet. He returned with a package, wrapped in manila paper and tied with a string, and placed it on the table. "All right, I'm going to quench that curiosity of yours, but on the condition this conversation doesn't leave the room. Got it?"

Matt looked at the package, saying nothing.

"Never mind then." Trey picked up the package and started back toward the closet.

Matt held up his hand. "OK. Mum's the word. What do you have there?"

Trey pulled a pocketknife from his pocket, cut the string, and unwrapped the package. "What's that look like to you? Pick it up. Have a look."

It was firm, the gray skin rough, a triangular shape, slightly rounded at the top, the base jagged and flinty yellow, where it had been cut from an animal. Matt inspected both sides, feeling the skin. "Seems to be a shark fin."

Turnbull snickered. "A shark fin? Of course not." He shook his head. "It's the wing of a Pacific skate. A big skate."

Matt's eyes narrowed.

"They're endemic to the Pacific Ocean. They first appeared in the waters north of Panama two years ago, and they've been working their way up the coast ever since. They reached Honduras eight months ago, and now they're in the waters of southern Belize."

Turnbull lifted a globe off his bookshelf and set it in front of Matt. "The skates migrated through the Panama Canal," he said, tracing the route with his finger. "They're bottom feeders, and they're better at it than our Caribbean rays and nurse sharks, so they're growing bigger and reproducing much faster than their native cousins. They call it lessespian migration. It happens wherever ship canals are built. Fish slip into one side and eventually come out the other. You can't stop it."

"And you're saying these," Matt waved the skate wing, "are Pacific skates?"

"That's just the tip of the wing. They're big animals."

"The Canal's been there nearly a hundred years. Why now?"

"No one's sure, but it's gone on for some time, and it's only been apparent in the last couple of years because of the population explosion. Anyhow, we've hired people to wipe them out. The Chinese use the wings in lots of their dishes, so we expect to sell most to finance the project, but the wings you saw had dried out before we could get them off the island. We'll be burning them and not bringing any more ashore."

Matt put the wing on the manila paper and leaned back. "A search and destroy mission."

"Exactly. You know, Honduras is where the Red Lobster chain gets its product. This is big business. We must wipe out these skates before they wipe out the lobster industry."

"An impossible job, don't you think?"

"We'll get rid of them."

Matt shook his head. "You're telling me that fishermen or divers or whoever you have will catch them all."

"At least enough to control them, keep down the breeding population so they'll be no threat."

"Why are you keeping this under wraps?"

"Because environmental lunatics like Greenpeace will call for a slowdown in Panama Canal traffic so someone can study the problem. Maybe even demand a total shut down. Even a slowdown would be disastrous. These skates are economically destructive. The U.S. government is not about to fight a battle over the Canal, so the Fund has taken on the task of destroying them."

Matt leaned back in the chair and tugged at his lower lip, saying nothing. He had made three dives and snorkeled Charlie's reef and had seen no skates. Jack hadn't mentioned them, and neither had Charlie. "I saw a few local divers out around Rum Caye. Is that what they were after?"

"Might very well have been."

"I've not heard any local divers talk about them. Certainly I haven't seen them."

"Then we're doing our job. When were you on Devil's Caye?" Trey leaned forward.

"Couple nights ago."

"I'll make a few calls. We need to secure the island and dump the trash. I'm thankful you brought this to my attention." He picked up the phone, and then set it back down. "You know, Oliver, don't get the Fund in the news about this. We have scientists out there from Audubon and World Wildlife. If someone makes the same mistake you did and goes public, all hell will break loose before we set things straight. The Fund will get tarred with a big brush."

Matt reached for a steel ball, pulled one back, then thought better of it.

"Our donors would withhold money first, ask questions later. That could cost the Fund millions and jeopardize scores of our wildlife projects. You wouldn't want to be the source of that mayhem, I trust."

Matt straightened up, surprised. "Of course not."

"Remember when the Red Cross didn't send all the money it raised to the victims' families after Nine-Eleven? Donors walked and cost the Red Cross millions. A false rumor about the Fund would cripple us. And you, Oliver, would find yourself the subject of a multi-million-dollar lawsuit. Do you understand?"

"You're saying the Fund would sue me?"

"In a New York minute, my boy, so no other son of a bitch would ever think to slander us." Trey sat back. "Now how long are you here for?"

Matt gritted his teeth, hiding his anger. "Not sure, why?"

"Call me in two days. I'll take you out to the island. The skate wings should be cleaned out by then, but if there are any left, you can take one with you. And then, I'll find you a Fund biologist who'll be happy to tell you all about our work."

"Fair enough."

"Now, I do appreciate your alerting me to our little security problem. Let me get on the phone and take care of things. The driver who brought you is outside. Are you taking the water taxi to Jack's?"

"My boat's at the hardware store."

"Too bad about what happened out there. Jack himself is a tourist attraction. Hate to see him in any kind of trouble."

"Jack's a survivor. He'll weather it."

"The country is changing, Oliver. Those old shipwreck survivors like Jack aren't always as lucky as they once were."

As soon as Matt stepped through the doorway, Trey dialed his phone and started shouting. "Chin, you bastard. What are you doing to me? I want you at the marina in fifteen minutes." He hung up without waiting for an answer.

27

T REY SAT ON the flying bridge of his *Texas Trigger,* a Sea Ray 44, listening to the smooth hum of the idling twin diesels. He glanced at his Rolex. Chin was half an hour late. If it were anyone other than Chin, he would rev the engines and leave him on the dock. He drummed his fingers on the wheel, but he kept his hand off the throttle.

It took another five minutes before Trey heard the sharp click of heels on the wooden dock. He recognized Chin's "oof" as he climbed over the transom. Chin entered the cabin, nodded and smiled.

"Martin, make yourself a drink, but stay inside. Let's not advertise our get-together. I'm going up on the bridge and take us out to where we can talk." Chin took a Crystal Water from the ice bucket and sat down in one of four stuffed swiveling chairs surrounding a round coffee table with a Belize chart under the thick resin coating.

Trey backed the *Texas Trigger* away from the pier and turned it toward the murky bay. Once they reached blue water, he climbed down the ladder and took his seat at the cabin wheel. Chin sat with his hands folded in his lap, his eyes fixed on Belize City fading in the distance.

"I'll head out past St. George's Caye. Nice day for a drift." Trey pointed at a small bar with bottles of Grey Goose, GlenLivet, Maker's Mark, and Bombay Sapphire. "Want something stronger?"

"I'll pass. Have you ever been in the harbor in Hong Kong? It looks like a parking lot. Here, never."

"That's why I like Belize, Martin, no one to stick his nose into your business, unless you make it too easy for them." Chin looked at the fading skyline, ignoring Trey's glare.

The twin diesels roared as they lifted the bow high. In thirty minutes, the *Texas Trigger* came to a stop a mile east of St. George's, the only sound the flap of the red, white, and blue Houston Yacht Club burgee. Trey poured two fingers of Maker's Mark into a tumbler embossed with *III* and motioned Chin outside. He lifted his glass, Chin his bottle. They nodded and sipped.

"Martin, a more diplomatic person than I might say he was upset, but I'm afraid that would be too kind. More to the point, you've betrayed me."

Chin's back stiffened. "Betrayed you? What are you talking about? Turnbull, you and I have a business arrangement."

"You're risking my reputation, Chin."

"And just how am I doing that?"

"By dumping a boatload of shark fins in the middle of my island. We had a simple drop arrangement. Your boat brings in what it can after nightfall and your boys sort them or whatever they do and get them off that island before sunrise. That's it. Quick and simple."

"I must apologize. You see, the captain had strict orders to drop off only half a ton for me and take the rest to my operation in Guatemala. He knew I couldn't keep those fins on the island, so he decided to extort me, and dumped all four tons, demanding more money. It's taken me four days to get the cash, which I will have in the morning, and his crew will go back tomorrow night and take what's left."

"You ought to shoot the bastard. In fact, I ought to shoot the bastard." Trey pushed the throttle up to half-speed.

"If he were working the Pacific, I would have shot him myself. But he's the only one willing to risk fishing the Caribbean. I have no choice but to pay him."

"Bullshit. Have your no-good kid take them to Belize City and dry them on your roof. You have a plane at the City airport. The one you should have used in that Guatemala fiasco, you cheap bastard. Load it up and get those fins out of there. And tell the captain to go screw himself."

"Too much risk. I must keep him working for me. No one else will fish this side of the Canal, no matter what I pay. It's too easy to be spotted. Besides, he finds sharks where there shouldn't be any."

"Chin, you're peddling those fins for a hundred U.S. each. You have half a million dollars piled up out there. Pay your people more."

"It's the risk, not the pay. I could get Chinese workers from Belize, but an all-Chinese crew is an advertisement to be boarded. I use Belizeans only, not even Guatemalans. This won't happen again."

"I don't care about next time, I care about now. I can't afford your carelessness." Trey started pacing, four steps to the cabin, four back to the stern. "Martin, I'm doing you a hell of a favor by charging you only twenty grand to use that caye. It's a favor to you because you're keeping the ambassador and his Washington buddies happy with those magic powders of yours. But if my ass gets caught up in this shark finning debacle, my reputation is ruined, and you're coming down with me."

"My people did what they could."

"Chin, if I go out to my island, and someone just happens to see both me and the fins, my only choice is to pretend to be shocked by the discovery and report it to Barnstable. He'll clean it out in a flash." Trey wagged his finger. "And he'll eventually come looking for you."

Chin stood up, his eyes wide, his jaw slack. "You would report this?"

"No, Martin, not this time. But those fins aren't a secret any longer. And if they get connected to me, as my little friend the American writer tried to do—"

"He knows?"

"You got it, pardner."

The *Texas Trigger* had drifted within a half-mile from St. George's Caye. Trey leaned over the railing to check the depth. Yellow fish darted about coral heads ten feet below.

"You didn't show him the ray wings I gave you?"

"Of course, I did. Told him the whole story about skates migrating through the canal. You might fool a Belize cop with that malarkey but how long do you think it will take that little turd to figure things out?"

Chin sat back down and rubbed his brow. "I can take care of that."

"Chin, right now he is my problem, and I'll address it."

Chin's weak jaw muscles rippled. "We'll both address it."

"Leave him alone, Chin. There'll be no blood on my hands. Don't forget that I bankrolled you when you climbed off that plane from Hong Kong carrying your little cardboard suitcase. I don't want any more trouble. Get the fins off the island and don't use it again until I tell you to. I'll deal with Oliver. No blood."

Turnbull rose from his chair and gestured to the cabin. "Go inside, pour yourself a real drink, and don't come out until we get back to the dock."

Chin held up a finger. "One more thing, Trey. The ambassador. He's asked me to get tiger penis for him."

"What?"

"Tiger penis. It's very rare. The best of the aphrodisiacs."

"And?"

"And almost impossible to get. And friends of the ambassador want supplies as well."

"Maybe I can help you." Trey lifted his glass. "Now, have you completed preparations for tonight's dinner?"

"Everything is in order. It will be a banquet never seen in this country."

Trey looked at his watch. "Well, I hope there's a lot of booze since we're both going to be late."

28

WHEN MATT LEFT Turnbull's residence, the driver was nowhere in sight. But it made no difference. Matt wouldn't think of getting back in that car. He sauntered toward the waterfront, pondering what Trey had shown him. Suppose it was a Pacific skate wing? That still didn't mean that's what he had discovered spread all over Devil's Caye. It meant only that Trey had devised a clever cover-up. If Pacific skates really were pouring into the Caribbean, how could the U.S. government possibly keep it a secret and off the Internet?

Trey Turnbull was full of shit. Matt had stumbled into something much bigger than a pile of shark fins. He shuddered.

As he crossed Bleeker Street, Matt spotted the ornate sign of the Black Coral restaurant, remembering that Laddie B. Baker had invited him to dine tonight, drinks at five and dinner at six-thirty. Thunderclouds were billowing, and a trip to Jack's through a summer squall was not on Matt's agenda. He peered in the window at Formica tables, a few booths, red tassels hanging from the ceiling, a door opening to a back room, and a framed sign: *Black Coral Restaurant. Belize's Finest, Martin Chin Proprietor.* "I'll be damned," he said aloud. He walked away, passing the time by poking through the cruise ship kiosks again and watching tired fishermen rigging their boats in Haulover Creek.

At a quarter past five, he walked through the Black Coral's double doors. In the back of the restaurant, at least thirty people mingled, half of whom were smoking Cuban *Romeo y Julieta* cigars they had taken from the humidor by the door. The rich aroma filled the restaurant. Most guests were Belizeans; a few seemed to be Americans or Canadians, maybe English. Matt slipped a couple of Romeos—*Hecho en Cuba, totalamente a mano*—into his shirt pocket, ordered a gin and tonic from a white-coated bartender, and stepped to the side of the bar. Laddie B. Barber was nowhere in sight. Matt introduced himself to a tall, slender Belizean, Police Superintendent Nigel Godwin, who asked Matt what he did.

"I'm writing a story on tourism in Belize."

The superintendent smiled, then turned to chat up the busty Creole server wearing a white apron skirt. She held out her platter to Matt and he took the last deep-fried pasty. Matt introduced himself to others but was brushed off by the mayor of Dangriga, by an Englishman who owned the Pepsi-Cola bottling plant, and by a member of parliament who never even looked him in the eye. Being a writer wasn't opening any doors with these good old boys, all puffing their cigars and drinking English gin.

The Creole woman returned with a platter of Swedish meatballs in one hand and a platter of crackers spread with a light yellow paste in the other. Matt popped a cracker in his mouth, speared a meatball, and moved to the edge of the crowd, where he exchanged a few pleasantries, trying hard to look engaged. As he ordered his second gin and tonic, Ambassador Laddie B. Barber tapped him on the shoulder.

"Oliver, the writer. What brings you to my party?"

"Well, sir, you invited me during our pleasant conversation on the flight from Houston."

"Oh yes. Glad you could make it. As you can see, the best of Belize is here. All my good friends."

"And very impressive. I guess America won't have to swing its big stick down here."

The ambassador took a step backward. "Swing a big stick?"

Matt flushed. "Uh, something Teddy Roosevelt said. 'Walk softly and carry a big stick.' Not in Belize, of course."

The ambassador laughed. "I get it. Big stick. Thought you were referring to an old Texas saying." He rolled his eyes upward, as if searching for the saying. The Creole lady returned with thin sashimi slices, each impaled by a toothpick. The ambassador excused himself and pushed through the crowd. Matt slipped a piece of sashimi in his mouth, and his lips immediately tingled. The Creole lady smiled. "Very special," she said, passing the plate to others.

As Matt took another sip of his gin and tonic, a burly Chinese man stepped in front of him. He spoke with his teeth together, in a hoarse whisper. "You have no business here. Come with me."

"I'm the ambassador's guest." Matt pointed toward Laddie B., but he had disappeared into the crowd.

"I said come with me." The man grabbed Matt by the elbow, digging his fingernails deep into Matt's flesh, and marched him into the hallway. "That door goes into the alley. Use it."

Matt realized it was useless to protest. With the man right behind him, Matt walked down the hallway and past the kitchen, where the chefs were busy carving up oily meat under Martin Chin's watchful eye. On the floor was a yellow bucket filled with dead puffer fish. *The Tuna* was painted on the bucket's side.

The man pushed Matt into the alley and locked the door behind him. Suddenly feeling sick to his stomach, Matt spit into the gutter, his mouth burning from the last appetizer.

The Tuna. That bastard was Chin's supplier. Matt stumbled down the street, so full of rage that he threw air punches at an imaginary Charlie, seeing each one landing square on his jaw. Charlie would have to answer for this. Tonight.

Six blocks later, Matt arrived at the hardware store dock. Jack's Whaler started quickly and he slowly moved down river, ducked under the swing bridge, and eventually left the river, where he jammed ahead full throttle. He would yank Tuna out of bed if he had to. To the east, a Sunflower cruise ship headed to its next port. From the deck, two women waved at him. Matt, still angry, gave them the finger. They reciprocated.

A half mile off Matt's starboard, a boat pulled away from a small key and began running a parallel course, a couple of hundred yards off his port and behind him. It would still take forty minutes more to reach Rum Caye, and he pounded ahead. Suddenly, his boat jerked, its bow dropped, and it slowed to a crawl. The engine choked and sputtered, and the boat went dead in the water. Shit. Out of gas. Jack had said he had filled it. Matt flipped off the tank cap and peered inside. Nothing. He yanked the spare gas can from beneath the seat, but it seemed weightless. It, too, was empty.

The drone of an outboard grew louder. The boat that had been running parallel soon pulled alongside.

"Need a hand, mon?" It was the Mestizo again, the scar running down his cheek looking more ominous than ever.

Matt took a deep breath. "Looks like I've run dry." He held up the can. "A couple of gallons will get me home."

The Mestizo looked at his younger partner with the Fu Manchu mustache, who was staring at Matt, and grunted. The Mestizo picked up a five-gallon gasoline can and held it out. As Matt reached for it, the Mestizo wrapped his other hand around Matt's wrist, squeezing it so hard Matt's fingers stiffened with pain. "I'll pour," he said, pulling on Matt's arm to move the two boats gunwale-to-gunwale. "Next time, you better check your gas before you leave town." The Mayan snorted.

The Mestizo stepped into Matt's boat, his motion rocking it and knocking Matt off balance and down on his knees. For a moment, Matt saw the setting sun, but when the gas can landed squarely on the back of his head, he saw nothing more.

When he awoke, he was shivering so hard he vibrated like a wind-up toy. The pain burrowing into his brain from the back of his skull outdid his worst hangover. Lying in a fetal position, he tried unsuccessfully to raise his leg, adjust his hip, or even lift his head, but the best he could do was wiggle his fingers and bend his ankles. He was paralyzed, immobilized. Voices in the boat began to rise above the engine noise.

"Another hundred yards, then cut the engine." The boat slowed and then stopped. There was a splash, a chain ratcheting over the side of the boat, then silence.

"Gringo, are you awake?" A sharp slap knocked Matt's head back, popping open his eyes in the dark night. The glowing Coleman lantern on the bow gave form to the face above him.

The Mestizo spit at him. "We don't want your Uncle Sam ass in our country. But you don't understand that, do you?" He spit again. Matt shut his eyes, the slime crawling down his cheek.

He was wrapped like a mummy, tied with a thin cord, his hands fastened behind his back. The Mestizo lifted him up like a laundry bag and plopped him on the gunwale. They were drifting off Goofy Bird Caye where a week ago he had spent the night fighting mosquitoes, wondering who had cut loose Charlie's boat.

"You know where you are?" the Mestizo asked. He picked up a dead mutton snapper by the gills, swung a machete, and half the fish dropped into the water. The surface boiled and he dropped in the fish head. Matt tried to speak but could only groan. His heart sounded like a snare drum. "This is where that guy in the ice took his last swim, and you're fucking going to join him."

The Mestizo lifted Matt over the water. Breathing as deeply as he could, he imagined his father telling him that he was going home, and then he felt himself falling for what seemed like minutes until he smacked into the sea. Holding his breath, Matt floated downward in the darkness, head first, then abruptly stopped. Something yanked at his ankles. He was tethered to the boat, surrounded by the midnight black sea.

A sharp jolt in his back sent him swinging like a pendulum, and then he was jerked up through the water, then dropped down, then pulled up, then down again, like a tea bag. A blunt blow to his stomach and then a sharp pain running up his arm, as if a metal file had been dragged across his bicep, startled him. As he opened his eyes the saltwater stung, but he could see a dark, blurry form move past, dimly lit from the lantern above.

Struggling to hold his breath, his lungs ached. Another blow to the small of his back shot pain, then hysteria, through his entire body, as if he were being besieged and prodded by invisible aliens. Worse. Sharks. Matt wanted to scream and most of all to breathe. But he clenched his teeth and shut his eyes, his thoughts vaporizing as carbon dioxide, a slow anesthesia, built in his lungs.

Then, just as swiftly as he had hit the water, Matt was dangling above it, his head clear of the surface. The Mestizo was yelling; he could not understand a word but he was still alive. He sucked in the night air, then exhaled and inhaled so rapidly he sounded like a train chugging up a hill. *The Little Engine That Could.*

He was dropped again into the sea. His body swung to the right then to the left, pushed by the pressure wave from a shark passing inches away. He felt another brush across the top of his head, and then he plunged downward until the rope was taut. He was an offal block without the ice. The shark feast was to begin.

Cat's face appeared as a point of light, growing larger and larger until he could see her golden hair, her emerald eyes, the soft curl in the corner of her mouth. "Does anyone ever call you Matt the Knife?" Oh, babe. The shark. It has such teeth, dear. Goodbye. I'll never know you. It shows them, pearly white. When the shark bites, with his teeth, babe, scarlet billows start to spread. Matt was back. He was. Now he's gone.

And then, up went Matt, again free from the water. He felt huge arms wrap around his legs, and in a flurry, he was dropped hard on the boat floor, gasping, rasping.

He tried to speak, but only bleated like a sheep. He lay there shivering, his heart beating so fast it sounded like one continuous hum. The deck vibrated as the engine started, and the anchor chain once again ratcheted over the gunwales. The boat lurched forward. Matt passed out.

When he awoke, the Mestizo was standing over him, cutting him free from the ropes. "So, you get the fuck out of Belize, gringo. If you don't, then we'll bring you back here tomorrow and cut you loose over the side. You'll be shark food." The Mestizo vaulted over the gunwale, yanked Matt from the boat, and pushed him into the sand.

"Your boat's down the beach. There's enough gas to get you back. Tomorrow, your ass is out of Belize." His partner turned the throttle handle, and the boat lurched forward. The Mestizo jumped back in, extinguished the lantern, and the boat disappeared into the dark, its roar slowly fading until only the sound of the night breeze through the palms remained.

Pushing himself up on all fours, Matt crawled into the undergrowth, his head aching, his heart pounding. His arms gave way. He passed out.

29

As the launch approached the mangrove channel on the southern end of Devil's Caye, Trey Turnbull
was hard pressed in the early dawn light to make out
the entrance, but his keen-eyed driver Winston headed
directly into the narrow, twisted canal, leaving the sea
behind. A hundred yards into the channel, Winston cut
the engine, and the launch slid quietly toward the dock.
A faint acrid smell drifted in from the north, waiting for
the trade winds to carry it away.

Winston grabbed a bulging string bag and headed
into the dense mangroves, using his machete to cut back
branches. Turnbull followed close behind. Thirty feet
into the bush, a narrow trail appeared. Two hundred
feet farther, they entered a small clearing with a table
and four canvas-backed chairs sitting in front of a cinderblock hut, its heavy metal door secured by two solid
steel padlocks. Winston retrieved a gallon thermos of
coffee, fresh cinnamon rolls and mangoes from his bag
while Trey pulled a key ring from his hunting jacket
pocket and unlocked the door.

Everything inside appeared as it should. Bottled water, cans of spaghetti, pork and beans, and corned beef hash, Jack Daniels, two first-aid kits, two machetes, a sheathed Bowie knife, boxes of nails, wire cutters, a hammer, six green ammunition boxes, and six 270-caliber Winchester 70s, double-locked into a steel gun rack, which Trey opened. Lifting a rifle from the rack, he headed back out the door and poured himself a cup of coffee. In the distance, he could hear the whine of an outboard. His first guest was arriving, and Winston set out to guide him in.

SUPERINTENDENT NIGEL GODWIN of the Belize Police Force was dressed smartly in gray slacks with a sharp crease down the center of each leg, a gray cotton shirt buttoned to the wrists, and leather hunting boots, his only concession to visiting a mangrove island. Trey gave him a perfunctory salute.

"Superintendent. I'm pleased you could make it."

Godwin smiled. "It's always a pleasure to join you, sir. I'm honored."

"Not as much as I. Here, sit down." Trey pointed at the chair next to his. "There'll be two more joining us. Coffee?"

"Yes, black." He brushed off the chair opposite from Trey, and then brushed off the front of his pants before sitting down.

"I understand you are quite the marksman, an able hunter, in fact. I appreciate that in a man," Trey said.

"I've been a hunter since I was a child, but I have no time now."

"I'm sure, what with all your law enforcement responsibilities." Leaning back in his chair, Trey crossed his arms. "And just how is Barnstable's investigation coming? Any breakthroughs?"

"It's progressing slowly. I know you have a great interest."

Pointing at the thermos, Trey snapped his fingers to get Winston's attention. "Seems like it's been dragging on far too long. Aren't you people tired of Jack Africa by now? He's sitting on the last sizeable island for development. Don't see how he can hold out much longer."

Winston handed the superintendent a mug of coffee "Jack's been there thirty years. Nothing we've ever done seems to affect him much."

"Well, no doubt he'll be implicated in that Iceman death, which will raise serious questions about the future of that island of his." He sipped his coffee. "Of course, the Fund has a major interest in acquiring it when the time comes."

"I'm sure that can be facilitated when he's gone."

Trey perked up, cupped his ear and looked at his watch. "Sounds like the boat. You stay here, superintendent, I'll go meet them." Winston ran down the trail, with Trey following. He didn't need to say more to Godwin. He was just the superintendent, not the chief.

When Trey was halfway to the dock, Barber appeared, dressed in ridiculous camouflage fatigues and puffing hard. "Mr. Ambassador, welcome to my little island."

Barber wheezed. "Delighted to be here, Turnbull."

"Where's the good doctor?"

"He got in late and arranged for another boat to bring

him. Said to start without him." Laddie wiped the sweat from his brow with his sleeve.

That bastard Herb was always late. Trey turned back down the trail, with Barber and Winston following behind. When they reached the clearing, Godwin was pointing a Winchester at the sky, peering through the scope.

"Have a seat here, Laddie."

Trey pulled out the canvas chair, and Barber slumped into it then nodded at Godwin. "Superintendent, nice to see you."

"I asked the superintendent to join us, Laddie. Sort of a multinational hunting party, if you know what I mean." Trey picked up the bottle of Jack Daniels with one hand, the coffee thermos with the other. "A little Jack in your coffee, Laddie?"

"A little coffee in my Jack would be more to my liking." Barber held out a cup, and Trey filled it halfway with coffee. The ambassador swirled it around, then poured most of it on the ground. He wiggled his fingers and Trey poured in a shot of Jack, then another.

"A little Jack for you, Superintendent?"

"Just coffee."

Trey refilled his cup and sat down. "Gentlemen, I told you I would fulfill a dream of yours, and today's the day."

The ambassador turned to Godwin. "I raised six million dollars for our president, and a good hunk came from this man right here," he said, pointing at Trey. "He doesn't owe me a thing."

"It's not about debt, Laddie; it's about making your friends happy. Now I know you two like trophy shooting." He handed the ambassador a photo. "Well, here's the trophy."

Laddie whistled. "I'll be goddamned. A jaguar? Out here?"

"Out here. As soon as the sun gets a little higher, we'll go look for it. Don't want it jumping out in the dark at us."

Godwin reached for the photo and then looked at Trey. "A jaguar on Middle Caye? Impossible."

"Not at all, superintendent. And whoever sees him first will get a crack at him."

Godwin looked at the photo again and shook his head. "Gentlemen, this is our national animal, so I won't be doing any shooting. You're taking a big risk here."

"But there's no risk from you, Superintendent, correct?"

"Of course not." The superintendent crossed his arms and leaned back. "However, my friends, what happens after it gets shot? I can't be on a boat heading to Belize City with a dead jaguar."

"None of us can," Trey said. "We'll go home right after our hunt. The jaguar goes later. By tomorrow night, there'll be nothing left but a drying pelt." Trey picked up a Winchester. "So, boys, grab a weapon, load them up, and Winston will lead the way."

30

Matt lay in a hollow of underbrush, wondering why he heard the traffic on Highway 101 heading south toward the Golden Gate Bridge. The cars came in waves. He couldn't remember how he had reached Sausalito or when he had climbed into the hills, but the fog had rolled in, bathing him in an eerie mist. He was glad to be home.

Opening his eyes slowly, he watched the out-of-focus lights dance along the road. He blinked and blinked again. The skies brightened. The traffic roar softened, morphing into the sound of slapping waves and palm trees moving in the breeze. Light glimmered off the sea. His teeth chattered. Then he heard voices. And he remembered the sharks and tasted the bitter bile in his mouth. He placed a finger on his wrist, barely finding a pulse.

His clothes were salt-stiff. Mud caked on his elbows and knees. His borrowed tattered and stained guayabera shirt looked like commando's camouflage, but a commando would have a plan, a weapon, supplies, a notion of what he was doing or where he was or why. Matt had nothing.

He lay still, listening to the voices, trying to distinguish the tones and inflections, but unable to understand the words. When he lifted his head, thorny leaves pricked his cheeks. He pushed himself up on one knee, then on the other. His ankles burned and bled. He remembered the rope. The voices grew louder. They were coming to get him. He had to move.

He stood slowly, and then crept through the brush until he found an overgrown trail. Moving carefully, he plodded through muck and decaying leaves, dodging branches. Behind him, a machete cracked, clearing the underbrush he had just struggled through. He pushed on, but the vines were thick, slowing him even more. Then he remembered. It had been dark, not just dim. He had a boat. They told him to drive it away. Why were they still coming after him?

He heard a low hiss. He stopped, more frightened than ever. A snake in the cayes? There couldn't be, at least none to be reckoned with. He stepped back. The hissing stopped. No leaves rustled. Dead calm. Then the leaves rustled again. Something was ahead.

A burst of energy exploded from the bush, flew through the air, slammed into the brush across the trail, and disappeared into the dense foliage—not an apparition, but a frightened jaguar on the run. For a moment, there was dead quiet, and then a voice came from far behind. "I think we found her."

Matt stumbled through the the lattice of vines for another hundred yards, finally stopping under the massive branches of a gumbo-limbo tree. Again, the hiss. This time above him, on a tree branch. It was the jaguar, staring at him, quivering. They were both terrified.

Matt backed away, keeping his eyes on the cat. What was it doing here? It had no business on this island twenty miles at sea, a hundred miles from its mountain home. The cat pricked its ears, as if listening to a distant call. It stiffened, on alert, its ears swiveling like parabolic antennae. It gazed at Matt, then turned back toward the bush. The cat could hear someone coming.

Slowly stepping backward, Matt watched the cat sitting quietly, tensing only when it turned its head to listen. Finally, Matt ducked behind a mangrove clump and peered at the animal from between the branches. The cat looked at him, then back into the bush. Matt could hear branches snapping.

He wanted to yell at the cat. Scram. Go. Get out of here. But a jaguar didn't need his help. If it had to run, it would.

It was Matt who ran, slowly, his arms and legs heavy, his mind unclear. He had no idea where he was, but finally, when he thought he had left the intruders behind, he dropped to his belly and pulled himself into a thicket.

"GOD DAMN, IT's hotter than a witch's tit out here, and we're almost to the water," Laddie said.

Trey glanced over his shoulder, shook his head, and said nothing.

"There's no cat out here." The ambassador had unbuttoned his camouflage shirt, revealing a hairless and mottled pink chest bathed in sweat. "We've been at this an hour and not so much as a pile of scat."

"Laddie, these are elusive animals. Be patient," Trey said.

"Tsst." Winston blew against his teeth, shook his head, and wiggled his finger. The ambassador froze. Slowly, Winston raised his hand and pointed to the branch above. The four men froze in place. Trey pointed at the ambassador's gun, then took his own from his shoulder and motioned toward the ambassador again. The ambassador slipped his rifle off his shoulder, planted his legs, and raised the weapon slowly. Ten feet away the jaguar, her eyes fixed on the ambassador, shifted her weight to her hind paws.

From behind the group, limbs crackled and snapped as if an elephant were charging. All four men spun around to see Dr. Herb Freeman rush into the clearing, screaming and pointing at the cat, but it was already in mid-air.

"Son of…" Slowed by four fingers of Jack, the ambassador froze, and the full one-hundred-and twenty-pound force hit him squarely in the chest, sending him sailing backward. The jaguar's claw swiped the side of his head and blood gushed from Laddie's ear as he fell.

Trey swung his rifle toward the fury, but the ambassador and the jaguar appeared as one. He grabbed Winston's machete, lifted it high over his head, and slammed it down hard. The blunt side of the blade hit the jaguar across the shoulder. Her howl was painful to hear—and then she fell limp, her legs buckling beneath her, her body shivering, her tail flicking, her ears twitching, her breathing labored, but she otherwise lay still.

The mighty cat, its dappled coat glowing in the morning sun, was paralyzed. The blow had crushed her spine.

Herb covered his mouth with his hand, his eyes fixed on the immobile cat. Trey turned to him and yelled, "You miserable bastard, Freeman." He started to swing at him but stopped. "You're an hour late, and you show up like this." Trey left Freeman standing there slack-jawed and rushed to the ambassador. "Winston, wrap your shirt around Laddie's head. Around that ear. We have to get him back to camp."

Winston pointed his gun at the jaguar. Trey pushed the gun away. "Don't spoil the pelt. She'll die here. The boys will get her later."

MATT HAD HEARD the scuffle, but he was too far away to see anyone and could make out only a few of the words he heard. He waited until long after the island had quieted, and then he stood and found his way back to the jaguar. He pulled off his shirt to dress her bleeding shoulder, but she was helpless, the fire gone from her eyes, her breathing punctuated by painful whimpers. He knelt beside her, breaking into tears as she looked up at him. He stroked her back, and then left for a moment, returning with a stone the size of a pineapple. "Forgive me, Dad," he whispered.

THE HUM OF a skiff skimming across the water awakened Matt. He tried to stand but fell back onto the sand, and then crawled away from the dead jaguar until he reached the underbrush and a small mangrove clump. He could see the Mestizo, standing in the bow. The engine cut and the boat nosed onto the squat beach.

The Mestizo hopped from the boat while his companion jumped over the gunwale. They gazed at the jaguar almost reverently. "Big animal. I never saw one before," the Mestizo said.

"You ought to see one alive."

"Where'd you ever see a live one?"

"The Belize Zoo. They got a jaguar there, just stares at you. Just the eyes, like a camera, following you."

"Not this one. Grab those legs. Let's get it on the boat and out of here before it starts to stink."

Matt watched them drag the limp jaguar across the sand and drop it into their boat. Still in shock, he passed out once again.

31

Matt recognized the street, or thought he did, with dozens of canvas-topped kiosks filled with silly souvenirs. But why was he there? He wore only mud-soaked, knee-length shorts and sandals. His hair was matted, his shirt was gone, his body was scratched and bruised. Tourists stepped aside, turning and mumbling as he passed. Ahead, a constable talked to a shopkeeper. Matt's first instinct was to ask for aid, but instead, he slipped between two kiosks and sat on an overturned plastic milk crate, watching the tourists pass.

Yesterday he had driven a small boat alone to town. It must have been Jack's Whaler because he could remember taking it into Belize City, seeing Cat, and then meeting Turnbull. He recalled roaring across the bay under a dark sky. Now, here he sat, his body rank like a decaying mangrove swamp, feeling like he had just washed up on shore. He had. He started to shiver, overcome by a fear he had not felt since he was a boy and a punk, half a foot taller, clobbered him from behind for no good reason. Then Matt had played dead, afraid to defend himself. Now he pictured sharks banging into his body with their blunt sandpaper snouts, his heart beating so hard it could crack a rib. He had been dunked like a tea bag and then dropped on the beach to dry out. A jaguar shot out of a tree and then was dragged away. Imagination? Memory?

He remembered a face across the way, the vendor who sold seashells. He dashed to her kiosk, startling her. He dug through his shorts, but his wallet must have drifted to the bottom of the sea. In the front pocket, he found several crumpled, waterlogged bills. Thirty-two dollars. He held out the money. "Can you sell me a shirt for this?"

She pointed at a table stacked with splashy tropical shirts marked forty dollars. "Pick any one."

Matt grabbed a long white shirt covered with toothy sharks and slipped into it. "And I need to use your phone, to call a friend to get a ride."

The vendor fished in her apron pocket and handed him her flip-top cell phone. He turned his back, thought hard to remember Cat's number, and then punched it in.

"Hello?"

"Cat, it's Matt."

"Matt! How did your meeting go at the Fund?"

"I'll tell you later. I'm in Belize City, near the cruise terminal, but I can't remember how I got here. There's a cop out there looking for me. Are you in town?"

"No, I'm at the lodge. Are you all right?"

"No. I mean… yes. They're after me, Cat."

"Who?"

"I don't know who. I lost a day. I don't have any money left. My wallet's gone."

"Go to the American embassy. They'll help. You'll be safe there."

"The embassy? Yes, the embassy. I will." Out of the corner of his eye, Matt saw the police officer stop at the kiosk. Matt kept his back turned, stuck the phone in the vendor's purse, then slipped through the back flap. Breaking into a sprint, he ran two blocks, turned left down a side street strewn with broken glass, took a right, and ran two more blocks. He stopped to get his bearings and then jogged straight ahead two more blocks, slowing to catch his breath when he saw the embassy gate. As he approached the guard station, the young Marine slid the window open.

"Sir? May I help you?"

"I'd like to see the ambassador."

"Sorry, the embassy is closed. Are you an American, sir?"

"Yes, Matthew Oliver. The ambassador told me to come by anytime."

"One moment, Mr. Oliver." She punched three numbers into a phone, looking Matt over as she spoke. Soon, a second Marine emerged from the doorway, motioned him to enter, and directed him to a small waiting room.

In an adjacent room, someone spoke. That voice. It was from a dream, a nightmare. The ambassador entered, a gauze bandage covering his right ear. "Oliver, looks like you've gone native on us. What have you been up to?"

That voice. Matt's hands shook, and he stuffed them into his pockets. "I'm not sure, sir."

"Well, what can I do for you?"

"Come to think of it, nothing right now. Let me return when I'm better dressed." Matt edged for the door.

"Please, have a seat."

"No. Thank you, though." Matt pushed open the front door. "I'll make an appointment." He walked briskly into the courtyard, past the guard booth, and turned at the first corner. Behind him, a white Belize City police car sped up to the embassy gate. Matt started running, down one street, up the next, around the corner, then five blocks straight ahead to the bougainvillea-covered gate of Randolph's.

Inside, behind the desk, sat Randolph, shaking his head. "I see you're back. Do you need a room?"

"Please. A room for the night, but I don't seem to have my wallet, so I don't have my credit card."

"Not a problem. I can get the number off your last receipt." He looked Matt up and down. "You need to clean up. And you look like you could use some food. Get what you want at the bar." He handed him a key to the same room he had been in on his first night in town.

Matt stopped at the bar for a Belikin and two sacks of Cheetos, then went to his room, turned on the light, and fell onto the bed. That voice, the ambassador's voice. *Son of a bitch.* Matt lifted the phone, but it was dead. He would have to wait until morning to call Cat. He stepped into the shower, wishing for hot water, but the faucet delivered only a cool trickle, barely enough to wash off the caked mud. He dried himself off and dropped back on the bed. Exhausted, he soon fell asleep.

HE AWOKE WITH a start. Light poured into the room, the beam dancing across the wall, then fixing on his eyes. "Oliver. Get out of that bed," Inspector Barnstable said. "You have a flight to catch."

Matt covered his eyes, and Barnstable turned the flashlight away. He grabbed Matt's arm and yanked him up. "You sleep naked like that? Get your clothes on."

Matt pulled on his dirty shorts and his new shirt and strapped on his sandals. Barnstable pointed him toward the door. The courtyard was dim, the office door open. Randolph, dressed only in a nightshirt, was shaking his head. Barnstable pushed Matt into the back seat of a waiting police car and climbed in alongside him.

"Your flight leaves in two hours." He handed Matt a small folder. "Inside is a one-way ticket to Houston, a facsimile of your passport that the ambassador had ready for us, and twenty dollars American. If you ever come back to Belize, you will be locked up, forever."

"How did you find me?"

"Your girlfriend called the embassy asking about you. She gave us an idea where to look."

"Cat?"

Barnstable said nothing. When they pulled up to the terminal, the sky was just beginning to brighten. The inspector pulled out handcuffs and placed them on Matt's wrists. "Just to make sure you get on the plane." He reached into his pocket and pulled out his cell phone. "If you want to call someone in the States, I'll dial for you."

Matt told him Maxie's number, which the inspector punched in, then handed Matt the phone.

"McCaw here."

"Maxie, it's Matt."

"What the fuck, it's four in the morning."

"Maxie, the police are kicking me out of Belize."

"Why?"

"I can't talk, but they're putting me on the seven-thirty flight to Houston. I have no money, no credit cards, nothing."

She groaned. "Let me think… OK. There's a bar called Pappadeaux upstairs by the Continental international gates at the Houston airport. Find yourself a stool and wait for me."

AFTER WAITING TWO hours in handcuffs at the Belize airport, Matt boarded his flight and arrived in Houston with the twenty bucks Barnstable had given him and the clothes on his back. He bought a bean burrito and sat at the bar waiting for Maxie, the missing day still a mystery. The bartender, a young woman with spiky frosted hair, flipped down a bar napkin.

He tried to smile. "Cheap white tequila, straight up, por favor."

"The only way."

Matt nodded. The world was going to hell in a hand basket, and the bartender made him feel even more depressed.

She returned with a shot glass filled to the brim and a slice of lime pierced by a tiny red plastic sword. He pulled out the sword and stabbed the lime again and again. He imagined sharks lying on the bottom of his glass, finless, dying a slow, cruel death so their fins could thicken the wedding soup of a Singapore bank president's daughter. Or Chin's. Or Turnbull's, the prick. Matt tossed down the shot, letting the burn in his throat linger. He could have another shot of tequila. Or he could find a pay phone and make a call.

He dialed Information for the number of the Global Fund in Washington, then punched in the number, then dumped in the roll of quarters he had gotten from the bartender. When he reached the executive director's secretary, he gave his name as Peter Hartman and explained he was writing a *Chicago Tribune* feature on the Fund and their Central American program. She put right him through to the executive director, Nancy Pareto. How they loved press attention.

Matt asked Pareto about the Fund's plans in Central America and complimented her on creating an open range for the jaguar. As she grew ever more chatty, he knew it was time for the kill. "Ms. Pareto, one of your directors, Robert Turnbull the Third, runs the office in Belize. What's his purpose there?"

"Trey's looking at land acquisition for both the Belize government and us. We need to ensure there's enough habitat for the jaguar and a large coherent ecosystem to protect the animal population. Trey is doing that for us."

"Isn't he one of your largest donors?"

"Our very largest. He's a generous man and a board member. We wouldn't have an office there if he hadn't volunteered to open it."

"As I understand it, the Fund owns a large island in Belize, right?"

"No, we don't own islands. As I said, we are looking at land in the Catscombs to preserve more jaguar habitat."

"Ms. Pareto, what would you say if I told you that Devil's Caye has a *Fund* sign on it telling people to stay off? And on that island, I found a thousand bloody shark fins? How would you say that reflects on the Fund?"

"What are you talking about? We don't own an island in Belize. Who are you? You need to do your homework."

"I have, Ms. Pareto, I was on Devil's Caye and found—"

"Look, I don't have time for this. Take your stories to someone else." The line went dead.

When he returned to the bar, Maxie was sitting at a table, talking on her cell phone, two margaritas on white cocktail napkins before her. She put her cell away. "Saw you on the phone so I ordered you a margarita. If you don't want it, it will save me from ordering another."

"You've always been able to read my mind."

"Which is why we split up," she said, raising her glass. Matt raised his alongside. "Jesus, Matt, you look like shit and your hand's shaking like you have Parkinson's. Getting thrown out of Belize couldn't be that bad."

"That was the easy part, Maxie." He told her everything he could remember, even if he could not explain the missing day, and then downed half his margarita. "And now I need your help. I have to go back as soon as I can."

"So, the hunted has become the hunter."

"Yes, but why are these guys so determined to get me?"

"You've seen too much, and you're probably the only

one in Belize they don't have under their thumbs. Why should they kill you if they can deport you?"

"But 'they' seems to be everyone. Turnbull, Chin—"

"And you had better watch out for Jack. And Little Man and Charlie. And Cat—"

Matt shook his head. "Charlie, maybe, but not the others. And Turnbull, for sure, who handed me this bullshit about Pacific skates."

"*Fortune Magazine* says he gave away three million dollars to conservation causes last year."

Matt pushed himself back from the table. "So, why does Turnbull care about shark fins worth half a million dollars? Makes no sense."

"Maybe not to you, Matthew, but it does to him. Look, I found out that before he joined the Fund, Turnbull was on the Natural Land Conservancy board and gave them millions. Then three years ago he switched to the Global Fund for Wildlife."

"Why? Most of those big donors usually ride one horse till it's dead," Matt said.

"Or until they're dead. I tracked down an ex-Conservancy board member who told me that the Conservancy wanted to prevent the development of a hundred thousand acres in Florida, mostly marshland that feeds the Everglades. Great place for wildlife and home to a dozen Florida panthers."

"There can't be more than a hundred panthers left in the whole state."

"Right. The Glades Sugar Company has owned that land forever but never did much with it, and over time all the surrounding land became protected, except for a one-hundred-acre access strip owned by a dirt poor guy named Hidalgo, who had leased the strip to Glades. Hidalgo does some subsistence farming, but not much because it's mostly swamp."

"Wetlands," Matt said.

"Whatever, but it's Hidalgo's land. Sugar is sweet again, so with all the tariffs and subsidies, Glades' hundred thousand acres has real value, but the only way they can get to it is by the road through Hidalgo's land. But Glades screwed themselves. They hadn't been paying attention, and the thirty-year land and road lease ran out, so all the rights reverted to Hidalgo."

"What difference does that make? Seems to me no one would ever let them farm that land anyway.

"You would think not, but some old parcels have been grandfathered in and Florida politicians like sugar better than they like environmentalists. Glades Sugar wouldn't have much problem getting that land filled and planted."

"So, what does this have to do with Turnbull?" Matt put up his hand. "Wait, I see where you're headed. The Conservancy is notorious for blocking development. They quietly buy a critical piece of land that maybe has the only source of water or the only access, and they kill the value of the larger tract, making it useless to developers.

"Right, and that's just what the Conservancy did. They had their eyes on the strip, and the day the lease ran out, they approached Hidalgo while Glades was asleep at the wheel. Within a week, the strip was theirs. Not long after, for whatever reason, Turnbull went ballistic and dumped his multimillion-dollar pledge to the Conservancy. Claimed they were wasting money because the government would prevent Glades from developing it anyhow, which sounds like a pretty weak excuse. Two months later, he joined the Fund's board."

"Turnbull, the great conservationist, should have celebrated."

"Well, he didn't, and my source says he never did offer another reason for changing horses," Maxie said.

"Makes no sense."

"For some reason, blocking Glades Sugar hurt Turnbull big time." Maxie leaned back and crossed her arms. "Otherwise, why would he walk out in a huff?"

"And end up in Belize with the Fund?"

"That's the question we need to answer."

Matt nodded.

"Along with other questions, like how can you even get back into Belize?"

Matt unfolded the photocopy of his passport Barnstable had given him. "There's got to be a way, but first, I need a valid passport, fast. And a credit card. Can you help?"

She smiled and tossed down the last of her margarita. "I've got my connections. You'll have them in forty-eight hours."

"Which should be just enough time to find out why losing that little road drove Turnbull batty," Matt said.

32

With forty-eight hours to kill, Maxie sprang for two tickets to Miami. They had discussed whether they should call Gregorio Hidalgo before they dropped in unexpectedly; Matt offered to pose as a *New York Times* reporter, but Maxie scotched that. "What sort of swamp rat wants to talk to somebody from New York or Washington, D.C.? Try the *Naples Florida News*. That might work."

"And what if Hidalgo calls them to see if I'm for real?"

"He probably wouldn't, but why chance it. We'll just have to wing it," she said.

At Miami airport, she rented a Prius and ninety minutes after they pulled out of the Avis lot they turned off the blacktop road onto a dusty washboard lane barely two cars wide. Two hundred yards down the road, bullet holes punctured a large white metal sign:

Thomas Jefferson Rod and Gun Club
No Trespassers. No Hunting. No Fishing.
Members Only

A hundred yards farther down the road, a wire gate sported a *No Trespassing* sign. To the left sat a disheveled clapboard house patched with tarpaper, a blue tarp covering half the roof. Matt knocked on the door, but there was no sign of anyone. After inspecting the lock on the gate, Maxie reached into her fanny pack and soon held the open lock in her hands. "Hop back in, let's take a drive."

After twenty-five minutes dodging potholes and scraping the undercarriage of their rental car, they ended in a clearing with a stone-lined fire pit surrounded by four wooden benches and scattered empty whiskey and beer bottles. They climbed from the car and walked over to the fire pit. "I don't know what we expected to find here," Maxie said, "but if this is it, we've just wasted a lot of time and money."

Crack! Gunfire. Slipping her gun from her waist pack, Maxie swung to her left, landing on her belly with both hands on her pistol, aimed directly at a grizzled, bent old man holding a rifle pointed skyward. Just as fast, he threw the gun in the dirt and raised his hands. "Ma'am, sorry, I didn't mean nothin'."

Matt hadn't moved. Maxie stood up and dusted herself off. "Then what's with the pot shot?"

"Just wanted to scare you. That's why I get paid. Ain't no trespassing down here."

"And you are?"

"I'm Gregorio Hidalgo."

Matt looked at Maxie. She picked up Hidalgo's rifle, cleared the chamber, put her Glock back into her waist pack and pointed to a bench. "Have a seat."

Hidalgo was ashen-faced, his eyes fixed on Maxie's fanny pack, but he sat down slowly while Matt and Maxie took the opposite bench.

"You're the fellow who owned this land once upon a time, right?" Matt asked.

"Can you tell me who I'm talking to?" Hidalgo asked.

Maxie turned to Matt. "Your witness," she said. "On-the-job training."

Matt looked at Hidalgo. "Let's just say we're investigators," he said. "As we understand it, the Natural Land Conservancy bought this land from you."

"Well, they cheated me out of it."

"The sign says the Thomas Jefferson Club."

"That's who I thought I was selling to. Didn't want no preserve here. All my people are hunters, been so all our lives. But that phony hunter's club buffaloed me."

"How'd they do that?"

Hidalgo said he had made his living by charging fees to wild boar hunters to use his road, which took them through his property to the Glades' property where they could hunt because the Glades' people never paid attention to it. In fact, Glades and the Hidalgos hadn't talked in years, he said, so when the Thomas Jefferson Rod and Gun Club from Tallahassee offered him a hundred grand for the land, he listened, unsure what to do. So they sweetened the deal and told him that he and his family could live on the land rent-free for the rest of their lives, as long as he didn't let anyone, other than Rod and Gun Club members, pass through and hunt. Hidalgo didn't know anything about real estate, so the Gun Club referred him to a Tallahassee real estate agent, who persuaded him to take the money.

"The day after the deal closed, a crew built the gate and hung up the Jefferson sign. Told me to keep everyone else out. A couple of weeks later, a fellow from Glades came around and made me an offer for three times as much, but I told him the land wasn't mine anymore. He'd have to talk to the Gun Club. He said there was no gun club, only the Conservancy. They hoodwinked me. Turned out the real estate agent was in their pocket. I was pretty upset, but my wife reminded me that we're living like we've always lived, free people, with a hundred thousand in the bank, more than we ever dreamed of."

"And that ends the story?" Maxie asked.

"Nope. I still didn't like the way they took advantage of me, so an old boy who used to hunt here hired a lawyer for me, and I went to court. But the judge tossed it out on some grounds I never understood."

"Who was the guy?" Matt asked.

"No one I care to mention."

Maxie put her finger on the pack and started playing with the zipper to the compartment that held her Glock.

"Actually, he never would tell me his name. Tall fellow, silver hair, had an accent, from out west, maybe Texas. I'd let him in many times when I was collecting tolls.

A hundred dollars a car and driver, twenty dollars for every passenger."

"Was his name Turnbull?"

Hidalgo looked at his feet. "Can't say as I ever knew, but when he came hunting he'd always give me three hundred dollars. Never saw how many people were in that SUV of his, because it had them dark windows. But for three hundred I never asked. On the way out, most folks stopped their car, told their tales, showed off their kill, which they usually had strapped on top. But those guys never seemed to have nothing. Never even stopped. In fact, he usually came back through, long after midnight. Didn't matter to me. As long as they passed before sun up, they didn't owe me no more money."

"What else do people hunt down here?" Matt asked. "Deer?"

"Mostly boar. Once a bear. I didn't allow no pig baiting, so they had to stalk them. That puts 'em all on even footing. Fellow got one over seven hundred pounds a while back. That's a mean pig. Think what that pig would do to you if you couldn't find a tree to climb."

"If they never had a pig strapped to a car, what else could they be doing down there at night?"

"Drinking whiskey, hiding out from their wives, maybe smoking a little weed," Hidalgo said. "Nothing else to do unless they were poachers going after panthers. You see a few around here now and then, but I never saw anyone lug a panther out of here. That gets you in a deep trouble. I don't think those fellas would do that."

"So, but if one were stuffed and covered in the back of that SUV, you'd never know it, would you?"

"Right, never would know it."

"And this silver-haired guy," Maxie said, "you ever see him again?"

Hidalgo kicked the ground. "You don't work for the Nature Conservancy do you?"

She shook her head. "No, sir, we don't."

"No, I guess you don't. At least, you don't look like it. Well, I still let him and his pals in now and then, but he pays me twice as much these days. I suppose I shouldn't, but then nobody ever comes to check."

Maxie looked at her watch. "Mr. Hidalgo, we have to be in Miami in two hours. Thanks for your time."

Hidalgo took a deep breath and put his head in his hands.

33

FROM THE CAPTAIN'S chair on the flying bridge of the *Texas Trigger,* Trey Turnbull studied the low-lying contours of Rum Caye. Next to him on the tall bridge chair, Inspector Barnstable, his shiny shoes dangling six inches off the deck, busied himself by cleaning the fingernails on one hand with the little fingernail on his other, flicking the dirt over the rail.

Mangrove roots covered most of the shoreline, but on higher ground red flowering cordial, poisonwood, and palmetto trees added color to the landscape. The island had never been properly surveyed, but Trey figured it had enough good land for a couple of hundred condominiums, twelve to a building more or less. Rum Caye's highest point, in the center of Middle Caye, rose about sixty feet above sea level, high enough for a club house view of the sea, even protection from hurricane-driven waters that occasionally flooded the low-lying islands.

"You don't seem to be enjoying the sights, Inspector. You get out to the cayes much when you're not investigating a murder?"

"No, sir. Got a fisherman brother living on one, but I rarely see him. I don't have a boat, and he doesn't like to leave his island unattended for any stretch of time."

"Maybe you should take me out for a look. There aren't many islands ripe for developing. Take Rum Caye. Perfect place, only it would run a hundred million or more to exploit its potential."

"The sooner, the better."

"I thought you didn't like Americans coming down, taking over this little country of yours."

"You're right. We prefer Canadian money. They don't have a history of treating people like slaves."

In the distance, the golden thatched roof of Jack's bar glistened in the morning sunlight. "Inspector, if Americans were to buy up this land, what would you do, just grin and bear it?"

"I'm a professional, Mr. Turnbull. Tourist money coming into this country has let us hire more officers and buy more vehicles."

"And put more cash under the table, I presume."

Barnstable pulled off his sunglasses and stared at him until Trey looked away. "I don't know what you're up to, and it's not my business. I'm here because the superintendent told me to be here."

Trey glanced at Barnstable. "You don't need to know my business, Inspector, other than I invest in Belize for the Global Fund. That's good enough. The superintendent wanted you to come along to make sure we're on the same page."

Trey cut the speed a few knots. "Did you know that I had dinner with the superintendent the other evening? I had nothing but praise for you. Said you should be next up for supervisor."

"Thank you, sir, that's nice to hear."

"But I'm surprised, Inspector, that Jack's still holding on to that island of his."

"He's tenacious, that man."

Guiding his boat in the shallow waters off the beach, Trey pointed ahead. "Looks like he's waiting for us." Jack was sitting at the bar, holding a coffee cup with both hands, the contents unknown. That was why Trey had arrived with the sun still low in the morning sky—he could not negotiate with a drunk.

Trey spun the *Trigger's* stern toward the shore, cut the engines, and lowered the bow anchor. Though wearing beige linen slacks, Trey hopped over the side into knee-deep water and walked ashore.

"General MacArthur walked through the water like that in the Philippines," Jack said. "Looks like you two have something in common."

"Like getting our pants legs wet."

"More like thinking they would stay dry."

Turnbull bit his tongue. "I hope I haven't disrupted your solitude, dropping in like this, Jack, but I wanted to arrive before lunch. I know you get busy later on."

"You know I get drunk later on. How can I get busy when guests aren't allowed anymore, Turnbull?" Jack pointed at the bridge, where the inspector stood with his back to them, looking out to sea. "Why's he here?"

"Just for the ride. He had a day off."

"Don't bullshit me."

"Now, Jack. Can we step inside, have a talk?"

Jack pulled himself up from his chair, walked to the picnic table, and sat down. "This is as far as we go."

Trey sat across from him. "I'm sure you know why I'm here. What's your response to our generous offer for your property?"

"I've considered it."

"And?"

"And you can blow it out your ass."

"Which means Jack Africa's Rum Point Inn is dead. The government is not going to let you reopen."

Jack pointed at Barnstable, who was studying Charlie's house with binoculars. "Your enforcer there can't shut me down forever. There's a semblance of British law in this country and he knows I had nothing to do with that dead body. Everybody wants me out of here, but I'm going nowhere."

Turnbull sighed. "Well, a few years back, the Fund paid you twenty thousand for first right of refusal. I trust that you remember signing that document."

"Of course, I do."

"And an iron-clad confidentiality agreement went with it, for both of us, right?

"I suppose."

"So, Jack, because we're going to own Rum Caye sooner or later, why not just accept our offer now? Sure, you can wait for the government to drive you off and expropriate your little island in the name of conservation. But when they do, we'll just buy it from them. So why let the politicians you think are scum make money from the deal?"

"They'll get Rum Caye over my spilled blood."

"Or when Barnstable finishes his investigation and locks you up. Be reasonable. The Fund will protect the land, keep it as it is."

"Just as you're protecting Devil's Caye?"

Turnbull ignored him. "Just think, you can go back to the states with a few million in your pocket, leave your problems behind."

"Turnbull, you don't get it. I live here. I'm fifty-eight years old, twenty years younger than my liver." He pointed toward the sea. "Out there is my sunrise, and back there," he gestured behind him with his thumb stub, "is my sunset. I live in between. As long as I'm here, the caye is already preserved. When I die, the Fund can buy it. If I don't give it away first."

"The Fund wants a guarantee that the island is protected. That's why they want to buy it now."

"You have my word. That's all you get."

"Perhaps another month or two without customers will change your mind." Trey lifted his legs from under the table, swung them out, and stood.

"I haven't told you, Turnbull, but in a few days, a dozen Denver divers are coming in. Tell your lackey out there that Jack is back. If he wants to stop me, he can arrest me. But he can't stop them folks from coming out here, and he can't shut me down."

"I wouldn't test his resolve, Jack."

"And he shouldn't test mine." Jack rose from the table, pouring the last of his coffee on the sand. "Nor should you, Turnbull. Come back here again and I'm giving this land free and clear to the Audubon Society. Or maybe the Natural Land Conservancy. Anybody but you."

Trey scoffed. "Be careful what you say, Jack. You violate our agreement, and you'll be selling this caye just to cover your legal bills."

34

T HREE DAYS LATER, from the Lido Deck of the *Norwegian Song*, the distant islands of Belize appeared like speed bumps on a flat sea, barely noticeable against the blue horizon. With Maxie's help, Matt had received a new passport, a MasterCard replacement, picked out a new wardrobe, bought a throwaway cell phone, and booked a Western Caribbean itinerary. He had suffered through stops at Grand Cayman and Cozumel, where guests milled around the pricey shops, buying bottles of rum to keep them on an even keel between ports. He had endured two dinners dressed in a blue blazer and white pants, dancing not so gracefully with women twice his age who were charmed by his manners. From the time he had boarded in Miami, no one other than his dance partners had paid him much attention.

On the way to Belize, Matt had signed up with the ship's concierge for an afternoon excursion to Ambergris Caye. With his passport in his pocket and a pink Norwegian Cruise Line card in a plastic holder pinned to his shirt, he waited with his fellow cruisers to board the next launch into town. Grinning at the purser as she checked off departing guests, he walked into the sweltering day and down the ramp, taking a bench seat on the launch next to two bleach-blond men wearing identical Tommy Bahama floral silk shirts.

Within minutes, Matt stepped onto the Belize City cruise ship pier and sauntered toward the gate, onto the sovereign soil of Belize. The uniformed immigration officer ignored him, distracted by jiggling bosoms.

Outside the exit, a woman in a flowery dress held a sign: *Marco's Water Taxi, Ambergris Caye.* "Excuse me," Matt said, showing his voucher, "I signed up for your tour, but I'm going to skip it. I want to see the town, museums, and what not."

She raised an eyebrow. "Museums? Belize City? Hah! You're supposed to go with the tour. They keep count that way. You have to talk to someone else. Not me."

"Maybe you can just take my voucher and include me in the count." He held out his folded voucher, with a twenty poking through. She grabbed it, covering the bill with her hand.

"Enjoy Belize."

Matt strolled down Front Street, past the canvas booths he had hidden behind just days before. He stopped to finger a woven basket, buy a coconut ice cream bar, and watch a blue-haired woman contemplating bleached barracuda jaws lined with razor teeth, all the while keeping an eye out for constables. A half-block ahead, he saw the Range Rover, just as he had expected. He walked up to it and climbed in. Cat leaned against the wheel, shaking her head, laughing.

"Matthew, I didn't recognize you in those fancy duds. You do belong on that boat."

"Maybe thirty years from now. You like my style?"

"I've made it a rule not to pick up men in white shoes; that's all I can say. If you walk a couple of blocks more in them, you can be sure someone will steal your money."

"But the shoes will be safe."

"You bet. Now take them off."

Matt unzipped his backpack, pulled out his polo shirt, shorts, and sandals, and changed in the car. Cat glanced at him from the corner of her eye, but Matt pretended not to notice. He threw the shirt, linen pants, socks and white shoes behind the seat, but kept the Panama hat.

He had stayed in touch with Cat via email, saying only that he had gone to the embassy, been given a new passport, and went home to the States. By email, she sounded angry that he had disappeared, yet encouraged him not to return, warning him that Belize was no place for a nosy writer. He had kept his intentions to himself, instead saying that he had a new assignment to write a story about cruise ships and would have a day in Belize City. Apparently, she had bought it.

She drove to Frankie's without asking any questions, but it was closed, so she continued to Welly's Cool Spot. They took a table in the courtyard corner, away from a raucous game of dominoes, and ordered bottles of *Crystal Water*. Matt wrapped his with a paper napkin and got down to business.

"The truth is, Cat, I'm in bigger trouble than I let on. The night before I called you, I was headed back to Jack's and two Belizean guys knocked me silly. It took me a day to remember that they had dangled me head-first into a nighttime shark frenzy. At night. The next afternoon I found myself wandering around town, the previous twenty-four hours wiped clean."

"My God."

"That's when I called you."

She leaned over and put her hand on his. She was shaking. "You must have been terrified. I was so worried after your call that I called the embassy looking for you."

Matt nodded, saying nothing.

"I talked to the ambassador. He said he would find you and asked where you might stay. I told him that you had stayed at the Radisson and even once at Randolph's."

"And that's how they found me."

"You were at Randolph's?"

"Barnstable pulled me out of bed in the middle of the night. I'm sure it was the ambassador who wanted me out. They put me on the first flight out."

"My call tipped them off? Oh, Matt, I'm so sorry."

"It's not your fault. By the time I arrived in Houston, I was pissed. I have to get this mess unraveled before the only living things left in Belize are the people chasing after me."

"Matthew, you're in over your head. Why did you come back?"

"Jack, a dead seahorse, a missing monkey head, a dead jaguar, it's a long list." His dead father, too, but he had no reason to share that tragedy with her. "I'm here now, and I'm not leaving."

"Like a poker player, 'all in.'" She swept her hands across the table as if she were pushing a pile of chips into the center. "The trouble is, you don't know what game you're playing or who you're playing against."

"It's not poker; it's a puzzle, and if I keep at it I'll put it together."

"Puzzle, poker, who cares? The end will be the same."

"Not if you help me. Chin has all kinds of people working for him, and the reefs have become wastelands."

"So, why isn't Jack raising hell? Or Charlie? They see those reefs firsthand."

"Charlie is shooting fish for Chin; Jack is just trying to hang on. Chin has the Fisheries people in his pocket. Nobody gives a shit about a few seahorses here and there, and God knows they hate sharks. And then there's Turnbull. You know, I saw him at your lodge."

"Turnbull?" She leaned forward and put her elbows on the table, fidgeting a little.

"I sat next to him at your bar. Silver-haired guy, midfifties, slick."

"I know who he is."

"What do you know about him?"

"That he's well respected, invests widely in Belize, has saved a lot of land. But I don't know his business." She hesitated. "I don't ask unless they want to be asked."

"Which means?"

"If someone wants you to ask questions, he'll talk about all the places he's traveled, about his important job, or show you a picture of his family. But when a man says nothing about himself, you don't ask."

"He's head of the Fund, and he's up to no good. When I told him what I had seen on that island of his, he told me what I found were not shark fins but wings from

Pacific rays that had migrated through the Panama Canal. That's such bullshit."

"Do you know for sure?"

"Could I prove it in court? Not today. But I don't need to."

She sat back. "I'm not about to take on the Fund. Or Trey Turnbull."

"I'm not asking you to, at least not now. Chin's first."

"And what does that require?"

"Helping me get inside Chin's place."

"Break into Chin's?" Cat shook her head.

"You don't have to go inside. All you have to do is drive."

35

"Y OU ALWAYS DRIVE like this?" Matt asked as Cat whipped around a slow-moving VW van on a narrow two-lane street, then ricocheted off the curb.

"Relax. If you don't drive this way, the drivers in this town will take advantage of you."

"And you're worried about my odds of survival?"

Cat maneuvered her Rover through a four-way intersection, then swung right, nearly knocking an old man off his bicycle. Two blocks later, pulling up alongside the curb and turning off the ignition, she pointed kitty-corner at a three-story faded yellow building that ran the full length of the block. "Chin's place." Splintered staircase balusters, some square, others round, formed a rooftop fence. "And that's his dog." A snarling black Rottweiler peered down at the street below. "Now tell me, how do you plan to get in there?"

"I'm not sure."

"Good, so then we can stop this silly little game." She looked at her watch. "It's nearly six o'clock. We can make it to the lodge before nine, and you can stay a few days."

Just then, a Ford Escort rolled down the street toward them, its right signal light blinking. Chin's garage door began to roll up and, when it stopped, the Escort turned slowly into the garage.

Cat put her hand on Matt's arm, but without a word, he opened his door, flipped his Panama hat to Cat, and dashed across the street. As the Escort nosed into the garage, Matt slipped behind it, dropped to his belly, and slithered under the car like a snake. The closing garage door landed on his heel and started back up.

Matt crawled forward slowly, gasping when his arm brushed the hot muffler. He saw Chin's hand touch the floor as if he were about to peer under the car, then he yelped, then groaned, just as he had when he had bent over in his office. Chin shuffled alongside the car, still moaning. The garage door motor started to hum again and then stopped when the door hit the ground. At the opposite end of the garage, a door creaked open, the light clicked off, and Chin shut the door behind him. It was pitch black. Matt took a deep breath, remaining motionless, wincing at the burning pain in his arm. Wiggling from beneath the van, he ran his hand along the wall until he felt a light switch and flipped it on. Not much light, just enough to see a half-dozen cardboard boxes stacked in the garage corner and a ladder leaning against the wall. Somewhere inside the building was Martin Chin. And his pistol.

But for how long? In an hour, it would be dark outside. Dropping to his hands and knees, Matt peered under the door that Chin had closed behind him, but not a ray of light poked through. He needed to make his move.

Matt flipped off the garage light and turned the door-knob. He heard a rough cough, another door open, then footsteps getting louder, Chin talking in Chinese.

Slipping behind the Escort, he peered through the car windows as Chin, flipping on the light, entered the garage with a cell phone pressed to his ear. He pushed the switch to open the garage door, and, concentrating on his conversation, climbed into the Escort, started the engine, and drove slowly into the street.

Matt duck-waddled alongside the car as it backed out. When the front bumper passed the garage door, he pushed the garage door button and remained inside. The Escort stopped.

He imagined Chin sitting outside, puzzled, trying to remember whether he had shut the door himself. Matt squeezed into the corner between the garage door and the wall as the door began rising. The Escort's head-lights bathed the interior of the garage. A moment later, the door lowered, and Matt heard Chin drive away.

Matt exhaled. He could see nothing. He slid his arm along the wall until his fingertips reached the doorknob. He turned it slowly, then pushed open the door. Not a sound, not a sight, not a light, but a wisp of aroma teased his memory. He sniffed, like a dog getting his bearings. Pungent. Dead. The sea. But what was the connection? He sniffed once more, and there he was again, in the middle of Devil's Caye, next to the fins cut from a thousand live sharks. The smell, like ether, stung his nostrils.

Enough light slipped through the corner of a boarded window for Matt to see a pull-chain dangling from a bank of neon lights. It took him three tugs before a light flickered, and then only one tube showed life. On one side lay three stacks of flat, unmarked cardboard cartons, about thirty to a stack. Several large cardboard stencils hung on the wall. *Lobsters, Republic of Honduras, 10 kg*, the same labeling he had seen on the boxes that had passed between the Mayan and the Mestizo. The lingering stink brought tears to his eyes.

Juvenile reef fish were jammed into two banks of aquariums, some with live antler coral, small razor corals, and lettuce corals, their tiny polyps flickering as aerators circulated water. Matt figured the fish and coral were destined for private home aquariums whose owners were unaware and probably unconcerned that Martin Chin was destroying living Belize reefs.

He moved down the hallway toward a single door. Opening it cautiously, he entered Chin's office, illuminated only by a glowing computer screen. He opened the filing cabinet behind Chin's desk, its drawers crammed with files tabbed in Chinese, their contents a mystery. A door opened to a staircase made visible by a dull light from above. Matt took each creaking stair carefully, his steps breaking the silence. At the top, several doors lined the hallway, and one door was slightly ajar. He peered inside. Two women sat with their backs turned, smoking cigarettes, and talking in Chinese. The burners on four large stoves were covered with massive pots. On the floor, two green turtles lay upside down, their eyes alert, but their flippers bound together with wire. Atop a cabinet, a droopy-eyed howler monkey in a cage picked at its arm, inspected whatever it found, and then ate it. Matt tiptoed backward, away from the door.

He moved to another door, quietly turning the knob. Exotic smells filled the air. In the dim light, he could see bags, jars, and bottles cluttering the shelves and bookcases. On one side were two stacks of boxes, their flaps tucked together but unsealed. Matt opened the closest box and reached in to paw through the feather-light, rough-feeling, thumb-sized objects: dead and dried seahorses by the thousands. On an adjacent table sat a large grinder, perfect for turning them into fine powder. But then, those Chinese voices again, the women. He backed into the corner. A woman smoking a cigarette entered halfway into the room, her back to Matt. Continuing her conversation with the woman outside, she turned off the light, and stepped back out, leaving the door slightly ajar. Matt held his breath as he heard them descending the stairs, still chatting, opening the door into Chin's office, and then shutting it behind them, their voices disappearing.

He turned the dimmer switch, careful to leave the lights low. In the corner lay something the size of a basketball, wrapped in butcher paper, atop a wooden box, *Washington D.C.* handwritten across it. He carefully lifted the tape so as not to rip the paper. "My god," he whispered. Staring at him were the golden eyes of a Florida panther, its face frozen in anger. Stunned, Matt retaped the paper around the stuffed head, fighting off an impulse to retch.

The cat's face lingered in his mind's eye and seemed to gain voice, but it now came from behind him. There, at the door, on its haunches, its jaws as wide as its head, its canine teeth glistening, crouched a growling Rottweiler, its fierce eyes fixed on Matt. It took a slow step toward him. If Matt were to turn his back, the dog would be on him like a wolf on a deer, going for his throat. It took another step. Matt swiped hard at a cardboard box on the table, and thousands of seahorses flew into the air. Snapping viciously, the dog gobbled up the air-borne kibble as if it hadn't had a meal in weeks. Matt slammed the door behind him and ran downstairs.

Back in Chin's office, breathing hard but feeling emboldened, he switched on a light. The walls held a gallery of photographs, showing Chin posing with every official Belize had to offer. Several photos waiting to be mounted lay on Chin's desk. Sweat poured down his brow, as he thumbed through them until he reached the last one. It was Chin, in camouflage fatigues, with Turnbull, the same photo he had seen at Trey's. The millionaire head of a conservation organization is conspiring with a guy whose warehouse holds thousands of dead animals. Blood brothers, eradicating what was left of the wilds of Belize.

In the corner, a thin polyester blanket covered the aquarium Matt had seen on his first visit. He lifted the corner and now saw only a few fish, all grouper, one nearly two feet long. It pressed its lower jaw against the glass, its fins fanning the water, helplessly trying to swim forward. The top of its speckled tail was missing. It was Nick, the last survivor from Charlie's reef. Nick couldn't see Matt, couldn't be asking for his help. It was a just fish, for godsake, a fucking grouper, the kind Matt had eaten with chips at the Miami airport. But it had been the last big fish on Charlie's reef. And if the bastards had grabbed Nick, they had grabbed everything.

Pulling the blanket back over the aquarium, Matt headed toward Chin's cabinet, slid open the file drawer and randomly pulled out papers from manila file folders, one or two from each file. Written in Chinese, some looked like bills, others cargo manifests, others printed emails, and some were brochures or memos. Chin would never miss a few here and there, so he folded and stuffed an inch-thick stack into his back pocket.

As he moved back down the hallway, that unmistakable Rover horn blared from outside in one long, forlorn tone, and then he heard the cacophony of cars colliding, crushing, and collapsing. Rushing down the hallway, he peered into the garage. The electric door was sitting on the roof of Chin's car, and Cat's Range Rover was jammed against the Escort's crumpled rear fender.

Chin jumped out, waving his arms, yelling in Chinese. Cat was motionless, slumped over the steering wheel, her horn blaring in the still night. Opening one eye, she looked straight at Matt, who ran around Chin's car and ducked behind a parked SUV, and then Cat started jabbering at Chin.

"Oh my God, I'm sorry, so sorry. I'll send you a check. I have to go," she gasped. "I think my leg's broken — I need to get to the hospital." While Chin stood there staring at his damaged fender, Cat threw the Rover in reverse, backed up ten feet, opened the passenger door, and Matt dived in. She jammed the shift into drive and lurched down the road, taking the first right turn on two wheels.

36

"You saved my bacon."

"I reacted without thinking," Cat said. "Chin's car startled me. As soon as I saw it come out, I drove right at him." She rubbed her head. "His Escort. That's what I saw on my road the other week."

"When the monkeys went missing?"

"Right." She picked up speed, bouncing down the rutted street as dusk fell.

"No wonder. Inside the building, I saw a howler in a cage. Turtles had been flipped on their backs and bound up. There were aquariums stuffed with live reef fish." He started to tell her about the panther head, but stopped, remembering her reaction to the decapitated monkey. "He's cleaning out Central America."

"I think Chin saw you."

"Maybe. But I know he saw you. You rammed his car."

"But he didn't see me pick you up."

They were soon outside Belize City. From the other direction, trucks overflowing with massive mahogany logs roared past them, horns blaring. Matt unfolded the sheaf of papers he had taken and flicked on the overhead light. He thumbed through them, checking the fronts and backs. "Unreadable," he said, shaking his head. "Everything's in Chinese."

"I'm sure you can find somebody in Belize City to translate," Cat said, her eyes looking straight ahead. "Oops, bad idea. Chin knows everyone." She turned on the Rover's headlights.

Matt put down the papers. "I do know who can do it." He slapped his leg. "My friend at the EPA. They must have interpreters."

"Who's your friend?"

"Her name's Maxie. My moral compass. Or so she'd like to think."

Cat glanced sideways, long enough for the car to swerve. "Friend?" Matt knew the inflection. The touch of jealousy surprised him.

"She's an old girlfriend. Now I use her as my sounding board, cheaper than a therapist."

"So, what does this Maxie actually do?"

"She's a Fed, an environmental agent. Goes after companies pouring crankcase oil down drains."

"Vital job, huh?"

"Of course it is. The oil ends up in San Francisco Bay." Cat bit her lip and glanced again at Matt. Ahead lay the turnoff from Hummingbird Highway. The blacktop gave way to a hardpan, red-clay road, bordered with drooping, dusty foliage waiting for the next rain to help it spring back to life.

Matt shuffled through the papers again. A few appeared to be shipping invoices, with lists in Chinese characters, but the money amounts were written in Arabic numerals with dollar signs. One item appeared to be a letter, handwritten on gray linen stationery; two were photocopies of magazine articles, and one—

"Stop. Pull the car over."

Cat hit the brakes, and swirling dust clouds enveloped the Land Rover as she swerved onto the shoulder. He tossed the paper onto her lap and jumped from the car. Holding the door with one hand, he took several deep breaths, coughing as the dust filled his lungs. His stomach churned, his throat burned, and he retched. "A hummingbird. I ate a fucking hummingbird!"

Cat picked up the paper.

Platters
Deep Fried Hummingbird

*

*Ground Manatee meatballs, traditional
vinegar and onion recipe*

*

Green Turtle Calipash and Calipee spread, on crackers

*

Fugu of Porcupine Fish

Dinner
*Traditional Asian Shark Fin Soup, with
chicken, seabird egg and vegetables*

*

*Mennonite-farmed salad greens with
poached hawksbill egg*

*

*Baboon Brain Stew Tienna, with
Chinese herbs and bok choy*

*Grill of meats: traditional manatee, mountain
cat, imported wild greater kudu*

Served with rice, plantains, greens

Fresh leechee

It was the menu from Martin Chin's high-roller dinner.

THREE HOURS AFTER leaving Belize City, they pulled into the Lodge's long driveway. They parked next to a green, mud-coated Land Rover then walked silently to the front desk, where Cat dug out a fax cover sheet for Matt. He wrote a long message to Maxie, filled in her fax number, and counted the pages. Seventy-four. He gave them to Cat, who disappeared into the back room. Matt plopped down on the bougainvillea-print sofa, shut his eyes and rubbed his temples, which ached from clenching his jaw. He didn't notice Cat's return until a frosty Belikin bottle clinked on the table.

She tugged at the rubber band around her ponytail, letting her hair fall upon her shoulders. Sipping her beer, she leaned back, gazing at Matt. "Last time you were in that chair I never thought I'd see you here again."

"And?"

"Well, you're back. And stupid me," she said, tapping herself on her chest, "picked you up and drove you here."

"Why stupid?"

"It pays to keep a low profile if you're doing business in this country, but now that I know what Chin's doing, I have to do something about it."

"A guy like that ought to get the same treatment he dishes out."

"We have to stop him, Matt."

"This from the woman who has constantly told me to mind my own business, that I was in over my head."

"You are in over your head. It's just that now I understand what you're doing." She looked at the clock on the wall. "It's almost ten. I'm bushed and tomorrow is a busy day. Let me get a key for you. Is the same room OK?"

"I was hoping the lodge was full."

"And may I ask why?" she said with a coy smile.

"Well, uh, well—"

"Matthew, it's been a long day for both of us. I need a good night's sleep." She took the last sip of beer and stood up. "Tomorrow afternoon a group of birders is coming by bus and tomorrow night every last room is booked." She smiled, one eyebrow raised. "But since you're on the run, I'll just have to offer you my private sanctuary."

"Well, how kind of you to harbor a fugitive." They laughed and said goodnight.

He walked alone to his room, knowing his ass was on the line. No doubt when the cruise ship left port, someone had reported a missing passenger; the cops were often the last to know anything in Belize, but surely by tomorrow Barnstable would know he had returned. No matter. He was too tired to care.

THE NEXT MORNING, after a walk in the forest, Matt entered the lobby. A dozen tourists were checking out while their bus idled in the parking lot. The receptionist behind the counter waved at Matt. "Mr. Oliver? You had a telephone call." She handed him a slip of pink notepaper. *Call Little Man, he says it is urgent, 622-7232.*

Matt tried using his cell phone but could not get a signal. "Is there a phone I can use?"

She pointed to a narrow doorway across the lobby. "In there."

He poked in the numbers and Little Man answered on the second ring. "It's Matt. I got your message. What's so urgent?"

"It's Jack, mon. He called me here in Belize City. They beat him up. Bad. He couldn't even see who they were, they hurt him so bad, but he said they wanted to know where you were. I guess they finally believed him when he said he didn't know and then they left by boat."

"OK, I'm heading down there."

"When?"

"There's a tourist van about to head back to Belize City. I should be at the Radisson in four hours."

"OK, boss."

So who in Belize City knew he was in the country? Who tipped off the thugs? Barnstable? Surely Jack's was the first place they would look for him. It had to be the Mestizo and his buddy. And when they didn't find

Matt, Jack took the beating. Eventually, they would find their way to the lodge, so the safest place to go would be where they had already looked, and that was Jack's. But were they getting him up? He went back to the phone and dialed Little Man again. "Little Man, who told you I was back in town? How do you know where I am?"

"You're not trusting me, mon."

"I'm not trusting anyone. Tell me, damn it."

"I saw you, mon, with that girl. I was playing dominoes in Welly's and saw you two come in. You looked serious, so I didn't bother you."

"OK, I'll see you at the Radisson."

Cat was out leading a morning walk. But the van was running, and the driver was standing by the open door. The best Matt could do was leave a note to say good-bye.

37

AIR WHISTLED THROUGH Jack's swollen nose. The skin on his puffy face was stretched so tight that the lines around his eyes and mouth had been flattened, and the bags under his eyes had disappeared. Matt swallowed several times, trying to get the lump out of his throat. Jack was too old to be slapped around. Lying in his beach hammock, he tried to open his eyes. When he finally got one open, he was looking directly at Matt.

"Back again, are you?"

"Thought you might take me diving today."

"Tomorrow, maybe. Not today." Jack closed his eye.

"Who did this?"

"Could have been anyone. I was walking past the scuba shack and next thing I knew I was face down in the sand, like a fucking ostrich. Somebody was yelling at me, asking where you were, kicking me in the ribs, telling me to keep my mouth shut or I would never open it again. Then I woke up looking like this." He pointed at his face, rubbed his skull above his ear. "Got a lump that feels like a brain tumor. But I'll live."

"Good, I'm sure you will, but stop bullshitting, Jack. Who did it?"

"Who knows? Get me a shot, would you?" Jack rolled his legs over the edge of his hammock, dropping his feet to the ground to steady himself. Matt poured a short shot of Appleton into a glass. Jack grabbed it and tossed down the rum.

"Where's Charlie?" Matt asked.

"Haven't seen him for two days. And Cleo went to her sister in Belize City. She was scared shitless. She had locked herself in her cottage when she heard the commotion and took hours to come out.

Matt sat down on the picnic table, studying Jack's battered face. "Jack, you have to tell me who's behind this. You know more than your saying."

"Matt, I've got a few enemies out there, but the only guy big enough to pull this bullshit is Turnbull. Plenty of people want this property, but he's been persistent and nasty. Even brought Barnstable with him a couple of days ago to scare me into selling."

"Why didn't you tell me Turnbull wants your land? And what's with Barnstable? You think he's helping Turnbull by shutting you down?"

"I don't know, Matty. Barnstable might have just been along for the ride."

"Maybe, but if you're not bullshitting me, then we have a piece of the puzzle. Call Barnstable. Tell him you were roughed up."

"Why?"

"Because you told me he's about the only guy in the department who isn't corrupt. Let's see if he comes to investigate."

JACK AGREED TO call Barnstable, but Matt was certain that he wouldn't hop a police launch this late in the day—he would not want to return to Belize City after nightfall. If he were to come out, it would be in the morning. Still, Matt wouldn't take the chance and wait for him at Jack's. He would spend the night at Charlie's, knowing that any commotion across the lagoon at Jack's would wake him.

With the sun setting, he slung his pack over his shoulder, grabbed a six-pack of Belikin from Jack's cooler, and walked through the mangrove swamp, swatting away the pesky mosquitoes and no-see-ums. He hadn't seen Charlie's boat on his beach, but he might still be home and, if so, Matt was ready to confront him.

Matt knocked on Charlie's door and called his name, but there was no answer. Pushing open the screen door, he stepped inside, trying to avoid the clutter. He pulled a Belikin from his stash, plopped down on the threadbare corduroy couch, and let a mouthful of cold beer trickle down his throat. He took another swig, wondering what took Charlie away, curious why Jack hadn't seen him. Maybe Charlie's office held a clue. He finished the beer, opened another, and climbed the narrow wooden stairs to the office, stepping over dried sea fans and dirty T-shirts.

On one long shelf, a dozen bleached sea urchin shells

were lined up, descending from softball-size to thimble-size. On the shelf above, a row of queen conch shells, whorls, and spiny oysters. Matt picked up a scallop shell from a cigar box overflowing with small shells. Running his finger across the wavy surface, he remembered Charlie admonishing any diver who plucked a shell from the reef. "All shells are living," he would say, pointing out a hermit crab that had taken refuge inside an empty moon shell. "Leave them alone." Who would have thought that Charlie had his own private collection?

Charlie's old Compaq laptop was open and, beside it, were several pages of notes on lined yellow legal sheets. Phrases jumped at him: *$48K on the 23rd.* Matt sat down and read on. *Get a copy of Jack's deed. Get Dallas attorney referral. Transfer accounts by Monday. Consider conservation easement.* Serious stuff. Who was Charlie in business with?

Matt thumbed through the pages, many with handwritten numbers and calculations, some in Charlie's scrawl and others in different handwriting. There were notes about potential septic tank leaches into the mangroves, drawings of two sewer pipes extending nine hundred feet into the sea and two hundred feet down, and a list of government regulations for septic systems. Charlie seemed to be after Jack's land, but Jack had said Turnbull wanted it. Matt logged onto his own email account but had no messages from Maxie, though he was eager to find out what she might have learned about Chin. As he logged out, up popped Charlie's login screen. Matt fished for a few passwords—*Charlie, Charles Tuna*—but without success.

On a shelf above the desk, two large chambered nautilus shells rested on a mahogany stand, shells from the South Pacific, the kind Chin sold. Lifting a nautilus carefully, he tilted it to look inside. Scores of dried, stiff seahorses stared back at him. He retrieved one, its horsey face immobile, its black eye fixed. As he tilted the nautilus farther, out rolled a small, gold-encased seahorse pendant, like the one Herb's wife had worn to breakfast. He had no doubt now that Charlie was working for Chin.

As he picked up the second nautilus and something inside slipped around, echoing in the chamber. Tilting the opening toward his hand, out slid the gold tooth — the tooth Matt had found buried in the sand, its original enamel showing through a small hole in the gold. Holding it between his thumb and index finger, he looked closer. It was a gold cap over a full tooth, and the hole was shaped like a turtle.

Matt dropped the gold-covered tooth into his pocket, hesitated, then pulled it back out and returned it to the nautilus. If it had been in the nautilus since he had found it, it was not going anywhere now. But if Charlie looked for it, and it was missing — well, Matt wanted no part of that.

He clambered down the stairs and opened another beer. He found a box of Triscuits and a wax-covered wheel of Gouda cheese, which he decided would be dinner, and opened another beer before he headed out to the guest cottage. His eyelids were heavy, his mind cluttered with so many questions that it had no room for answers. He imagined a jigsaw puzzle — a Belize map — with key pieces missing. Too many people held a piece.

As the first light of day shone through the cracks in the cabana's wall, Matt felt his pulse beat inside his head. Too much beer. He splashed cold water on his face to wake himself up and headed out the door.

The screen door to Charlie's house was wide open. Charlie's bag was on the table, the light on, and the door was open to his upstairs office.

"Charlie? You here? It's Matt." Matt looked at the clock: 7:15 AM. He climbed the stairs to Charlie's office and stopped abruptly in the doorway. Charlie was slumped over his desk, his back covered with blood, the dead flesh exposed in a crevice running from the bottom of his shoulder blade to his waist, where the dark membrane of his kidney poked through. It was the indelible death mark of a vicious machete.

38

"Did you cover him up?"

"I did. The poor son of a bitch." Matt stepped over the Zodiac's gunwale, carrying Charlie's laptop and papers. Jack, whose dark glasses shielded his sadness, twisted the outboard handle and headed the Zodiac back to his dock.

"First time he's been covered up as long as I've known him. Never saw him with a shirt on. Not even shoes. Almost seems like a shame." Jack shook his head. "At least, it'll keep the flies off."

They walked back toward the tiki bar, both staring at their feet. "I've known him for twenty years," Jack said.

As they passed the overturned freezer, Matt said, "How come Barnstable's not here yet. Didn't you call?"

"I talked to him twice. Last night he didn't say shit when I told him I'd been beaten up, but this morning, dead Charlie caught his attention. Though the first thing he asked was whether you were here. Like he figured you did it."

"What did you tell him?"

"That I hadn't seen you." Jack walked behind the bar. "Say, you want a drink?"

Matt took a bar stool but waved off the drink. "No thanks. That won't help anything."

Jack grunted and pulled two water bottles from the refrigerator, giving one to Matt. "Well, at least he's not sending that Ambergris cop. Said he'd handle it himself."

Matt unscrewed the cap, took a sip, then another. "So, Jack, who could have done this?"

"The question is, Matty, who paid someone to do it? Charlie didn't have any enemies. Come to think of it, not many friends either." Jack hesitated. "Like me, I guess."

"What about his girlfriend?"

"She was make-believe. You think anyone would want him?"

"A phony girlfriend?" Matt took another swig. "So where did he go all the time?"

"Beats me. He was always worried about money and liked to say his photo book would save his ass, but that was bullshit. I once looked at his camera after he said he'd been shooting all day. Nothing on it."

The papers on Charlie's desk. The seahorses. Matt would tell Jack about them only when he knew for certain what was going on. "Jack, let me have a look at your computer, the one Charlie uses here."

"Be my guest. It's in my office."

Matt ran up the stairs to the lodge and returned with the computer, booting it up as he walked. "It needs Charlie's password. You wouldn't happen to know it, would you?"

"Nope. I don't know anything about those machines."

Matt tried variations of Charlie's name but got nowhere. He glanced over at Charlie's house. The shed door was open. "Jack, did you go into Charlie's shed?"

"No, why?"

"The door's open." Matt grabbed the binoculars from Jack's bar. Inside the shed, he could see the vague outline of someone's back.

"Give me those binoculars." Jack focused on the shed, and the same vague outline.

"I'm going over there," Matt said.

"Don't be an idiot."

"Why stop now?" Matt asked, jogging toward the dock. As he passed the dive shop, he grabbed the speargun leaning against the wall. He considered taking the boat, but then his approach would be too obvious. He headed for the mangrove path and soon trotted up behind Charlie's shed. Inside, he could hear drawers being opened and closed. He edged around the building, holding the spear gun like a rifle with a bayonet. Peering around the doorway, he recognized that filthy yellow T-shirt.

"Yo, fuck," Matt yelled.

The Mestizo sprung up on the balls of his feet and spun around, his face flushed with fear. Matt pointed the spear where his cut-off T-shirt ended and his shorts began. The Mestizo threw up his hands. "Hey, mon, no. That spear gun got a hair trigger on it."

"And if you move a hair, I'll pin you to the wall." Matt brandished it like an AK47. "Man, do I owe you big time." He jammed the spear gun toward the Mestizo's navel, and the Mestizo tried to jerk back.

"You almost killed me and then you killed Charlie." Matt thrust the spear tip at the Mestizo's crotch.

"No, mon, I don't kill no one. Shit. What are you doing with that?" He kept his hands over his head but wiggled his index fingers at the spear gun.

"I'm pointing at your nuts. You ought to be neutered like a dog, so you don't reproduce yourself."

Sweat poured down the Mestizo's grimy forehead, running into his eyes. "No, no, mon, don't do that. It goes off too easy. Please, please."

"You killed Charlie, you fucker."

"No, I don't kill no one. I go fishing with him. Just looking for my fishing gear."

"Sit your ass in that chair. Who do you work for?"

"Uh— the Chinaman."

"Chin?"

"The Chinaman. Chin."

"He told you to kill Charlie?"

"I don't kill no one. I just—"

"What do you do for Chin?"

The Mestizo looked at the spear point getting closer to his groin. "I help with his shark fins."

"How?"

"Take them to Guatemala. Sometime pick some up from the fishing boat."

"What boat?"

"The one out there catching them. I don't know. It has a Chinese captain, that's all I know."

"What about Turnbull?"

"The American?"

Matt moved the spear tip inches from the Mestizo. "Yeah, the American. You work for him, too, don't you?"

"Drop it." The shout came from behind him and, as Matt turned his head, the Mestizo's foot came up between Matt's hands and the spear gun flew skyward. From behind, the Mayan lowered his shoulder and charged, knocking Matt into the sand floor. Matt got to his knees but with the next blow to the back of his head, he tumbled forward, his face again hitting the sand, and this time he didn't move.

DRUMBEATS POUNDED IN Matt's head. He imagined dancers in yellow T-shirts with red bandanas around their necks, smelling of sweat, rum, smoke from cooking fires — and Aqua Velva.

"I see you're waking up, Oliver. Did you have a nice nap?"

Inspector Barnstable was only a blur. Matt groaned. "I didn't do it."

"Maybe not, but you've done enough."

Alongside Barnstable, Matt could see Jack's puffy face. "The inspector arrived just as those bastards took off."

Matt rolled over and pushed himself up from the sand floor. His fingertips were purple as if he had been crushing grapes.

"We took your fingerprints. And we have the machete. For now, we will presume your prints are not on it. But, Mr. Oliver, why are you back in my country?"

Matt brushed off his clothes, his face reddening.

Jack stepped between them and glared at Barnstable. "Inspector, open your eyes, for godsake. My dead partner is upstairs with a two-foot gash down his back, and you're complaining about Oliver. Do your job."

"Mr. Jack, this is my job. I reported the escapees to headquarters, and my constable is upstairs investigating Charlie's murder." He leaned into Jack's face. "But this illegal alien is destroying us by putting up blogs about the so-called Iceman, how Belize is contributing to illegal shark fishing, and God only knows what else. The word is out, and the tourism bureau has reported hundreds of canceled reservations. Some crazy conservationists are calling for a boycott. Even if this man's prints aren't on the machete, I will jail him."

"You can't be serious. We've got bodies, and you're shooting the messenger? Who are you working for?" Jack said with disgust.

"My country, something rich Americans like you don't understand."

"Rich American? Shit, Barnstable, I owe more money than I'll make in the next two years."

"Sell your land, Captain, just sell your land," Barnstable said, wagging a finger.

Matt held up both hands. "Gentlemen, please. With all due respect, Inspector, you ought to be worried about who is destroying your wildlife rather than chasing me around. And what about the body in the ice?"

Barnstable pulled off his sunglasses. "That crime is solved, even without the body. We have enough evidence to make our arrest. We will announce it shortly."

Jack glared at Barnstable. "And it better be the same

guys who killed Tuna." Jack pointed at his right cheek. "See this big welt on my face? Or this eye? If you had answered my call last night, the Tuna might still be alive."

Now Matt stepped between the two men. "Inspector, you need to know something. Charlie and I went diving where the Iceman was. I found one big clue in the sand and gave it to Charlie. He said he'd give to you."

"Charlie gave me nothing."

"I know. It's still in his office. Come upstairs with me."

They climbed up to Charlie's office. A constable was taking photos of Charlie, still slumped over his desk. Flies worked the canyon-sized gash down his back. The breeze through the open window circulated only the smell of death.

Matt lifted the chambered nautilus from the shelf and tipped it. The gold tooth fell into his palm. "This is what Charlie was supposed to give you." He handed it to Barnstable.

"A tooth?" Barnstable rolled it around in his hand.

"It's from the body that the sharks devoured. It was in the sand."

"And how do you know that?"

"I had a witness." He motioned toward Charlie.

Barnstable held the tooth inches from his eye, inspecting all sides.

Matt leaned close and pointed. "Look there. It's a tiny engraving in the gold cap. You can see the enamel through it. It's a decorative cap."

Barnstable stared, then handed Jack the tooth and looked away. Jack picked up Charlie's reading glasses to inspect it. "Looks like a little gold turtle to me." Four tiny legs, a head, and tail showed through the enamel. "Whoever the dentist was, he knew what he was doing."

Matt reached for the tooth. "So, Inspector, if you know who smiled with this little turtle tooth, then you will know who's dead. Maybe that's why Charlie didn't give it to you. Maybe he recognized it. Or he didn't want you tracking down the dentist."

Barnstable looked it over again, pulled a handkerchief from his back pocket, and carefully wrapped up the tooth. He slipped it into his shirt pocket, pulled off his reading glasses, rubbed his eyes, and put on his sunglasses. "I'll look into this."

39

With the Mestizo and the Mayan looking for him, and with Chin or Turnbull or maybe both pulling their strings, it was time for Matt to get lost in Belize City. He thought of staying with Little Man, but he had been too friendly with Charlie and, besides, anyone pursuing Matt would certainly track down Little Man. And Cat's was no place to go. Maybe Randolph would help. After all, he had seemed sympathetic, having reacted with horror when Barnstable hauled him out in the middle of the night. Before, the locals at the bar had ignored Matt, and the barmaid never made eye contact. He would be as anonymous there as he could be anywhere, now that Barnstable was no longer after him. He would see what Randolph had to say.

Matt took Jack's Whaler to the Princess Hotel Marina and hailed a cab. He found Randolph sitting behind the desk, his hands folded, watching his bar patrons through the open door. When he noticed Matt, his eyes opened wide. "Well, my American friend. You're back? Please come in."

Matt entered, and Randolph shut the door behind him. "I had nothing to do with Barnstable's raid," Randolph said. "Before he pulled you out of your room, he was talking on the cell phone to your embassy. They're the ones behind the raid. They have no right coming onto my property and dragging a paying guest out in the middle of the night. Gives me a bad name and all."

"Then you won't be calling the embassy if I stay here."

"You have my guarantee. I'll give you the same room you had last time. I can't imagine anyone would think you'd come back here."

"How about the local rate, now that I'm a regular?"

"Stay six nights and the seventh is on us. Otherwise, it's forty dollars American."

"Let me think about it." He walked into the court-yard. The Giants were two up on the Cubs, and the bar-tender didn't look away from the screen. Matt pulled his cell phone from his backpack and tried to dial Maxie. Unable to get a signal, he went out on the street where he finally made a connection just as a battered yellow school bus full of shouting children rolled past.

"Maxie, it's Matt. What did you find out about Chin?" He pressed the phone to his ear.

"Not as much as I'd like, but enough from the trans-lators to know this guy is more than the king of tchotchkes. One bill of lading had him sending twelve-hundred cases of shark fin soup to Mexico City, enough for a presidential banquet or two. And he's shipping live fish and coral to Mexico City, Panama City, any-where he can find a market for them. Oh, he also sent eight-hundred cases of turtle soup to Hong Kong and is paying people from Mexico to Honduras to gather turtle eggs, and even live turtles off beaches. He makes big money off the turtle shells."

"I saw a little cannery in his building."

"Have you seen his big cannery in Livingstone, wherever that is?"

"That's Guatemala, about a hundred and fifty miles south as the crow flies. He has a cannery there?"

"Big enough to ship four-thousand cases of soup and thirty-two-hundred boxes of lobster into Panama and south as far as Peru. Just in the past month."

"Those aren't lobster. They're shark fins. He ships them in boxes marked *Honduran Lobster*," Matt said.

"Clever man. He's even harvesting sea cucumbers for dog treats. And he keeps meticulous records, even of the officials he bribes."

"Good. Anything else about the finning?"

"Get this. He has half-a-dozen boats in the Pacific, and he's got one scow working blind spots in the Caribbean, areas no countries care much about. Looks like Chin's the main man, according to his papers. Maybe number two, but he's no street-corner vendor."

"Anything about the fins on Devil's Caye?"

"Nothing in his papers referenced them. But you faxed me a schedule that shows in three days someone's going to pick up fins from a long-line fishing boat eighty miles off the Belize coast. Those boats troll miles of line and hundreds of hooks. Chin's a scribbler, and his notes are almost unintelligible, but it looks like they're even hunting whale sharks. He sells their fins as trophies."

"Those fish weigh tons."

"How do they get them?"

"They harpoon them with lines tied to empty oil barrels. The shark tries to dive, but the flotation holds it back and eventually exhausts it. Then they jump on the animal's back with a chainsaw and cut off a trophy."

"Jesus."

"And no one gives a shit."

"Well, there are two U.S. Coast Guard vessels down there, but unless Chin's boats are moving drugs, they're not going to be interested. You're on your own, Lone Ranger."

"I'll get help. Maybe Little Man."

"Right. A name that strikes fear into everyone's heart. Or take Charlie along."

"Charlie's dead, Maxie. Murdered."

"No!"

"I found him whacked from behind with a machete." For the first time that he could remember, Maxie was speechless. "I think they've upped the ante."

Her voiced dropped. "Well, that would be enough to get me to come home."

"I'm just getting started, Maxie."

It took Matt's taxi ten minutes to get to the Municipal airport. From behind the single counter, the Aussie pilot waved at him. "Hello, mate. Fancy seeing you again. I thought you went back to the States."

"I did. Came back just a few days ago."

"Splendid. Are you flying up to the Lodge?"

"No, I'm looking for a charter flight down toward Placencia. I want to see if the whale sharks are still there."

"Righto. When do you want to go?"

"The sooner, the better."

"Well, I need to make a freight run south to Dangriga, so I can take you out for a look-see. If you ride along, I'll only charge you for one way."

"Can't argue with that."

Two hours later the Cessna 172 lifted off the Dangriga airstrip, climbed to four thousand feet, then headed due east, over Glover's Reef. "I flew out here last week," the Aussie shouted over the engine noise, "and the sharks were about twenty miles out." He pointed toward the horizon. "Look for the birds overhead. The sharks are dark shapes in the water. They call them dominoes in Mexico because of the white spots on their backs." He grinned, his eyes hidden behind dark aviator glasses.

"What were you looking for last week?"

"The chap who runs the Global Fund for Wildlife — Turnbull, the guy I took up to Jaguar Lodge a couple of weeks ago. Said he has high rollers coming to town. He wants to take them out whale watching but won't waste a boat trip if they've migrated north looking for better plankton waters."

Matt could understand if Chin were looking, but why Turnbull? One doesn't take a boat out to watch whale sharks. They don't breach, they don't spy hop, and they don't cruise by with a soulful eyeball fixed on you. You have to get in the water with a snorkel to make your trip worthwhile. Unless you wanted to pick out your own personal trophy and have someone take a chainsaw to it.

"Frankly," the Aussie said, "this is no time to go whale watching in a party boat. Weather's coming in. Lulubelle's looking to turn into more than a tropical storm. She's supposed to get up to a hundred and twenty knots around Tulum, maybe even work her way down to Ambergris. She shouldn't get this far south, but there will still be plenty of commotion. Anyhow, keep your eyes out for the birds."

After flying ten minutes past Glover's Reef, the Aussie made a slow, right-hand ninety-degree turn, flew fifteen miles south, then a slow hundred-and-eighty-degree left-hand turn and headed north. "If they're around, this is where they'll be."

In the distance, Matt saw a boat bobbing in the whitecaps. "Got any binoculars?"

The Aussie pointed under the seat, and Matt fished them out. "It's tough to spot birds with binocs when the plane's moving," the Aussie said. "You're better off with your own eyes. In fact, look there." He dipped the Cessna's nose. "See that? There they are."

"Wait." Matt held out his hand. "Head toward that boat."

The Aussie turned the plane sixty degrees. The boat, maybe a hundred feet long, was a junker—a Panamanian flag, a tarp on the back deck, two huge winches, and orange floats attached to long lines stretching to the horizon. "You see boats like this out here often?"

"Nope, looks like an old fishing scow, probably Colombians."

Matt stared at the miles of floats supporting long fishing lines and dangling hooks. He could imagine the surly crew, covered with blood and guts, throwing back dead tuna and wahoo and sailfish, even turtles, all useless by-catch to shark finners. Their job was to haul in sharks, slice off their fins, then let the animals flail around the deck until someone kicked them overboard to die a labored death.

The pilot tapped the fuel gauge breaking Matt's spell. "We're getting low, so let's say we have a closer look and head back. No sense pushing our luck." The Aussie dropped the plane to five hundred feet. Below the circling seabirds, the lumbering whale sharks appeared, a dozen or more, some twenty-feet long, their dorsal fins breaking the surface, the white spots on their chocolate bodies shimmering in the sunlight.

"I've got a fix on the position. They don't stick around too long, but my guess is they'll be here a day or two. These are headed south. This time of year they're supposed to be up north in Mexico, but it looks like they found a local banquet." The Cessna took a wide sweep and headed northwest toward Belize City, eventually passing two miles off Devil's Caye. Off the north end, a small boat slowly moved west in the choppy sea.

"By the way," the Aussie said, "don't know if you want more details about the crash that killed your father, but after we talked I got curious and called the pilot's wife. Turns out they had overloaded the plane with freight from a cannery in Livingstone. The guy who owned the plane also owned the cannery, a Chinese guy in Belize City named Chin, Martin Chin."

40

D<small>RY PAPER-THIN FRANGIPANI</small> blossoms had floated down from the treetops in Randolph's courtyard and covered the cracked cement floor. Drinkers shuffling back and forth had cleared the area around the bar, but in the corner, a carpet of faded pink petals waited for the next rainstorm to flush them into the gutters. Matt sat at a rusty wrought iron table studying the spots on a domino. Six on one end, five on the other. He set it face down, alongside twenty-seven other tiles, 168 spots in all, staring at him like the spots on a miniature whale shark.

Ten days had passed since he had stumbled across the shark fins, and by now they must have been hauled away. However, Chin was greedy, and Matt was sure that hundreds more sharks were now dangling from hooks dropped by that broken-down Chinese shark-fishing scow sixty miles at sea. And the crew would be harpooning whale sharks if they could find any.

And Chin. He had crammed every last case of shark fin soup he could into the plane that carried Matt's father to his death.

Matt fingered the dominoes, standing them on edge, flicking them with his finger, watching them tumble. He had to stop that shark boat. But he needed help.

Matt called Cat and explained his scheme. She happened to be in Belize City and said she would be right over. He also tracked down Little Man at his girlfriend's house near Welly's, and he arrived before Cat.

Matt told him about the shark fins, his meeting with Trey, the rusting scow trailing miles of hooks he had seen from the air.

"No place for them in Belize, mon, but why you telling me this?"

"We're going to stop them, Little Man."

"You and me? The only way we could stop them is with prayer, mon, and nobody ever listens to mine. How about you? You're the parson."

"Only in name, Little Man. And that's why we're going to steal a boat."

"Do what? You steal it. Not me."

"We. And we're not really going to steal it. Just borrow it."

"Those Chinese fishermen out there have guns. Big ones, I bet. The only way you could slow 'em down would be if you had a bigger gun."

"Well, we don't."

"No, and you won't, since I heard you don't shoot people. I don't either."

Matt took a deep breath then felt his heart race when Cat, wearing a tight white tank top, walked into the courtyard. "Well, Matthew," she said, "you won't give up, will you?"

"Not if I can get you to come along."

She pointed at Little Man. "And what does he say about your latest scheme?"

"I told him we're going to borrow a boat."

She turned to Little Man. "But he has to call his girl-friend back in the U.S. to figure out how to do it."

"Ex-girlfriend," Matt said.

"Right," she said.

Little Man smiled.

LITTLE MAN MOTORED the Zodiac out of the mouth of Haulover Creek, around the bend, directly toward the pier opposite the Radisson. Matt sat on a house stoop across the street, the bill of a baseball cap pulled down over his eyes. It was midnight. The sea was barren of ships. Not even a cruise liner lay at anchor. When Little Man pulled up to the pier, Matt darted across the street and jumped down into the Zodiac.

"Where to, boss?"

"Go up to the Princess Hotel pier. Slowly. No one should be paying attention this time of night. I'm going to slip over the side and swim to that new Belize City fireboat docked there."

"Do what?"

"Swim to the fireboat. You'll drop me off then come back here very quietly and pick up Cat so you can join me off St. George's Caye. We're going for a ride."

"How are you gonna drive a fireboat?"

Matt held up his cell phone. "Maxie."

The phone rang. "Speak of the devil." Matt grinned at

Little Man then turned his attention to the phone call. "Hey, what did you find out?"

"Plenty. What time is it there? Nine o'clock?"

"No, it's one in the morning. We're two hours ahead, not behind."

"It's past your bedtime, so I guess you're still going through with this."

"I recruited my crew, and we're ready to go. Now how do I fire up that boat?"

"You have to find the key, but that shouldn't be hard. They don't want some fireman fumbling through his pockets while a cruise liner's on fire so the boat should be open and the key inside. The ignition might not even be locked. It's a FireMarshall 32 built in Southampton, England. The cabin isn't much bigger than an English loo. You shouldn't have to look hard to find the key."

"Then what?"

"The manual says a switch on the right, below the fuel gauge. Flip it up, turn the ignition. Controls are much like any other thirty-two-foot boat, fireboat or not. It should be fueled and ready to rumble."

"What about the water cannons?"

"There are two, one you can operate from the bow, the other is on top of the cabin, and you control it from the inside. The boat has twin diesels. You flip a toggle switch and one diesel stops turning a prop and starts pumping water. You'll have to figure out how to aim the water yourself, but you're a guy so you should have learned that trick early on."

"Thanks for your vote of confidence. What else?"

"That's about all I can help you with, but do me a favor, Matthew."

"What's that?"

"Don't forget to untie the lines before you pull away from the dock."

"Maxie, you're a sweetheart. I owe you."

"Of course, you do. Now, have fun. And be careful."

"I didn't know you cared."

The call went dead. Matt slipped his cell into his back pocket. "Ready to roll?" he asked Little Man.

"Mon," Little Man replied, "all I wanted to do was to make a living running old Jack's boat. You're the worst thing that ever happened to me."

TEN MINUTES LATER the Zodiac approached the *Princess Anne*. Most lights in Belize City had gone dark, and only a few shone behind curtained windows of the Princess Hotel. Laughter from the dockside bar echoed across the water.

"Little Man, stay about sixty feet off the docks. Cut the engine to idle and coast. I'm going overboard. Go pick up Cat and I'll see you at St. George's, south end. No running lights."

As soon as Matt heard the engine slip into neutral, he tossed Little Man his cell phone, slid off the Zodiac, and started silently dog paddling toward the *Princess Anne*.

"Hey, boss? What if you don't show?"

"I don't know. Hadn't thought about that," Matt shouted back. And kept swimming.

MARTIN CHIN SAT on the flying bridge of his Bayliner watching the action below. He often spent the night on his boat to get away from the constant smell of death wafting through his building. The jaguar's head had been mounted, its pelt hung to dry, its bones and organs cooked, treated, dried and packaged. Now Chin needed sleep, but the noise emanating from late-night drinkers and karaoke at the marina bar destroyed the quiet. However, it was the idling Zodiac just off the dock that held his attention.

He had seen it approach slowly from the south, hugging the shore, unusual for a craft on the water well after midnight. It had slowed and then stopped briefly. Chin thought he saw a second person crouching low. There. In the water. Someone swimming slowly. Chin lifted his binoculars and watched the swimmer until he disappeared behind the city fireboat. The swimmer pulled himself up on the fireboat, hesitating just for a second before entering the cabin. Martin Chin's heart dropped. It was Oliver, the American writer.

Chin watched the Zodiac turn around and head down the shoreline. Seconds later, he heard the low rumble of the fireboat's engine as it pulled cautiously away from the dock and headed southeast. Fear struck Chin, then anger. The writer could be going only one place. The shark boat. Chin grabbed his phone, punched the number for his water taxi company, and started screaming. "This is Chin. Bring me a boat right now. Fast. To my Bayliner at the Princess Pier. Now!"

41

THE FIREBOAT CREPT to the leeward of St. George's
Caye where Matt helped Little Man and Cat climb
aboard and then hauled up the Zodiac. Matt jammed
the fireboat throttle forward. The power surge knocked
him back on his heels.

"Whoa, Nellie," he shouted over the screaming engines,
as the *Princess Anne* ripped through the water. With a
half-moon high in the sky, the crest of the three-foot
seas glimmered faintly. He drove hard for a minute,
skimming the surface like a water bug, and then cut the
throttle, realizing that he could be on top of an unsus-
pecting night fisherman in no time, destroying him and
the fireboat. "Little Man, you had better drive this thing.
It's too damn dark. I can't see the coral heads."

Little Man grabbed the wheel. "No problem, mon,
but this don't draw water like Jack's boat. You won't hit
nothing."

Standing at the console, Cat pored over a manual. "I
can barely understand this. You'd think they'd have a
Fire Boats for Dummies book."

"I'll propose it to my agent," Matt said, flipping through another manual.

Little Man inched the throttle forward. Twenty knots, twenty-three knots, twenty-seven knots, then thirty. "Mon, that Whaler don't even do this." The moon reflected off the rippling surface, mesmerizing Matt as the boat seemed to fly above it.

Little Man pointed at the gas gauge. "Look at that, mon, half full."

"Probably costs too much money to keep it topped off. Cat, does the manual give the range of this thing?"

She ran her fingers down the table of contents, and then flipped to the back page. "Nope, only says it has a hundred-gallon fuel capacity."

"So we have fifty gallons left. Any idea how much we burn, Little Man?"

"Maybe ten gallons an hour. Maybe less, I don't know."

Matt unfurled the chart of Southern Belize waters. They had already traveled thirty miles. If Chin's documents were correct and if the shark boat had remained where he and the Aussie had spotted it, then they were still twenty-five miles away. Forty-five minutes. "Fifty gallons should give us five hours, maybe a hundred-and-fifty miles."

"But that ain't enough to get back, mon."

Matt shrugged — they would have to play the return trip by ear. As the boat skimmed along, he and Cat scoured the manuals and notebooks filled with technical drawings and instructions, but there was no operating manual.

"Matthew, I can't find anything about firing the water

cannons. Looks like they expect people to know what they're doing, not to be thumbing through a manual when a fire's raging."

"Keep looking." Matt went back to the chart and checked the compass readings. "Little Man, head one-hundred-fifty degrees. That ought to put us in the right neighborhood."

Little Man gazed at the screen. "Don't these fancy boats have a GPS tracker?"

"Boat's too old, I suppose."

"Then how are we supposed to find them guys?"

Matt flipped on the radar, watching the glowing band crawl around the eight-inch screen. "When we get near enough, we'll let the radar find them. Holler if anything shows up."

As they roared past the tip of Glover's Reef into open water, Little Man turned the *Princess Anne* to starboard, fixed on 205 degrees and powered ahead at thirty-two knots. For ten minutes, Matt watched the radar beam circle. Suddenly, a blip appeared at 150 degrees. "There she is." Matt pointed and Little Man altered course. Now, dead ahead, five miles, ten minutes away.

He watched the beam circle, with Glover's Reef dropping rapidly from the screen. Then another blip. As the beam completed its next 360-degree sweep, the blip appeared closer, as if it were following the *Princess Anne*. "Look at that." He pointed at the screen. "There's a boat behind us, coming hard."

Cat closed the manual. "Who could it be?"

"No idea," said Matt. "The Navy, maybe?"

Little Man shook his head. "No, mon, they never get involved, especially this time of night."

"Slow down, Little Man. Let's watch it."

Little Man cut the speed to twenty knots, and the three stared at the radar screen, watching the blip catch up to them. The *Princess Anne* was four miles from the shark boat, with the blip four miles behind them. Then three miles.

Matt grabbed the wheel. "Maybe it is the Navy. Let's get out of its way and let it pass." He swung the bow 90 degrees left, pushed the throttle forward, and the fireboat leaped ahead. In minutes, it was more than a mile off course. Matt cut the engine to idle. The shark boat appeared at the edge of the radar screen, and the moving blip headed right toward it. They watched until both crafts seemed to merge into one.

"They're alongside each other. What now, mon?"

"I say we wait a few minutes, and then get close enough to see who it is. If they're no threat, we go ahead with the plan."

Cat cocked her head. "And what plan would that be, Matthew?"

"Neither of them can catch us if we need to get away."

"That's no plan," Cat said.

"It's a start." Turning off the cabin lights, Matt watched the distance narrow between the blip and their boat position. "When we get a mile away, let's cut back to five knots or so." It was four-thirty, an hour before sunrise, but the first light would soon appear. "No need to give them a wake-up call."

The best he could tell, the blip had disappeared

behind the shark fishing boat. Through binoculars, the shark boat's dark hull, a Panamanian flag drooping from a pole, appeared like a deserted island against the night sky, displaying no running lights, no cabin lights, nothing to indicate people were on board the vessel. "It's bigger than I thought. Maybe a hundred and fifty feet. And low in the water." On the stern, in faded letters, Matt could read its name, *Scorpion*.

The *Princess Anne* was a half-mile east of the shark boat, passing across the stern, when the second boat came into view. "That's a water taxi," Matt said, "Nothing to worry about." He lowered the binoculars. "Shit, quick to the right!" Matt shouted, and Little Man swung the wheel, just missing an orange, basketball-sized float. "They have floats a half-mile out, no telling how many miles of line they're running."

Once they were far enough from the floats, Little Man swung back and headed for the *Scorpion*'s port side. In the dim light, Matt could make out the enormous stern winch, fifty feet behind the cabin. Two hatch covers were propped over entrances to the hold. "You have to wonder how many fins they have down there. The boat's riding low, but they're still hooking sharks." Matt held up his hand, and Little Man slowed the fireboat to a crawl. Leaning forward, Matt pointed at the nozzle on the front deck. "Let's get that pump working."

Cat pointed at the toggle switch. "The manual says you have to disengage one of the two diesels and use it to pump water."

"That's what Maxie said. When we get a hundred feet away, disengage it. We're going to blast that captain right out of the wheelhouse." Matt ran to the deck. A dark form rushed across the *Scorpion*'s deck, shouting and pointing at the *Princess Anne*. Matt waved to Little Man and instantly a thick stream of seawater gushed from the nozzle but fell short of the *Scorpion*. The torque from the jet spun the bow, pushing the *Princess Anne* off course nearly ninety degrees, pinwheeling the boat and tossing Matt to the deck. Little Man switched off the water. "What happened?"

"I don't know, but for one thing, we're not close enough."

Shoving the throttle forward, Little Man drove *Princess Anne* within fifty feet of the *Scorpion*. Two people were on the deck, waving their fists at the fireboat.

Matt grabbed the water cannon again. Little Man switched the diesel engine from powering the propeller to pumping seawater, and a powerful spout shot from the nozzle, hitting one man broadside and sending him sprawling on the deck. As the *Princess Anne* pin-wheeled again, the spout shot helplessly into the air. Little Man flipped off the water pump.

"The torque spins the boat," Matt shouted. "Try it again, but steer the boat into the spray, fight the torque." Matt grabbed the spout, Little Man flipped the switch, struggling to steer the boat against the spin, but the spray whipped back and forth like an uncontrolled garden hose, unfocused and ineffective.

From the *Scorpion*, two bright flashes were followed by loud pops. Matt scurried inside the cabin.

"Mon, these guys are shooting at us." Little Man ducked behind the console.

"I can fix that nozzle so it doesn't turn," Matt shouted.

"I'll aim it dead on, and you drive right at them. Cat, there's a spotlight on top. Shine it on them. Blind them, or at least bother them."

Matt jumped on the bow, tightened the nozzle, saw two more bright flashes as two pings echoed off the fireboat's steel cabin. He dropped to his knees, the pump his only protection. Now five people were on *Scorpion*'s deck. Matt adjusted the nozzle and Little Man turned the *Princess Anne* directly toward the shark boat. The powerful waterspout hit two men, knocking both to their knees. They slipped and slid as they crawled into the cabin, the water hitting them broadside. Another jumped into the hold; the fourth ducked. Muzzle flashes now came from the cabin.

"Spot the cabin, Cat. Blind them!"

She rotated the light, illuminating the cabin and the two men inside shielded their faces.

Matt jumped into the fireboat cabin and pushed Little Man aside. "Watch this. I have a plan now." He threw the *Princess Anne* in reverse, bringing the bow around to aim the water plume directly at the open cabin door. Water rushed into the cabin, and the two men inside struggled to shut the doors against the powerful stream. Finally, as the boat swerved, the waterspout swung wide of its mark, and the men slammed the cabin doors shut.

Matt squared away the fireboat, now aiming the cannon at the deck hatches. The mighty stream blew off one hatch cover and the spray's full force poured into the hold. He held the boat steady for a minute, two minutes.

"Look, boss, the stern. It's lower in the water."

"Hot damn, the water's filling the hold. We're going to sink that thing." As the water kept flowing, a shadowy form crawled out the starboard cabin window and rolled over the gunwale. Thirty seconds later the water taxi shot out from behind the *Scorpion*, raced around the bow, and headed toward the fireboat. Guns flashed. Matt turned the boat toward the taxi, but the water cannon fired far above it. Jumping on to the bow, Little Man slipped to one knee, but lowered the water cannon, aiming it straight at the taxi, just as it pulled an immediate left. Matt followed it, and as the taxi turned, the waterspout hit the hull full force, lifting the boat into the air and capsizing it.

Matt spun the *Princess Anne* back toward the *Scorpion*, continuing to pummel it as the sea began covering the stern. Six men climbed over the railing and leaped into the sea.

On top of the overturned water taxi sat Martin Chin, soaked to the bone, silhouetted by the rising sun. Matt turned off the cannon and stared at him for a moment. "Little Man, pull the motor off our Zodiac and scuttle it overboard. Leave the paddles here. We'll let them float for a while." He turned away from the sight of the water taxi. "We have a storm to beat, let's get out of here."

42

"Dere's a guy in the water, mon," Little Man yelled into the microphone. "Big shot. Martin Chin. Latitude sixteen degrees, twenty-three minutes, longitude sixty-six degrees, fourteen minutes. Copy dat? Go find him."

Little Man put the mic on the console. "I hope de Navy goes out to get him, mon, but they don't always do what they should."

"Name-dropping never hurt. The government's not going to leave Martin Chin wallowing at sea for long. But when they learn what he's been up to, they may not treat him kindly."

"Don't be silly, mon. He got too many friends."

Matt shrugged. "Maybe so."

The weather had turned; the sea churned. Matt stood behind the wheel, the fireboat skimming the surface at thirty-five knots. Cat looked smug, as if she had an eternal secret. Little Man balanced himself with both hands, looking out the open cabin door at the floating shark carnage, the bow of the WWII-era Chinese fishing boat submerging, and eight men in a Zodiac, gazing at the *Princess Anne* speeding away.

Cat tapped him on the shoulder, speaking. Unable to hear her, he cut back on the throttle.

"Matthew, do you know where you're going?"

He turned to her, an eyebrow raised. "Belize City, I guess."

"You expect we'll arrive with our water cannons spraying in the air, like fireboats on the Fourth of July?"

Matt scratched his head. "We didn't have an exit plan, did we?"

"Not just that," Little Man said, "we didn't have a battle plan either." They all laughed.

"But Cat's right, we won't be celebrating. You both need to jump ship before I take this back. Little Man, you'd get ten years for stealing this boat, and Cat, my sweet, you would probably be deported and lose your lodge."

Cat put her hand on Matt's arm. "And what about you?"

"Me? If I'm caught, I'll call my friend, the ambassador. He would be more than happy to deport me. So, where's the closest settlement to drop you off?"

Little Man pointed starboard. "That way. Parrot Caye. Fishermen live on one side, and an English guy has a house on the other."

Matt reached for the throttle, but Cat leaned over him and touched his hand. "Matthew, are you sure?"

"Yep. I'll drop you off and call Jack to have him meet me if I run out of fuel."

Cat shook her head. "Let's stay together until we get to Jack's."

It seemed like a plea. "Nope, that's thirty miles—too much risk. Get off at Parrot. You can get a boat in, or we'll come get you later."

"You need to listen to him, lady," Little Man chimed in. "He's right."

Ten minutes later Matt guided the fireboat into a palm-lined inlet on the south end of Parrot Caye. As Little Man and Cat jumped into the shallow water, a boy waved from shore. Cat took a few steps, then turned around and vaulted back over the gunwale to give Matt a long hug. "Take care of yourself." When Cat cleared the boat, Matt powered forward toward Rum Caye.

He steered well away from two fishermen in a skiff, and a sailboat pointing toward Belize City, ducking his head in case they were curious about the visiting fireman. Knowing his cell phone wouldn't connect, he radioed Jack, got no answer, and tried again five minutes later, but no one picked up. No matter. At thirty-five knots, he would be at the lodge in less than an hour. He looked at the fuel gauge; the needle was pushing empty, not quite to the stopper. He cut the speed to twenty-five knots to conserve what fuel remained, hoping there was a reserve.

A mile ahead, Devil's Caye drew him like a siren, but Matt stayed a hundred yards offshore, on the east side. Waves slapped hard at the hull, and even with two engines running he had to pull hard to port to stay on course. Weather was coming, maybe a tropical storm, but so far the sea wasn't angry, just annoyed. Matt would follow the island's curve, running behind Turneffe on the leeward side to shield him.

Still, he was curious. Anything happening on Devil's Caye? He took a risk and turned inward, dropping the speed to twenty knots, gliding no more than fifty feet off shore. He was running on fumes but confident he could make it to Jack's.

Suddenly, his chest slammed forward into the wheel. Bouncing backward, he landed on the floor so hard that his legs flew over his head. It sounded like two giant millstones grinding together, followed by a horrible, piercing high-pitched whine as the propellers spun free of the water. He jumped up and threw the engines into reverse, but the propellers had no purchase, the boat did not budge, and the engine sputtered and stopped. Wind-driven seas had covered Devil's coral plateau, and the *Princess Anne* was sitting on top of it. A wave crashed into the window. The next wave hit even harder.

Another night on Devil's Caye? Shit. Well, he would survive. At least, he thought so until he looked shoreward and saw the Mestizo glaring back.

THICK, OMINOUS CLOUDS blotted the sun, casting daylight in depressing shades of gray. Matt hunkered on the ground, his shirt and shorts stiff with dried salt spray, his arms resting on his knees, his head bowed. He fixed on the Mestizo's hammer toes gripping the sand, his thick yellow toenails caked with dirt and fish blood, the hard-leathered skin of his bare feet looking like hiking boot soles. The tip of his machete dangled inches from Matt's nose.

"So now what do we do with this one?" It was the

Mayan, his tattered pants rolled calf-high, his stubby feet covered with rough-cut sandals three sizes too large.

"Like they did with the jaguar, bust his spine."

"And take his head to the Chinaman."

The Mestizo laughed.

The Mayan raised his machete. "The Chinaman wouldn't care. He didn't care about the old man in the hammock, why would he care about this guy?"

"The American would care. He's a big shot. He never killed nobody."

"But the American ain't here. And he ain't coming. Look at those black clouds."

"The storm's coming fast, mon, too fast, and we got work to do. Tie the fucker to a tree until we get the fins loaded."

The Mestizo yanked Matt up by his hair, and the Mayan stuck the machete tip into his back, marching him to a palm tree. "Put your arms around that tree, motherfucker. Get up close like it's your girlfriend."

Matt put his chest against the coconut palm and hugged the tree. The Mayan pulled a roll of monofilament from his pocket, wrapped the nylon line around one of Matt's wrists, and then started on the other. "Hey, man, I can't even wiggle my fingers, you cut off my blood," he said.

The Mestizo pulled at the nylon. "Loosen it up. I don't want to hear this gringo screaming while we're trying to get those fins out of here."

After the Mayan unwound the monofilament and rewrapped it, it still cut into Matt's skin, but he could wiggle his fingers.

"Tie his legs!"

"He ain't going nowhere. The wind's picking up, and we haven't done shit. We got to get out of here." They disappeared into the bush.

Water slapped at the shore, the sky darkened further, the wind rattled the sea grape branches. Lulubelle had turned and was coming his way. Matt pulled at his bonds, but the brittle nylon line only cut into him more. Stepping back from the tree, he yanked the line against the trunk, hoping to break it, but he didn't have the strength. He dropped to his knees and leaned forward, resting his head against the bark, feeling like a small child, alone and afraid. Then he jumped to his feet. "You bastards, you rotten bastards," he screamed.

An outboard engine roared and then dropped to a hum. Matt cocked his head and listened as the sound grew faint and then all that remained was the roar of the wind.

43

GUSTS WHIPPED THE small beach into a frenzy, spinning sand particles into the air that peppered Matt's back, the stinging so severe he imagined being lashed with a cat o' nine tails. Behind him, the ocean boiled. Whitecaps became waves, and then breakers, crashing against him, jamming salt into his cuts and scratches, setting him afire. His chest bled from the coconut palm bark scraping against it, but his shackled wrists still held him firmly. Whenever he tried to break the monofilament line by yanking it against the palm's tough bark, it cut into his skin with a sharp, knife-like pain, forcing him to stop. Warm blood dripped into the dark water.

Twigs and branches flew skyward. Category One winds? Seventy-five miles per hour? More, much more. His palm tree surrendered to the wind, bending and bowing until the crown was nearly parallel to the ground, then snapping back only to bow again. No longer a tropical storm, this was a hurricane.

The water rose higher, reaching Matt's waist. Each time a wave crashed against his back, water filled his nose.

He lifted his arms above his head, as high as he could reach before the nylon shackles stopped him. Grasping the trunk with his hands, he jumped up a foot, digging his rugged sandals into the rough bark. He slid his hands higher and jumped again, another foot higher. And then another short leap. Now his feet were above the water.

He leaped again, digging his feet into the tree and squeezing his knees against the sturdy trunk. He was ten feet up the bending trunk, four feet above the rushing sea. A sharp wind gust pulled him sideways, and he lost his grip, but he dug in and held tight. Shimmy, Matt, for godsake, shimmy. He crept up farther. Below him, a rope, a metal pail, and plastic water bottle were tangled in the brush. A gust lifted the bottle, sent it sailing into a tree, and then it bounced to the ground near a mound of shark fins abandoned by the Mestizo. The fins danced, buffeted by the roaring winds.

The water continued to rise. Gritting his teeth, Matt wrapped his arms around the trunk. The Aussie said Lulubelle might hit Category Three, winds 120 mph or more, and that could raise the water fifteen feet and drive it back half a mile, maybe flooding the entire island. He couldn't survive this. He prayed to whatever god would listen to him. He had no favorite. He asked only to survive.

Matt lay nearly flat on the palm tree as it bent from the force of Lulubelle. Two coconuts flew off the tree next to him, lifted skyward like twin balloons. The tree snapped back against the wind, lifting Matt off the trunk, his wrists still lashed, throwing his feet into the air as if he were on a bucking bronco, then dropping him downward so violently that the weight of his plummeting body snapped the line, setting him free. He crashed through the surface of the surging water, then jumped up, choking, coughing, oblivious to the blood running from his wrists. He struggled through the rising water, twice bowled over by the raging wind, before he reached higher ground, though still knee-deep in seawater.

Lulubelle sounded like a calliope, with different pitches and tones as it whipped through the maze of vegetation. Water crept higher. Sand pebble welts throbbed on his back. Wind-driven raindrops pierced him like needles. A flying mangrove branch slammed into his kidney, knocking him down. Covering his vibrating eardrums with both hands, he shut his eyes. He wanted only to slip beneath the water and seek silence. And just let go.

He steadied himself. Ahead, he could see . . .a tangle of mangroves that the rising water had yet to reach. But it, too, would soon be submerged. He had but one chance to survive. He stumbled back the way he came, against the wind, waist deep in water. Branches slapped him, sticks hit him, the rain beat on him. He was walking the gauntlet—Lulubelle's gauntlet.

A coil of rope dangled in the brush near his palm tree. He jerked it free. Struggling against the ocean's surge, he managed to flip the rope around the trunk and tie a slip-knot around his waist with one hand while gripping the tree with his other. Shimmy. Shimmy, he told himself. Certain he could not withstand Lulubelle's full force on the ground, he slid the rope higher, pushed himself upward, wrapped the remaining rope around the tree and himself, and tightened the knot. Below him, scores of shark fins tumbled about in the frothy water.

Climbing higher, he tightened the knot again, and then pushed even higher. He wrapped the rope around himself and then around trunk, three times, four times, five times, and tied it off with a bowline. The trunk, now nearly parallel to the ground, snapped back with such a force when the wind shifted he thought it would catapult him to the next caye. But the line held. And then Matt passed out.

WHEN HE AWOKE, the wind had redirected, and it was now coming from the west. The palm weaved viciously side-to-side. The shifting wind picked up flotsam it had hurled in one direction and threw it back at him. He was on the exit side of the storm. He felt himself slipping down the tree trunk, but he was too weak to retie the knots. Rain hit him sideways with such force it seemed to pierce his skin. But it slowly lessened. And lessened more. And finally, the rain stopped. The wind softened and soon only whispered. Lulubelle had moved on.

Fifty yards ahead on the mound of mangroves lay a jaguar, its coat covered with mud. It rose slowly, shook its emaciated body, and then stepped through the rubble, disappearing behind a jumble of broken branches. Then Matt remembered another day. The jaguar in the tree. Flying through the air. Lying paralyzed. Dying at Matt's own hands. But this was not the same jaguar. And it was not a dream. Matt closed his eyes.

44

After Lulubelle had slammed into Belize, she changed course and headed up the Mexican coast before turning inward south of Cancun, one hundred and fifty miles north of Devil's Caye. She tore apart countless islands while ripping off roofs and knocking out power. Nearly all the Americans on the islands had been evacuated. Only Belizeans were left behind.

Klaas Thiessen had told his fellow Mennonites living in Spanish Lookout that he would take the community-owned boat from the hurricane hole where it had been safely moored to Lord's Caye and assess Lulubelle's damage to their Bible camp, which was to open in two weeks. Mennonite children from Shipyard and Upper Barton Creek to the south, where technology was still forbidden, would attend, so it was important to show the horse-and-buggy Mennonites that a boat ride in the name of God would do their children no harm.

At the dock, his wife and daughters—Sara, eighteen, and Marie, twelve—carried baskets of bread and cheese and fruit onboard. Klaas wiped the salt spray from the

windows of the twenty-six-foot handcrafted hardwood boat and started the engine. Lulubelle had passed
only yesterday, and while the seas were still choppy,
he expected to get to Lord's Caye by noon, make his
inspection, and return well before dark.

An hour out, the sea was muddy with flotsam
everywhere. The two sisters sat on the bow, their legs
stretched out under long plaid dresses that touched the
tops of their socks. They played a game to see who could
first spot and identify anything floating in the water.

"Soda pop," shouted Sara, as she spied a red can floating in the distance.

"Where, where?" asked Marie.

"I'm not going to point it out, little sister. You need to
exercise your eyesight. You need to be able to see things
far and away."

They turned their eyes back to the horizon, searching
the water. On an island more than a mile away, a sandy-
colored lump caught Sara's eye. It seemed to move. She
had passed that lush island every summer, but now it
was stubble, as if shaved by the hurricane's sharp winds.
She tried to make out the crumpled shape on the shore,
uncertain what it could be, but it moved again. Maybe
a tarp. Or a ripped sail. She crawled down the bow on
her hands and knees, walked around the edge of the
boat, and jumped down into the cabin. From a drawer,
she retrieved a pair of old binoculars and trained them
on the island.

She lowered them from her eyes, and then raised
them again so quickly she hit herself in the nose with
the eyepieces. Holding her breath, her heart racing, she

whispered to herself, "Please, dear God," unsure whether she was asking for help or forgiveness.

Her father, tight-jawed, concentrating on keeping the course, grasped the wheel with both hands. She tapped him on his arm. "Father," she said. "Father, please." Her mother, busy crocheting a prayer cap, did not hear Sara's soft voice over the engine.

"Father, look." She pointed at the island, and now she could clearly see what was onshore. A man waving.

Squinting, Klaas reached for the binoculars and peered through them. "Heaven forbid. Sara, what are you looking at, child?" He slammed the binoculars down.

"Father, that man is in trouble."

"Sara, that man has no clothes on." He turned the boat to the port, away from the island.

"Father, please. He's in trouble."

"He is naked. He is crazy. Sit down." Klaas pushed open the window and yelled at Marie. "Come off the bow and come inside." Marie followed her father's orders and jumped down.

Sara grabbed the binoculars and looked again at the man. He was entirely naked, hunched, barely waving.

"Father, you have to help him."

"And you must obey me and sit down. Do not look again."

She grabbed her father's arm. He shook her off, restraining both her arms, and sat her down. "Now stay there. We have a schedule to keep."

The man on the island — it was he, the one she had wronged, not because of what she had said, but because she had remained silent. Her father had been the accuser; she had not. She did not know whether the man had been sent to jail, sent back to America, or put in front of a firing squad. But there he was, naked as everyone is in God's eyes. And she could not turn her back on him again.

She stood and faced her father, realizing for the first time that she had grown as tall as he. They were standing eye to eye. "Father, that man needs help. Now, you don't want us looking at a naked man, so we will look away. But you go see what you can do. He needs help, I swear."

Klaas looked up at his daughter. "I told you to sit down. We have a schedule to keep. Some fisherman will pick him up."

She stepped to the stern, lifted up her dress knee-high, and put one foot on the gunwale. "Father, you pick him up, or I will swim to him." He stared at her, his mouth wide open.

Sara's mother picked up the binoculars. Klaas tried to take them from her, but she fixed them on the man. "Heaven forbid," she said, slamming down the glasses. "Klaas, we must help him."

He glared at his wife and began to speak, but said nothing and turned the boat east toward Devil's Caye.

45

M ATT STARED INTO the mirror, fixated on what had once been the white of his left eye but now looked like a blood orange. So did his upper lip. He gazed at his chest, crisscrossed with scratches in patterns like primitive weavings. Sand grains were embedded in his skin. Creases and cuts circumscribed his wrists where the monofilament had bound him. He looked like a villain in a horror movie, with a make-up artist named Lulubelle. He had slept nineteen hours, and he might have slept longer had the searing pain shooting up his back subsided.

Matt dragged himself to Jack's main lodge. The sea had carried away Jack's picnic tables. The tiki bar's thatched roof lay upside-down in the mangroves, two hundred yards behind the lodge. But before the storm, Jack had shuttered and latched the windows of the lodge, cleared out the bottles and glasses from his bar, and taken his boats to the lee side, so the only other casualty was a crack in the cistern's roof from a flying tree.

Matt stepped onto the porch, gripping the railing to

steady himself. He perked up when he smelled the deep aroma of Guatemalan coffee. Jack, holding a cup in his hands, nodded then pointed across the water at Little Caye. The bright rays of the rising sun reflected in the morning mist.

"Have a look at the sunrise over Little Caye, Matty. You might think you died and went to heaven." Jack sipped his coffee, looked at Matt, and shook his head. "In fact, you almost did, didn't you?" Jack looked older than Matt remembered, much older than just a week ago.

"I thought I had. More than a few times. Guess I was hallucinating. I could see Belize City, the Cayes, even saw you. You were sitting right here with my father."

"I don't know how you survived it. It was bad enough here, with the building rattling and shaking like it was a ten-hour earthquake." Jack put his hand on Matt's arm. "Let me get you some coffee."

He returned with a mug of steaming coffee and a plate with four Johnnycakes with a slab of butter alongside. Matt grabbed one and held it up. "First food in two days." He slathered butter on it, devouring it with two bites, then finished off the others and wiped his hands on his shorts.

He looked over to Jack, who held a Canon digital camera in his hands, running through photos on the back screen. "Charlie's camera." He handed it to Matt. "Click through a few shots. You'll know when to stop."

Matt glanced at several photos, mostly underwater shots of colorful reef fish. And then he stopped, stunned by a picture of a thin old black man wearing only shorts, face down in the sand, with Bucky's ramshackle house behind him. Matt didn't recognize him, but it didn't look like Buck. The next image was a night shot, with an illuminated Little Man in the frame, his eyes wide, as if he had been caught by paparazzi. Draped over Little Man's shoulder was the body of that old man. Matt stared. He went to the next frame, the Kelvinator filled with offal. The old man's ear, hip, and ankle protruded through the surface as he lay in a fetal position. The next frame was more of Charlie's fish. Matt returned to the first shot and stared again at the night shot of Little Man. Matt handed the camera back to Jack. "Where did you find this?"

Jack pointed at Charlie's house, where Charlie's overturned skiff lay covered in sand. "Over there. With Charlie dead, I didn't get the house shuttered up, and after the blow, his stuff was scattered from hell to breakfast. I heard a commotion yesterday and came out to find a village guy ransacking the place. I shot over in the Zodiac. Another guy was almost out the door with Charlie's computer, but as soon as they recognized me, they put the stuff down and took off. One guy had this." Jack lifted a yellowed *Belize Times* from the table. Under it was a .36-caliber pistol. "And he had that camera there on your lap."

"Little Man put the body in the freezer? And Charlie took his picture? Jesus, Jack. Why?"

"I want Little Man to tell you about it. You judge for yourself." He turned his head toward the screen door. "Little Man, get your ass out here."

Little Man walked out, his head down, his hands in his pockets.

"Here. Sit down. Tell the parson what you told me. Confess. It'll do you good."

Little Man sat in the wicker chair, his knees together, his hands folded in his lap, looking half his normal size. He didn't raise his head.

"The guy in the ice was a fisherman, mon. They called him 'Wickets.' He lived on the island near Buck. Charlie told me that two days before the shark dive he had stopped by Bucky's island to say hello. Bucky wasn't there, but Wickets was, Charlie said, and he was face down on the sand, like he had a heart attack. So he brought him back here for proper burial."

"A proper burial in a Kelvinator freezer?"

"Let him finish, Matty."

"That same night I went to Charlie's," Little Man said. "I lit up a spliff, and we sat around smoking weed till it got late. Then somebody called Charlie, and when he hung up, he told me about Wickets. He was in the shed and Charlie said for me to help him bring the body over here. I hardly knew the old guy, so he didn't matter to me, but when we got him here, Charlie told me to dump him in the freezer. Said it would be a practical joke on Jack. I told him I wouldn't do it, but that was strong weed, and I wasn't thinking much and Charlie was dragging him, so I lifted him up and put him in." Little Man, a tear welling in one eye, looked up at Jack. "Next morning, when I woke up, I was scared, mon, scared. I went over and woke up Charlie and told him we had to tell Jack and get that body out, give him a proper burial. Charlie said no way, and then he pulled out that gun, there, and told me to sit down. Never pointed it at me, just put it on his lap. Said we'd been friends a long time, would always be friends, but he was in trouble, and that body was going to stay in that freezer. Charlie said he'd be dead if we didn't do it. Then he got a scary look on his face. He put the gun away, but he scared me." Little Man looked up. "And that's all I know."

"That's all?"

"Well, I got no video, either."

"Intentionally, right Little Man?" Jack said.

Little Man nodded, staring at the floor.

"Nothing more?" Matt asked.

"Swear to God."

"Do you believe him, Jack?"

"Sounds like bullshit to me, but then I've always trusted Little Man. And we do know Charlie was up to no good, don't we?"

"Charlie probably figured he could use the photos to keep Little Man quiet."

Jack put down the camera and patted Little Man on the leg. "There's more to the story, Matt. I know the guy who tried to heist the computer, so I looked him up in the village. He told me he had received a call from some-one who told them to clean out Charlie's house. Told them to get the camera and the gun and said a guy from Belize City would come by and pay them for everything. They don't know who called."

"I'll tell you who called." Matt pumped his fist. "As the Mestizo would say, either the Chinaman or the American."

Jack shook his head. "That prick Turnbull wants my land, bad."

Matt nodded. "So he gets you charged with the murder."

"And he pushed Barnstable to hassle me — maybe even chase my ass out of here."

Matt held up his hands. "I appreciate the confessions, gentlemen, but they don't mean much now, do they? Little Man, you put a dead man in a Kelvinator. Now I suppose if that diver who got bent found out about it, he might want to throttle you. But Jack told me that guy is walking fine these days, so forget about what you did with someone who was already dead."

"I suppose you're right, Matty," Jack said. "Charlie's the real issue."

"So, Jack, did he use your computer for his emails?"

"No idea, I never looked."

The three went upstairs into the dining room, and Jack walked into his office, returning with a Compaq laptop and a slip of paper. "Here. Charlie's email address."

Matt turned on the Compaq. "We still don't know his password. Jack, he must have written it down for you, somewhere. You were his boss."

Jack scratched his head and frowned, "Nah, I don't think so." Jack hesitated. "Wait. Maybe there is something." He went to his office again, this time returning with a black notebook. "Here," he said, pointing inside the cover. In Charlie's handwriting, was *PW: tunafart-follies.*

Matt typed it in, and Windows sprang to life. He scrolled through Rum Point Inn email, searched for other accounts, but everything he found was legitimate business.

Little Man poked Matt's shoulder. "So, boss, maybe Charlie used that password on his computer?"

Jack sprang up and walked into his office, returning this time with Charlie's Compaq. Matt booted it up, typed in *tunafartfollies* and Windows played its welcome tune.

"Little Man, you're the smartest guy in the room."

And there they were, a string of emails running back two years, hundreds sent to Martin Chin. Matt scrolled through those from the last month. *Martin, I saw those shark fins and I'm finished. No more scouting for your divers or fishermen, no more seahorses, no more crap, you rotten little bastard—you still owe me $4K. Fisheries might not do shit about this, but someone will put you out of business.*

Matt read Chin's responses, brief yeses, and noes. "Doesn't look like Chin has implicated himself in any way, but we know who did in Charlie."

"But I don't think Charlie was talking to Chin the night we was smoking weed," Little Man said.

"Why not?"

"He was too polite. Kept saying 'sir,' like he was talking to a big shot."

"Sounds like he was talking to Turnbull," Jack said.

Matt nodded. "The first thing we do is that Little Man and I are going to wash away our sins."

"And how we do that, boss?"

"By burning what's left of those shark fins. It's not enough just to put Chin out of business. Maybe when he knows we're not going away, he'll leave the sharks alone. Who knows? But that's what I need to do. There were thousands of fins inside the fence on Devil's Caye, and I doubt the water rose high enough to float them all away, so I say we have a bonfire."

"Here, let me help you." Jack picked up a matchbox from the bar and tossed it to Matt, who stuffed it into his shorts pocket.

"I haven't told you, Jack, but I have a personal score to settle. That was Chin's plane my father died in."

"Chin owned that plane? Jesus, I need a drink." He grabbed a bottle of Appleton, then put it down, shaking his head.

"It couldn't get enough altitude. It was way overloaded with cases of shark fin soup from his Guatemala cannery."

"Why that son of a bitch. I'm coming with you."

"Nope, it's my job. Little Man's all the help I need."

Jack crossed his arms, and then rubbed his chin with one hand. "And what're you going to do when the bonfire's over?"

"I'm going to honor an invitation from Cat," Matt said.

46

"Matthew, I was so worried about you. Belize Radio said they found the fireboat upside down in the middle of Devil's Caye." Hearing Cat's voice on the phone, Matt felt warm for the first time since Lulubelle hit him.

"Well, the *Princess* and I did run into a little trouble and by the time I got back I couldn't get through to you. Cells were dead."

"This is the first call I've received. Two cell phone towers were blown over, and our house phone was down. Are you at Jack's now?"

"That I am, helping him clean up a little debris."

"You rode out Lulubelle there?"

"Ah, no. I'll tell you about it. I'm just glad to hear that you and Little Man made it to Belize City OK."

"Everyone was evacuating to the mainland, so we hitched a ride and hunkered down in a community center. But you? What happened to you?"

He told her the story, how the fireboat had run out of fuel, how he had survived the hurricane, the rescue.

He talked so rapidly that he felt out of breath when he finished.

"My God. That's incredible. Come up to the lodge and hide out a few days. No one will look for you here."

"Not until I torch those fins. I'm pissed at all those people, but the best I can do is get rid of those last fins and send Chin a message."

"Matt, don't be stupid."

"Look, he'll be busy in Belize City cleaning the mud from his building and kiosks. Jack heard that half the city was flooded. We can get out to Devil's Caye and back in a few hours."

"It's too risky."

"Maybe, but it's all I can do right now."

"Then come here afterward to recuperate. We'll figure out how to get you out of the country."

"Oh, Jesus, I forgot I'm not legal. That might be a problem. What if I can't get out?"

"Do you know how to chop tomatoes and onions?"

THE SKY HAD turned a perfect blue, the sea almost flat again. Nearly forty-eight hours after the hurricane and the earth was healing. He picked up the Belize phone book and turned to the government section. The Records Department was in Belmopan, the inland capital city, which the hurricane hadn't touched. Matt dialed the number on Jack's phone.

It rang a dozen times on the other end before a hurried voice said, "Records Department."

"I'd like to get information on land ownership, a caye in fact, Devil's Caye. Can you tell me the owner?"

"Sir, we're too overwhelmed handling hurricane calls. You'll have to phone back later."

"Well, uh, I am calling about a hurricane problem. You see, I'm out on the caye now, and it looks like the owner, at least we think he's the owner, is dead. A tree fell on him. We need to find out who he is to notify next of kin. His house and all his records were washed away."

"I can try. Where did you say you were?"

"Devil's Caye."

"OK, let me see if I can help." A click told Matt he had been put on hold. It was nearly two minutes before the clerk returned. "I have the folder. It's owned by a Landon Billy Barber."

"What?" Matt nearly dropped the phone, "Well, it's not Mr. Barber's body, so can you tell me who owned it before?"

"One minute please." He was placed on hold for another minute. "It was owned by the Bodden family as far back as the records go. Peter Bodden."

"He's an African-American, right?"

"Sir?"

"Sorry, a Belizean, African descent, right? Well, this isn't him either, but you say Bodden sold it to Mr. Barber?"

"Sir, the Bodden family sold it to the Global Fund for Wildlife about four months ago. Mr. Robert Turnbull signed for the Fund as Executive Director."

"And Barber purchased it from them?"

"Looks that way. Just last month."

"Well, it sure isn't Mr. Barber under that tree."

"I guess I can't help you then. Sounds like a terrible tragedy. But can you hold again?" She didn't wait for Matt to answer but returned in less than a minute. "Sorry, sir, I didn't check carefully enough. There's a second file. Barber transferred the title the same day he bought it. To Robert Turnbull the Third, but acting for himself, not the Fund. Mr. Turnbull owns Devil's Caye outright."

47

As the Zodiac approached Devil's Caye, Matt, rubbing his ten-day stubble, admired his still-standing forty-foot high palm tree hurricane perch. It had resisted everything Lulubelle had thrown at it. Had it been uprooted, he and the tree would have crashed into the surging water, and he would have drowned. Although his palm had bent and bowed, it had remained unbroken, as if it knew that for him to survive, it too had to survive. Other palms lay scattered and shredded. Seagrape trees had been ripped from the shoreline. Mangrove trees, stripped of their leaves, stayed firmly rooted, like inverted candelabra. The entrance to the channel, once nearly invisible from the sea to any passerby, stood out clearly.

Little Man guided the Zodiac into the channel and cut the engine. Broken branches slapped at the hull as the boat slipped through the murky water. Sitting in the bow and watching for obstructions, Matt held up his hand. Just below the surface, he could see a telephone pole-sized palm trunk.

"Hold it. Back off a bit." He grabbed a paddle and poked at the log, but it didn't budge. "Go as far to the right as you can. I think we can get around it."

Little Man steered toward the bank, cut the engine, and lifted the prop from the water. Matt pushed with his paddle and Little Man pulled branches to move them along, both of them ducking under the brush. Once through the maze, Little Man lowered the motor, and they continued down the channel. Five minutes later, they reached the remains of the dock, which Lulubelle had torn away from the muddy bank.

Matt jumped to tie off the boat, catching himself on a piling when his foot went through a space where Lulubelle had ripped out a board. Little Man handed Matt two full five-gallon gasoline cans, leaving two others in the boat, then leaped across the four-foot chasm.. They started down what had been a cleared trail, but stopped after ten feet. "This is a hell of a tangle," Matt said.

"I'll get the machete, boss," Little Man said, and soon he was hacking away, taking nearly half-an-hour to clear the fifty-yard path to the fence. The gate was intact, but scores of fence posts had been toppled and the winds had twisted the chain link into odd ribbon-like strands. Scores of shark fins had been trapped under the fallen fence. Others had been scattered in the mangroves. And a single fin topped a mangrove branch like a one-armed star on a Christmas tree. But that was all that remained of the fins.

"We can forget the bonfire. A thousand shark fins have been sent back to sea. Looks like the gods did their work for us."

Little Man smiled. "Shark Gods?"

"Sure. Good as any."

Little Man's head perked up. "Listen. You hear a boat?"

Matt cocked his head, hearing nothing.

"There, listen." A faint whine, muffled by the mangroves, grew louder. "Somebody's coming in. They just cut their engines."

"Whoever it is, it's not good news. Let's get out of here."

They ran back up the trail. Matt stopped and put his finger to his lips, and they both slipped into the brush. Matt hunkered down, with Little Man alongside him. A voice sounded close, a Texas voice, and in his mind's eye, Matt saw a jaguar dying, with Turnbull, the ambassador, and Herb watching. And the day Matt lost suddenly came rushing back.

"We're not letting that prick get away this time." Trey Turnbull trailed the Mayan, who pushed away the branches already cut by Little Man's machete. "The phone call said he was coming out here. He's a dead man when we find him." Turnbull spoke in half a whisper, "He'll bring down the ambassador, even embarrass the president, goddamn it. I'm going to hold this gun to his head, but you're going to chop it off, got it?"

Matt held his breath; his eyes were fixed on the Mayan pushing past the branches, with Turnbull right behind. After the two disappeared into the bush, Matt exhaled and motioned to Little Man. They struggled back to the trail and walked the opposite way, glancing behind them with every step.

Just then, Matt put out his arm, like a crossing gate. It was the Mestizo, standing three feet away, waving a machete over his head. As it came crashing down, Little Man bulldozed under Matt's arm and buried his shoulder directly into the Mestizo's groin, sending the machete flying. The Mestizo doubled over, gasping for air. Little Man jumped to his feet; Matt jumped over the stunned Mestizo, and they both rushed for their boat.

"Shit. The line is over the piling." Matt leaped out, whipped off the line and tumbled back into the boat as Little Man began maneuvering down the channel. As they rounded the bend, a poacher's net filled with decaying snappers bridged the canal. Matt reached for the machete, but the net was so entangled in the branches he didn't swing. "There's no way around. We have to go back."

Spinning the Zodiac, Little Man raised the speed to seven knots. Near the dock, the Mestizo rolled on the ground, still moaning. Behind him stood Turnbull and the Mayan. Little Man threw the Zodiac in reverse, made a tight turn in the channel, and then pushed the throttle forward. The Mayan jumped the dock chasm, landing on the broken board, and fell to his knees. Lurching sideways, he rolled off the dock, gasping just once as the massive jaws of a crocodile wrapped around his torso and dragged him below.

Mesmerized, Matt almost missed seeing Trey lift his rifle, but he dropped quickly to the boat deck. A bullet whistled overhead. Then another. Quickly Little Man powered the boat back around the bend, separating them from Turnbull by a massive mangrove clump.

Little Man gunned the boat, forcing it up on the bank. As he cut the engine, Matt leaped out, and Little Man was right behind. They slogged through thick, oozing mud and clusters of mangrove and sea grapes and branches, now so knotted they looked impassable.

What once had been a trail Matt had easily traversed, Lulubelle had turned into a jumble of brush. Matt climbed over one branch, and then stumbled over the next. Little Man pulled him up. And there stood Trey Turnbull, fifty feet away, his pistol pointed directly at them.

"This is it, you little—" And then a blur, a yell, the gun's roar, flashes of blood and patches of cloth. Everything froze for a single second before Matt saw the furious jaguar hanging on Trey's back like a fur coat, its sharp claws wrapped around Trey's head. Matt shouted and charged. Startled, the jaguar looked up, then leaped into the tree above where he looked down at Trey, who lay on the ground whimpering, his head wrapped in his own arms. The jaguar licked its paw, then leaped from the tree and scampered away.

Trey reached up to Matt. "Help me." Blood poured from his right eye, clear, vitreous gel dripped from the other, its lens ripped out and lying in the palm of Trey's hand. Matt pulled off his muddy shirt and wrapped it around Trey's head, telling him to press both eye sockets to stem the blood. Matt covered his mouth, trying not to retch.

Little Man and Matt guided Trey into the Zodiac, helped him step over the gas cans, and sat him on the center bench. Moaning, Trey held both hands to his face, one fist tight. Little Man started the engine, and the Zodiac crawled back down the channel. The Mestizo had disappeared.

They continued down the canal toward the opening, swerving toward the bank to avoid the sunken trunk they had passed when they entered. As they rounded the next bend, Matt sat up with a start. A Colt 45 was pointed directly at his head.

Behind it was Martin Chin, standing on the bow of a boat. "Cut your engine, boy."

Matt looked at Little Man and back to Chin.

"I said cut your engine."

Little Man cut it.

Chin wiggled his gun at Matt. "I came to see whether my shark fins survived, and I find you instead."

"They didn't make it through the hurricane, Chin. Now, we have an injured man here. Trey Turnbull. I think you know him. He'll die if we don't get him out of here. Have some mercy."

"You have destroyed my business, Oliver. Stand up. With your hands over your head."

Matt stood up slowly, raising his hands. Trey didn't move, only moaned.

Chin gripped the Colt with both hands, as if he had been trained for the moment. He lifted it carefully to eye level. Matt glanced left, then right, looking for some way to escape.

"I've never done this before, Oliver, but I might enjoy it."

Matt stared into the Colt's barrel, the muzzle appearing as wide as a cannon's. Was his father's heaven just another fable? He would soon know.

The water rippled to Chin's left, catching his attention. A hawksbill turtle surfaced, a small hole visible in its shell. Then Matt saw a flash. Bright. Brief. Then a deafening blast. He waited for the light, the tunnel, the end. But instead, Chin's arms jerked upward, and his head fell forward. It wasn't until Chin splashed face-down in the canal that Matt realized he wasn't the one who had been shot.

Inspector Barnstable stepped out of the brush, Jack behind him.

"I thought you might be in for a little trouble, so I called Belize's finest," Jack said as Barnstable disappeared back into the bush. "He met me here. I don't want to say much more than that because of your passenger there," Jack said.

"I don't think he's going to be an eye witness."

"Doesn't look like it."

Matt perked up at the sound of an engine and looked down the canal. "Jesus, there's still one left."

"Who's that?" Jack asked.

"The Mestizo. He might have Turnbull's gun."

The roaring engine resonated up the canal. Jack ran to the boat. "Hand me those cans. Quick." Matt lifted up the two gas containers and handed them to Jack. "Now, get your ass down the channel."

Little Man took off with a roar as Jack pulled the cap off one can and dumped the gas into the water. He pulled the cap off the second, poured out more fuel, and then tossed both cans into the water. Pulling a wooden matchstick from between his teeth, he lit it with a flick of his thumbnail and threw the flame into the floating gasoline. It was a bonfire meant for the shark fins, but it was now destined for the shark hunter. When the Mestizo's boat hit the submerged log, it flew six feet into the air and then into the wall of fire. Now a ball of flames, it slammed into the bank. Covered in flames, the Mestizo jumped up and ran into the brush, the stench of gasoline, burning rubber, and seared flesh filling the air.

48

An ambulance and two technicians were waiting when Little Man guided the Zodiac up to the Princess Hotel dock. The EMTs lifted Turnbull out of the boat, strapped him on a gurney, and rushed him down the dock, Matt's shirt still wrapped around his head.

Little Man and Matt walked the six blocks to Randolph's in silence, a wave of sadness rolling over Matt. After washing up, he sat down at a courtyard table and put his head in his hands. "Jesus."

Little Man placed his hand on Matt's shoulder. "Is that a prayer?"

"Maybe." He thought of his father, his death now avenged, but he felt no better. "It's tragic seeing anyone go out the way those guys did."

"They were not good men."

"No, they were not." Though Matt had washed his hands, Trey's blood was still deep beneath his fingernails. His body scratched, bruised, and covered with dirt, his eyes blood red, his toenails turning yellow from fungus, Matt could only mumble. "Eight days in beautiful Belize."

"You don't look so good, boss, with them red eyes and everything."

"I need a shower. Clean clothes. Sleep."

"You can stay with me and my girlfriend tonight."

"Thanks for the offer, but I'm sure Randolph has a room. I'll buy you a drink, and we'll call it a day. Later on, can you send an email for me?"

"Sure, my girlfriend has a computer."

"Then, I'll give you David Mallard's email address and a message to send." Matt walked to the bar, returned with a pencil and a notepad, and began to write:

Dr. Mallard, you will soon hear of a horrible tragedy on Devil's Caye—Martin Chin is dead. Trey Turnbull is seriously injured and in the Belize hospital. However, you should know that a jaguar is living on the Caye, beaten up pretty badly by Hurricane Lulubelle. All I can figure is that somehow it must have swum there, but if you were to get out there pronto, you could save it and return it to the Catscombs. Matt Oliver

IN THE MORNING, Matt called the Belize Medical Associates Hospital on St. Thomas Street. With no ophthalmic surgeon on staff, they had called in an eye surgeon visiting the British Army Training Support Unit at Ladyville.

"Sorry, sir," the doctor said when he was able to pick up, "there was nothing I could do for him. Just patched him up and gave him a stiff dose of antibiotics. Poor chap will never see again, but other than that, he's jolly well, not in much pain, just a lot of misery. His family just picked him up. No reason for him to stay here."

The next day Matt watched the grass runway approach from below, involuntarily putting out his hand to steady himself as the Cessna's wings wobbled in the shifting wind. He winced when pain shot up his back as the wheels slammed down on the ground. "Not an easy strip," the Aussie shouted. He pulled the plane up to the palapa and shut down the engine. "How long are you planning to stay?"

"A couple days. I need a little mindless R and R." Around the bend came the Range Rover, swerving back and forth as it dodged potholes before stopping along-side the palapa. "I'll call you in Belize City when I know when I'm leaving," Matt said.

"I'll ride to the lodge with you. I'm waiting for some cargo to take back."

Both men opened their doors and climbed out. The Aussie waited for Matt, who carried only the Dopp kit he had bought when he purchased a new polo shirt, khaki shorts, and Teva knockoffs.

"By the way, I don't mean to get into your business, but between you and me, mate, I think the proprietor sees you as something more than a paying guest."

Matt stopped. "Cat? How's that?"

"She doesn't stop talking about you. I've flown her back and forth half-a-dozen times since your first trip. She talks about getting someone to help her run the lodge, and then she talks about you, but she's not refer-ring to employment."

"I'm flattered."

"You ought to be."

The Aussie climbed into the back of the Land Rover, Matt into the front, disappointed to see Luciano, the bartender, behind the wheel. "Looks like you've been in a hell of a fight."

"Yup, it was a Lulu."

"I bet." He turned the Land Rover around on the airstrip and headed up the rutted road to the Lodge. "Didn't know you'd be on the plane. Just thought I was picking up leftover baggage."

"I tried to call, but couldn't get through this morning."

"Power's been off and on; cells are spotty. It's been like this for days."

When Luciano stopped at the entrance to the Lodge, Matt jumped out and went to the front desk, where the clerk was shuffling papers.

"Mr. Oliver. We weren't expecting you."

"I know. You probably don't get many drop-ins. Where's Cat?"

"I'll get her for you." She disappeared into Cat's office, and a moment later Cat emerged, her arms crossed in front of her. Matt walked toward her, reaching out his arms, but she remained motionless. Matt stopped.

"Matthew, you look terrible."

"But I feel great. I couldn't wait to see you."

She looked at the ground, then back at him. "I'm glad you're OK — but I didn't want you to come out here."

"No? What's wrong?"

She looked at the ground again and shrugged her shoulders. When she looked up, a tear rolled down her cheek. "I'll show you. Come with me." She led him down the cinder path, saying nothing, stopping at the first cottage. A light breeze passed through the open windows, fluttering the white curtains inside. She tapped on the door, then opened it and stepped inside, motioning Matt to follow.

Inside, a Belizean woman, dressed all in white, sat next to the bed, humming softly. Trey Turnbull lay atop the bed, his arms folded across his blue guayabera shirt, his linen slacks stopping short of his bare feet. A gauze bandage covered his eyes and the shaft of his nose. He might have been sleeping, but his index finger tapped on the back of his opposite hand.

Matt stopped breathing.

"Hi, Daddy, I just wanted to check on you. How are you feeling?" Matt straightened up and looked at Cat.

"Who's with you? I don't want to see anyone. Who is it?"

Cat, her eyes soft, sad, glistening, extended her hand to Matt, who stared at Cat, unable to speak.

"No one , Daddy. I just wanted to check in. I didn't mean to disturb you." She leaned down and kissed him on the cheek, then led Matt out the door and back to the lounge, without saying a word.

They sat across from each other. "I didn't know," Matt said.

"I didn't tell you."

"Why?"

Cat shook her head, as if she were trying to shake loose an explanation. "He's been trying to get into my good graces for years, but I never fully forgave him for abandoning my mother. He's a rich, rich man, and for years, he refused to give her anything. She worked her fingers to the bone to keep me in school, until I headed to the Caribbean."

"Where you got arrested and jumped bail."

Her face didn't change; her eyes fixed on his, and then she dipped her head.

"That was six years ago." She hesitated. "My father came to St. Lucia to reconcile with me. I wanted nothing to do with him. I even wished he were dead, but while we were there, a guy broke his jaw trying to rob him and put him in a coma for three days. I went after the guy with a gun. Turned out he was a local cop and they arrested me. You can get years for possession of firearms in those islands. They released me so I could be with my father. When he was OK, I went to the docks at midnight and sailed to St. Vincent with a good friend, then flew here the next day.

"You wished your father was dead, but you were willing to kill for him."

"Sounds silly, doesn't it?"

"No, not to me. And the lodge?"

"He's the money behind it, all the money. After St. Lucia, he claimed he regretted turning his back on his family and wanted to get back into our favor. He started supporting my mother again and then moved her to a care home in Florida. Her mind is gone."

"And you?"

"He knew the Lodge was my dream."

Matt nodded, but could say nothing.

"I'm sorry, Matt. Sorry for what might have been."

He saw the tears in her eyes. "I'm sorry, too." They sat in silence for several moments. Then Cat stood. "The plane will be heading back to Belize City soon. I'm sure you can catch a ride."

49

"So, MON, WHAT dey put you in dis piece of shit place for?"

Matt tried to ignore the huge man. He turned his back and peered through the window bars into the courtyard below where a dozen policemen milled about, their catcalls chasing women to the other side of the street.

"Dey calls me 'teacher,' mon. Hear dat? So when I ask a question, you answer. Otherwise, you get a lesson in disrespect." He took a step toward Matt, who turned and held up his hands, palms out.

"Sorry, I meant no disrespect. It's a long story."

"Don't fuck wit' me."

"Teacher, leave the American alone." Inspector Barnstable stood at the cell door, his jaw tight. Teacher folded his arms and stared at Barnstable, but didn't move.

Matt rushed to the door, grabbing the bars with both hands. "Inspector, why am I in here?"

"That's what I wondered, too, when I saw your name

365

on our inmate list, Oliver. The American ambassador demanded your arrest."

"The ambassador? And you listened to him?"

"No, not me. My superintendent ordered you arrested when you got off that Tropic Air flight from Jaguar Lodge."

"Can you get me out of here?"

"No, I can't, but I can get you away from Teacher." The inspector unlocked the door. "Come with me." As they walked past other cells, prisoners hooted. They went up a flight of stairs to the third floor and another closet-sized cell that smelled of pine oil. Matt hesitated when Barnstable unlocked the door, but he stepped inside when he felt Barnstable's gentle push on his back.

"You won't have any problem here."

Through the bars, Matt looked at Barnstable. "Inspector, I do have to thank you for saving my life."

"And I should apologize for your treatment these past weeks."

"I'll forget about it if I get out of here alive."

"You will. I owe it to you."

"Why's that?"

"You solved the mystery of the body in the ice." Barnstable held up the tooth.

"The tooth. Whose was it?"

"Just an old fisherman who tried to make an honest living."

Matt took the tooth from Barnstable and looked at the engraving. "A fisherman?"

"My brother."

"Your brother? Wickets?"

"That's what they called him, bow legs and all. Last time I saw him, maybe a year ago, he told me Chin tried to get all the fishermen to work for him—catch sharks, seahorses, bring him live fish, anything. My brother said he wouldn't do it, but Chin had threatened him, saying he would sink his boat or burn down his cottage. I think Chin killed him to frighten the other fishermen."

"Not a heart attack like Charlie told Little Man?"

"From looking at the pictures, I think his neck was broken." Barnstable shook his head, shuffled his feet. "He was an independent old chap. He never wanted me to look out for him. I could have never saved his life."

It took twenty-four hours for Maxie to arrive, but when she did, she was the second hurricane to hit Belize in a week. She walked up to Matt's cell door, with Barnstable in tow. "Good for you. If you're looking to get a Pulitzer for journalism, there is no better way than to spend a night in jail. Are you going to open your story with the author behind bars, or is that your ending?"

"Maxie, I need to get out of the country first."

"Wrong. You need to get out of jail first."

Barnstable unlocked the cell door. "Officer McCaw here did what I couldn't do, Mr. Oliver."

"Yes," she said, "Mr. Oliver, you're now under my custody. For illegally entering Belize."

"Hah! The Environmental Protection Agency?"

"Well, one thing an agent should do in a foreign country, if appropriate, is to inform the embassy of your presence. So, I made a courtesy call." She pulled an embossed business card out of her waist pack. *Ambassador Laddie B. Barber.*

"He likes to hand them out," Matt said.

"He is all hands. Told me how lonely he was down here in Belize and tried to put on the moves." She pulled a black leather luggage tag from her waist pack, slid the ambassador's card into it, and dropped it back into the pack. "He said anything I wanted was mine."

"You should have asked for his ranch."

"Hadn't thought of that. He is kind of cute, though, with only half an ear. Anyhow, he's taking the afternoon flight to Houston, so you and I, my prisoner, are going to be on it. Superintendent Barnstable will get us to the airport, right, Superintendent?"

"Superintendent?" Matt said.

"That's right. When Godwin, now the ex-super, saw a few of Charlie's email messages, he made a quick departure." Maxie turned to Barnstable. "Congratulations."

"Thank you, sir."

She didn't flinch when he called her "sir."

Barnstable turned to Matt. "Of course, you're welcome to return to Belize, Mr. Oliver. I still hope you write kindly about us."

"I'll keep that in mind, Inspector."

"Superintendent," Barnstable said as he shook Matt's hand.

THE LINE FOR the Continental flight to Houston was sixty deep, weaving out the front door of the airport. Matt had only the clothes on his back, and Maxie carried her briefcase in one hand and a large yellow plastic bag labeled *It's Better in Belize* in the other.

"I'm getting on first, an agent's prerogative. Must pay my respects to the pilot—let him know I'm carrying a Glock and that I'm legit. See you on board."

Matt stepped behind a short man in a powder-blue jumpsuit taking his last puffs from a Cuban Cohiba cigar, when he heard the familiar rattle of Jack's Ford pickup. "Hey, Matty, my boy." Little Man had pulled his truck to the curb and out jumped Jack, wearing one of Matt's polo shirts over his Speedo.

"Jack. Little Man. You made it!"

"Damn right. We have our first group of divers coming in from Colorado on the incoming flight. Want to start them off right. But no more ice blocks. Just a few fish heads here and there to tease the sharks."

Matt opened his arms, first hugging Jack, then Little Man.

"When you coming back?" Little Man asked.

"I haven't left yet."

Jack grabbed him by the elbow. "Then why don't you get out of that line and come out to the lodge? Get wet. Go diving."

"Tempting, Jack. Maybe in a month or two, when things settle down."

"Got to make it soon. Otherwise, your bloody eye will be white again, and I won't recognize you."

Matt laughed. "So what are you going to do, Little Man?"

"Jack says I don't have to go diving no more, mon, just run the boat."

"I'm giving him Charlie's job. In fact, I'm giving him Charlie's house. Seems to me if my liver turns black, Little Man's Scuba Shack can keep the customers happy. Say, have a look at this." Jack walked over to his dusty old pickup truck and pulled a blue plastic tarp off a rusty five-foot-tall wire cage. A bald scarlet macaw flapped up to the swinging bar, jumped down and pirouetted.

"A little freedom dance for you, Matty. We're taking her to the Belize Zoo. Sharon out there will have her healthy in no time."

The Continental queue had moved inside the door. "Guys, I better get going."

"And we have to meet our divers," Jack said. "But you come on back, Matty."

"I will, Jack. Yes, I will."

MATT FINALLY CHECKED in and headed to the security line. He recognized a squeaky voice coming from behind him. "Laddie B. Barber here, pleased to meet you." Matt lowered his head and stepped forward, hoping to disappear into the crowd, while the ambassador introduced himself to passengers as if he were running for office. His aide, carrying a suitcase, ushered him past Immigration and into the Customs area. When Matt entered Customs, the ambassador, with his aide behind him, was being escorted directly onto the tarmac.

Once on board the plane, Matt found Maxie sitting on the aisle in the first row in cabin class, seat 7D, directly behind the first class section. With no one in the center seat, Matt took the window seat, falling asleep even before they took off. It wasn't until he felt a finger in his ribs that he woke up. They were at thirty-one thousand feet, crossing the Belize border into Mexico. "Here, you can use an eye opener." Maxie handed him a can of Snappy Tom and a plastic glass with two ice cubes. "No booze. We need to keep our wits about us."

"Thanks." He looked out the window, down at the verdant rainforest, trying to keep his mind off Cat, but the smell of the rainforest lingered.

"You have to let go of that one, Matt. She has her hands full, if not with her father then with her guilt."

"I suppose."

"She didn't know what her father was up to, you know."

Matt looked back out the window. Below, smoke from farmers and developers clearing land obscured the Mexican landscape.

Ninety minutes later, after the ding of the cabin bell, Maxie and every other aisle seat passenger jumped to their feet and started snapping open the overhead bins. Matt, right behind Maxie, stepped into the well between the first and cabin classes. Barber, a bandage on his right ear, crawled from his seat and yawned, but when he saw Maxie his brows popped up, his eyes opened wide, and a sly grin appeared. He pushed his way past three passengers. "Why, I didn't know you were on this flight. Had I known, I would have had you come sit with me." He looked at Matt. "I suppose you had to stay with your prisoner."

"Yes, duty calls. But I appreciate the offer, Mr. Ambassador."

As the ambassador pushed his way toward the exit

door, Matt stepped in front of him. "Excuse me, sir, but I think you forgot one of your bags." Matt reached into the overhead compartment. He lifted down a yellow plastic sack labeled *It's Better in Belize* and handed it to the ambassador. "I think this is yours."

"No, not mine. My aide has everything."

Matt looked inside and then thrust the bag at Laddie. Its open end revealed a large box wrapped in string. "There's a luggage tag on it. Have a look."

Laddie slid the box part way out of the bag and fingered the black leather luggage tag attached to the box. "*Ambassador Laddie B. Barber.* Well, I'll be..." As Barber looked at the tag, Matt pulled the box out of the bag. The bottom of the box sagged, stretching the string, and with a snap, the flaps fell open. An object the size of a soccer ball bounced on the floor. The flight attendant jumped back, a woman screamed, and Matt smiled as he watched the ambassador's face. Between Laddie's feet lay the stuffed head of a Florida panther.

The only thing that broke the ambassador's horrified stare was Maxie's hand, as she held out her badge. "Mr. Ambassador, this is an endangered animal." She waved her badge in his face. "However, I'm going to do you a favor." She put her badge back into her pocket. "You like girls, so I'm going to introduce you to a real hot one." Laddie B. smiled and stepped closer. "Her name's Miranda. You see, sir, you have the right to remain silent. Anything you say can and may be used against you in a court of law. You have the right..."

Epilogue

~~~~~

DATELINE, BELIZE CITY, September 23: Catherine
"Cat" Mandell, the President of the Turnbull Foundation,
today announced a new thirty-eight-million-dollar
(US) project to purchase land and expand the jaguar
habitat in Belize and other Central American countries.

The news comes just a week after the Global Fund for
Wildlife announced that it had closed its Belize office.

The project will be headed by Dr. David Mallard, who
figured prominently in the news last month after he discovered an emaciated jaguar living on an outer caye that
had been ravaged by Hurricane Lulubelle. Mallard res-
cued the jaguar and nursed it back to health at his camp.
Yesterday he released Belize's national symbol deep in
the Catscomb Basin.

Author's Note

~~~~~~

THIS YEAR, AT least fifty million sharks will be pulled aboard fishing boats, their fins sliced off, and then dropped alive back into the sea, unable to swim while they await their grisly death. The only purpose is to provide chefs with the primary ingredient for shark fin soup, an expensive Asian delicacy. The fins add a sinewy texture, but no flavor. A bowl may cost as much as $100 and you can still find it in restaurants in many American cities.

Millions of swimming reef fish will be stunned with drugs, collected, bagged, and shipped halfway across the world for display in home aquariums. Most of those lucky enough to survive the journey will die within a few months. Untold numbers of fluttering seahorses will be gathered from reefs, dried, and powered to create an imaginary male aphrodisiac. Millions of live animals in shells will be scavenged from coral reefs, their bodies discarded and their shells turned into lamps, exhibited on bookcases, or strung onto necklaces. In many nations, wealthy trophy hunters will track and kill rare endangered animals, to be remembered with a mounted head or photograph of the proud hunter standing over the magnificent corpse.

While *Tropical Ice* is both thriller and mystery, I set out to describe the extent of useless wildlife destruction, hoping to encourage some readers to act. While scores of important groups are tackling these issues, WildAid in San Francisco stands out. And, for broader conservation issue, the Wildlife Conservation Society in New York is a leader. I'm indebted to the research conducted by WCS scientist Dr. Alan Rabinowitz and chronicled in his important book, *Jaguar: One Man's Struggle to Establish the World's First Jaguar Preserve*.

As fiction writers are wont to do, I took a few liberties with the setting, both in Belize and Houston. America's embassy in Belize moved from Belize City to Belmopan earlier than my story. I borrowed a famous old bar and a family name from Grand Cayman. I adjusted the landscape, failed to give credit to Belize's jaguar preserve and the government's effort to protect their national animal, and even modified the jaguar's range a bit, inadvertently even stretching a behavioral trait or two. That's fiction.

Tropical Ice is an imaginary tale, as are its characters, and I've not witnessed the tragic treatment of animals in Belize that I describe. I have spent many weeks on Belize's reefs and in the mountains and rainforest, and while it's a beautiful country with fine people, the fine people of every nation do have their dark secrets.

Acknowledgments

Some say a writer is only as good as his editor—that's true for me, at least. I've been lucky to have two extraordinary editors: Jennifer Sawyer Fisher, who taught me more about fiction writing than a dozen classes might have, and Lynn Vannucci, who showed me how to cut the fat and push the reader to turn the page. My deepest thanks to both of you.

Tropical Ice would still be in a drawer had not my literary agent, Elizabeth Trupin-Pulli, taken a liking to it, but not until I cut six thousand words…and then a few thousand more. Each time, my story got better.

Several friends offered helpful criticism: talented scuba divers and real pals, Larry Clinton, Chuck Ballinger, and Dr. Michael H. Smith; Dr. Rodger Schlickeisen, a true defender of wildlife; forever undiscovered humorist Arthur Hardman; Ayris Hatton, a fine artist and writer; and eagle-eyed Michelle Jordan. My cousin, Canadian poet Steven Ross Smith, and his wife, novelist J. Jill Robinson, provided early encouragement, even after suffering through an uncured draft. I'm grateful for everyone's generosity.

I received technical help from Lee Schwartz, MD, Steve Carnes, Jim Lummis, Rich Gelber, and Neil Ostgaard, as well as scientists at the Wildlife Conservation Society, where I consulted long ago. Fred Good, with whom I dived many weeks as a paying customer at his St. George's Caye Lodge in Belize, shared a few of the country's dark secrets. Two superb mystery writers' conferences at Book Passage in Corte Madera, California, stimulated my imagination, as did a course taught by Anthony-award-winning mystery novelist Judy Greber, who read the first draft and encouraged me to go for it.

Finally, I must thank my beautiful wife, Lucia Christopher, who always gave me the space to write. Many times, she would say, "Why don't you get out of the house and go write," and perhaps only a couple of times did she really mean, "Why don't you just get out of the house."

ABOUT THE AUTHOR

KL SMITH is an international travel reviewer and the publisher and editor of the newsletter, Undercurrent.org, the private guide for traveling scuba divers.

He has visited more than fifty countries and dived in twenty-six of them. He was a partner in a management consulting and fund-raising firm, with clients such as Greenpeace, the Sierra Club, the Wildlife Conservation Society, national political candidates, and public television stations. He has taught graduate courses at three universities, managed a successful California political reform ballot initiative, and served on several nonprofit boards, including the Marine Mammal Center. His articles have appeared in *Skin Diver Magazine*, *Outside* and *Men's Journal*. He lives in Northern California with his wife and two dogs.

READERS GUIDE

1. What role does Matt's memory of his father and religion play in Matt's motivation?

2. What motivates Trey Turnbull?

3. Did David Mallard do what he needed to do to preserve the jaguar range, or by allowing a jaguar to be sacrificed, did he break his obligation to his profession and employer? Did he behave morally?

4. People who criticize the exploitation of nature—harvesting seahorses for aphrodisiacs, hunting tigers for their penises to be used for erectile stimulants, harvesting sharks only for their fins for rich people's soup—are often then criticized as attacking the Chinese culture and, at times, are accused of racism. Are these valid criticisms?

5. Why is Matt so loyal to Jack that he takes on the task of proving Jack's innocence? Is it, in fact, loyalty, or rather some other, more personal motivation?

6. How would you characterize Cat's relationship with Trey?

7. Is it reasonable in today's world for someone like Matt to take on Turnbull, Chin, the thugs and the shark-finners if he is unwilling to arm himself with anything other than a fire-hose cannon?

8. The boats of most fishing nations—the United States included—pursue one or two species and throw away the unwanted fish, injured or dead, that are inadvertently captured in their nets. For some fisheries the weight of this so-called "bycatch" may be greater than the targeted fish they keep. There is little pressure by environmentalists to solve the bycatch problem, but great pressure to stop fishing boats from throwing back live finless sharks. Why go after one cause and not the other?

The Grand
Dennis D. Wilson

Chicago cop Dean Wister takes a forced vacation when he is on the brink of a breakdown after the death of his wife. During his summer solstice in Jackson Hole, he is called in by local police to consult when a notorious Chicago mobster is found dead in the Snake River. What has drawn the hit man west to murder a popular local citizen and pollute the pristine mountain enclave of the rich and famous—is it love, sex, money, or power? Or is it somehow related to the Presidential campaign of Wyoming's favorite son? Dean's investigation threatens to uncover the secrets of a group of memorable suspects—rich tycoons and modern day cowboys, with political consequences reaching far beyond the small resort town. A funny, romantic, sexy, roller coaster thriller!

WATER STREET
CRIME

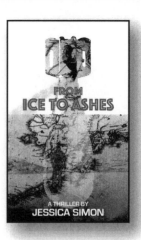

From Ice to Ashes
Jessica Simon

Who would expect a terrorist infiltration of Alaska on foot in winter? No one, until it happens. *From Ice to Ashes* propels the reader off-road and into the frozen Northland on the course of the Yukon Arctic Ultra—the toughest and coldest human-powered race on earth. For race official Markus Fanger and his reluctant helper, Donjek Stoneman, a brief lull at their checkpoint shatters when Muslim racer Omar Ahmed arrives, battered and blue. In short order, Fanger and Donjek discover the extreme athlete is also an extreme militant. From Dawson City, Yukon, to Fort Greely, Alaska, the race is on to defend northern sovereignty. Against a backdrop of the North's beauty and brutality, within the tension of a daring endurance race, it's up to the local heroes to keep a terrorist from his target, Ground-based Missile Defense.

WATER STREET CRIME

Stained Fortune
Joe Calderwood

It wasn't his plan to land back in a Mexican jail. But from nighttime prowls through seedy backstreets of Merida, to the roar of the bull ring, to the gleaming towers of Miami's most prestigious banks—in the company of old friends, beautiful rent-a-boys, and South American drug kingpins—relishing the finest in French cuisine at a private banker's restaurant and the freshest tacos at the most glorious dive on the road to a fortified bunker built under a Mayan ruin—it was all an adrenaline rush. And jail was almost inevitable.

Bloody Paradise
Jame DiBiasio

Travis Mitchell lands on the Thai resort island Samui with a broken wrist, a bag of cash, and a seriously pissed off Hong Kong crime boss on his tail. There he bumps into Mazy, a yoga instructor with a penchant for booze and abusive boyfriends. Trav is convinced he needs to save her from Gordon, a cockney Londoner developing K-Love, the world's perfect date-rape drug. Mazy flees Gordon's villa, but running away with Trav triggers a hunt by Thai gangsters, Chinese triads, Samui cops, and a pathetic janitor who cleans up after the tigers in the local zoo. As her escape brings them all into collision, Trav wonders if the beautiful yoga teacher is worth it – while Mazy, unsure if she should trust him, decides to take matters into her own unsteady hands.